CHRISTIAN NATION

— A Novel —

Frederic C. Rich

W. W. NORTON & COMPANY

NEW YORK • LONDON

For information about permission to reproduce selections from this book,
write to Permissions, W. W. Norton & Company, Inc.,
500 Fifth Avenue, New York, NY 10110

For information about special discounts for bulk purchases, please contact
W. W. Norton Special Sales at specialsales@wwnorton.com or 800-233-4830

Manufacturing by Courier Westford
Book design by Brian Mulligan
Production manager: Louise Mattarelliano

Library of Congress Cataloging-in-Publication Data

Rich, Frederic C.
Christian nation : novel / Frederic C. Rich. — First edition.
pages cm
ISBN 978-0-393-24011-5 (hardcover)
1. Religious right—Fiction. 2. United States—Politics and government—21st century—
Fiction. I. Title.
PS3618.I33275C48 2013
813'.6—dc23
                        2013009640

W. W. Norton & Company, Inc.
500 Fifth Avenue, New York, N.Y. 10110
www.wwnorton.com

W. W. Norton & Company Ltd.
Castle House, 75/76 Wells Street, London W1T 3QT

1 2 3 4 5 6 7 8 9 0

CONTENTS

AUTHOR'S NOTE

THIS NOVEL IS a work of speculative fiction. The speculation is about one possible course of American history had the McCain/Palin campaign won the 2008 election. Except for certain historical events and statements by public figures prior to election night 2008, the narrative is entirely fictional. Accordingly, all statements and actions of actual public figures and organizations following election night 2008 are the product of the author's imagination; the appearance of such statements and actions in a work of fiction does not constitute an assertion that such person or entity would speak or act in that way in those circumstances.

In contrast to the actual public figures and organizations appearing in the novel, the other characters and organizations are purely fictional, and any resemblance to actual persons, living or dead, or actual organizations, is entirely coincidental. As Evelyn Waugh put it so well, "I am not I: thou art not he or she: they are not they."

Religion begins by offering magical aid to harassed and bewildered men; it culminates by giving to a people that unity of morals and belief which seems so favorable to statesmanship and art; it ends by fighting suicidally in the lost cause of the past. For as knowledge grows or alters continually, it clashes with mythology and theology, which change with geological leisureliness.

—Will and Ariel Durant,
The Story of Civilization

CHRISTIAN NATION

CHAPTER ONE

What They Said They Would Do

2029

> *The struggle of man against power is the struggle of memory against forgetting.*
>
> —Milan Kundera,
> *The Book of Laughter and Forgetting*

> *[W]ould-be totalitarian rulers usually start their careers by boasting of their past crimes and carefully outlining their future ones.*
>
> —Hannah Arendt,
> *The Origins of Totalitarianism*

ADAM TOLD ME TO START by writing about what I feel now. Sitting here, I don't feel much except the faint phantom ache of a wound long since healed. It was only six weeks ago that I met Adam Brown. He and his wife, Sarah, are downstairs asleep. In front of me is a beige IBM Selectric II typewriter, disconnected and without memory, immune from the insatiable probings of the Purity Web, and thus the ultimate contraband. A man I hardly know has seated me in front of a typewriter and told me to remember and write. I've spent a long time staring at the egg-like ball of little letters wondering why I am here and what they really want from me.

Here are the facts. I was a lawyer and then a fighter for the secular side in the Holy War that ended in 2020 following the siege of Manhattan. Like so many others, I earned my release from three years of rehabilitation on Governors Island by accepting Jesus Christ as my savior. For the past five years I have lived as a free citizen of the Christian Nation. This is the only truth I have allowed myself. Can I really now think and write the words that express a different truth? Here they are then: I am no longer chained in my cell, but for five years I have been bound even more firmly by the fifty commandments of The Blessing and the suffocating surveillance of the Purity Web. The cloak of collective righteousness lies heavy on the land.

Before coming here, I did not ask myself how it happened. I have neither remembered nor grieved. But now I discover that recollection is there, a paper's edge from consciousness. When I close my eyes I find flickers of memory: Emilie's empty martini glass on our terrace, drinking in the sun, the day after we broke up. And I remember looking at the hard empty glass and remembering her skin soft and warm and full of the same sun only the day before. Hard and soft. Stone and skin. Memories flicker and stutter, old film freezing in the projector, slipping, lurching forward. Dissolving.

Before, I was a lawyer. I was good with words. I was organized. I was not, frankly, much interested in my feelings, although I was pretty good at telling a story. A story should start at the beginning, but exactly where this one began is still a mystery to me.

What *is* clear to me is that they did what they said they would do. This morning, Adam pulled from the wall of old-fashioned gray metal file cabinets a tattered manila folder marked "2006" filled with clippings. In the folder I found a small glossy pamphlet from a group promoting "Christian Political Action." An affable-looking man stares back at me from the cover. Inside is a letter dated November 2006, just a year after I started at the law firm.

*When the Christian majority takes over this country, there will be
no satanic churches, no more free distribution of pornography, no*

more talk of rights for homosexuals. After the Christian majority takes control, pluralism will be seen as immoral and evil, and the state will not permit anybody the right to practice evil.

That certainly is clear. I have read this little brochure over and over, trying to remember when I first heard this message, this promise. Was I listening? I was twenty-five in 2006. I was not very good at listening at that age, at least to things I didn't want to hear. But what about the people who should have been listening? My parents, for example. I try to imagine my father picking up this brochure from the table in the foyer of our little wooden Catholic church in Madison, New Jersey. What would he have thought when reading these words? Closing my eyes, I can see him, still sandy haired at fifty, his athletic frame softened by scotch and a desk job. A decent man, reading a letter from a fellow Christian threatening to remake his world. He would have looked up, a shadow crossing his handsome face, then thrown the brochure in the little box where people neatly discarded the copies of hymn lyrics. He would have gone to play golf.

They promised, in 2006, that if they succeeded in acquiring political power, "the state will not permit anybody the right to practice evil." In 2006 I was a first-year associate at the law firm. I try to remember. Had I ever heard of Rushdoony, North, Coe, Dobson, Perkins, or Farris? Did I know anything about Brownback, Palin, Bachmann, DeMint, Santorum, Coburn, or Perry? I do remember watching maudlin confessions of adultery from buffoonish TV preachers, stoic big-haired wives at their sides. I knew vaguely that out there somewhere in America, in an America that was to me a dimly understood foreign land, there existed people—lots of people—who called themselves "born again" or "evangelical." I wonder what I thought that meant. Something ridiculous about believers flying up to heaven in a longed-for event called "the rapture," leaving behind those not saved to endure the tribulations of the apocalypse. But I do remember being surprised when a banker client told me that the *Left Behind* series of apocalyptic novels and films had a US audience not so far behind that of the *Harry Potter* franchise.

Both were fantastic stories of magic and miracles—one benign and one that proved to be an early symptom of something far darker.

It was 2009, I think, after President McCain's sudden death, that my best friend, Sanjay, first explained to me that behind the public face of the Christian right was a strange mix of fundamentalist theologies, all different and often at odds with one another but aligned in support-ing the election of politicians who believe they speak to and for God, aligned in seeking to have their religiously based morals adopted into law, and aligned in rejecting the traditional notion of a "wall of separa-tion" between church and state. Of these fundamentalist theologies, the most extreme, and in many ways most influential, were dominionism and reconstructionism.

"Dominionism," Sanjay explained, "holds that Christians need to establish a Christian reign on earth *before* Jesus returns for the second coming. Dominionists also believe that Christians in general have a God-given right to rule, but more particularly, in preparation for the second coming of Christ, that Christians have the *responsibility* to take over every aspect of political and civil society. And dominionism is often associated with a fringe theology called reconstructionism, which emphasizes that this reconstructed Christian-led society should be gov-erned strictly accordingly to biblical law."

How bored we were at first with Sanjay's preoccupation with this dark strain of American belief. I didn't know, and Sanjay only later discovered, that this dominionist outlook had influenced not only the Wasilla Assembly of God, the Pentecostal church attended by Sarah Palin in Alaska, but many thousands of others around the country. What had once been a fringe of exotic beliefs and schismatic sects had entered the religious mainstream in America.

Before the start of the Holy War, I delivered dozens of speeches warning of the political ambitions of the fundamentalists. Most of the time, I illustrated the meaning of dominionism with a single quote from a prominent evangelical "educator" from Tennessee, George Grant. I still remember it:

Christians have an obligation, a mandate, a commission, a holy responsibility to reclaim the land for Jesus Christ—to have dominion in civil structures, just as in every other aspect of life and Godliness. But it is dominion we are after. Not just a voice. It is dominion we are after. Not just influence. It is dominion we are after. Not just equal time. It is dominion we are after. . . . Thus, Christian politics has as its primary intent the conquest of the land—of men, families, institutions, bureaucracies, courts, and governments for the Kingdom of Christ.

Of course, it was only later that I made those speeches. After I made my choice. Before, for many years, I just couldn't take it seriously. Closing my eyes again, I can hear Sanjay's voice at a dinner at the East Side apartment I then shared with my girlfriend Emilie.

"It *is* serious," he said, leaning forward. "What I am telling you, Greg, is that when they speak of turning America into a Christian Nation ruled in accordance with the Bible by those who purport to speak for God, this is not just rhetoric. It needs to be taken at face value. Right now, tens of millions of your fellow citizens believe—fanatically believe—there is nothing more important, and have been working for decades to acquire the political power to make it happen."

"San," my girlfriend Emilie replied, "I love you dearly," which was not exactly true, "but on this you're seriously off base. We've always had big religious revivals. Think of the Great Awakening. It's just mass hysteria—it flares up when people feel anxious about change, and then it burns out. And the evangelicals are, what, only a quarter of the population? Fact is, most of the people are drugged out on shopping and reality TV and couldn't give a crap. It's just not going to happen, San."

I agreed with her.

★　　★　　★

THE TYPEWRITER SITS on a table directly in front of a large picture window that frames a view of three overgrown rhododendrons in the foreground, the narrow lake below, and the rocky shore opposite, dominated by a single large gray-green granite boulder. A dense oak forest punctuated with tall hemlocks rises sharply behind it. The lake is flat, so free of ripple or blemish that every cloud is rendered perfectly on its surface. I hear no sound other than the unfamiliar mechanical hum of the typewriter, in which—I suddenly hear—the dominant note is G, with strong overtones. Secular music has been missing from my life since the end of the Holy War. All we had at Governors Island were Church of God in America hymns, which were so insipid as to kill the joy that I normally found in any music. I listen to the hum of the IBM. It isn't Bach, but it isn't *Walk with Jesus Mild* either. I hum a fifth interval, over and over, harmonizing with the IBM, then stop when I suddenly remember the face of the redheaded kid I killed with a grenade. He ran at my position in Battery Park, alone, screaming, his face twisted in hate. I couldn't hear him, but his mouth suggested, "Die faggot." They called everyone left in Manhattan "faggot." He exploded in a fine red mist.

This was not the first time that the world didn't listen. In college I read Hitler's *Mein Kampf.* Fourteen years before the first shot was fired, Hitler announced his plan to destroy the parliamentary system in Germany, to attack France and Eastern Europe, and to eliminate the Jews. Why, I asked the professor, did neither ordinary Germans voting in the Reichstag elections in July 1932, nor foreign leaders reacting to the rise of Nazism, believe him? Why was anyone surprised when he simply did what he said he would do? She had no answer.

The fall of my senior year at Princeton, nineteen deeply religious young men flew planes into the World Trade Center and the Pentagon. During the decade before 9/11, Osama Bin Laden had shouted out his warnings of mass murder using all the means of modern communication. And still we were surprised when he did what he said he would do.

So I suppose what happened here is that they said what they would do, and we did not listen. Then they did what they said they would do.

CHAPTER TWO

Indian Lake

2029

> *An exquisite pleasure had invaded my senses, something*
> *isolated, detached, with no suggestion of its origin. . . .*
> *Whence did it come? What did it mean? How could I*
> *seize and apprehend it? . . . And suddenly the memory*
> *revealed itself.*
>
> —Marcel Proust,
> *À la recherche du temps perdu*

SITTING HERE OVERLOOKING INDIAN LAKE, it feels strange to be outside New York City for the first time in ten years. For the past five years, I have worked at the Christian Nation Archives in New York, in what formerly was the Bobst Library of New York University. The old libraries are closed, of course, but not all the collections have been destroyed. As "indexers," we are charged with the task of coding the remaining books for preservation or destruction, and occasionally retrieving books requested by public officials or scholars whose research has been sanctioned by the Church of God in America, universally referred to as COGA. All academic and cultural organizations operate under the supervision of COGA, a sprawling enterprise. Most of us from Governors Island were placed with COGA-affiliated employers, which allows them to keep a close eye on our progress. GI has faith in its graduates, but even for them there are limits to faith. I find the physical presence of the books to be a comfort. We are constantly reminded that the eradication of evil is vital work entrusted only to those of us who know Christ and thus have the fortitude for the task.

Six months ago, a new indexer named Adam settled in to work at a table two rows behind mine. He is the only African American in our group, and his rimless glasses, tweedy garb, and strong vocabulary immediately suggested to me that he had been a scholar. For the first two weeks he ignored me, nearly to the point of rudeness. Then, during his third week, seeing that I was heading to Washington Square Park for lunch, Adam casually asked if he could join me. He chose a remote bench facing a dense stand of shrubs. He asked lots of questions about work and dodged most of my questions about him. When we finished our sandwiches and rose from the bench, he glanced to see that no one was near and then said simply, "Greg, you need to know that I am here because of you." Before I could respond, he shook my hand, giving it that distinctive extra squeeze I had felt from a few others, and then turned to walk back to the library by himself.

Two weeks later, Adam and I had become friends, which is what we now call the sort of superficial acquaintance that is the only relationship possible when people are unable to discuss anything important. I know that Adam is married, has no children, and had spent his career before the siege as a lay professor of theology at the General Theological Seminary in Chelsea. I knew from that first day in the park that he wanted something from me, but I waited patiently for him to ask. He would ask when he was ready. When he proposed the risky enterprise of a long vacation during which I should write a memoir, I refused.

"Why, Adam?" I asked. "You've got to tell me why you want me to write this thing and what you plan to do with it."

"You need to trust me."

"How the hell can I trust you? I hardly know you."

"You trust me enough to have this conversation. You know we're careful," he replied.

"True. But talking to you is something I might survive if they found out. But leaving town, somehow going off the Purity Web—which by the way I sincerely doubt is possible—and then writing everything that happened, telling the truth . . . That's entirely different." I paused. "And by the way, who is 'we'? Are you telling me that Free Minds is real?"

"No. I'm *not* saying that." He looked annoyed with me. "Please, Greg. I know about you. I know what you did. I know *he* was your friend. We need you to tell your story. That's all I'm asking."

"You're asking me to commit suicide. No."

A few days later, I changed my mind. You may think that I harbor some kind of self-destructive urge. Perhaps so. Not sure what I was going to do or why, I decided to do what Adam had asked. It had been a long time since anyone had asked me to do anything, and it felt odd to be asked, for someone to suggest that I was needed. Saying yes suddenly seemed easier than saying no. You should know that. Coming here was *not* an act of courage.

Adam and I departed Manhattan by train. We were met at the station in the Hudson Valley town of Peekskill by the owner of a small inn located in the nearby hamlet of Putnam Valley. After both of us scanned in as guests, Adam wordlessly handed his Device across the counter to the innkeeper. They both looked at me, silently indicating that I should do the same. The day I left Governors Island, the out-placement officer informed me that I was required to have my Device with me at all times. In the five years since then, I have obeyed. So I hesitated. Although not a suspicious word passed between them, the owners of the inn, Adam said, were "friends." I had stopped asking about FM. The feds denied the existence of the Free Minds movement, and even I, on balance, assumed it was more secret longing than reality. After all, with the Purity Web encompassing every possible means of communication, observing every meeting and movement, analyzing everything one read or wrote—with the big machines knowing us better than we knew ourselves—how could a movement like that organize or function? But Adam was real, and Adam had "friends." I handed over my Device and immediately felt more abandoned than liberated.

We walked out the back door of the inn and entered the woods on an old dirt road, now a narrow path kept open by deer. I was over-whelmed by the smell. The woodsy air, damp and infused with the dusty fluff kicked up by our steps, carried odors of mold, decay, fungus, and scat. The only nature I had known after Governors Island was the little wild garden behind our communal house on Commerce Street. It had been sunny and dry. When had I last smelled the woods? I couldn't remember. I inhaled deeply, and my head felt light. Adam gave me an odd look.

"You OK?" he asked. "Don't worry about your Device. I've gone up to five weeks without touching, and didn't go pink. My friend knows what he's doing. He'll take care of us."

I nodded, distracted. The smells of the woods told a story, the story of an approaching hemlock stand, of a distant carcass, and of granite ledge rock radiating back the heat of the morning sun. I had forgotten how rich, complex, and without judgment were the smells of nature. For the moment, I was glad I had come.

We hiked for three miles, until the path ended abruptly. The rocky cut, through which the old road crested the hill, had been blasted closed. It appeared impassable. Adam led me through dense brush down along the ridge to an ominous-looking gap between two large boulders. We squeezed through, crawled under the corner of another enormous rock, and emerged on the far side of the ridge, where I saw a gem-like lake at the bottom of a steep valley.

We scrambled down the boulder-strewn slope to the lake's edge. The water was clear. I could see the algae-covered stones on the bottom, and tadpoles swimming erratically among them. We walked along the shore for about a half mile and suddenly came upon a decrepit two-story cedar cottage, set into the side of the hill, with a partially collapsed covered porch running along the water side of the building. From the outside, it gave every appearance of being abandoned. Inside, it was clean and dry, powered silently by solar panels that looked at least twenty years old.

This is the second day I have sat in front of this machine staring out at the lake. I have underestimated the difficulty of this project. A great stone seems to have been rolled across the only door to that part of my brain in which the past resides, and I don't have the strength to push it aside. It protects me from memory, keeping the demons behind it from penetrating my consciousness. It even keeps them out of my dreams. I realize that not once have I dreamt of the past. And now Adam says I must remember. Recollection, synthesis, and meaning he repeats like a mantra.

I close my eyes. This time I suddenly remember opening them that warm summer day in August 2020. Only nine years ago. The feds had finally ended the siege of Manhattan and invaded through Battery Park. When I came to I was lying facedown on a lawn. My eyes and cheeks were caked with dried blood, and I could see only a few blurry blades of grass beside my nose. I could hear the sound of the harbor waves, and knew that I was still in the park. My wrists were secured behind my back with a thick plastic zip tie. My shoulders ached, and I surmised that I had been lying there, hands tied, for at least a few hours. My ankles were also secured with a zip tie, but I didn't care. I was too exhausted to move in any case, and quickly slipped back out of consciousness.

When next I woke it was nighttime. A soft warm August night. I hadn't been moved, but this time my eyes could focus. I later learned that almost six thousand secular fighters had been captured and brought to the Battery. During the day, teams of army medics had performed triage, evacuating the seriously wounded to hospital ships in the harbor. While I was passed out, my shallow but bloody scalp wound had been cleaned and bandaged and the blood wiped off my face. My arms by this time were numb, and the pain in my shoulder had disappeared, replaced by a sharp headache centered on the place where the bullet had gouged a neat pencil-thin groove in my skull. I shifted my legs and managed to roll onto my side. I could see only bodies. Seventeen acres of bodies. The white plastic zip ties shone with a weird iridescence in the moonlight, an effect that was oddly decorative. Some of the prisoners had managed to turn over and sit upright, arms behind their back and legs stretched out front, but most remained facedown and still. Other than the sound of the harbor waves against the Battery breakwater, all I could hear was the occasional stifled sob. No one screamed. No one spoke. Regular fed army and marines stood casually on guard, looking bored. When I closed my eyes, I daydreamed that I was an African deep in the hold of a slave ship. Shackled. The sound of waves slapping against the hull. Silent stinking African bodies my companions and only comfort.

My mind was sluggish, like an agonizingly slow computer. Churning and churning, and ultimately failing to put the thoughts and words into coherent order. I should be dead. These four words repeated themselves in a demented feedback loop. I should be dead. I, a corporate lawyer with no aptitude for violence, stood up and shot at a company of charging US Marines. They wanted me dead. I stood up to die. I should be dead. And now they had bandaged my wound.

Later that night, civilian Red Cross volunteers were allowed into the Battery with drinking water. A solidly built Chinese lady who looked about seventy years old squatted beside me and dipped a battered paper coffee cup into a large bucket of water. She gently lifted my head and gave me a drink and a sad smile. On the side of the blue coffee cup I saw the familiar white Greek key rim and the large gold letters "WE ARE HAPPY TO SERVE YOU." This offbeat symbol of New York City's cheesy, ironic culture reminded me of all that we had just lost; and bound and facedown on the ground, for the first time since the shooting started, I wept.

CHAPTER THREE

Sanjay

1998

*[S]incerity becomes apparent. From being apparent, it
becomes manifest. From being manifest, it becomes brilliant. Brilliant, it affects others. Affecting others, they
are changed by it. Changed by it, they are transformed. It
is only he who is possessed of the most complete sincerity
that can exist under heaven, who can transform.*

—Confucius,
Doctrine of the Mean, chapter XXIII

*It is characteristic of the most entire sincerity to be able
to foreknow.*

—Confucius,
Doctrine of the Mean, chapter XXIV

"THIS IS GOOD," ADAM SAID. The "but" was left unspoken. It
has become clear that I am not to have the usual privacy enjoyed by a
memoirist at work. Adam is careful not to interrupt when I am typing,
but if I leave the desk he picks up the typed pages and reads them. If
catharsis is what Adam is pushing, erupting memories and sudden
insights should be just the thing. But he is insistent in his call for order.

"One thing leads to another," he said. "Think dominoes." Order is
hard for me to find. The last twenty-five years sometimes seem to be a
singular moment, the beginning not appreciably more distant than the

end, like a single point of collapsed time. Like time suspended during an intense conversation, or immersion in a poem. That single point of collapsed time is dense and heavy, like a netsuke with tightly wound grains, turning and looping in three dimensions, its superficial features providing only subtle clues to its inner meaning. It is not, for me, a thing easily deconstructed. But deconstruction is what I must do.

Looking out the window, I see Adam standing on the shore of the small lake, which he tells me is named Indian Lake. He is casually skipping stones across its calm surface and then staring at the ripples as if they tell a riveting story accessible only to him. For the first time in over five years, I force myself to activate that part of my mind that sits apart, and observe the wisps of recollection as they arise and drift across the rest of my brain. And for the first time in a long while, I allow myself to think about my best friend, and the finest person I ever knew, Sanjay Sharma.

We met on my first day of college in 1998, moving into the freshmen dorm room we shared. I could tell that my parents had doubts. Not that they were prone to racial prejudice, but aristocratic Indians were simply outside the scope of their experience. Sanjay's mother wore a beautiful purple sari. His father's English tweeds seemed not very practical for hauling in boxes from the Land Rover parked outside. We quickly learned that this task was delegated to a darker-skinned Indian man introduced only as "our helper." I think my dad, who was dressed in jeans and a sweatshirt, felt outclassed. But Sanjay himself—putting aside his Indian ethnicity and striking good looks—seemed to me like an ordinary eighteen-year-old American, his choice in brand of jeans, polo shirt, and sneakers the same as mine. As I soon discovered, there was nothing ordinary about him.

★   ★   ★

MY FINGERS HAVE hovered over the keyboard now for a good five minutes. I am surprised at how much the Sanjay I met that day in Princeton was the same as the Sanjay who, fourteen years later, I worked with, fought with, and then did not die with. He was the same person at ages eighteen and thirty-two. I used to try to imagine him as a child—thinking he may have been one of those bizarre old-men children, a Little Father Time from *Jude the Obscure*, unnaturally wise, scarily seeming to know what children should not know. But he assured me he was not like that as a child, and I believed him. He was not that sort of saint.

Sanjay spent most of his childhood in the United States. His English was unaccented but slightly formal in the manner of his parents, including an aversion to contractions. He retained a ghostly trace of the Indian head wobble and a more pronounced shadow of the typical Indian mannerism in which the head is slightly cocked to one side when considering a question. Few people noticed these habits in Sanjay, but everyone noticed how he looked at you. He had an unusual gaze that was completely attentive. His eyes were a deep warm amniotic brown, and these soft liquid eyes stared out at you as if you were the focus of his world. And you were, at that moment. This is easy to misunderstand. Sometimes attentive people seem to skewer you with their eyes. It can feel aggressive and unnerving. Not so with Sanjay. Although his focus was complete, his attention was tender, neither judgmental nor threatening. I don't know anyone who ever met him who was not affected by the way he looked at them.

I didn't have the words when we first met, but I later realized that these qualities—of being present, focused, and "mindful"—were not natural attributes of his character but qualities carefully cultivated over his short lifetime. When he was a child, his immigrant parents urged him to shun all things Indian and become completely American. So with the typical contrarianism of precocious children, he insisted on taking up yoga at age ten. By thirteen he had mastered the full Ashtanga series of yoga poses.

One night early during freshman year, a female friend called and asked if Sanjay wanted to join her for a drink after an evening lecture. He demurred, and she asked why. I overheard his strange reply: "I hope you will forgive me, Patricia, but your conversation, although entertaining, I generally do not find *intellectually* stimulating. It may be selfish of me, but tonight I am looking to be intellectually stimulated, not simply entertained."

"San, buddy, you can't say things like that," I admonished him after he hung up.

"Like what?"

"Like telling a friend that you don't find her conversation stimulating and that's the reason you won't go have a drink with her."

"But it is absolutely true."

He eventually learned that minor falsehood is a lubricant without which social life cannot run smoothly, and he mastered it to that minimum extent. But Sanjay remained a natural truth teller. This complete sincerity, more than anything else, was what later made him such an effective leader at Theocracy Watch. And, as it turned out, his enveloping focus and obvious sincerity survived the intermediation of the television camera. He was spectacular on TV.

It didn't hurt, of course, that unless someone was the type who could never see beauty in a person of another race, people usually thought that Sanjay was one of the most handsome men they had ever seen. Over the years a great deal of airtime was devoted by the media to the subject of Sanjay's extraordinary face, in which all elements were in perfect harmony—"super-symmetry," joked one of our physicist friends at Princeton. His skin was the color of warm polished cinnamon except below the perfectly defined edge of his beard, where a fine pixilated black shadow was visible even though he was always clean shaven. His jaw and cheeks were strong and slightly wider than usual for a Brahmin. The resulting face straddled, or perhaps combined, the elegance that Indians celebrated in their aristocratic men and the more robust masculine qualities that were considered desirable in the West. His hair was a black so luminous that all other colors were visibly collected up in each strand.

For our fundamentalist opponents, this perfect face was evidence of dark forces at work. This was because the Antichrist, according to prophecy, would take the form of a handsome young man. Sanjay was the popular champion standing against the establishment of the Godly Kingdom. The fact that he was also Indian (which they always referred to as "pagan"), and gay, certainly seemed to them to complete the satanic profile.

Before the time that President Palin first cited Sanjay's physical appearance as evidence of his demonic nature, it was a feature that he wore lightly, neither viewing it as a burden nor deliberately wielding it for effect. He never denied he was good-looking, but neither did he use his looks to charm or flirt or persuade. He was too honest and too confident of the power of his words for that. This unself-conscious innocence merely magnified his appeal to women and men alike.

Sanjay told me the first night we met that he was gay. It was news he delivered without drama as we got to know each other over a beer. I told him about my sister and my parents, my undistinguished career as a high school jock, and the casual high school girlfriend I had sensibly broken up with over the summer. He told me about his family's life in India, why his parents emigrated, what it was like to be an only child, that he was gay, and that he did yoga. I confess that I worried for a few days that having a gay roommate might impair my own social life. To my shame, I felt compelled to have a very public fling with a cute girl in the next entryway to ensure there would be no room for speculation about my own sexual preference.

In a few days, I realized how stupid I had been. Sanjay was extraordinarily popular with men and women alike. He had an ease that allowed him to circulate among the different circles of college social life in a way few other students could. And from freshman year on, it was I who was carried along in the wave of friends and fans who gathered around my roommate.

I've often wondered why Sanjay chose me for his most intense and long-lasting friendship. After freshman year he could have switched to any number of accomplished and fascinating roommates. But he never waivered. By October we were best friends, and no one—neither the occasional boyfriend of his nor my girlfriend Emilie, with whom

I lived for six painful years—changed that. Ultimately, that is. Emilie came close.

One thing about me that I know did interest Sanjay was this odd gift that I have. In another age, I might have thought of myself as some sort of seer or clairvoyant. But it really is just a knack for sudden, sometimes extreme situational awareness. It's not a habit of mind that I can call up at will; it just happens.

"It feels like a kind of out-of-body experience," I told Sanjay one night in the dorm after we had watched *Saturday Night Live* and had a few beers. Thinking about it today, I remember the sounds of the campus on a late Saturday night floating in through our open casement window.

"The first time it happened, at least that I can remember, was the day of my first middle school football game," I told Sanjay. "We were in the locker room, dressed in brand-new uniforms. I was excited, but mostly just scared—not that we would lose, but scared that I would do something stupid or embarrassing, like run down the field in the wrong direction or fumble. You know how it is." Sanjay looked empathetic, but he was too honest to signal that he did indeed have experience with that type of anxiety. It seemed clear that he didn't. Anyway, I continued.

"Just before we ran onto the field, San, the coach told us to get down on our knees. We all knelt. Then he said a prayer." I did a bad imitation of the coach's flat midwestern accent:

"Lord, as we prepare to join the field of battle, we ask you for strength, we ask you to lead us to victory. Victory in your name, and in the name of your son, Je-sus. Help us to vanquish our foe, to defeat our enemy, to . . . , you know, to defeat evil. Take the field with us, Je-sus. Well, you know. Screw the other bastards. Amen."

"And you know what happened then, San? Suddenly in my mind's eye I was looking down at the locker room from somewhere up in the air, looking down on twenty scrawny teenagers, dressed ridiculously, on their knees, invoking the personal intervention of the deity—the deity responsible for the spinning galaxies and the quantum flux—to take their side in a pissant football game. I had absolute situational clarity. I didn't have the vocabulary at the time to articulate it, but I completely and profoundly understood what I was seeing. I felt—so strongly that I had trouble keeping my composure—the absurdity, futility, humanity, and pathos of the moment. I . . . Let's say I didn't play very well that day."

"Fascinating," Sanjay said, considering carefully what he had heard. "I do not think that any young person should have to carry that kind of baggage. I know, G, how hard it can be to know such things. Perhaps this burden is one of the things we have in common."

Memory, I'm finding, is not very reliable. But I cannot remember any conversation, other than this one, where Sanjay or I ever alluded to the basis of our friendship. And by the way, although I thought I saw things clearly at the time, it was only much later that I finally understood that about half of those teenagers had earnestly adjusted their cosmology to accept that God was quite literally on their side.

Sanjay practiced yoga every day. Early each morning, usually starting while I was still asleep, he unrolled a thin green rubbery mat in the center of our living room and proceeded through the identical sequence of yoga postures. Most mornings I awoke to the sounds of his breathing—slightly constrained extended inhales and exhales that accompanied his movement. While engaged in this practice, including ten minutes of motionless meditation, he was oblivious to the noise and commotion of the dorm. At the end, he was always covered in a thin layer of sweat.

One morning I woke up unusually early, when Sanjay was just starting his practice. I passed through the living room in my boxer shorts on the way to the bathroom down the hall. For the first time, Sanjay stopped what he was doing. He looked uncertain, and then said, "May I teach you?" This was a surprise, as a kind of invisible wall had always descended around Sanjay when he was doing his yoga. Each time before this, when Sanjay was practicing, we had both behaved as if the other was simply not present.

"Sure," I said.

We stood side by side as he patiently taught me to breathe deeply through the nose, find the rooted ease of mountain pose, and then progress through the simple sun salutations with which he started his practice. He made adjustments to my posture, pulling my hips back to achieve an arched lower back in down-dog, and pushing the upper back to a flat and relaxed position—adjustments that allowed me to get a glimpse of the energy released by proper alignment. By the end of the hour, I too was covered in sweat. At the end, we sat with folded legs facing each other.

"G, I want you to understand. You need to understand what yoga means to me. You cannot really know me otherwise."

Yoga, he told me that morning, was not a religion, and it had no supernatural elements. Nor was it a purely physical practice, although many Americans enjoyed it only at that level. Instead, he said, it was a system of external "cleansing" practices that laid the foundation for internal mental practices. The external practices included yama, or the determination to live an ethical life; niyama, a type of enhanced self-awareness; and then—what I saw him doing every day—a physical practice of asanas, or postures, accompanied by controlled breathing. These, Sanjay explained, laid the foundation for the mental practices— concentration and meditation—which in turn could lead to *Samadhi*, which was, he admitted, something like the Buddhist nirvana, but was really just an advanced state of meditation that brings an insightful understanding of a person's oneness with the rest of that which exists. He had not, he assured me, reached *Samadhi*, nor did he expect he ever would.

"So," I asked, "what's the point? I mean, why devote an hour a day to practicing if you're never going to cross the finish line?"

Sanjay laughed in a way that never gave you the sense that he was laughing *at* you. He did not laugh at the misfortune or embarrassment of others. He laughed like a child at things that were silly, and laughed when he saw—sometimes by himself—the deep humor in a situation.

He never laughed out of politeness when others saw humor that he did not, but his own laugh was unusually infectious.

"I like that, G," he answered, laughing, ". . . 'the finish line.' Apt. You know that Indian culture is patient and accepting of destiny. But you have spotted that there is, in much of yoga tradition, a striving for result, including the ultimate result of *Samadhi*. I prefer another strain that puts more emphasis on simply doing without striving. I want to live an ethical life and a life that is well suited to the person I am. I have discovered within myself a strong moral compass, and it is difficult to enjoy serenity while engaging in immoral acts."

"So you are striving for serenity, then?" I asked, provocatively. Sanjay spoke quite a bit about serenity. It was ironic at the time, since college life is anything but serene. And it would prove to be a fruitless quest for my friend, whose ethical impulse led him to a life filled, externally at least, with drama, agitation, and, ultimately, suffering.

He ignored my provocation and continued his answer. "I admit, the postures and breathing make my body strong and healthy, and clear the mind. But even these things, although desirable, are not really desired as ends in themselves. Yoga, G, is not about striving. For me, desiring *Samadhi* would be wrong—as wrong as being good only because you desire the eternal reward of heaven or merely wish to avoid the punishment of hell. I agree there is a contradiction. Think of it this way, perhaps. You are walking down a road aware of the fact that at the end of the road there is a city. In one sense, the city is your destination, since if you keep walking along the road you will arrive there. But the fact is, that is not *why* you are on the road. You are on the road because you are a walker who wishes to take a walk on that road; you wish only to live in the moment, and walk well. I am sorry. I understand that this is not an altogether satisfactory answer."

It wasn't, and I had a hard time getting my mind around Sanjay's relationship with yoga. It was such a central part of his life and one that I didn't share. I envied Sanjay the equilibrium and peace of mind that was so obvious to all who knew him. He was often alone, and almost never lonely. I, on the other hand, was not—am not—an introspective person. As a young man, I did harbor a secret fear that I was a superficial person whose shallowness was well disguised by a glib cleverness. But I don't think that now.

I don't want to write about college. Princeton itself was a kind of nirvana, but like all temporal and physical varieties of paradise, it passed quickly. And I have always been profoundly vulnerable to the pain of loss and change.

My choice to go to law school did show a latent self-awareness. I couldn't have articulated it at the time, but I was right to intuit that I would be a good lawyer. I am a linear organized thinker, comfortable with abstraction and with a knack for insight. Good with words, and disciplined when I need to be. Of course, law school was also a safe choice. So safe as to be almost a non-choice. So like me at the time. Maintaining options, taking few risks.

Sanjay, in contrast, showed no interest in any of the conventional options. I overheard him on the phone one night with this father.

"Yes, Father. It is true that I could get into Harvard Medical School."

He listened impassively.

"Yes, I do want to help people and be a responsible member of society."

He saw I was listening, but he did not wink or grimace. When his words were attentive and respectful, he *was* attentive and respectful.

"I do not know, and yes, I agree with you that I am not ambitious. Respectfully, Father, I do not believe that ambition is an altogether good and safe thing. You misunderstand yoga. It is not passive. It accepts what we must accept, and arms us to engage with the world in a positive way. That is my ambition."

The day after graduation, when Sanjay and I drove out of Princeton headed for New York City and the rest of our lives, I was gripped by a deep sadness and unsuccessfully tried to stifle a few tears. Sanjay put his hand on my shoulder and said, "G, to be happy, you must always look forward." And here I am now, risking everything to look backward.

By the time I graduated from law school three years later saddled with student loans from seven years of tertiary and graduate education, Sanjay was rumored by the press to be worth $100 million and had just appeared on a list of the hundred most successful twenty-somethings in the country. The source of his wealth and his fame was *You and I*, a social networking website that he founded and, like the most successful such ventures, was hard to explain and, when described, sounded highly improbable.

"All relationships," Sanjay told me on the phone when I was taking a break from studying for my exams, "are bilateral. A social network of multiple individuals—a virtual community—is necessarily superficial. The other sites have it all wrong. The measure of success is not *how many* online friends or contacts you have, but the *quality* of the relationship you have with each individual. *You and I* is about deepening the online contact between two people. It is not a dating site. These are not romantic relationships. It is not necessarily even about friendship. It is about deep engagement with another mind and another character. And, most importantly, it does not make the mistake of all the other sites that base their networks on shared experience or shared interest. Zuckerberg has it all wrong, feeding the Facebook friending fetish with people who went to the same schools, grew up in the same town, or work at the same company. Relationships based on affinity are essentially narcissistic—it is like looking in a mirror."

"But isn't shared experience at the root of all sense of community? I mean, what's the alternative?"

"In yoga we spend lots of time looking at our own minds. We know ourselves. What enriches and completes us are other minds that are different. And engagement with those minds is best achieved when both parties are at peace with themselves: centered, mindful, and open. That is the alternative. So while our site is not restricted to yogis, it is where we are starting. For among yogis, you are far less likely to find people for whom friendship is needy, grasping, and demanding. That is the gift of *You and I*."

It was a gift that many people accepted gratefully. In 2003, *You and I* attained cult status among the thousands of young yogis in New York.

It was, they claimed, the only "authentic" online experience, bucking the very essence of wired society by providing depth not breadth, and substance instead of spectacle. In an early interview, making an analogy to the slow food movement, Sanjay called his site the "slow web." By 2004, he had reached a million members. Sanjay did not take advertising, and *You and I* had no source of revenue. He instead relied on donations from members to defray the costs of the site. Just before I graduated from law school and returned to New York to start my job at the firm, he sent me an e-mail: "Just been offered $80 million cash for *You and I*. How can this be? Please explain. You are coming to Wall Street, G; please be careful. I fear something is seriously wrong."

CHAPTER FOUR

Tomorrow Belongs to Me

2005

> *I don't see how you can be President . . . without a relationship with the Lord.*
> —President George W. Bush, 2005

> *The second coming of Christ is everything that I'm living for. And I hope the Rapture comes tomorrow.*
> —House Majority Leader Tom DeLay, 2007

> *America has no King but Jesus.*
> —Attorney General John Ashcroft, 2004

> *The Republican Party of Texas affirms that the United States of America is a Christian Nation . . .*
> —Official platform, Republican Party of the state of Texas, 2004

SEVERAL MONTHS AFTER STARTING WORK at the law firm, I handled the closing of an initial public offering for a company that previously had been taken private by a private equity firm, entered Chapter 11 when it could not service the debt it incurred to fund its own acquisition, was again bought and re-leveraged by a different set of private equity firms, and was then being re-sold to the public. Nothing about that seemed to me to be unusual or untoward. It wasn't that I failed to think about my work in any sort of larger context; I did. But what I thought was that facilitating the free flow of capital to where it was needed was a necessary and an even noble calling. After all, the removal of regulatory impediments to the free flow of capital had led to three consecutive economic booms, freed billions in emerging markets from poverty, created the wealth that brought New York back from the brink of disaster, and created the glamorous world city, of unprecedented energy and cultural vigor, that I enjoyed. So when I, with unbecoming self-importance, cleared the deal to close—harvesting $7 billion in cash from the public markets for the private equity firms that were our clients—I felt very good about my day.

It was on that early deal that I met Emilie Craig. She had just graduated from Tuck Business School and started as a vice president at Credit Suisse. With all that has happened, can I really see her again as I saw her back then? When I close my eyes, I cannot see her twenty-five-year-old face, but I do hear her twenty-five-year-old voice before it acquired the strain and exasperated edginess that later caused me such pain. That twenty-five-year-old voice was lively and fun. Our roles as the most junior team members on a big deal, and our mutual professional insecurity, formed the basis for an easy camaraderie. I kidded her about the unconventional spelling of her name, which was the result of a Francophile father. She joked and said I was the best lawyer with whom she (with all of three months' experience) had ever worked. After the deal closed, I asked her out on a date.

Emilie looked great in a suit. At work, she was comfortable with the role of being a strong professional woman, but, like the suit, it was something she put on. The Emilie I first fell in love with was not the banker. Behind the amusingly flip and confident professional woman was a warm and sometimes vulnerable girl from a small town in the Midwest. She let me see that vulnerability, which for her was an act of great intimacy. I think it also contributed to the disproportion of her subsequent bitterness.

I cannot honestly say she had a great gift for friendship. But initially this did not matter, since we were lovers before we were friends. We had sex after our first date. Emilie was a free and uncomplicated lover. For both of us, sex became a critical part of coping with the stress of our new lives. And in many ways she communicated better and more honestly with her body than with her words. After a few months I convinced myself that I had fallen in love.

Nothing in Emilie's past had caused her to care much about money. She went to business school because she was good with numbers. At the beginning, she and I looked at our new lives in New York with a degree of detachment, but it was a perspective that—for her—faded quickly. She proved to be a chameleon, efficiently absorbing and reflecting the tastes, prejudices, and values of the people whose world she had entered. I did so more slowly and less completely. And therein lay the root of our problem.

I was of course nervous about introducing Emilie to Sanjay. I knew he would be genuinely delighted that I had a girlfriend. But I also knew he could not dissemble, and I greatly feared that he would betray either doubt about, or disapproval of, my choice. Being in the first stages of love, or perhaps just being dense, I didn't have the slightest worry about how Emilie would react to Sanjay. I simply assumed she would find him as fascinating as everyone else did.

"Well?" I asked Sanjay after their first meeting, which occurred over my trademark swordfish dinner and seemed to me to have gone well.

"She is most delightful," he said. "Lovely, smart, and clearly interested in you. You are lucky." I didn't read anything into the brevity of Sanjay's verdict, and I was vastly relieved at the time that he hadn't felt compelled to point out any of her flaws.

At first Emilie didn't fully understand my friendship with Sanjay. She was perfectly cordial in a disinterested sort of way—in the way, I suppose, that lots of women are not terribly interested in their boyfriend's male friends. But once she started spending frequent nights at my place, and realized that I spoke to Sanjay almost every day and saw him at least once a week, she could not hide her annoyance.

"What does he give you that I can't?" she once asked. And, after too many glasses of an old and expensive Armagnac, she made a statement she never would have made sober: "*I* want to be your soul mate."

After we had been a couple for a couple of years, Emilie and I reached an accommodation on the Sanjay issue. She and he became friends, and she adopted a role of motherly concern for a not very practical child, mocking his idealism and occasional spectacular lack of understanding of the ways in which human beings usually relate to one another. She simply chose to ignore the irritating fact that Sanjay's continuing role in my life was a symptom of something missing from our own relationship.

★　★　★

THE YEAR 2005 was a good one. I graduated near the top of my class from law school, started a job in the best law firm on Wall Street, and acquired an attractive and successful girlfriend. I did not take these things for granted. Nothing in my background—even four years at one of the country's most elite universities—had prepared me for my life in New York City during the boom period that preceded the financial crisis in 2008. I made $125,000 my first year as a lawyer— more than the salary that my hardworking father was making after thirty years at his job. The Wall Street that I entered was not the Wall Street that became so reviled following the 2008 financial crisis, with its lethal brew of myopic focus on short-term profits and faith in financial alchemy. At the firm, I found a truly diverse group of men and women, from across the country and the world, who had risen to the top of their law school classes through extraordinary academic performance and were attracted to the firm by its culture of quality and integrity. And it really was a meritocracy. No one who started in my class of lawyers at the firm had obtained their positions through family or connections.

There were, of course, rewards. In addition to the salary, we got first-class training and great work. We also ate with clients in the city's best restaurants, learned not to feel guilty when drinking hundred-dollar bottles of wine, rode around town in radio-dispatched "black cars," and—when entertained by RCD&S partners at their penthouse apartments and perfect country houses—received a glimpse of the life that we too might have. Despite the suddenness of our immersion in this world, within a few months it seemed entirely natural and completely deserved that we now sat near the top of the vast pyramid that was New York City.

The quid pro quo for our provisional access to this rarefied world was total dedication to the firm. The first rule was that the clients were to be treated like gods. Their phone calls and e-mails were to be answered promptly. Their requests and deadlines, no matter how unreasonable, were to be met—and met with perfection. The firm was obsessive about quality. We aspired for our work product to be perfect. In doing legal research, no stone was left unturned. Every possible solution to the client's problem was explored and analyzed. I quickly came to have pride in the firm, while at the same time doubting constantly that I was really up to the job. For a young lawyer, the sources of stress were manifold. I was often exhausted from lack of sleep. Worse was the uncertainty. You made plans but never knew when a last-minute assignment or crisis would keep you at the office. Your friends quickly became used to empty seats and unused tickets. And for overachievers accustomed to excelling at everything, having memos and drafts come back from senior associates and partners covered with corrections and comments was deeply disturbing.

★   ★   ★

EARLIER TODAY I looked up and was startled to spot a person walking along the far bank of Indian Lake. I quickly convinced myself that each time the man stopped and turned toward the water, he was staring across at the cottage. If I could see him, I thought, then he could see me through the large plate glass window. My heart raced. I didn't know whether to be still, so as not to attract attention, or to go and alert Adam. I chose not to move. Sitting here, ridiculously frozen, I was overcome by a feeling of guilt: guilt for being off the Purity Web, guilt for lying to Lurlene at the archives, guilt for breaking their rules. But quickly guilt turned to anger. Faced suddenly with the possibility that this project, which I had taken on so reluctantly, would be interrupted or terminated, I became angry. I have not been angry for a very long time.

When the person moved farther down the lakeshore, I went downstairs and found Adam. He could see I was shaken.

"What's wrong?"

"Someone is out there," I said, my voice trembling slightly.

"Let me see."

"You can't. He's gone," I answered.

"Are you sure it was a he?" I nodded. "And where was he? On the other side of the lake?"

"Yes. He was staring across at the cottage."

"OK, thanks for letting me know. Don't worry about it. It's probably nothing. Some of the old-timers remember the lake and walk here."

"Not an easy place to take a walk," I said.

"No, you're right. It could be a deacon. But if so, there's nothing we can do. Don't worry about it."

When I seemed reluctant to return to my desk in front of the window, Adam asked me a strange question.

"There's something I want you to think about, Greg. When you remember 2005 and the start of your career, what were the things you believed or assumed then—the certainties you embraced—that ultimately proved most wrong?"

Whether or not it was his intention, he succeeded in distracting me from worrying. It was an odd question, and a hard thing to think about. Of all the things I held certain at the beginning of my adult life, which one was most mistaken? Of course, there's my family. I never imagined I would lose them so early. But that's not what Adam meant. At the start of my career, I knew that the exact path of my career would not be clear or certain. But I did think that the ground over which that path would lead would be more or less stable. I believed that the stage on which my life would play out—this country and its institutions— would be essentially static and unchanging. I see now that this was a spectacular failure of perspective. I should have known from history that the ground on which we take the walk of our lives is shifting and unstable, and that change is unpredictable and spasmodic. Nothing seems to us—in human time—to be more solid than the ground. And yet in reality the earth's crust jerks across the globe in devastating spasms. Centuries or millennia of rock-solid calm punctuated by a few minutes of heaving and rolling readjustment. This is the perspective of geological time.

But after the cataclysms of the twentieth century, it seemed to me in 2005 that the ground was stable. Indeed, the framework within which I thought my life and career would unfold seemed so settled as to be invisible. The status quo—a stable federal union, an open society, democracy, personal freedom, or indeed basic civil order—was so expected, so much a given, that not once did even a flicker of appreciation for these things cross my consciousness. What I gave no thought to then, though, has for the last fifteen years never been far from the center of my mind.

★   ★   ★

WITH NEW YORK having recovered from 9/11, and the credit and housing bubbles being in full flower, life in New York seemed strangely detached from the broader trends of the Bush years in America. When one of our Princeton friends got married in central Pennsylvania, I rented a car, and Sanjay, Emilie, and I drove together to the wedding. These excursions out of the city often gave us a sense of dislocation, a sense that the suburban and rural America of our youths—not so many years before—was changing beyond recognition.

"There it is again," said Sanjay.

We had been driving through a sprawling landscape of shopping malls and housing developments, grotesquely ugly beads strung randomly along a strand of four traffic-choked lanes. The cars—windows up cocooning their passengers in air-conditioning on a lovely spring day—mysteriously shuttled among malls even though most seemed to contain exactly the same blend of national chain stores and fast-food outlets. The rare undeveloped pockets between commercial strips and sprawling housing developments hosted overscale billboards carefully angled toward the slow-moving traffic. Sanjay had noticed a particular billboard advertisement, repeated over and over, that featured a recognizable image of Jesus, looking rather more stern than I was used to, looming over the dome of the Capitol building in Washington with the strident message "The time is now" floating above on a banner supported by two angels. It seemed there had always been religious billboards, most of a fairly anodyne variety, announcing, for example, that "Jesus Saves." But this seemed different.

"Tomorrow belongs to me," I said.

"What?" asked Emilie.

"The song. That's what the billboards remind me of. In *Cabaret*, when the young Nazi starts singing. You know, 'Fatherland, Fatherland give us a sign . . .' I can't remember the rest. But it ends with 'Tomorrow belongs to me.' It always gives me the creeps. I mean serious creeps. Not sure why. Every time I hear it I get goose bumps."

"You are a sentimental twit." Emilie had started to pick up all sorts of anglicisms from the British bankers at Credit Suisse, a habit that had started, even then, to annoy me.

The wedding was in a suburban "mega-church"—a large gray metal building seating thousands and surrounded by acres of blacktop parking that entombed the fertile soils below that had been farmed for centuries. I had never seen anything like it. It was near the intersection of two state highways, far from any village or town center. Other than a grossly overscaled cross mounted on the roof, the architecture was not at all ecclesiastical. It could have been a factory. The complex included a vast sanctuary with a platform at the front that was more stage than altar, with elaborate theatrical lighting. In another bit of stagecraft, a large crucifix, which looked to me as though it was made from fiberglass, was suspended by invisible wires, giving the appearance that it hovered over the back of the stage. A rock band was positioned on one side, and a large choir in shiny purple robes was on the other. Enormous video screens were arrayed, stadium-like, around all sides of the room. During the service, a talented producer chose images for the large screens. He projected close-ups of the preacher but frequently interrupted that feed in favor of ecstatic faces from the audience and angelic choir girls who then appeared in flashing superscale all around the room. This clearly was religion as entertainment. It made me remember that so much of the historical success of Christianity was owing to its ability to embrace and incorporate popular culture from all parts of the world and all eras. The pagans are wedded to celebrating the winter solstice? No problem, we'll shift the birthday of Christ to accommodate.

I reflected how different this was from the Catholic Church of my childhood, holding fast to the old hymns and refusing to make any expedient accommodation to contemporary sensibilities. What we saw that day, in contrast, was religion finely and completely attuned to every nuance and preference of contemporary American popular culture—attuned, that is, in terms of experience and presentation. Content, as we found out, was another thing altogether.

The sanctuary stood at the center of a complex that included several schoolrooms, a library (which contained mostly religious DVDs and few books), a senior center, and a kindergarten, among other facilities. This church seemed to loom large in the life of the bride's family. The church, our friend Jim said, had given back the sense of community that this suburb had been missing. He also had called it a "Bible-believing church," but he didn't elaborate.

At the dinner after the ceremony, the three of us were seated with the sister of the bride, who was slightly older than we were and worked at an accounting firm. Sanjay was talking about *You and I* and happened to mention that the first group attracted to the website were yogis.

"Oh," the sister said, suddenly looking troubled. "And that was . . . well, ok?"

"Oh, yes," said Sanjay. "Really perfect. They got it immediately."

"But . . . well," she asked, "aren't yoga people, you know, atheists?"

Sanjay, who had been polite but clearly bored, suddenly looked interested.

"Well, some are, I suppose. But no more or less, I would think, than the general population. Why do you ask?"

"I don't think so," the sister said. "I mean, yoga is a religion, an atheistic religion, so that means that yogis don't believe in God. In our church, we believe that yoga is one of the ways that Satan recruits souls."

I had rarely seen Sanjay at a loss for words. He looked genuinely confused.

"Sue, with all respect to your church, I have to tell you that is not right. You can be a Christian or a Buddhist or a Muslim and still do yoga. It is true that it emerged from the Hindu tradition and that there is a spiritual dimension in addition to the physical practice. But many devout religious people do yoga. And," he added, attempting to lighten the mood, "I have done yoga since I was ten, and have never encountered Satan."

"You cannot know that. Satan doesn't announce himself, you know. And anything that calls itself a spiritual practice that doesn't have Jesus at its center is . . . well, you know, an illusion."

Sanjay was just about to say something conciliatory when Emilie, who had drunk too much wine, jumped in.

"And I suppose your church teaches that evolution is also an illusion?"

"No," she answered, "not an illusion but a theory that is incorrect because it conflicts with the Bible. We're a Bible-believing church. The Bible is pretty clear about creation. But even if you don't believe the Bible, there are so many problems with evolution that many eminent scientists don't believe it, you know. Surely you understand that much."

Emilie opened her mouth, but nothing came out.

The sister, sensing success, went on.

"Last year our church did a field trip to Kentucky to visit the Creation Museum. It was awesome. It explained the right way to understand fossils and about all the evidence for the flood, and showed how man and the dinosaurs coexisted with all the rest of God's creation. You've got to go, really. You'd never think the same way about it if you went. There's just so much nonsense you hear from the mainstream media—it's really important for people like you to be exposed to both sides of the story. Oh, and there was a fantastic exhibit at a nearby museum proving the existence of hell. So clever. They put microphones down some abandoned oil wells in Texas and recorded the screams of the damned. Terrifying. You really should go."

I could tell that Emilie was on the verge of saying something she would regret, so I interrupted and changed the subject. Sanjay clearly wished to probe and explore the woman's beliefs and views, but with one look I warned him off. He looked very thoughtful during the rest of the dinner.

In the car on the way back, Sanjay was animated and clearly fascinated by the experience. I was driving, and Emilie was in the back, with a hangover.

Sanjay was looking down at his Palm Treo. "Amazing. Did you know," he asked, "that 84 percent of Americans believe that Jesus is the son of God, 80 percent believe in the Day of Judgment and in miracles, 50 percent believe in angels, and 40 percent believe in the literal truth of the Bible? Fifty-five percent say God created humans in their present form, and only 13 percent believe in evolution without divine guidance."

"Impossible," said Emilie. "I don't know anybody who believes in angels or who doesn't accept evolution. Who are these people?"

"Those numbers are true, I am afraid," continued Sanjay. "I am looking at the latest Gallup Poll. It says that 25 percent of Americans describe themselves as evangelicals and 40 percent self-describe as born-again Christians—40 percent. I had no idea."

"So what?" asked Emilie. "I mean, these people say 'I believe this, I believe that.' I'm supposed to care? Why? I mean, these people cannot get the small stuff right. Did you see on the news that Miss South Carolina said on TV that she thought Europe was a country and she had never heard of Hungary? Unbelievable. So if they can't get the small stuff right, why should I care about what they believe about the really big stuff, like creation and infinity and the universe? It's absurd. Why do we pay attention to these people?"

"I am not sure, but I found the weekend very interesting," Sanjay answered. "Those people are not what I thought fundamentalists were like. We were not in the Deep South or a stereotypical 'red state.' We were in Pennsylvania. And the family. Well, they did not appear to be unreasonable people. But the sister at dinner . . ."

"Wasn't that a scream?" Emilie interrupted. "When she started explaining to you why yoga was satanic . . . oh my God, it was classic, classic. Sanjay, dear, it's not often that I've seen you at a total loss for words. And she's an accountant. What an idiot. Unbelievable. My head hurts."

That weekend in Pennsylvania is what first got Sanjay interested in the evangelical movement and eventually in its quest for political power. Would something else have triggered the same interest, or would he and I have had completely different lives if our friend had married someone else or if Sanjay hadn't gone to the wedding? A frivolous thought. Coincidence and randomness create opportunity and choices, and our lives then take a path determined by the opportunities we take and the choices we make.

Within days I realized that Sanjay had become fascinated by the mega-church phenomenon, by the theology of fundamentalist Christianity, and by the rapid rise of the Christian right to the pinnacle of political power. Running *You and I* at that point was not really a full-time job, and Sanjay immersed himself in the topic and spoke of little else. It was not, at the time, a topic of great interest to me. In fact, as I immersed myself in my work and had my eyes opened to the worlds of business and finance, Sanjay's preoccupation seemed to me to be more than a little quirky. I had the sense that, after years of academics, I was finally learning how the world really worked. The people with whom I spent my days were what we pretentiously called at the time "players," and San—despite his success with *You and I*—seemed to have taken a turn back to a world of abstraction, theory, and academic speculation. Despite our closeness, I occasionally was tempted to see Sanjay as an artifact of my past life as opposed to a major part of my current life—a view that Emilie did nothing to discourage.

It is painful for me to realize how far things already had progressed by 2005. Even Sanjay didn't have the full picture at the time. After the 2004 election, not only were the president of the United States, the Speaker of the House, numerous cabinet members, and other senior federal officials born-again Christians, but *forty-two out of a hundred* US senators were entirely supportive of the Christian right agenda, holding ratings of 100 percent from the Christian Coalition. Extreme fundamentalist Christians entered the US Senate, including Tom Coburn of Oklahoma (calling for the death penalty for abortion doctors) and Jim DeMint (wanting to ban gays and unmarried pregnant women from teaching in public schools). Fundamentalist Christian theology was already driving our federal policy on medical research (with the ban on stem cell research), sex education (which the government decreed should focus exclusively on the promotion of abstinence), and US foreign policy in the Middle East (where an important driver of US policy was the need to have Jerusalem in the hands of the Jews in order to satisfy a biblical condition to the second coming of Christ). The federal government was channeling billions in taxpayer funds to faith-based organizations—nearly all evangelical. And, perhaps most significantly and least noticed, much of the legislation that would eventually implement the theocratic program, including the Constitution Restoration Act (preventing federal courts from hearing church/state separation cases) and the Houses of Worship Free Speech Restoration Act (allowing tax-exempt churches to engage in partisan political activity), had already been introduced in Congress, ultimately failing to become law but attracting significant pluralities. We had already been given, unknowingly, a preview of what was to follow.

★　　★　　★

MUCH LATER, WHEN working for New York governor Bloomberg, I read a lot about revolutions. Revolutions are rarely if ever majoritarian but instead are usually propelled by a small group that is disciplined and fanatical to which a passive majority then acquiesces. Incredibly, by 2005 the first phase of the Christian revolution was already over, yet few people other than its proponents understood at the time that this had happened. The small band of fanatics, headed by James Dobson, Tony Perkins, and Doug Coe, among others, inspired by Rousas J. Rushdoony and funded by Howard Ahmanson, Jr., had succeeded in bringing their brand of fundamentalist Christianity from the fringes of American life to the very heart of political power. A theology that had been intolerable to mainstream Christianity before had achieved legitimacy. In 1981 Gary North had written that "to smooth the transition to Christian political leadership . . . Christians must begin to organize politically within the present party structure, and they must begin to infiltrate the existing institutional order." This was, they were clear, to be a revolution from within. Twenty-five years later, evangelicals, through carefully incremental political work at the precinct, county, and state level, had seized control of the Republican Party. It was a movement that was at once cultural and political, and it was the largest such movement in the country by far. All that by 2005.

Very few people at the time noticed what had happened. There were, admittedly, many moderate Republicans who fully understood this takeover of one of our two major political parties, without, of course, anticipating its eventual implications. But the general public was largely blind to the enormous role that religion was playing in politics, in part because evangelical Republican candidates used a veiled code in their communications with the faithful, what political pros referred to as "dog-whistle politics" for its ability to arouse the faithful while passing undetected by others.

As a result, the rest of America still associated the word "Christian" with benign mainstream Protestant denominations and Roman Catholicism, which had no theocratic tendencies and for whom the dominionist, reconstructionist, and similar theologies were heretical and abhorrent. Non-fundamentalist Christians thought that John F. Kennedy had disposed of the issue of religious belief and politics when he said: "I am not the Catholic candidate for president. I am the Democratic Party's candidate for president who also happens to be a Catholic.

I do not speak for my church on public matters—and the church does not speak for me." But the world had changed. Now, when it came to politics, "Christian" meant something very different.

By 2005, Christian fundamentalism, self-identified by various types of congregations referring to themselves as "Bible-believing churches," had migrated from the Deep South to northern suburbia, where loss of community and empty consumerism had left a void that the evangelicals were all too ready to fill. They filled the void not with a traditional Protestantism but with a dumbed-down Christianity where "faith" was not a private embrace of the mysteries inherent in the human condition but a requirement for complete dogmatic credulity—where the ultimate measure of devotion and religiosity was the willingness to dismiss empirical reality and profess absolute belief in bold and improbable lies (such as the coexistence of man and dinosaurs), and where the primary values were not the dignity and integrity of the individual and the realization by that individual of the whole and spiritual self but total submission by the individual to biblical law and Godly authority. And perhaps most tragically, what had migrated north was a redefined Christianity in which the singular voice of Christ called the faithful not to modesty, charity, meekness, love, and social justice but to a theological imperative for the accumulation of wealth and political power in order to establish Christian dominion over the country.

The evangelical Christianity that spread from the south to the rest of the country was, in effect, an ideological system demanding complete obedience to the word of God as revealed by the Bible. The Bible was no longer a book of instructive parables whose teachings were limited to the sacred and the moral. Instead, the Bible had become what the evangelical faithful called a "guide to everything": facts, history, science, politics, and civil life. The non-evangelical majority was bemused by the evangelical preoccupation with biblical literalism as manifested most prominently by creationism, but in retrospect these specific beliefs were trivial distractions. What so few people saw at the time was that this mind-set of credulity was a form of brainwashing that completely undermined the role of rational argument that lies at the heart of democracy. This, more than anything else, laid the groundwork for the totalitarianism that would follow.

Like any populist movement, the evangelical right depended on enemies. By 2005 they had largely settled upon what their prime enemies would be: secularism (which, they argued, was really a competing religion) and "the homosexual agenda." Anti-Semitism, which had served other nascent totalitarian movements so well in the past, had been rendered off-limits by the Holocaust; and communism, the prior bogeyman, had faded as a credible threat following the fall of the Soviet Union. By the 1990s, the anti-gay message had proved itself as a successful vehicle for crystalizing political action, largely centered around repeal of civil rights laws protecting homosexuals. Christian broadcasting was filled with ridiculous canards: Nazism was really a gay movement; gays were born with a missionary zeal to convert others (especially children) to the "gay lifestyle"; a whole range of diseases, not just AIDS, was spread by homosexuals; all male homosexuals were pedophiles. Preachers preached that the rise of homosexuals was the surest sign of the coming end times; they were the Antichrist's army, predicted with startling clarity by the Bible. They reminded the faithful again and again that the rise of homosexuality was God's way of testing humanity—if we tolerate the abomination, then we are irrevocably lost and abandoned by God. They preached that the idea of homosexual "rights" was absurd, no more sensible than speaking of the "rights" of murderers, rapists, and child molesters. The relentless preaching had the desired effect. By 2004 the official platform of the Republican Party of the state of Texas stated: ". . . the practice of sodomy tears at the fabric of society, contributes to the breakdown of the family unit, and leads to the spread of dangerous, communicable diseases. Homosexual behavior is contrary to the fundamental, unchanging truths that have been ordained by God, recognized by our country's founders, and shared by the majority of Texans."

A few years later, the anti-gay message had been honed and refined for maximum effect: The problem was not only that homosexuality was an abomination in the sight of God but that the existence of and tolerance for homosexuality was a vital threat to marriage, to Christianity, and to the nation. This core message was echoed every Sunday, week after week, at thousands of churches around the country: "The religious freedoms of all Americans are under attack from radical homosexual activists . . . gay marriage will destroy your marriage and your family." Or, as James Dobson put it quite comprehensively, gay marriage "will destroy the earth."

Finally, having enemies was not enough. In a strategy common to fundamentalists the world over, evangelical preachers successfully tapped into the meme of the "persecuted church." The growth of a modern, secular, and tolerant society, they argued, really is about the tyrannical suppression of Christianity because the idea of a secular and tolerant society is inconsistent with Christian claims to dominion over civil society. In the ultimate Orwellian perversion, the core "secular" value of religious tolerance becomes *in*tolerant and tyrannical. Extension of basic civil liberties to those who engage in a sexual practice that is taboo to fundamentalists becomes an attack on the Christian church in which Christians, and not the historically persecuted homosexuals, are the true victims. Permitting gays to marry becomes an attack on marriage in which married people are somehow victimized, threatened, and undermined. Abortion is seen as an attack on life itself. Even ordinary non-evangelical Christians started to look at modern secular society differently. Perhaps the big city atheist intellectuals really do *not* mean "live and let live." Perhaps, they began thinking, the patina of tolerance really is part of a program to abolish my religion and prevent me from believing and worshiping as I see fit. Fear is contagious and, when accompanied by economic distress and social alienation, turns easily into the comforting cloak of victimhood, providing absolution to the wearer for his misfortune, solidarity with his fellow victims, and an enemy on whom to project his anger and resentment.

I found in Adam's file a clipping on Pat Robertson, the strange Christian media mogul with reconstructionist tendencies who ran for president of the United States in 1988. It was Robertson who first introduced the idea of Christian fundamentalists as a persecuted minority.

In a 1993 interview he said, "Just like what Nazi Germany did to the Jews, so liberal America is now doing to the evangelical Christians. It's no different . . . More terrible than anything suffered by any minority in history." Reading that now, I can't help wondering what the journalists first hearing these words thought. Did they have even a glimmer of their implications? A former candidate for president asserting that the treatment of evangelical Christians by "liberal America" was more terrible than the treatment of Cambodians at the hands of Pol Pot, of the Tutsi minority by the Hutu majority in Rwanda, the Bosnian Muslims by the Serbs, the Jews by the Nazis, the early Christians by the Romans? Because such an assertion was manifestly untrue as an empirical matter, did the journalists not see that it must have been uttered for a purpose? Did they not sit up in their chairs, faces pale at its enormous implications? After all, what do such victims do? What are they *entitled* to do? What would we *expect* them to do? There is no moral or legal code under which a minority so terribly victimized would not be entitled to rise up and vanquish their persecutors and claim the mantle of history—and the mantle of righteousness—in doing so. But neither Sanjay nor I saw it at the time, or could even have imagined how quickly the self-described victims would become the victors.

CHAPTER FIVE

Striving

2007

Christianity and democracy are inevitably enemies. . . .
Christianity is completely and radically anti-democratic;
it is committed to spiritual aristocracy.

—Rousas John Rushdoony

It is the quality of patriotism to be jealous and watchful,
to observe all secret machinations, and to see publick
dangers at a distance. The true lover of his country is
ready to communicate his fears, and to sound the alarm,
whenever he perceives the approach of mischief.

—Samuel Johnson,
The Patriot

"G, YOU ARE A LAWYER. Please explain something."

"I'll try," I answered cautiously, as Sanjay's questions were rarely capable of being answered.

"I have just read a book called *A Christian Manifesto* by a man named Francis Schaeffer. This is a popular book; it sold two hundred ninety thousand copies in its first year and is still selling briskly almost twenty-five years later. It advocates the end of a pluralistic secular democracy and advocates violence to restore biblical morality. I understand that the crime of treason includes advocating the overthrow of the Consti-tution of the United States. So tell me, when evangelicals say that God's law, as set forth in the Bible, should trump all civil law including the Constitution, is that not treason? Should that not be illegal? It is very confusing because instead of prosecuting promotion of this idea as a crime, the federal government subsidizes those who are advocating it by making them tax exempt. What is more, at a time when the author of this book was advocating violent resistance to the US government and constitutional law, two presidents invited him to the White House. You are a lawyer, Greg. What am I missing?"

"San, I'm sorry, I'm really tired, and that's not my kind of law. And it's a naïve question. We don't prosecute people for treason for writing books."

"We did when those books advocated communism," San said.

"This is different," I answered.

"How so?"

"San, do you think I can make partner? I want you to tell me honestly."

"I do not know."

"Come on, you're supposed to say that I can do whatever I put my mind to."

"Sorry, but that would not be true. You know I have great confidence in your abilities. But I do not know what it takes to make partner; therefore, I cannot appraise whether you have what it takes."

"OK. Well, that's the problem. I don't know either. And I don't know whether I want it. But I'm beginning to think I do."

I waited for his comment. He gave me one of his gently probing looks but did not speak.

"San, I want to know. I really want to know what you think. Am I cut out to be a lawyer? Should I try to make partner? Should I spend my life being a corporate lawyer?"

"Those are, perhaps, different questions," he replied. "I think you can be—I think you probably are—a fine lawyer. You have the brains. Your mind is orderly. Analysis and logic come naturally. You are articulate."

It was my turn to be silent.

"But," he continued, "*should* you stay at RCD&S and become a partner? This is a question only you . . ."

It was my turn to give him a dirty look.

"OK," Sanjay continued. "I have enormous respect for the profession. And to have the opportunity to practice at the top of your profession would be a privilege. But yes, I do have a worry. I know you, G. You are a fine person. But you will be at the heart of Wall Street. It is a culture that does not merely accept self-interest but celebrates it. There is a tendency toward grasping and shallowness that is endemic. There is striving always and, I fear, much disappointment. Such a place could change a person."

"San, I'm sorry. And no disrespect, but that's yoga talking. The world is not an ashram. The economy and political system—hell, the society—is built on self-interest. Evolutionary biologists teach us that even altruism may be a form of self-interest. You know that. Wall Street is no utopia, but it's a lot of bright people doing things that are really important. And are there sharks? Of course. But give me a little credit, San. I think I can swim with the sharks without turning into one of them."

"Yes," he said, "you have put your finger on the issue."

And so went many of my conversations with Sanjay during this period. He slowly and methodically connected the dots and assembled a coherent picture of the Christian Nation to which the fundamentalists aspired. I increasingly immersed myself in my practice and slowly developed the determination to make the sacrifices required to become a partner of RCD&S. If I stayed at the firm, it would be a marathon, requiring five more years of long hours, high stress, and low odds of ultimate success.

Emilie had no doubt what I should do, and 2007 was the year I moved into her two- bedroom East Side apartment. I asked her to move into mine, but she declined.

For about six months we did not see much of Sanjay. It was actually Emilie who felt badly about it, and to my surprise one weekend she suggested that we do something with Sanjay. "Friends are precious," she said, "and it is far too easy to let them drift away." There were still many moments like these when I was glad I was living with this woman and was completely convinced that she was different from the bankers whom she increasingly resembled, at least superficially. And so Emilie called and invited Sanjay to the opera.

We were all guests of Emilie's boss at Credit Suisse. He was an enthusiastic member of the Metropolitan Opera Club—a group of opera fans who maintained a dining room within the opera house and a row of boxes for the use of the members. The club maintained a strict dress code, with black tie for men and evening gowns for ladies and, in an anachronism remarkable even for New York, a requirement for white tie and tails on Monday nights. Emilie's boss, of course, preferred Mondays.

We were seated at a large round table in the center of the gold-leafed dining room when Sanjay arrived. There was a noticeable lull in conversation when Sanjay turned the corner from the coat check and stood in the front of the room. And it was not simply the relatively rarity of a brown face. Even I was stunned. Sanjay in white tie presented a striking image. The black and white played off his brown face and ebony hair. The long line of the tailcoat emphasized his height and lean body. He could have been an Indian prince entering the court in Edwardian England.

Emilie was obviously thrilled, and I wondered momentarily if this was all about the plaudits she would earn from her mentor and his wife for bringing such a striking figure to their party. It was an unkind thought.

The partner's wife and other women were fascinated, and Sanjay charmed them without effort. The opera that night was Massenet's *Thaïs* and the Credit Suisse partner led a spirited discussion of its plot: the monk who leaves the monastery to save the courtesan and ends up with his love for her eclipsing his love for God, while at the same time the courtesan whom he comes to save ends up renouncing her life of pleasure and entering a convent to devote her life to prayer. What were we to make of this, he asked? Was this just an O. Henry–like plot twist, or was Massenet taking sides? Was the hero the monk or the prostitute?

After allowing others to speak first, Sanjay then offered his opinion.

"I would imagine," said Sanjay, "that we are intended to conclude that neither is the right path to follow. Instead, both paths illustrate the same fallacy, the fallacy that religious devotion can lead to real redemption or salvation. The monk learns from hard experience that he cannot be complete as a human if his only relationship is with an imaginary being, and that striving for eternal life is a futile quest. The courtesan spends her life striving for pleasure, but when she finally realizes that she is in need of redemption from an immoral life, she makes the same mistake as the monk in seeking it in an equally futile marriage with God. Massenet is telling us that we humans make the same mistakes over and over—the mistake of striving and of endlessly seeking unobtainable extremes. This opera is, I think you will see, a tragedy."

Emilie looked momentarily uneasy. We both knew from prior experience that Sanjay's earnest frankness, especially on matters of religion, could easily offend.

"Yes, yes," the investment banker exclaimed. "Brilliant. You are right. I've seen the opera a half dozen times and never thought of it this way. But that's it. A carefully disguised polemic against religion. Faith and religious enthusiasm leading where they always do, to tragedy. Heh. Heh. I wonder if any of the French clerics got it. You had to be careful back then, you know."

"You have to be careful now," Sanjay observed.

"Oh, don't worry. We're Episcopalians; we're not offended. We don't believe; we go for the music, and so our kids have someplace nice to get married."

"I am glad that you and Mrs. Mettrick are not offended, but that is not what I meant. I was referring to the evangelical political movement. They *are* easily offended. Did you know that 40 percent of Americans believe that blasphemy should be a crime?"

"No," said the wife. "You don't mean America; you must mean

Afghanistan or Pakistan or some such place. It's the Islamics who go on and on about blasphemy."

"You are right—but actually it is all fundamentalists—Islamic, Christian, and even Hindu—who are not only offended by blasphemy but believe that it should be a crime. A capital crime, by the way."

An uneasy silence settled over the table, and Emilie shot Sanjay an imploring look.

"But," said Sanjay, "I think what is far more interesting is the structure of the violin meditation. Have you ever studied the music? Its structure is fascinating."

And at this the wife of another young banker—she had played violin at Brown—took the bait and engaged in a discussion with Sanjay about the musical form of the famous instrumental interlude.

The evening was a great success, and Emilie told me the next day that all the guests were fascinated and enthralled by Sanjay. It was typical of Sanjay at the time. He could capture any audience, but he had not yet figured out how to work his preoccupation with the religious right into his everyday interactions.

The next weekend we started to settle back into a mode of regular visits with Sanjay. He came over Sunday morning, one of the few times when Emilie and I were unlikely to be needed at the office. Emilie was on the couch reading the paper wearing, without having asked, a pair of my boxer shorts and one of my shirts. It was, in fact, a shirt that I had intended to wear that week to an important meeting in Dubai. Also, I resented that it cost me eight dollars every time I had to send it to the laundry.

"Fucking unbelievable," she said. Emilie had not only picked up anglicisms from the bankers with whom she worked but also a casual vulgarity that had not been part of her vocabulary when we met.

"What's that?"

"Look. Pakistan. A stoning. Of a couple. She's only seventeen. She ran off with this boy, and they were both convicted of sex outside of marriage and sentenced by this mullah judge person to death by stoning. Stoning? It's completely medieval. What are these people thinking?"

This was not an isolated incident. After 9/11 and the fascination with the Islamic world which it engendered, Western media coverage of Islamic punishments exploded. Sentences of lashing, whipping, stoning, flogging, amputation, and the like were reported with shock and outrage. Humanitarians, lawyers, and assorted do-gooders were dispatched to Arab capitals to plead for suspended or commuted sentences. What was largely unnoticed at the time was that American evangelical leaders were not among those condemning these barbaric practices. And what went largely unreported at the time was the newly public enthusiasm of the Christian reconstructionists for the literal application of Old Testament penalties.

I found a clipping in Adam's file from 1998, my sophomore year in high school. It reported a speech made by Gary North, Rushdoony's son-in-law, to an evangelical audience. He did not even bother to make the general case for capital punishment for adultery, homosexuality, and blasphemy (among other crimes), as he would have correctly assumed that his audience already accepted this as a biblical imperative. Instead he addressed the *method* of execution and explained the great wisdom of the Bible in specifying stoning as the required method for these particularly heinous crimes:

> *Why stoning? There are many reasons. First, the implements of execution are available to everyone at virtually no cost . . . Executions are community projects—not with spectators who watch a professional executioner do "his" duty, but rather with actual participants. That modern Christians never consider the possibility of the reintroduction of stoning for capital crimes indicates how thoroughly humanistic concepts of punishment have influenced the thinking of Christians.*

As usual, North was being utterly transparent. Those who focused simply on the perceived barbarity of stoning entirely missed the point. He was correct that the essence of stoning as a punishment is indeed community participation. In the accounts of stoning in Afghanistan,

Pakistan, North Africa, and Indonesia, the detail most often overlooked is the determination of the religious authorities to force entire
villages to participate. And why? Because afterward the entire village
is complicit and completely invested in the continuance of religious rule
for the absolution of its guilt. Only religious law can justify the stone
thrower's act. Without religious law, the villager has been reduced to a
brutal thug who killed his neighbor in a particularly heinous manner.

I could tell that Sanjay was hesitating to engage with Emilie on this
topic.

"Did you know," he said, "that there are many people here who
believe that all Old Testament punishments, including stoning, should
be restored?"

"No way," said Emilie. "Impossible. Maybe some nutcases in
Oklahoma."

"Well, since you mention Oklahoma, did you know that most statewide executive offices in Oklahoma are now held by an evangelical?
Together with 85 percent of the state legislature. Most of them support
the entire agenda—criminalization of homosexuality, adultery and
blasphemy, the death penalty for abortionists, reinstatement of school
prayer, a requirement that creationism be taught in public schools—
and all based on the Bible as ultimate law. They call their vision of
America a Christian Nation—and all that stands in the way of that
vision is the federal court system."

"Well, if that's true, and I doubt it is, then it really doesn't matter.
Who's ever been to godforsaken Oklahoma? They can worship corn
for all I care."

"They do," said Sanjay, "have two United States senators. You
would not believe how bad things have gotten there. It's this ugly mix
of anti-immigrant sentiment, over-the-top patriotism, and Christian
fundamentalism. Did you know that in a poll, 60 percent of Oklaho-
mans said they did not believe that Christians and Muslims worship
the same God? Even on the subject of their own religion, they display
astonishing ignorance. Most believe, like the bride's sister at Jim's wedding, that God created man and the dinosaurs at the same time. This

is possible because *almost a fifth* of the children are homeschooled and exposed *only* to Christian fundamentalist doctrine. They've never been to a public school and never been exposed to any non-fundamentalist views. And it is not just Oklahoma; Idaho and some other western states are not far behind."

When he noticed that Emilie wasn't really listening, he stopped.

I reflected on all this the next day in one of the places I did my best thinking, the first-class cabins of the really good international airlines, such as Emirates. En route to Dubai, I was settled into my own small cabin, with a sliding electric door cutting off the distractions of my fellow passengers, sipping Arabic coffee and—through four windows —enjoying the view of the clouds below and the dark edge of the atmosphere above. During my first two years at RCD&S, much of the actual work was ministerial—routine research, drafting documents based on precedents with little need for variation, and the review of large stacks of contracts and corporate documents known as due diligence. But instead of complaining that the work was not sufficiently challenging, I forced myself to think about the reasons the transactions were structured the way they were, and I tried to figure out whether I could conceive a more efficient or less risky alternative. This critical and creative habit of mind stood me in good stead, and I quickly was given more advanced work than was customary for associates at my level. Powerful partners with interesting work, including a senior partner in line to be the firm's chairman, increasingly sought me out to be assigned to their transactions. To emerge as a star in a group of the country's brightest and hardest-working young lawyers was, honestly, a source of some surprise to me, but I was truly delighted by the fast pace at which my career was advancing. My determination to stick it out and become a partner was firming.

Six hours later, after a good sleep on a flat bed covered with a starched linen comforter, I was eating a breakfast of freshly scrambled eggs, crisp bacon, and fresh figs. The flight map on the large plasma screen at the opposite end of my small cabin indicated that we were directly over Baghdad. Here I was, cosseted with every indulgence, and 39,000 feet below me were other Americans my age fighting a needless war and dying by the thousands, mostly by being blown up by a faceless enemy. I wondered why I was here and not there. The skies were cloudless, and I could see the Euphrates and even make out the Green Zone, familiar from so many maps on the television news.

Perhaps being in the air so much contributed to a feeling of separation from the rest of humanity. I realized that the way the world really worked—how things got done, who had power, and why things actually happened the way they did—was almost completely opaque to ordinary people. I felt an increasing sense of estrangement from those not living a similar life. They didn't "get it," we would say. The handmaiden of justifiable pride is an ugly undercurrent of arrogance from which I was not exempt. Many of my colleagues came to see the rest of humanity as idiots, ordinary people bumbling through life in a fog of imprecision with no real knowledge of the world, easily duped, analytically handicapped, and generally clueless. I suppose you could say that I had "drunk the Kool-Aid," but at least I remained aware that I had done it. During the rare times Emilie and I were not working, we tended to socialize with other bankers and lawyers who lived in the same world. They shared our experience and understood our lives. It was easier.

★   ★   ★

ONE WEEKEND Emilie proposed to me that we ask Sanjay to dinner the following weekend.

"I want him to meet George. He's the cutest associate in Financial Institutions. I mean, really, really cute. I don't know a girl who wouldn't want him if he weren't gay."

"You're trying to set up Sanjay?" I asked.

"Why not? He may be filled with yogic equanimity, but he's still got to fuck."

"Jesus, Emilie. I wish you wouldn't be so crude."

"Yeah, so what, you think he doesn't want to fuck cute guys? He doesn't want a relationship? I guess you think as long as he's got you as his best friend, he doesn't need another man? Is that it?"

The long argument that ensued ended, like all arguments during that time, with Emilie doing exactly as she intended. She invited Sanjay and her friend George, neglected to tell either of them he was being set up, and then fussed to create a "romantic" atmosphere. To this day I don't know whether this was the "good Emilie" actually trying to do something nice for two friends, or the "bad Emilie" desperate to drive a wedge, any wedge, between Sanjay and me. Although I was careful not to let her know, the later mission was unnecessary. I already was distracted by doubts that my closeness with Sanjay could survive my turning into the person I was becoming. Could I really talk to him about my life, which was now dominated by my work? And I just didn't want to hear any more about the fundamentalist Christians. I was not looking forward to the dinner.

Upon arriving and meeting Sanjay, the Credit Suisse associate, George, instantly deduced Emilie's intentions and flushed with embarrassment. Sanjay later told me he found this most charming.

Emilie painfully tried to steer the conversation to gay topics, and I, mortified, pushed around my plate the forty-dollar-per-pound white asparagus that Emilie had ordered from the most expensive market on the East Side.

Sanjay, largely oblivious to everyone else's discomfort, was excited by his most recent research. It was the first time that I learned about *The Institutes of Biblical Law*, a tedious text in excess of a thousand pages on which I later became expert, having been asked by Governor Bloomberg time and time again to search out clues about the strategy and behavior of our theocratic foes.

"Have you ever heard of Rousas John Rushdoony?" Sanjay asked, ". . . usually known as R. J. Rushdoony?"

We all looked blank.

"Neither had I, but I have finally found what I was looking for . . . the intellectual underpinning of the more extreme parts of the Christian Nation movement. This is it. *The Institutes* is the Bible, so to speak, of reconstructionism. Rushdoony was funded by Howard Ahmanson, Jr., whose father founded and owned America's largest savings and loan.

The son was at one time a committed reconstructionist and provided much of the funding for Rushdoony's Chalcedon Foundation. These people don't always completely agree with Rushdoony—for example, just three years ago one of them said that he 'no longer consider[s] [it] essential' to stone people to death for certain crimes of immorality. But it is Ahmanson's money that allowed Rushdoony to promote—and successfully move toward the mainstream—what started out being viewed, even by evangelicals, as pretty extreme views."

"It always comes down to money, doesn't it?" Emilie observed.

"In this case, yes. The Chalcedon Foundation is still going strong, run by Rushdoony's son. Gary North, who is Rushdoony's son-in-law, carried the project forward with Jim Dobson, Tony Perkins, and the others we all have heard of. It all fits together now."

"I haven't heard of any of them," Emilie said, with an inflection that signaled boredom and the hope that Sanjay would change the subject. He was oblivious.

Sanjay continued. "Rushdoony started out as a fairly traditional Calvinist but then promulgated the simple and powerful view that no law made by man can ever have authority or legitimacy. Instead, the civil man-made law must be replaced with, or at least be subordinated to, the law of God as revealed in the Bible. They argue that man cannot create law; man can only embrace or reject God's law. Under this view, of course, the idea of individual rights is anathema or, as one of them said, 'an assault on God's sovereignty.' Is that not fascinating? Within their frame of reference, it makes perfect sense. If God is supposed to be omnipotent and rule all things, then to speak of men as having rights is nonsense. And of course you will appreciate the other implication."

No one answered, but George had the courtesy to say "What?"

"Democracy, of course. Democracy is rule by the majority, not God, with the minority protected by inviolable individual civil rights. So democracy too is anathema. As Rushdoony himself has said, 'Christianity and democracy are inevitably enemies.'"

George looked shocked.

"And here is the most important thing," Sanjay continued. "This isn't just a philosophy or political ideology. Rushdoony believed that living in a society ruled solely by God's law is so important because this in turn is required as a condition for the return of Jesus, for the second coming of Christ. Do you understand? No theocracy, no second coming. Before Rushdoony, most evangelicals were, and I believe still are, what is called 'pre-millennial,' believing that when Jesus returns, all born-again Christians will go up to heaven, physically, in the rapture, leaving the unbelievers to endure the tribulation and the apocalypse. But Rushdoony believes in 'post-millenialism,' meaning that Jesus will come only *after* Christians succeed in establishing Christian rule over the earth. This urgent imperative for Christian rule over civil institutions in order that Jesus can come again is at the heart of what they call dominionism. Dominionism simply means that Christians have a God-given right to rule, and that in preparation for the second coming of Christ, Christians have responsibility to take over every aspect of society and to govern solely in accordance with biblical law. The pursuit of secular power, of control over the legislature and the courts, is a theological imperative, and the most important one there is. And all this with its roots in a man you never heard of, R. J. Rushdoony."

"Oh for God's sake," said Emilie, impatient at the turn of the conversation, "please Sanjay, not all the theology. Although I like his name. Rushdoony. Rhymes with looney. Rushdoony is a loony. Easy to remember."

"We also have Rushdoony and his followers to thank for homeschooling. It is hard to get a precise number, but some scholars estimate that 10 percent of American children are either homeschooled or taught in fundamentalist Christian private schools. As a percentage of all children, this is significantly higher than the proportion of Pakistani children attending fundamentalist madrassahs. That translates into roughly two million children in homeschool, almost all from evangelical families. And it was largely Rushdoony's idea—he argued that establishing Christian rule required little more than indoctrinating a couple of generations of children. It is not just about filling them with Christian doctrine and protecting them from immorality; it has the effect of undermining reason and science as a mode of knowing the world. Children are taught that faith and acceptance of the revealed wisdom of God are the highest values and the only legitimate and reliable ways to know the world. With children thus trained, it is an easy step to get them to accept as true the things that are manifestly false, such as that the earth is only a few thousand years old, that Iraq was behind 9/11, or that Senator Obama is foreign born. As one writer said, they are 'redefining faith as deliberate blindness to big lies.'"

Emilie interrupted. "Greg, that can't be legal, can it? I mean, you cannot pull your kids from school and fill their heads with bloody nonsense. Why doesn't someone do something?"

Even though Emilie had addressed the question to me, Sanjay answered.

"No, it is perfectly legal, and the Christian right defends home-schooling most energetically. The Home School Legal Defense Association litigates anything that could limit the right of parents to cut their children off from mainstream society and fill their minds with superstition and hate. I believe it is child abuse, I really do. In America last year more than a billion dollars was spent on homeschooling texts. These texts are increasingly political, emphasizing a Christian-ized American history, with little basis in fact, to emphasize the divine destiny of America. Wait—"

Sanjay pulled a wad of paper scraps from a pocket.

"Did you know that much of this is not online? I spent today at the library. They actually have these homeschooling books. Here's the one I remembered from a high-school-level history text. I was really struck by this: 'Who, knowing the facts of our history, can doubt that the United States of America has been a thought in the mind of God from all eternity.' I mean, talk about American exceptionalism. The essential lesson of history is that America was invented by God for the sole purpose of being the vehicle by which godly Christian rule will be imposed on the earth in preparation for the second coming. Just think, please, what it will mean for our futures if one in ten American children believes this absolutely."

"Oh, I don't know," said Emilie. "One in ten? That's not so bad. Has there been any time in American history when at least ten percent of our people *haven't* been utter lunatics?"

"Perhaps," answered Sanjay. "That is an interesting perspective. But I fear that this may be something different. That their influence may be greater than their numbers. The evangelicals call these cadres of homeschooled children Generation Joshua after the military commander of Moses. You know, the one that marched seven times around the walls of Jericho? That's what they call them, GenJ for short. A generation of little soldiers. There is a homeschooling video titled *Putting on the Whole Armor of God*, which asks, 'Boys, are you ready for warfare?'—and they mean warfare against secularism and warfare to obtain control of all civil institutions. And when they are teenagers, these kids are made to join GenJ clubs that focus on political action. They are organized by congressional district, and they do things like getting their older brothers and sisters to register to vote. And in addition to homeschooling, Mr. Rushdoony promoted the organization of the Christian so-called colleges, like Patrick Henry."

At this point George, who had been extremely quiet, interrupted. "I was a White House intern."

This seemed to be a non sequitur. We all looked at him, puzzled.

"I had never heard of Patrick Henry College. But during 2004, my year at the White House, 7 percent of all the White House interns were from Patrick Henry."

Sanjay looked at George with new interest. "How do you know that?"

"We calculated it from the intern program facebook. It tells you where all the other interns went to college. Almost one in ten—for perhaps the most competitive position for young people in Washington—were from the same small school we had never heard of."

"And a school whose stated purpose is to train 'warriors to take back the land,'" Sanjay reminded us. "I suppose the White House is a good place to start."

"It wasn't just the White House," said George. "Evangelicals are everywhere in Washington. There are prayer cells in the Senate and almost every federal department. My year there was a bit of a scandal because senior civilian and military leaders at the Pentagon appeared in a video for a group called Christian Embassy talking about the platform that their jobs provided for doing evangelical work. But lots of people were not even surprised, and it blew over quickly. Many federally paid congressional junkets are really evangelistic missions. I went to a talk by a congressman who described a recent trip to Africa by saying he was there to represent the Lord, that he went to tell the people about Jesus. I *was* surprised by that."

"Wait a second," I said. "That's hard to believe. Not with federal funds. That wouldn't be legal."

"G, you are not often naïve, but you have been working hard," Sanjay said.

I gave him a dirty look.

George continued. "Not only are public displays of religion ubiquitous in the military and civilian services, but federal money is flowing directly to evangelical causes in large amounts. When I was at the White House, we bragged to the base that we dedicated a billion dollars for abstinence education alone, with the result that a third of US public schools have so-called sex education that teaches only abstinence. And this solely for reasons of religious doctrine. You know about Bush's so-called faith-based initiative, which seems fairly innocent in its funding of church-affiliated social service agencies doing charitable work, and yes, sometimes more efficiently than the federal government. But you know I discovered that there are faith-based offices not only in the Department of Health and Human Services but also in Education, Commerce, and many other agencies. Why? There is no conceivable proper reason."

Sanjay was listening intently but stayed quiet. George continued.

"How much of this money do you think goes to Presbyterian churches or Catholic congregations or synagogues? Virtually none. And did you know that evangelical and Pentecostal churches, which receive nearly all faith-based funding, are free to discriminate against non-Christians and gays on the grounds that it would conflict with their own religious freedom if they were not free to do so? I found that strange."

"Where the hell is the *New York Times*?" asked Emilie.

"You know," answered George, "they do sometimes cover these things. We just don't always notice, or quite believe it. I mean, Emilie, really, Sanjay is right. None of this is news to anyone who lives in DC or works in the federal government. People are almost beyond noticing; it's—sorry to use a cliché—the 'new normal.'"

"So did it bother you?" asked Sanjay.

George answered carefully. "I was brought up to respect people and be tolerant of differences. I try not to be too judgmental. I always thought that devout religiosity was something to be admired, not feared. But after 9/11, I started to see parallels between Islamic fundamentalism and what I had seen in DC. And yes, as a gay person I felt threatened by their . . . well, I felt there could be some real hatred there. I was not 'out' when I was at the White House, so . . ."

Sanjay looked thoughtful and then smiled warmly at George. Emilie was suddenly looking pleased.

"You know," continued George, "I just remembered another thing that did surprise me. Do you know who I was told had a weekly conference call with the White House while I was there? Ted Haggard. I mean, every Monday. I don't think anyone else did, except maybe Cheney."

"Wait," asked Emilie, "which one is Haggard? Is he the one who tried to get a blow job in the Minneapolis airport?"

"No," answered Sanjay. "He's the crusader against gay marriage, married with children, who was accused in a scandal involving allegations of drug use and gay sex. He was head of the National Association of Evangelicals, representing forty-five thousand churches with thirty million members, and pastor of the New Life Church—a mega-church in Colorado Springs with over twelve thousand parishioners. And a confidant of the US president."

"Yes," added George. "You know that most of the evangelical leaders who get caught just say the devil made them do it, that they regret their sin, and that they now accept Jesus totally and that Jesus has forgiven them. Their fellow pastors usually cry '*alleluia!*' and let them be. But the Haggard case was unusually egregious. He lost his job."

"Well, George," Emilie responded, "I hope all this talk of gay sex has put you in the mood."

Sanjay rescued him by interrupting, "Emilie, I am very happy that you have introduced me to George."

Until the next day, we didn't know whether that meant that Sanjay was happy to have met George as a source or whether he had taken Emilie's bait. Emilie called me the next day at the office with the news that Sanjay had spent the night at George's apartment. She was very pleased with herself. I should have called Sanjay but didn't, and then got deeply immersed in a deal and didn't speak to Sanjay again for a couple of weeks.

He and George were together for almost a year, and it always seemed highly improbable to me that Sanjay was dating a banker. But I recall George as a thoughtful and gentle person, and as sympathetic and supportive of Sanjay as he could be, given his own work life. When they finally split up, I was sorry for Sanjay but not surprised. I realize now that I never really liked George, but I cannot put my finger on why. I do wonder now, writing these words and thinking about the man for the first time in many years, where he is today. I never saw him in New York during the siege. He was not at Governors Island. Had he married and kept his position as a banker? It was possible. Or fled to Canada or Sweden after 2016? He certainly would have had the money to get a visa. Or perhaps I'm not giving him enough credit. Perhaps he fought with us and died, or languishes even today in one of the gay reorientation camps scattered in remote locations around the country.

When John McCain picked Sarah Palin to be his running mate in the summer of 2008, Sanjay was so agitated that he founded a not-for-profit organization to pursue his interest in spotlighting the growing political aspirations of the Christian right. I helped him get his tax-exempt status from the IRS, and strongly advised against the name he was considering, Theocracy Watch.

"Theocracy," I argued, "is an egghead word. Ordinary people don't know what it means. And besides, it doesn't sound all that bad—kind of like 'democracy.' Also, 'watch' is too passive. Who wants to support an organization that only watches? You need to use a word like 'campaign'—something active."

Sanjay usually took all my advice seriously, so I really needed to be careful about what I said. He was earnest and apologetic when he told me he was sticking with Theocracy Watch.

"Sorry, G. Your points are excellent ones, and I considered them carefully. But there is no good synonym for theocracy. It is exactly the right word. All the alternatives suggest that I object to religion in general, or to religious people exercising political power, or to the advocacy of morality in politics or civil life. I do not oppose any of these things. The only problem I have is with a state where law and policy are based on divine revelation, and government officials purport to speak for God—a theocracy. And it *is* a 'watch'—the purpose of my organization will be to watch and report. It will not be a campaign. I do not want to be politically active. I want to watch and then shine a spotlight on what they say and what they want. Only that is necessary. The people and the democratic political process will take care of the rest."

And so, in the fall of 2008, Theocracy Watch was born, and what Emilie liked to call Sanjay's "hobby" became his full-time job.

At the same time, he sold *You and I* to a tech fund for $400 million. The closing was only three weeks before the collapse of Lehman Brothers, and Sanjay put all the cash into treasury bills. He was now, without "striving," wealthy beyond anything he could have imagined, or anything that I could hope to attain, even as a successful Wall Street lawyer. At the time I thought it highly ironic that he owed his fortune to the Alaska governor who worshiped at a dominionist-influenced church in Wasilla where worshipers spoke in tongues, who did not read books, and who epitomized the woeful ignorance of much of the extreme evangelical subculture. But for Sarah Palin being yanked from deserved obscurity, Sanjay would not have sold *You and I* before the market crash, would have labored in noble poverty, and would never have had the resources to mount the vigorous campaign he did against the theocratic effort. From that point in time, the fates of Sanjay and Sarah Palin were closely intertwined.

CHAPTER SIX

Sarah

2008

It is not the forces of darkness but of shallowness that everywhere threaten the true, and the good, and the beautiful, and that ironically announce themselves as deep and profound. It is an exuberant and fearless shallowness that everywhere is the modern danger, the modern threat, and that everywhere nonetheless calls to us as savior.

—Ken Wilber,
Sex, Ecology, Spirituality

She absolutely believes these are what the evangelicals call the Last Days. She absolutely believes . . . that the earth is six thousand years old and that dinosaurs and man once lived together. And she absolutely believes that Jesus will return to earth during the course of her life. These beliefs are at the core of everything she says and does. She is locked into that worldview. If you don't appreciate how totally she is governed by these beliefs, you'll never understand Sarah Palin. Sarah feels chosen. She feels called. . . . She knows herself to be on a mission from God. . . . [I]f you're on a mission from God to destroy evil, there are going to be all kinds of expendables along the way. Collateral damage.

—Rev. Howard Bess, quoted in Joe McGinniss,
The Rogue: Searching for the Real Sarah Palin

*I want to be invisible. I do guerilla warfare. I paint my
face and travel at night. You don't know it's over until
you're in a body bag.*

—Ralph Reed, 1991

HALF THE NATION WAS DISAPPOINTED when the dream of
an Obama presidency died. Although the popular vote was close, 51
percent to 49 percent, the entire nation was relieved that there was no
replay of the electoral litigation drama of 2000. And though I had voted
for Obama, I was content with the outcome. I believed that McCain
was fundamentally a good man: experienced, independent, and well
intentioned. I was hopeful that the McCain administration might even
bring us a few years without the bitter partisan divide that character-
ized the Clinton and Bush years. Moreover, the continuing financial
crisis was truly scary, and despite McCain's apparent lack of economic
savvy, I assumed that the Republicans would nonetheless be better
stewards of financial markets and the economy. But none of us could
have anticipated the bizarre way in which the McCain administration
began and ended, or the disastrous start to Sarah Palin's presidency.

The Palin factor had weighed on the minds of many Republicans
during the election, myself included. Most of the Republicans I knew—
the moderate types found in New York—believed that John McCain
either had been careless to the point of negligence or had made a distasteful but perhaps clever bargain with the right wing of his party.
It was a difficult subject to discuss. All Democrats, and a few of my
Republican friends who had particular reasons to know something
about Palin, were disdainful and, I could tell, genuinely disturbed by
McCain's choice of her. For them, politics seemed to have turned a
corner. Never before had someone as ignorant, naïve, uncultured, and
unprepared been elevated, for the most cynical reasons, to be a candidate for high national office. Never before had the voters seemed so
mesmerized by the personal narrative of such a person, so driven by
emotional appeal, and so accepting of a candidate with only the most

superficial grasp of policy. But most Republicans I knew were willing to overlook it. After all, they said, both parties had a history of choosing "lightweights" for the vice presidency. This was the favored euphemism. Yes, she was a lightweight, but this was not enough to override their conviction that Barack Obama would surely raise their taxes.

"Don't you understand," said a partner I respected, "that this means money out of your pocket? Do you really want to be poorer?"

It was apparent from election night on that President-elect McCain and his running mate were not on good terms. She was not permitted to speak that night. The next day, the "McCain-Palin" campaign morphed into the coming "McCain" administration, with the word "Palin" never again appearing in a public statement or press release from the transition team. She was given no special assignment and no responsibilities, and she became invisible until the moment of the inauguration. She reappeared on the steps of the Capitol to be sworn in immediately prior to John McCain, and then again retired from public view. Although the press amused itself for a while speculating about the relationship between the two, they quickly tired of the story and settled into a "new normal" where the vice president was to be neither seen nor heard.

President McCain allowed his Treasury secretary to take the lead on the continuing fallout from the financial crisis, and decided to focus his own activity on foreign policy—his traditional area of strength. Relations with Russia having hit new lows during the second Bush term, the McCain team negotiated quietly with the Russians for a series of major cooperative initiatives, to be announced at the new president's first overseas visit, to Moscow.

When President McCain left in early March 2009 on his first overseas trip, the vice president was not present at Andrews Air Force Base to see him off. The press, already accustomed to the invisibility of the vice president, hardly made any comment.

For whatever reasons, the Russian government did everything possible to flatter the new US president. Crowds lined the streets from the airport, and he was invited to address a joint session of the State Duma and the Federation Council. The speech must have been in midafternoon Moscow time, as I heard the news on the radio in the morning while shaving.

The seventy-two-year-old president walked to the podium looking vigorous. He delivered about three sentences of his remarks, paused, gripped the back of his head, and then crumpled to the floor unconscious. Surrounded by Secret Service, he was taken to the nearby Kremlin hospital by the ambulance always flown in on a presidential visit. A CAT scan revealed a cerebral aneurysm. Kremlin doctors, with the president's doctor in attendance, opened his skull in an attempt to intervene, but the president was declared dead from massive cranial bleeding before the ruptured artery could be repaired.

I stayed at home with Emilie watching the endless video replay of the president collapsing at the podium and the scene of reporters mobbing the gates outside the Kremlin hospital. When the president's American doctor emerged to announce McCain's death, around nine in the morning in New York, I felt a grip deep in my gut and bent over slightly to relieve the pain.

Emilie, who focused intently on the unfolding story, did not notice my reaction. After a while, no new details were released and the coverage became completely repetitive. "I'm going to work," Emilie said. "See you tonight."

I too went to work, but not before calling Sanjay.

"San. What do you think?"

"It was my worst fear. And now that it has happened, it somehow feels like it was inevitable."

His voice sounded weak.

"You OK?"

I heard a deep breath.

"Talk to you tonight" was all that he said in reply.

Not a lot of work got done that day. The firm tuned the plasmas in the conference rooms to CNN and allowed the lawyers and staff to watch. All the protocols for this situation had been executed efficiently. Palin had been spirited away to the White House Situation Room from her home at the Naval Observatory (where a cleaning lady later revealed that the vice president had been watching reruns of a television reality show, *Bridezillas*, and not the president's address). One hour after the announcement of the president's death in Moscow, Palin appeared on television reading remarks announcing that she had been sworn in as president by the chief justice, that all the cabinet members and Joint Chiefs not with the president in Moscow had gathered with her in the Situation Room, and that the US military had gone to DEFCON 4, as is prescribed by protocol, although no enhanced threat to the United States was known or anticipated.

By midday, the news coverage had shifted from the medical aspects of President McCain's death to a considerable state of confusion over the location of his body. In these circumstances, everyone expected that the president's body would be promptly removed to Air Force One and returned with the rest of the official delegation to the United States. The president's staff, cabinet members, and others had returned to Vnukovo International Airport. The president's doctor was apparently still at the Kremlin hospital, and none of the press had seen the president's ambulance leave the facility.

At 5:00 p.m. on the East Coast, the Kremlin released a one-line written statement to the effect that under Russian law an autopsy and inquest were required before the president's body could be released. These would be scheduled and conducted in accordance with normal procedures, and the public would be advised of the results when complete. In the meantime, the president's body would remain in the custody of the Federal Security Service, the successor to the Soviet-era KGB.

Few people in the United States slept much that night. The Russians held the president of the United States, dead or alive, and refused to release him. Commentators speculated wildly on the motives of the Russian government in what could only be construed as a remarkably bold and aggressive affront to the United States. Experts explained how the international law of diplomatic immunity, if asserted, would exempt from autopsy or inquest a government official who died on the soil of another country. Others noted that wars had started over far less serious offenses. Congressmen advocated ultimatums. I thought that Putin and Medvedev were, in a typically Russian way, simply testing their new adversary, Sarah Palin.

The White House pressroom was in a state of near riot, with no spokesman emerging to speak for the new administration. Around midnight, the deputy press secretary, who had not traveled to Moscow, emerged, ashen faced, to announce that President Palin was in touch with Russian authorities and would have more to say in the morning.

But in the morning, the unthinkable happened. Instead of a statement from the White House, the website Wikileaks announced that it had secured two transcripts of the call from the night before between Presidents Palin and Medvedev—one in Russian leaked from the Kremlin, another in English leaked from the White House (the latter from a loyal McCain aide who had been one of the chief architects of the vice president's invisibility). The two transcripts matched exactly:

"Mr. President, this is Sarah Palin."

"Madam President, please accept my sincere condolences on the loss of your president. A terrible tragedy. And to happen here in Moscow, we are inconsolable."

"Yeah, well, it was God's will, ya know. So. I mean, um. I want to talk about the, you know, body."

"Yes, Madam President."

"Well, what's this about not . . . about keeping it, uh, him. The American people want him. I mean, they want him to come home."

"Ah. I'm afraid it's the law, Madam President. Due to the circumstances of his death, an autopsy is required and then an inquest must be convened to determine the cause of death. I'm sure it will be quite routine; I understand that President McCain was not in the best of health. When it's complete the body will of course be turned over."

"But . . . I mean. Dim . . . Dim . . . Dim-i-triss . . . I'm asking

you. Can't you give a waiver or something? The man deserves a Christian burial."

"But of course, and he shall have one, I'm sure."

"But, now . . . When I was governor of Alaska, ya know?"

"Yes. Alaska . . ."

"Yeah. Well, when I was governor the law thing was not always crystal clear. Ya know, not carved in stone . . . not like the Ten Commandments. Some of my people said the law was one thing, and some said another thing, so, ya know, it wasn't really always clear . . . So, well, I kinda got to decide."

"Uh-huh." [pause]

"So, I mean, can't you decide? Look here, I know that God really wants him back in Washington. He does. It's what God wants."

[pause] "I have decided. We will obey the law of the Russian Federation, do an autopsy and inquest as quickly as possible, and then return the body to your government."

"But, so . . . [pause] so, there's nothing really you . . . really can do?"

"No, I'm afraid not. I was sure you would understand. [pause] Well, again Madam President, my deep condolences. I do look forward to working with you. I'm sure this unfortunate tragedy will not affect the good working relationship between our two great countries."

"Oh no. I want a good . . . I mean . . . We should . . ."

"Good-bye, Madam President."

After the public release of this transcript, pundits from right and left called for her resignation. There was no way to spin it. In a moment of crisis, she had been revealed to be as totally out of her depth as her critics had claimed. The argument "it's what God wants" did not work as well at the pinnacle of international statesmanship as it had in Wasilla. In a well-timed leak about a week later, Putin was quoted by a source in Moscow as joking at a cocktail party, "If God wants the body back in Washington so much, why can't He just take him? I guess this means that Russian law is stronger than the firm intention of the omnipotent being with whom this woman claims to be on such good terms." The European press indulged in an orgy of collective sniggering. Americans were not amused. Americans really don't like to be made fun of. It looked like Sarah Palin was history.

Two days later, an unmarked black town car pulled up to the gates of the White House. Unnoticed by the press, Steve Jordan entered the White House by the side door to the West Wing. Actually, come to think of it, he has never left.

Jordan had a remarkable history. The Holy Spirit found him when he was relaxing in his dorm room at Alabama State and he was born again in Christ that night. He led protests at abortion clinics in the mid-1980s and was then hired by James Dobson as a political strategist for the relatively new Family Research Council. Jordan proved to be a political genius. By 1996 his political machinations on behalf of the evangelical cause had firmly established him in the top leadership ranks of the Christian right, although, unlike Pat Robertson or his boss Jim Dobson, he preferred to work outside the public spotlight.

That changed in 2006 when he emerged from obscurity to run for governor of Alabama. His campaign ended ignominiously when the IRS prosecuted him for failure to file federal income tax returns. But, as Sanjay and I were to learn, Jordan was a survivor. His telegenic face, corporate dress, and unassuming manner distinguished him from the other leaders of the evangelical right. There was no teary-eyed confession from Jordan. Instead, he simply retreated, regrouped, and teamed up with Ralph Reed to build a new network called the Faith & Freedom Coalition (FFC), intended to harness the energy of the new Tea Party movement and ensure that the fiscally oriented Tea Partyers stood solidly behind the broad cultural and religious agenda of the Christian right.

Jordan and Reed were remarkably open about their plans for the new group. They centered around four principles. First was inclusiveness. "This is not your daddy's Christian Coalition," Reed said. "It's got to be more brown, more black, more female, and younger." The second principle was stealth: "Rather than nab the publicity as I did at the Christian

Coalition, I want to cultivate the rising generation . . . We're less focused on pyrotechnics than on being a strong grassroots presence all the way to the precinct level. . ." Third was consolidating political power at the state and local level first. Jordan and Reed argued that there was little national liberal money flowing into state legislative campaigns, so evangelical funding could have a big impact. Their aim was "huge majorities," of the sorts already achieved in Oklahoma and Wyoming, in state legislatures. The fourth principle was embracing the power of the web. Most of the chapters of the Faith & Freedom Coalition would be virtual. "The Internet's first wave was e-mail," Reed explained, "and the next wave was social networking, which Obama perfected. There's going to be a third wave, which we're still developing." If we should have listened to anything, it was that. During their partnership at the Faith & Freedom Coalition, Reed was the spokesman and public face of the organization, but those in the know believed that the brilliant and politically ambitious Jordan was the chief strategist behind the FFC.

True to their promise, until that moment the Faith & Freedom Coalition had worked stealthily, quietly preparing for the "next wave" of the revolution. So when the rest of the evangelicals were ready to write off Sarah Palin as damaged goods, Jordan finally saw the opening for which he had waited.

Jordan was installed in a room two doors down from the Oval Office, but he was not given a title and did not become a US government employee. He remained as political director of the FFC, which paid his salary. This arrangement proved useful, as Jordan was exempted from the record-keeping and disclosure requirements that would otherwise have applied to paid presidential advisors.

In 2009, although Sanjay's new organization, Theocracy Watch, had been in existence for over a year, it was not a success. Although the website was state of the art, there were few visitors, and fewer still clicked on the "donate" button. Although Sanjay could have funded the organization more lavishly from his own fortune, Theocracy Watch worked out of a small loft-like office in the Financial District that was directly adjacent to the World Trade Center site and thus available at a highly discounted rent. I was rather pleased by this, however, as it meant we could easily meet for lunch on those rare days when I could get away from the firm. Sanjay employed one person full-time, a recent religion PhD from NYU, and a rotating staff of part-time undergraduate and graduate students who surfed the web trolling for speeches and writings illustrating the increasing penetration of dominionist thinking into the mainstream evangelical community.

Despite Sanjay's persistent outreach to the media, Theocracy Watch (TW) had labored in almost complete obscurity since its founding. But within a month of Steve Jordan's arrival in the West Wing, Sanjay got his first major break. The occasion was a leaked memo from Steve Jordan that Sanjay was the first to reveal on the TW website. This generated some attention from the mainstream media, including a full segment on PBS's *NewsHour*. Many of us thought that this segment contributed to PBS's firing, within the year, of the show's longtime executive producer.

The memo leaked by Sanjay read as follows:

RE: FIGHTING HOMOSEXUAL AGENDA IN FIRST TERM

Recommend going slow in first term. Priority now should be to lay groundwork for acquiescence by mainstream culture to re-criminalization in second term. How? Religious arguments ineffective beyond Family, and non-Family simply does not see tolerance of homosexual lifestyle as attack on family/marriage. Key problem is diminishing revulsion at homosexual behavior— traditionally most powerful motivator in prejudice against gays. We must refocus on gay sex and thus restore visceral disgust. Best strategy is to conflate all homosexual behavior with extreme sexual practices, especially sexual abuse of young boys.

Goals: (i) everyone has vivid picture of what this depravity involves and (ii) all parents of young boys become viscerally fearful of all male homosexuals.

Tactics: Personify victims. Ensure that physical acts against young boys are graphically depicted in major films and TV.

Action items:

(i)   *Provide stealth support to pedophilia promotion groups to allow them to raise their profile, prompting sponta- neous backlash even from mainstream culture.*

(ii) *Fund mainstream films, one with explicit pedophilia, one gay S&M. J2 and J3 have agreed to fund.*

(iii) *FFC to place abuse victims into mainstream talk radio and TV to tell their stories, coach to ensure graphic detail and maximum impact.*

This strategy fully cleared with and supported by leadership.

SJ

Sanjay argued that the memo revealed that the Palin administra- tion's goal was the eventual re-criminalization of homosexuality. Per- haps more importantly, he said it vividly evidenced Jordan's patient, methodical, and strategic approach to achieving his goals, together with his casual disregard for the truth and his willingness to cynically manipulate the sentiments of the American people. It also demon- strated that Jordan himself was fronting for a broad coalition of evan- gelical leaders. We didn't know for sure, but Sanjay speculated that this included both James Dobson (founder of Focus on the Family, whose radio programs already reached 200 million people) and the younger Tony Perkins, who spun off his Family Research Council from Dob- son's larger group.

The administration took the position that Jordan was an unpaid political consultant whose words and ideas could not be attributed to the president and that there was no evidence that this memo was ever intended for or read by the president or anyone in her administration. Moreover, the president's spokesmen reminded the press that evangel- icals such as Jordan had been utterly transparent for years about their views on so-called "gay rights," so they didn't understand why anyone should be surprised by any of it.

The memo stayed in the news for a couple of cycles, but as far as I can remember, it was never mentioned again by the major media. As

I write this, I am wondering whether the plan was implemented after the memo was leaked. I cannot remember any film during this period that might have resulted from Jordan's machinations. But that doesn't mean much, for between 2009 and 2012 my work at the firm did not leave a lot of time for going to the movies. And, besides, Emilie didn't like films and instead ensured that the few evenings I could get away were spent at whatever restaurant was, that week, at the top of Manhattan's mercurial dining scene.

For me, the shock of Sarah Palin becoming president was soon transcended by another, far more severe. I was in the elegant conference room of one of London's best law firms when my secretary transferred a call from a state trooper in New Jersey. My parents, together with my sister, had been in an accident on the New Jersey Turnpike. A tractor-trailer had blown a tire and veered across the highway into the opposite lane. Our trusty green Volvo station wagon had been obliterated, and, along with it, in an instant, my entire family. These things, as you know, happen to other people, unless they don't. I endured a full-length Catholic funeral mass at our family church in Madison, New Jersey. Only when I was forced to stand alongside the three neatly dug holes and watch as all three caskets were simultaneously lowered into the ground did my grief finally erupt. I knew I was expected to be stoic, but instead I collapsed to my knees sobbing convulsively. Emilie looked terrified. Sanjay knelt beside me and held me tightly, and did not let go.

CHAPTER SEVEN

Passionate Intensity

2009

> *The best lack all conviction, while the worst*
> *Are full of passionate intensity.*
>
> —William Butler Yeats,
> "The Second Coming"

AFTER THE LEAK OF THE PALIN/MEDVEDEV transcript and Palin achieving the lowest presidential approval rating in the history of that poll, not a single voice from the right spoke out in her defense. Even Fox News was silent, seeming to wait to sense the national mood and then make a judgment whether Palin could recover or should be jettisoned as a mistake.

About a month following President McCain's death, the first politician spoke publicly in defense of Sarah Palin. He was the Republican senator from Kansas, Sam Brownback, well known for his support of the intelligent design movement and his determination to abolish the Departments of Education, Energy, Commerce, and Housing and Urban Development, as well as his anti-gay agenda and desire to ban abortion unless necessary to save the life of the mother. Brownback freely admitted that as a senator he looked to scripture and guidance from God to inform his legislative program.

Appearing on all the Sunday talk shows, and echoed by local

spin-masters around the country, he explained his view that God doesn't require brilliant leaders or erudite lawmakers, just those who submit to His will. Brownback argued that President Palin was the first president who would do her best to submit totally to the will of God, which is all that really matters. She had his total support.

Put this way, many of the country's 70 million evangelicals soon decided to overlook the McCain body incident; accept that intelligence, knowledge, and competence didn't matter; and focus instead on the fact that finally they had a president who, like themselves, spoke to God and obeyed His instructions. Soon after Brownback, Rep. Michele Bachmann, who studied with Pentecostal reconstructionists at Oral Roberts Law School, and Texas governor Rick Perry came out strongly in support of Palin. A cascade of endorsements from the religious right followed. There was much talk of Joan of Arc, a simple unschooled girl who had only her unshakeable faith and who succeeded in freeing France when statesmen, scholars, and soldiers all had failed. The president's poll numbers started to recover. A grateful President Palin named Senator Brownback to fill the vacant vice presidency, and Congress confirmed him by a narrow margin.

Jordan had been hard at work on a political strategy for Palin. As an accidental president, she needed to acquire two things: a public persona and a political message. For the former, Jordan adopted one of the oldest archetypes in politics, the "common man." Palin's "thing" would be to be absolutely ordinary. It was one of several roles she had auditioned during the campaign, and Jordan correctly judged that it was her best performance. It was a risky choice, though, and a clean break from the traditional wisdom that Americans want their president to be "presidential." As for the political message, it also was risky, as it required the leader of the federal government to condemn as "socialistic" virtually every federal government program or action other than defense. She would seek systematically to starve the federal government she led by zero tolerance for either increased taxes or increased deficits. These twin strategies suited her perfectly. She could speak freely, and her errors, ignorance, strident anti-intellectualism, and naiveté would simply reinforce her "common man" image. And she needed to master only a single idea and a single policy, and repeat it in answer to every question.

When the outlines of the Jordan plan were leaked, David Brooks, a thoughtful conservative commentator, wrote, "If all government action is automatically dismissed as quasi-socialist, then there is no need to think. A pall of dogmatism will settle over the right."

"Exactly" is what Jordan must have thought upon reading those words. And of course Brooks was prescient.

The financial crisis inherited from the Bush administration was in full swing, and although the bank bailouts that commenced under Bush were allowed to stand, the administration did not extend any further support to the financial sector, allowed Chrysler and General Motors to go bankrupt, and specifically promised to veto any spending that appeared to be in the nature of a fiscal stimulus. The economic decline that year was precipitous. Unemployment rose to 15 percent, home foreclosures reached unprecedented levels, and middle-class savings and pensions were decimated by a stock market that languished at Dow 5000. The national mood turned ugly.

But Jordan had a plan, and like any good political plan, its first step was to "shore up the base." And so, in June 2009, the nation suddenly became completely distracted from its economic woes. During the first week of that month, Rupert Murdoch, Ralph Reed, and Steve Jordan announced the merger of the Faith & Freedom Coalition with Fox News to form Fox Faith & Freedom News. This was truly something new, with a major network abandoning all pretense of journalistic neutrality (the "fair and balanced" slogan was dropped) and becoming part of a national political movement. The mainstream media, professional journalists, and academics were all aghast, but public reaction was muted. Democrats in Congress called for an investigation, but this was quashed by the majority. The Federal Communications Commission, whose budget authority had been held up by a small group of extreme conservatives in the House, did nothing. Some liberals even saw this as a positive development, arguing that Fox would be finally exposed as an entity whose raison d'être was to act as agent provocateur for the far right. They were wrong. And no one at the time, not even Sanjay, appreciated the true enormity of what had just happened.

Although the Fox/FFC merger was highly visible, few focused on the parallel—and almost invisible to non-evangelicals—world of Christian broadcasting. At the time when Palin became an accidental president, all six national Christian television networks, and virtually all the two thousand Christian radio stations, had come under the control of the dominionist branch of conservative Christianity. The aspiring theocrats had thus already completely highjacked the Christian mass media, controlled the most-watched mainstream network, and had just merged it with the principal political action group working toward the creation of a Christian Nation. It was a good start for Jordan.

Only one week later, the majority leader of the Senate, the Speaker of the House, and the vice president joined the president in hosting a meeting in the Rose Garden attended by four hundred "religious leaders of all denominations," according to the White House. Sanjay's Theocracy Watch revealed that the group actually consisted exclusively of evangelicals other than two conservative Catholics, one representative of Jews for Jesus, and an imam who advocated the deportation of all American Muslims to an Islamic country of their choice, provided it was governed by strict Islamic law. Surrounded by the most committed fundamentalists in the nation, the president laid out her legislative program.

First, she announced, a joint resolution of Congress would declare America to be "a Christian Nation, which devoutly recognizes the authority and law of Jesus Christ." As a resolution, it was non-binding and would have no legal effect and thus was not subject to review by the Supreme Court. This was, the president argued, little different from the addition of God to the currency in 1863 and to postage stamps in 1912, or from the amendment in the 1950s of the Pledge of Allegiance to include the words "under God." Declaring the United States to be a Christian Nation was, she said, a simple and uncontroversial statement of fact and perfectly consistent with these many prior affirmations of the role of God in our national life. America was conceived as a Christian Nation by the founders and remained overwhelmingly Christian. She hit the majoritarian theme relentlessly, reminding the members of Congress who were present that in a recent poll 57 percent of Americans surveyed agreed with the statement, "Members of Congress and other political leaders are ignoring our religious heritage." "No more," she said, to the tumultuous applause of the assembled preachers.

The president did go off message with a reporter the next day when she attempted an extemporaneous explanation that America was "ya know, kind of like Israel, a Jewish state, but also of course with the right of people at home to also practice those minority religions too." When asked whether this meant that people could practice "those minority religions" in public as well as "at home," she declined to answer. When reminded that the "God" in the pledge and on the currency was the God of Abraham, common to Judaism, Christianity, and Islam, she professed doubt that this was indeed so, and—showing some confusion over Trinitarian theology—stated that "it was always understood, in an American context, that God meant Jesus, you know, and also his Father too, of course, together." When later asked why—if this was a Christian Nation—there was no mention of God or Christianity in the Constitution, she looked surprised and started to answer "That can't be . . ." before she was interrupted by Vice President Brownback, who explained that mentioning the fact in the Constitution would have been superfluous. "Christ in the eighteenth century," he said, "was like the air and water. He was everywhere, part of the accepted background of life. You wouldn't send an e-mail to your folks from a vacation and think to mention that there was air to breath, would you? No. Just read the words of the founders. America was a religious project from the moment the first Pilgrim set foot on Plymouth Rock. And when the Founding Fathers, our Christian godfearing founding fathers, got together in Philadelphia and, with the assistance of God, gave us our divinely inspired Constitution, they gave us a Christian Nation. They knew it, and the people knew it. No reason to say it."

Brownback's comments were lauded by David Barton on Fox Faith

& Freedom News, or F3, as it was already starting to be called. Barton was the wildly popular evangelical pseudo-historian, whose life's work was to recast American history to support the core proposition that America's origins were as a Christian Nation. That day was the first time I heard him speak. He explained to Glenn Beck and the country his version of American history:

"The old world was irredeemably corrupt, so God conceived of a completely new nation, a 'Shining City on a Hill,' to be born on the blank slate of the New World, in which Christianity could flourish and establish dominion over civic and political life. This is what the Pilgrims and other early settlers came to do, and it is what they did do. As you know, Glenn, the Massachusetts Bay Colony was for all intents and purposes a theocracy. Then we won the Revolution —a bunch of ragtag farmers against the greatest army and navy in the world. You think that would have been possible without God's intervention? Then the Lord, through our godly Christian Founding Fathers, gave us our Constitution—a template for creating a nation like none other on the earth before or since. How else do you think this small country rose up and overtook so rapidly the nations of the Old World? The great religious revivals of the seventeenth and eighteenth centuries were manifestations of Godly religion deepening its hold on American life. But in the twentieth century, Glenn, God's people in America began to lose their way."

Sanjay turned the channel. An historian from Princeton was speaking on CNN: "Even in Salem, Massachusetts, *in 1683*, 83 percent of taxpayers stated that they had no religious allegiance. There is not a single mention of God in the US Constitution. Although theocrats and religious dissidents of all types constituted many of the earliest settlers of the New World, the political project that climaxed with the birth of America was first and foremost a project of the enlightenment, where freedom *from* state religion—the source of so much turmoil and tragedy in European history—was among the core objectives."

The second announcement made by President Palin in the Rose Garden that day was that Congress would again take up the Houses of Worship Free Speech Restoration Act, which in 2002 had been only thirty-one votes short of passage by the House and was reintroduced in 2003 and 2005. The act would allow, on "free speech" grounds, tax-exempt churches to endorse candidates for public office and otherwise engage in political activity without imperiling their tax exemption.

"How can we say we are free," asked the president, "if our religious leaders and religious people are not allowed to exercise their most fundamental political liberty, the right of free speech and engagement in the political process?"

And third in the trinity was the Academic Freedom Bill of Rights, a surprising choice that was based on legislation proposed by Florida Republicans in 2005. The bill gave students standing to sue their universities if they believed they were subjected to "liberal bias."

"It's only fair," said Palin, "that students paying for an education get a real education, with all of history, and all points of view, and not simply political indoctrination. It's a matter of freedom, academic freedom. Let the courts decide; I think we can trust our courts—especially our state courts, which are close to the people—to distinguish liberal bias from real academic freedom." Or as Fox Faith & Freedom News put it rather more candidly, the act was necessary to "fight leftist totalitarianism by dictator professors."

With deft handling by Speaker Boehner and Majority Leader McConnell, the Joint Resolution and both pieces of legislation passed one week later with only a single amendment, which added to the Joint Resolution a reference to the constitutional protection of freedom of religion. This allowed moderate Republicans and Democrats to put the best possible face on it, emphasizing that as a joint resolution it meant nothing legally and that by insisting on an express acknowledgment of freedom of religion, they had specifically rebutted any implication that the status of the country as a Christian Nation in any way derogated from the rights of other religions.

The next morning Sanjay called me at work and asked if I had access to a television and insisted that I tune in immediately to see what was happening. In a reaction unanticipated by both right and left, small groups started to gather throughout the country in shopping malls, mega-church parking lots, and the occasional town square and celebrate their new Christian Nation by burning books.

"Isn't it joyous?" one typical pastor was quoted as saying. "All that filth, all that pornography, so-called gay literature, abortion manuals, irreligious filth forced on our children, evolution nonsense, so-called science, the Koran—all the work of the devil and all purified in God's great light and heat. I knew this day would come," he said, breaking down in tears, "but I just wasn't sure I would live to see the day. And now, by the grace of Jesus, my nation, my America, has been redeemed. Praise God. Praise God."

The bonfires were ringed with families and typically included hundreds of children. A festival atmosphere prevailed. New families arrived with lawn chairs and coolers of beer. But for the fuel source and the absence of cheerleaders, the scenes could have been college pre-game bonfires.

Soon the media, including Fox Faith & Freedom News, had switched to nonstop coverage of the phenomenon. Book burnings continued in all fifty states, with over two thousand specific locations indicated by little flames on the CNN national map. In Colorado Springs, the crowd in the parking lot of the New Life Church was estimated at twelve thousand. SUVs drove up and off-loaded new piles of books to keep the fires going. Reporters asked irreverently whether the celebrants had been stockpiling gay pornography in their houses and, if not, where they had gotten the books. The answers were evasive, although it soon became clear that teenagers were checking books out of public libraries to provide fuel for the bonfires, after which almost all public libraries closed by midday and locked their doors. It also became clear that, having little use for books of any sort, families were just emptying out the dusty bookcases at home, where the volumes, many inherited from their parents, hadn't left the shelves for years. Reporters spotted Reader's Digest Condensed Books, 1950s encyclopedias, American Heritage dictionaries, lots of Danielle Steel and Harry Potter books, and many other works that hardly seemed to fit the stated criteria for destruction (although, when asked, a number of pastors explained that the Harry Potter series, which promoted the false religion of witchcraft, had to go).

I remember being startled by a CNN interview that morning with a woman from the National Institute for Literacy. When asked to offer her explanation for the orgy of hostility toward the written word, she said, "I'm not sure that it's really hostility; more like indifference probably. After all, one survey showed that one-third of high school graduates in America, after they leave high school, never read another book for the rest of their lives. And do you know what the percentage was for college graduates? Forty-two percent. That's right, 42 percent of American adults who have had the benefit of tertiary education will never read another book after graduation. Putting aside what that says about the quality of college education, I think part of this is that for many American households, books are simply an anachronism."

By midday, the media other than Fox were asking why the president, the political leadership of both parties, and the governors were not calling for these crowds to disperse. Only a few governors spoke out against the fires. To their great credit, the Catholic archbishops of New York, Boston, and San Francisco held news conferences at which they called book burning "abhorrent," reminding the reporters of the sad history of their own church and the great evils that had sprung from this sort of intolerance. Fox Faith & Freedom News was jubilant—pressing the theme that the rights of majority Christians had been denied for so long that this sort of jubilant release was perfectly understandable and appropriate. The theme for the F3 news coverage was a clip, played over and over, of Dr. Martin Luther King speaking the words "Free at last, free at last, Thank God Almighty I'm free at last."

Late in the day, crowds at malls across the country swept into Borders, Barnes & Noble, and small locally owned bookshops and started pulling almost everything off the shelves to feed the fires. Police appeared on the scene, and the usual mix of hotheads and provocateurs on both sides created dozens of violent incidents, with mobs surrounding the police and demanding the release of "celebrants" accused of looting. In Oklahoma, Wyoming, and Texas, "Minutemen" and other "Christian Militia" appeared on the scene to protect the "celebrants" from the police. Police and officials seemed uncertain about how to deal with these armed groups, referred to by F3 as Second Amendment Militias, which were "simply exercising their rights to guard the people from tyranny."

No one was killed in the few episodes of violence, and by nightfall the families had packed up and gone home. A few days later, the malls and parking lots were back to normal, the media had dropped the story, and most people settled into the comfortable illusion that this ugly spasm was an aberration, a letting off of steam, a reaction equally attributable to popular discontent over jobs and the economy as to religious fervor.

Sanjay, of course, saw things differently and was relentless in arguing that capitulation on the Christian Nation resolution was a mistake, not because it had any legal effect now but because the declaration itself could later provide a justification for the more tangible parts of the theocratic vision. Emilie and I, and most other people, thought he was overreacting. Palin seemed right—the cash in our wallets had the motto "In God We Trust," and we had grown up pledging allegiance to one nation "under God," and after fifty years these simple symbols and gestures had not undermined the Constitution.

"It's actually smart of her," said Emilie. "Throw the crazies a few bones where it doesn't matter. I mean, presidents have been saying 'God Bless America' for years at the end of every speech. Even the Clintons went to the prayer breakfasts and made necessary obeisance to the Jesus freaks. You think Bill believed a word of it?"

As a lawyer, I had more sympathy with Sanjay's horror at the other two pieces of legislation. Worst was the Houses of Worship Free Speech Restoration Act, which drove a stake through the principle that partisan political activity was not to be subsidized with a federal tax deduction but did so in a way that gave the benefit of the deduction to a single party. The evangelical and Pentecostal churches of America were, of course, overwhelmingly Republican and the largest single part of the charitable sector. Although the Christian right had long been politically active, pastors were not allowed to endorse specific candidates or invest their charitable revenues in political advertising. Although there were many egregious violations of these rules, most clergymen obeyed because loss of the federal tax deduction would have been devastating to the tithing and other contributions on which the movement relied. This would now change, with the $100 billion given to religious causes each year (about one-third of all annual charitable giving in America) suddenly available to support partisan politics. And "speech" included paid advertising. The act was challenged in federal court the day after it was signed. It was declared unconstitutional in the lower court, but after the government appealed that decision, it became clear that the matter would slowly wind its way to the Supreme Court and only there be resolved. In the meantime, the evangelical churches were stopped from leaping into the midterm election cycle.

The Academic Freedom Bill of Rights was more subtle but perhaps even more insidious. It wasn't really expected that masses of students would sue their schools for liberal bias, but a few, funded by F3 and others, would. And the mere threat of such litigation might cause the universities themselves to think twice about promoting academics with liberal views or seek to balance the liberal faculty with conservatives who would not otherwise have been advanced on merit.

The schools with strong principles and, more importantly, vast financial resources, such as the Ivies, proved immune to this pressure, further provoking the wrath of the Christian right. But after a few years, in community colleges and small liberal arts schools around the country, the most liberal professors seemed less lucky when it came time for tenure, and Christian youth social networking sites systematically identified teachers with "liberal bias" and organized boycotts of their classes. With fewer students signing up for their courses, these professors retired or drifted off toward the larger schools and the coastal cities where the evangelical forces were less potent. This vacuum in talent at colleges and universities throughout the most conservative parts of the country was quickly filled by the graduates of Patrick Henry, Regent, Liberty, and other purveyors of "Christ-centered" education who did not conceal that their primary mission was not education in the traditionally understood sense but "taking your faith to the next level."

★   ★   ★

ONE NIGHT AT dinner, Sanjay seemed unusually subdued.

"What's up, San?" asked Emilie. "No doom and gloom for us today? No yogic pearls of wisdom?" Emilie had become somewhat more tolerant of Sanjay since he sold *You and I* and pocketed $400 million. It was impossible for her not to look differently at someone who had founded and grown a business and sold it to a well-respected tech fund. Sanjay, in Emilie's eyes, was now a "player."

I could see Sanjay wondering whether to take the bait.

"Have you seen F3 lately?" Sanjay asked.

"Can't stand it. Did you know that the reason there are no coffee tables in front of the couch on F3 is so that the women's legs aren't hidden? They hire only girls as news readers and reporters who have truly outstanding legs. They're on to something, because they make a shitload of money for Murdoch. I wish I had bought Newscorp stock five years ago. Not, that is, that I would ever want to profit from misogynist exploitation of women's legs . . . and not their brains."

She trailed off, vaguely aware of the mild incoherence resulting from the fourth glass of her favorite white Burgundy.

"You are right, Emilie. Nothing is left to chance over at Fox. And I have noticed something recently." He seemed reluctant to go on. "You will say I am overreacting, but there has been a deliberate shift to a rhetoric of violence. I did not notice it until they fawned all over the Christian Militias who popped up during the book burnings."

"Oh Sanjay dear, you really need to get out more," Emilie said. "If you stare at the Internet all day, you'll start seeing whatever you want to see. This is America. We've used the language of guns and war forever. Remember the war on drugs? And the war on . . . I can't quite remember the other one. But it doesn't matter. No one is talking about civil war. That's utter bullshit."

"Perhaps," Sanjay said, looking thoughtful. "But think about this. When we were young, the religious right—groups like the Moral Majority—was obsessed with sex *and violence* on TV and in movies. They got the rating system introduced. They campaigned incessantly against gratuitous violence. Remember?"

Both Emilie and I nodded skeptically.

"When was the last time you heard a mega-church preacher criticize a film or television show or video game solely on the grounds of being too violent? Sex—yes, they still go on about that. But violence, not so much."

He was right.

"It started in the mid-nineties. Their disapproval of violence in popular culture abated at the same time that their own use of violent rhetoric increased. I think it was deliberate. If you want people to take up arms and fight, you need two things. You need the people to have arms, which is what our forty-year fight over the Second Amendment and gun control has been all about. But second, you need to make the use of those guns acceptable. People have to lose their fear and abhorrence of violence. It has taken more than a generation, but they have almost succeeded."

"I can't believe that," Emilie interjected. "You're seeing ghosts."

"Sorry, but it is true. The rhetoric of violence has exploded on their websites and in the speeches of the movement leaders. And, most oddly, it is not a rhetoric in which the evangelicals are talking of being at war or in violent struggle with their secular enemies. It is the opposite. All of a sudden, what they are speaking about is how the secularists are at war *with them*. The gays, they say, are conducting a war against marriage and family. Those who advocate separation of church and state are 'at war with believers.' The governor of Texas keeps saying that America has 'declared war' on religion. It is a rhetoric in which the evangelicals and their friends are 'under siege.' In which they are relentlessly and brutally attacked by what they call 'the culture.' It is remarkably clever. You do not advocate violence against your enemies;

you just tell people that your enemies are engaged in a violent struggle against you. What follows is then natural. You fight back."

"San, darling, all religious crap is violent as hell. They're always smiting one another over something or other, especially in the Old Testament. Why do you think they call it 'fire and brickstone'?"

"Brimstone," I said. Emilie shot me a look; she hated it when I corrected her.

"What is brimstone anyway?" asked Emilie.

"I have no idea," I answered.

"It is the sulfuric rock often found at the throat of a volcano," said Sanjay matter-of-factly. "An apt metaphor, I've always thought, for divine wrath. Like the spewings of a volcano."

Emilie went to the kitchen to open another $130 bottle of Chardonnay.

"Sorry," I said to Sanjay.

"She meant no offense. But really, Greg, this is something new on F3, a militancy that was not there before, and it started shortly after the Christian Nation resolution and book-burning day. For example, there is a new series of reports on F3 called War Room. One episode had Glenn Beck interviewing right-wing generals and others about a civil war scenario. The basic message was that if their agenda is not respected, ordinary people will rise up in violent rebellion to 'do the right thing' and defend the Constitution. They said that if the federal authorities tried to arrest or resist what they called the 'bubba militias,' then the people would rise up and defend the militias, exercising their Second Amendment right to resist tyranny. It ended by saying that civil war may be inevitable, that history repeats itself. To be clear, this was all painted as 'just one scenario.' But the first step in making something real is to talk about it openly. Civil war, G—when was the last time you heard mainstream media talking about civil war? I think the taboo against violent means has been lifted."

"San, you know the expression 'to a hammer, everything looks like a nail'?"

"No, I have never heard that expression. A very interesting aphorism. Most apt."

"Yeah, well, it is apt. You are Theocracy Watch. You are looking for evidence of theocracy. You want to find it. You need to find it. You have to be careful. This is a big country. There have always been lots of crazies. The militias were big under Clinton. There has always been a violent undercurrent in this country, and now with the Internet all the nuts preaching violence are there for everyone to see. They were there before, San, but with the web, now you can see them. Don't confuse visibility with prevalence. It's a question of perspective."

Sanjay cocked his head in a slight echo of that typical Indian mannerism, and gave me one of his penetrating looks.

"You are right, my friend. Desire is a strong force. I must not will into existence that which I most fear."

"That's not exactly what I meant."

Emilie came back in, and Sanjay knew it was time to stop talking business. Emilie entertained us with stories of her new boss, whose every word and action annoyed her terribly and provided further evidence of his essential character as an irredeemable jerk.

"What about George?" Emilie asked. "I mean I know you guys broke up, but do you ever talk to him, San? Do you know he's left Credit Suisse?"

Most people betray some sort of emotion—whether lingering pain or anger—at the mention of an ex. I looked carefully at Sanjay's face, which was entirely passive. This, I knew, was not Sanjay hiding his emotions but a reliable sign that pain or anger, if there had been any, had passed.

"I did not know. And no, we have not spoken recently. Have you?"

"Nope. Too bad. I mean I hope you don't blame me," Emilie said.

"Of course not. That would be irrational," Sanjay answered.

"Right. So, how 'bout it, want me to set you up again?"

Sometimes Sanjay's transparency was revealing. He paused, and you could sense the neurons firing as he weighed the tempting aspects of Emilie's offer against all the negatives and complications.

"That is very kind, Emilie. But no thank you." He obviously did not think that any further explanation was required, but I sensed that perhaps he had just made quite a major decision. I changed the subject.

"I had my review yesterday."

"My God," said Emilie, "why didn't you tell me?"

"Sorry, forgot. It went fine. Well, not to be immodest, better than fine. They said I was doing fantastic work and was in the very top part of my class. That's a pretty strong signal for RCD&S, especially after fourth year."

Emilie got up from the table and, oblivious to Sanjay's presence—or, perhaps, because of it—straddled me on the chair, took my head in her hands, and delivered an intense and passionate kiss, which I reciprocated. Sanjay slipped out without our saying good-night.

*   *   *

DESPITE MY ADVICE, Sanjay was not to be deterred from his increasing preoccupation with the notion that the long-standing battle over gun control and the theocratic program of the Christian right were deeply synergistic. In a blog on the TW website, Sanjay wrote that it was entirely possible that the most radical evangelical leaders understood well that their ultimate goal of Christian dominion could never be achieved without force of arms. Suspecting that Christian militias were already organizing, he decided to spend a week in Tulsa and see for himself. A few days before he left, I called his office, and the receptionist who answered the phone asked if I had a moment.

"Greg, he probably wouldn't want me to tell you this. But, well, he listens to you. We had a comment on the website that, well—it was a death threat against Sanjay. It's probably nothing, you know, but . . . Well, I wanted you to know."

I was not worried. Given his subject, it was inevitable that abuse and threats of all sorts would ricochet around the web. But I did insist that he report the threat to the authorities and take two staffers with him to Oklahoma.

When he returned a week later, Sanjay reported that his worst fears were confirmed. He found that the Christian media there was filled with talk of apocalyptic violence. Informal militia and military groups were springing up everywhere, including branches of the Christian Identity movement, which believed that religious war was inevitable. The ranks of these nascent militias were filled with what one brave investigative journalist called "thugs, felons, and low-lifes." His exposé showed that the shadowy organizers of these militias recruited ex-cons on the day of their release, gang members, and the chronically unemployed who had become homeless.

Sanjay told me he had attended a rally of twenty-five thousand young people organized by the Battle Cry Campaign, a fundamentalist youth movement whose founder wrote, "This is a war. And Jesus invites us to get into the action, telling us that the violent—the 'forceful' ones—will lay hold of the Kingdom." In the stadium, the chant was "We are warriors." San showed me the transcript of the speech by an Ohio pastor, Rod Parsley:

> *"The secular media never likes it when I say this, so let me say it twice. Man your battle stations! Ready your weapons! They say this rhetoric is so inciting. I came to incite a riot. I came to effect a divine disturbance in the heart and soul of the church. Man your battle stations. Ready your weapons. Lock and load . . ."*

"I was really not expecting this," Sanjay told me. "They cite Romans 13:1 all the time: 'For there is no power but of God; the powers that be are ordained of God.' In other words, follow orders as long as those giving the orders wear the cloak of an earthly government ordained by God. They say that violence in the service of God is an act of devotion. At these rallies in Oklahoma, I met homeschooled evangelical kids who referred to themselves as Generation Joshua. They told me their purpose in life is to retake the land for Jesus."

"San," I said, "that's got to be a very small slice of the population. It's not going to amount to anything."

"Perhaps. But they are not content to leave it at kids and stadium rallies. The Oklahoma legislature is actively considering a proposal that the state officially recognize and sanction a Christian militia."

This surprised me.

He continued. "Do you know about the Militia Act—a law originating in 1792 that is still on the books in modified form? It provides federal sanction not only for the state national guards but also for something that is called an 'unorganized militia.' That concept has been hotly debated in far right circles for decades, but most believe it means that the states are free to recognize and permit private armies in their own states. The so-called Constitutional Militia Movement really got going sometime in the mid-1990s, and the motivating concept was that the people needed to be well armed and organized to defend themselves against unconstitutional regulation by the federal government, such as gun regulation. They are firmly convinced that the Founding Fathers so distrusted both the federal government and the idea of a federal standing army that they insisted on an armed population ready to resist federal overreaching.

"What the Oklahoma legislature is now trying to do is somewhat different," Sanjay continued. "Most of the militiamen call themselves Liberty Boys or Freedom Fighters. But the Oklahoma legislation proposes to recognize what it calls a Christian Militia. Imagine, G, all the red states. The most committed fundamentalists organized into armed militias. With ranks, regimental headquarters, advanced weapons, Saturday drills—all sanctioned by the state but not subject to state or federal government control. Most people would have thought it impossible in America. After all, only a few years ago private militias, like the white supremacy groups and neo-Nazis, were hunted down by the FBI and prosecuted. Now they are being sanctioned by the states themselves. What has changed?"

It was a rhetorical question. I had to concede that Sanjay was right about the cultural undercurrent of violence and its embrace by the Christian media and F3. But, as always, it was a question of perspective. America's libertarian streak, its infatuation with arms, and the use of militarist rhetoric all had deep roots in American history, waxing and waning with the ebb and flow of popular content and discontent, prosperity and distress. Was this different? That was the question. During the siege, we spent many evenings debating whether our collective blindness to the militarization of the Christian right was in fact an understandable error of perspective or some lethal combination of historical myopia and wishful thinking. Does the explanation matter? I'm starting to think that it might.

In any case, when Sanjay returned from his trip to Oklahoma, I expected him to write aggressively about the militias, the quasi-official status they were being granted by that state, and the threat posed by the gradual development of an armed wing of the Christian right. Instead, to my complete surprise, he wrote and published, above the fold on the opinion page of the *New York Times*, a concise essay on virtue. In the face of the potential for political violence, his instincts turned to the stronger power of the traditional personal virtues celebrated across all human cultures and religious traditions. He wrote of the civic and political fruits of a society in which generosity, gentleness, humor, and politeness were practiced and celebrated. He explained how these simpler virtues in turn depended on a foundation of humility, tolerance, and sincere truthfulness without which the other virtues could not flourish. He demonstrated how, in turn, the practice of these qualities leads inevitably to the more profound virtues of compassion, mercy, and love. He then asked, with the gentleness and spirit of forgiveness indicated by these great virtues, how those who advocated a "more moral society" could engage in behavior that was, by this standard, anything but Christian. He picked quotes from Palin and Jordan to show that their own morality was arrogant, full of pride, and fundamentally intolerant. If these were their words, Sanjay argued, their behavior was inevitably going to be rude, devious, and intemperate, as it was. Their idea of justice, he argued, was harsh and bereft of charity. For them, the enemy was to be defeated, not, as Jesus had preached, to be loved. Evangelicalism in America was a movement, he concluded, launched in the name of the most compassionate role model man had ever known but was now on the verge of being irrevocably infected by bitterness and hate.

I and many others were profoundly moved by this essay. The rhetoric of obedience to God's will, of revealed truth and biblical authority seemed hollow compared to Sanjay's vision of a society that valued generosity, compassion, mercy, humility, tolerance, truthfulness, gentleness, and the rest. And it revealed that Sanjay was a profound thinker and a good man. Although I had known him at that point for twelve years, I discovered in him a depth I had not seen before. Sanjay was growing and becoming a better man, I remember thinking. But was I? He had written an essay designed to move hearts and change history. I was spending my time, and my own powers, writing indentures and loan agreements.

A year after Palin's legislative program had become law, even her harshest critics had to admit that their lives had not been changed by the largely symbolic acts of her presidency. And the attention of the nation was again focused almost exclusively on the lingering "great recession."

The economic situation was the most serious since the Great Depression. The Dow had not budged. The savings and retirement plans of middle-class Americans were worth about a third of what they had been, and retired people had to work to pay the rent, if they were lucky enough to find a part-time job. Unemployment rose relentlessly, reaching 18 percent in the summer of 2010. The collapse of the US auto industry had the exact devastating ripple effects on the US economy, especially in the Midwest, that the advocates of a bailout had predicted. Few jobs were available to college graduates. Abandoned and foreclosed houses with unmowed lawns, collapsing gutters, and, increasingly, broken windows languished in every town, depressing the spirits of even those who were still employed and gutting the pride and morale of previously prosperous communities. The homeless returned to the streets of the big cities in numbers not seen since the early 1980s.

The Republican-controlled Congress had steadfastly refused to support any federal action. Despite a public letter to the US Congress from every living Nobel Prize–winning economist calling for fiscal stimulus, no new appropriation could pass the House, and federal spending actually decreased, exacerbating the economic decline in exactly the way predicted by the Keynesians. Moreover, unemployment benefits were allowed to expire. All the president said, repeatedly, was "Washington is the problem, not the solution."

On November 2, 2010, the people of the United States, suffering and fearful, handed control of the US House of Representatives back to the Democratic Party. For the second time in Sarah Palin's national political career, the pundits declared her to be finished. Emilie smugly reminded Sanjay that for our entire history, American politics flirted periodically with the extreme but always reverted to the centrist mean and now had done so again. In the face of the largest economic challenge for a generation, the risk of Christian fundamentalism seemed the least of the country's problems. Sanjay was once again ignored by the media, and I immersed myself in my work.

CHAPTER EIGHT

Currents

2011–2012

When opinions cannot be distinguished from facts, when there is no universal standard to determine truth in law, in science, in scholarship, or in reporting the events of the day, when the most valued skill is the ability to entertain, the world becomes a place where lies become true, where people can believe what they want to believe. . . .

The culture of illusion thrives by robbing us of the intellectual and linguistic tools to separate illusion from truth. It reduces us to the level and dependency of children.

—Chris Hedges,
Empire of Illusion

It was characteristic of [authoritarian movements] that they recruited their members from this mass of apparently indifferent people whom all other parties had given up as too apathetic or too stupid for their attention.

—Hannah Arendt,
The Origins of Totalitarianism

THIS MEMOIR PROJECT HAS BECOME ADDICTIVE. I rise early, make coffee for the house, and most of the time take a swim in Indian Lake.

Yesterday we had a visitor. I was writing at the desk overlooking the lake when I had that feeling of being observed. I turned to see a woman, about my age, standing in the doorway with Adam, silently watching me. I don't know how long she had been there. I started to stand and Adam raised his hand. "Sorry to interrupt, we'll be going now." He did not introduce me, and I watched through the window as Adam and the woman walked along the shore of the lake to a small stone platform at the water's edge with two old Adirondack-style chairs. They sat and talked for at least an hour.

When neither Adam nor his wife raised the subject of the mystery guest at dinner, I did.

"Who was the woman? And why weren't we introduced? Why the secrecy?"

"Our being here is forbidden. This house is forbidden. The typewriter is forbidden. What you are doing is forbidden. And you ask 'why the secrecy'?"

It was the sharpest tone he had taken with me during our entire acquaintance.

"Let me be more precise. Why are you keeping secrets from me?"

"Ah," he said, smiling at his wife, "that's different. What do you want to know?"

"Who was the woman? And while we're at it, are you part of the Free Minds movement, how did you get the job in the archives, and what are you going to do with what I write? That's for starters."

Adam's wife left the table. "I'll answer what I can. The woman today belongs to my FM cell. I did not introduce you because I don't know her name, or at least her real name, and even if I did, I couldn't tell you. Or Sarah. What's my role in the movement? Honestly, I'm not entirely sure. I was told to get a job at the archives to get close to you. And what I want from you is what I have asked you to do. To remember and to write exactly what happened and why."

He rose from the table and signaled with his body language that the conversation was over. Nothing he said surprised me, though I knew it wasn't the whole truth. For the moment, it was enough. We had begun the conversation, and a certain taboo had been lifted.

I feel oddly confident, even strong, as I pick up my story. The stars are bright and the North Star is crisply reflected in the mirrored surface of the lake. I stare at the reflection and will the water to ripple. A breeze obliges and I indulge the fantasy that I have caused a minute wrinkle in space-time, and I wonder, momentarily, what might be its consequences.

It was almost a year before the midterm elections in 2010 that I had started work at the firm on the most important matter of my career. By 2009 some farsighted engineers in the world's largest mining company had started to worry about the near monopoly the Chinese government had obtained in an esoteric class of minerals called rare earths. These metals—with names like cerium, neodymium, scandium, and yttrium—are not used in bulk quantities, as are copper or bauxite, but are absolutely essential to a whole range of applications, including aviation, computer monitors, and medical imaging. Previously, rare earths were produced from mines located in North America and southern Africa, but every one of those mines had been shut as the result of low-cost competition from China. Customers didn't mind, though, as the Chinese supplies were reliable and cheap.

But once the Chinese consolidated their near-monopoly position, they limited supply and achieved a gradual increase in prices to a level exceeding that at the outset of Chinese competition. Some vague talk of export quotas had been heard from Beijing. The US and EU governments sounded the alarm, and Harco, a global conglomerate based in the United Kingdom, saw an opportunity. It quietly bought up the mining licenses for the world's largest non-Chinese rare-earth deposits, located deep in the Highlands of Papua New Guinea. Development of these deposits to compete with the Chinese would require negotiating a long-term agreement with the government of PNG, assembling a joint venture, and raising most of the US $8 billion project cost.

When Harco came to RCD&S with the assignment, the general

counsel specifically requested that I should be the lead attorney. It was a remarkable opportunity for a young lawyer.

I spent the next two years in a peripatetic international existence, traveling many times to Port Moresby, the sometimes violent and dangerous capital of PNG, to negotiate with the government. On a particularly bad day I remember the freshwater supply to the city having been cut off by rebels. The hotel staff responded by bringing two buckets per day of salt water to my room—"one for flushing, one for washing," the bellman cheerfully explained. Negotiations with the relevant ministry were held in a Quonset hut dating from the Second World War. I also traveled frequently to Tokyo, Frankfurt, and London. One day I would be patiently explaining the joint venture arrangements to the senior executives of a Japanese trading company in Tokyo, and the next would find me in Frankfurt explaining the same provisions to German businessmen in a wholly different way. I found I was able to communicate to different audiences with remarkable success.

★   ★   ★

I HAVE BEEN silently staring out the window overlooking the lake for ten minutes now, startled by my ability to feel again what it was to be that person. I remember vividly my immense productivity and the exclusive claim made by the job on my life. I felt again the almost guilty satisfaction of really understanding when those around me were confused, and the rewards of listening well, bringing solutions to the table, and bridging interests and cultures. I recalled the gratitude of the clients. I had been truly happy in my work. After I left the law firm, I never looked back in this way. And now I have, and I'm surprised by the magnitude of what I lost.

My work on the rare-earths deal marked the beginning of a new phase in my relationship with Emilie. She didn't mind my working long hours because she did the same. She didn't mind the stress that I brought home because we had that in common. She never complained about my not being around, about missed dates, or about not attending weddings of our college friends. When I called her from a car in Tokyo to say I would not be back for the wedding of one of her oldest friends, the other RCD&S lawyer in the car cringed. When I reported her curt reply—"I understand, no problem"—he said simply: "She's a keeper."

On the other hand, nothing annoyed her more than my periodic doubts about whether I wished to spend my life as a corporate lawyer. She mocked anything I said that had about it even a whiff of diluted ambition. In that sense, the rare-earths deal should have been good not only for my career but also for my relationship with Emilie. This is because after a few months of working on rare earths, I was so interested and fulfilled by the work that most of my career-related doubts evaporated. I allowed myself to be defined by the job, and I acquired the confidence and ambition of a fast-rising star. For her, it should have been an aphrodisiac.

Perhaps it was. As our time together became scarcer, our physical relationship became more intense. We were still cathartic lovers. I remember one night in bed, after sex, I told her about my most recent trip to Japan, particularly how fascinated I was by the contrast between the refinement of Japanese culture and the misogyny and potential for cruelty that seemed equally embedded. I told her about the Zen rock garden at Ryoan-ji.

"Did Mitsubishi commit to a billion?" she asked.

"What?"

"Isn't that why you went? Did you get them to sign up for a billion?"

"Yes, but—"

"Good. Keep your eye on the ball, Greg. No one is interested in the Japanese. They're has-beens. The money is in China now."

She turned away and went to sleep. I remember staring at her back, as if it was the first time I had ever seen it. I was stung by her complete indifference to the things that fascinated me. I see now that in a lifelong quest for perspective, the years I dedicated to rare earths were the great leap forward, and the experiences that propelled me were those that Emilie disdained.

During the same period, Sanjay was deeply frustrated by his forced inactivity. The loss by the Republicans of the House of Representatives had effectively paralyzed the White House, and the president and Steve Jordan's religious and cultural agenda was at a standstill. The fear of the theocratic tendency, urgently felt by millions following Sarah Palin's first year, now itself seemed extreme. Sanjay pointed out to anyone who would listen that the fundamentalist movement was famously patient and that the Internet revealed continued plotting and intrigue by dominionist groups. Millions of children each year were still being withdrawn from public schools so their minds could be locked in the cage of fundamentalist dogma. But very few people had time for such arguments.

Instead, the entire attention of the country was now focused on what was being called the Second Depression. It was three years after the housing crisis and near financial meltdown, and the American economy had not budged. The newly Democratic House seized the initiative and adopted a series of strong fiscal stimulus measures. Republicans continued their relentless accusations that these measures were taking the country down the road to socialism, but they sensed—and shared—the fear of permanent economic stagnation, and allowed the measures to pass the Senate. The president did not use her veto.

A couple of weeks after my return from Japan and the strange moment in bed with Emilie, I dropped by Sanjay's apartment downtown after work. Honestly, I can't remember whether I was going to cheer him up or vice versa. But I do remember we both were feeling low. I described my attempted conversation with Emilie about Japan and how her response had troubled me in a way that was completely out of proportion. For the first time, I found myself sharing with him doubts about whether my relationship with Emilie would survive— doubts that I had not even allowed myself to entertain consciously until I found myself speaking them out loud to Sanjay.

"G," he said, "I am no expert, but I think there may be only one question, which is whether she makes you happy."

"Sometimes, yes. But I think we want different things. Don't you think that's a problem?"

"You and I may want different things and we are still friends."

"Friends. That's different."

When she was angry, Emilie often called me "clueless." After all this time, I am starting to understand what she meant.

The conversation about Emilie was a short one. And then, for the first time ever, Sanjay admitted to me that he was dealing with his own doubts.

"What if," he said, "I am wrong? Most people think I am missing or undervaluing the factors that doom the theocratic program to failure. What if they are correct? What if I have been deeply egotistical in becoming so invested in my own analysis?"

After a long pause, he continued. "What if I am just another gay man afraid of a heterosexual world? Or a mind deluded by an illusion of prophetic powers? Or even worse, an insecure person seeking status and validation? What if, G, that is what this all is? I would find it unbearable."

I was shocked to hear Sanjay articulate so precisely my unarticulated disquietude about his crusade. Yes, I thought, those are the right what-ifs. You are, my friend, finally worrying about the right things. Of course these were words I did not say. But the more profound surprise was seeing the usually imperturbable Sanjay so vulnerable. He routinely questioned his actions and plans, but always in the language of reason. That night, I heard the language of fear.

I got up and went to the kitchen and came out with two cold beers. Sanjay had a weakness for an artisanal lager from Brooklyn.

"San, tonight we are going to give birth to something completely new. I call it 'brewga.' It's going to be big. Bigger than *You and I*, and a lot more fun. A nice big gulp of Brooklyn lager between every pose. This is the way I want to learn yoga. Will you teach me?" We hadn't done yoga together since we were in college.

Without comment, he took the beer and started teaching. Three hours and four beers each later, we had run through all the poses of the Ashtanga primary series, stupidly chanting "brew-ga, brew-ga" at the end of every pose. Sanjay told me he had never before laughed out loud while doing yoga. At the end, we sat cross-legged on his brown carpet facing each other, knees almost touching. I remember the smell of his sweat, slightly sweet, mixed with my own, more acrid, and the stale odor of the beer we had spilled on the carpet. Empathy aligned our inhales and exhales. His breath wafted across the small distance between us and was drawn inside me. His tender gaze gently held my eyes. We sat like that for a very long time.

★ ★ ★

I AM RETURNING to the typewriter after a long break. I did not write at all this afternoon, but I walked to the other side of the lake and sat on the large boulder opposite the cottage. I realize that the last time I did any yoga was the morning before the invasion of the Battery. The last day of my former life. Tonight I feel my body in a different way. I feel the strength and upward thrust of my skeleton and the relentless pull of gravity on the muscles and soft tissues. I plant my feet on the floor, feeling the four corners of the foot. My muscles remember. I realize I could stand up now and do my practice. But I'm not ready for yoga. Not yet.

★ ★ ★

ONLY A MONTH after brewga with Sanjay, everything changed again.

Like 9/11, July 22, 2012, was a perfectly clear day in New York. The sky a May blue, unusual for July, with no trace of humidity. It was no accident. The terrorists had planned their attack for the previous week, but on the appointed day nearly half the airports were plagued by low ceilings, fog, or drizzle. On July 22, 2012, though, the nation sat under an enormous high-pressure system, and each of New York's three airports—together with Boston, Washington National, Atlanta, Miami, Houston, Chicago O'Hare, Denver, LAX, San Francisco, and Seattle—had unlimited ceilings and visibility of over twenty miles. At 9:30 a.m. eastern time, 6:30 a.m. on the West Coast, none of the terrorist teams had received the agreed abort signal.

At that moment, the situation at Newark Liberty Airport, just west of Manhattan, was typical. Anyone looking west from Manhattan could see six planes on final approach strung along an imaginary ramp in the sky leading down onto Runway 4 Right. All these final approach patterns were well defined and publicly known. Because none of the planes was a "heavy"—planes like 747s and A380s, whose heavier weights create a larger and more dangerous wake vortex— they were separated from one another by only three to four nautical miles, making the approach "ramp" along which they were arrayed extend about twenty to thirty miles south of the airport. When taking off and landing, passenger jets are at their maximum vulnerability and minimum maneuverability, flying at a low airspeed, close to the "stall speed" at which the wings lose their lift, and at the nose-up angle of attack, or attitude, in the air. Uninterrupted, one of these planes would have touched down on Newark's Runway 4 Right every forty-five to sixty seconds. On the other side of the airport, planes taking off to the north from the parallel Runway 4 Left were fewer in number but even more vulnerable: close to the ground, heavy with fuel, and flying slowly, usually around 250 knots below 10,000 feet. Not a single terrorist team at any airport failed to destroy the two most recent jets that had left the runway. And in no case was a second missile required.

The terrorist teams were spread out below these final approach and climb-out ramps at intervals of about three miles. Each had a laptop open to a website showing, in real time, the air traffic around the airport. Their radios were tuned to the frequencies used by both approach control and the airport tower. Numerous politicians later expressed shock that the radar approach images were available to anyone and that these radio channels were not secure, but this was totally disingenuous. Everyone had understood for years that this information was available to anyone.

The terrorist plan was simple. At the appointed moment, each team was to fire its first missile at the plane immediately behind it, that is, in the direction away from the airport for those on the landing side, and in the direction toward the airport for those on the takeoff side. This then allowed the next team along the route to fire a second missile at the same plane as it passed overhead.

At Newark, as was typical for many of the airports, there were ample abandoned industrial sites, unused parking lots, swampy fields, and other places in the towns of Perth Amboy, Port Reading, and Carteret, to the south, and Harrison, Kearney, and the Ironbound section of Newark to the north, for the terrorist teams to set up their positions. Only one, the position in Carteret, was in a residential neighborhood, where the risk of interruption was significant. The close-in missiles were heat-seeking MANPADS (man-portable air-defense systems), a type of SAM (surface-to-air missile) that can generally be launched by a single operator and that targets the heat signature of a jet's engines. The simplest of these missiles is five to six feet long and weighs only thirty-five pounds. The price on the black market: several hundred dollars. At a few of the sites more distant from the airports—where the planes' altitude would be higher and the chances for recovery and safe landing greater—the terrorists used fancier laser-guided assemblies mounted on the back of jeeps. These cost the terrorists up to $250,000 each. When President Palin expressed surprise that such sophisticated weapons could have found their way into the hands of terrorists, the PBS *NewsHour* correspondent read to her from a Pentagon report addressed to her three years previously citing intelligence estimates that between 5,000 and 150,000 SAMs were in terrorist hands, with twenty-five to thirty separate groups estimated to be in possession of the weapons. Nor was the use of such missiles against airliners unprecedented. The CIA put the total number of previous missile attacks on civilian airplanes at thirty-five, all outside of the United States. Of these previous attacks, twenty-four were successful. Terrorists had been practicing this technique for years but had reserved for the United States the novelty of simultaneous attack on multiple planes and multiple airports. Later that afternoon the Al Qaeda website ran a single ironic headline in Arabic: "Shock and Awe."

The chaos caused by simultaneous attacks on between three and nine planes at each of thirteen airports cannot, even today, be fully grasped. At Newark, where the maximum number of hits occurred, three planes were destroyed instantly, their wreckage scattering over downtown Newark and Harrison and starting scores of ferocious fires fed by fully fueled planes. Six other planes simultaneously declared an emergency and sought clearance for immediate landing. Of the planes on final approach, only two succeeded in making controlled landings with survivors. Some were struggling to land on one engine when the remaining engine was hit with a second missile. Within less than a minute, all semblance of air traffic control collapsed. The controllers had no idea what was happening or why. Within minutes most runways were littered with the wreckage of planes. In a horrific pattern repeated over and over around the country, crippled jets plowed into the wreckage of the plane ahead of it on the approach that had crashed only moments before on the same runway. Hundreds of people who survived the landings were killed in these fiery collisions. The total lack of situational awareness was such that one plane waiting for takeoff clearance when the attacks began received that clearance and flew right into the line of missile fire, notwithstanding that the two planes that had taken off just before it were already burning on the ground below. On the ground, emergency services were confused and unequal to the unprecedented challenge. A ten-square-block area in the Ironbound section of Newark, directly under the climb-out line at Newark Liberty Airport, burned to the ground before a single firefighting vehicle reported to the scene.

LaGuardia and JFK airports experienced similar losses, and both Queens and Brooklyn suffered heavily from the number and severity of the crashes. Manhattan, this time, was spared. I was in the office that morning. As the news broke, we scurried from the east to the west sides of our building to see the numerous wreckage sites and the plumes of ominous black smoke. My secretary came into my office and told me it had happened in Washington too. Then Boston, Atlanta, Houston, Denver, Miami, Chicago, Seattle, LA, and San Francisco. First, dozens of planes. Then scores of planes. And again, the drama, for the first time since 9/11, of having to get every other plane in the air safely on the ground, but this time with many major airports completely closed. By that evening, the numbers were in: attacks at thirteen airports on thirty-nine planes; more than six thousand dead in the planes and over five hundred on the ground; six cities still on fire.

Pearl Harbor had been an attack on a single remote state. The targets in 9/11 were the power centers of New York and Washington. But 7/22 hit seven states, eleven major urban centers in all parts of the country, and the sprawling suburbs around large airports in all those places. Looking at the map on CNN, with the small symbols of crashed planes and fires on the ground evenly scattered across the continent, anyone could see that this truly was an attack on all of America. And all of America received the message that was sent: Nowhere in your country is safe.

Eighty-one terrorists had been found dead in the places from which the missiles had been launched: all men, all Muslim, and all in America legally. By 10 a.m. eastern time, there were no planes left for the terrorists to shoot. Not a single terrorist team had been discovered or interrupted by law enforcement. Each group consisted of a commander and one or two others. At each location, once the missiles were used up or the planes stopped flying, the senior man shot the junior and then himself. Not one of these men suffered a failure of courage. Just short of the tenth anniversary of 9/11, the whole thing was over in thirty minutes.

America again had the sympathy of the world. But this time there was an undercurrent of doubt or even derision. Each of the terrorists had been allowed into the country *after* 9/11. How could that have happened? One or two or ten maybe, but eighty-one? Moreover, the terrorists had not come up with something new or unexpected but simply exploited what the US government itself had identified as the prime remaining vulnerability of the air system, a known vulnerability that went completely unaddressed by federal authorities. Instead of figuring out how to defend airliners against missiles, the government had spent the decade having ordinary Americans and frequent travellers like myself remove their belts and shoes and pack their toiletries into little plastic bags. And now, eighty-one terrorists operating in thirteen cities; terrorist teams setting up missiles at thirty separate sites around major American cities. The number noticed and stopped: zero. Were the terrorists that brilliant, or did we have a competence problem, a failure of will, or perhaps both? Perhaps, said many around the world, perhaps America's best days were over. And the mood in the country, initially one of shock, grief, and solidarity, turned ugly.

CHAPTER NINE

It Can't Happen Here

2012

Repeatedly I heard anti-Nazis say, "If only 1,000 of us in the late twenties had combined in heroic resistance, we could have stopped Hitler."

> —Dr. James Luther Adams, dissident in Germany in the mid-1930s and later a professor at Harvard Divinity School, "The Evolution of My Social Concern"

Hannah Arendt dated her awakening to February 27, 1933, the day the Reichstag burned down. From the moment Adolf Hitler began using the fire as a pretext to suspend civil liberties and crush dissent, Arendt said, "I felt responsible."

> —Samantha Power, introduction to 2004 edition of Hannah Arendt's *The Origins of Totalitarianism*

IT IS OBVIOUS IN RETROSPECT that only an external attack like that on 7/22 could have saved the Palin presidency. Without it, would any of what followed have happened? I doubt it. The Democrats would have recaptured both the White House and Senate that fall. The culture wars would have simmered on, but the evangelical movement's momentum on the path toward political power would have been lost. I would be installed in my corner office downtown, practicing law. I would probably have children with Emilie. I might be having dinner with Sanjay tonight instead of sitting here with people I really don't know, trying to remember and record all that happened since then.

But 7/22 did happen. It was truly horrible, and the American people were understandably scared and angry. 7/22 opened a door, and Sarah Palin walked through it.

On July 24, 2012, President Palin, for only the second time in the history of the republic, declared martial law over the entire country. Instead of appearing alone in a televised address from the formality of the Oval Office, she addressed the nation from the Situation Room in the basement of the White House flanked by all the Joint Chiefs of Staff, with Vice President Brownback and Steve Jordan the only civilians present. Her speech was direct and forceful. After 9/11, she said, our enemies had counted on our weaknesses. They knew of our preoccupation with rights, laws, and political correctness of every sort. They counted on it. And what did we do? We acted true to form: no profiling of Muslims; continuing to welcome Muslim immigrants; hauling terrorists into federal courts as if they were common criminals; and having some of the brightest legal talent in the country come to their defense. "No more," she said. Nearly seven thousand of our fellow citizens died because of it, hundreds of thousands more were heartbroken, and six American cities were still smoldering. This was a war. Islamic fundamentalists were our sworn enemies. Each of the eighty-one terrorists had been welcomed to our country like the millions before them seeking freedom and a better life. But they had betrayed us and used our freedoms against us. Thousands more were doubtless still in the country plotting the same betrayal. She swore to find and deport or punish every last one of them. Every one. Nothing would stop her.

The president reported that the Joint Chiefs, her cabinet, and all her advisors were unanimous in their advice that fighting this war here in the homeland required a declaration of martial law. The protections of the Constitution were not intended for our enemies, she said. Moreover, this was a war to be fought by soldiers, not policemen, and when the terrorists were caught, they needed to be tried in military, not civilian, tribunals. Nothing else mattered. She would devote her presidency to this and only this. The emergency and her duties as president required her full attention. She would not conduct a normal political campaign. She would appear at her party's convention but would neither debate nor travel the country for public appearances in the run-up to November 6. This was not, she said, a time for politics. If the American people chose to reelect her, her promise was simple: she would eradicate all the other Islamists lurking here in the homeland and keep out any new ones. That was it. She hoped everyone understood her priorities.

The speech was wildly popular. Article 1, Section 9 of the US Constitution states, "The Privilege of the Writ of Habeas Corpus shall not be suspended, unless when in Cases of Rebellion or Invasion the public Safety may require it." During the Civil War, Lincoln had selectively imposed martial law through unilateral suspension of the writ, but the Supreme Court ruled that congressional authorization was required. Lincoln got it. But after the Civil War, the Posse Comitatus Act limited the role that the federal military could play in domestic law enforcement. The bill submitted to Congress by President Palin authorized her to suspend habeas corpus—the constitutional guarantee of judicial supervision of detention and civil trial—*and* it sanctioned unlimited involvement by the US military in investigating, pursuing, and prosecuting terrorists found within the country. Largely overlooked in the legislation was a provision that allowed the president to take direct control of the state National Guards without the consent of state governors. In a rare display of unity, Congress authorized the martial law legislation on these terms and, unwisely as it turned out, failed either to prescribe limits to the president's authority or to provide a "sunset date" following which martial law would terminate unless extended by Congress.

The weekend after 7/22, Sanjay was at our apartment and the three of us were flipping channels and comparing the coverage. F3 was, as usual, the most dramatic and compelling. The network had suspended regular programming and was running stories on the prior uses of martial law in an attempt to dispel the widespread disquiet by numerous commentators that the loss of constitutional protections represented a victory of sorts for the terrorists. F3 cited, in some cases incorrectly, the Chicago Fire, Hawaii after Pearl Harbor, coal riots in West Virginia, and even hurricane Katrina as prior uses of martial law. They argued that martial law was routine and necessary in times of national crisis.

Of course, it was not. What was new here was the remarkable cognitive shift required for the states'-rights and individual-freedom-loving opinion makers of F3 to now show unbridled enthusiasm for *federal* usurpation of fundamental state prerogatives, suspension of the Bill of Rights (including, notably, their precious Second Amendment), and an unprecedented projection of Beltway power into the heartland. Not two years before, F3 itself speculated that, faced with a far more limited projection of federal power, the "bubba" and Christian militias would rise up and defend the Constitution and the people from the threat of tyrannical abuse. This time around, there was no talk of militias or tyranny.

Emilie was not surprised. "It depends, of course, which side you are on. If Barack Obama were in the White House and 7/22 happened exactly as it did, the Christian right would be screaming bloody murder about martial law. But since they're in charge, it's OK. It's that simple. Surely you understand that much."

To be honest, I did have trouble understanding even that much. My mind expected and sought principle and coherence. I was not programmed to deal well with pure expediency, and I found it difficult to accept that people could be so easily manipulated into supporting positions that contradicted both their self-proclaimed values and their own interests. But Karl Rove, Steve Jordan, and the other brilliant political strategists of the Republican far right had made their reputations and fortunes doing just that.

"Emilie is right," said Sanjay. "I think it is that simple. Power is good if it is in your hands and bad if it is in the hands of the enemy. And by the way, the corollary rule is that once extraordinary power is in your hands, risking that same power transferring into the hands of your enemy through free and fair elections is difficult to accept."

"Are you saying she'll suspend the election?" asked Emilie.

"Not at all. She doesn't need to. This is an election that now she cannot lose. But I am saying that the Christian right has backed itself into a corner. Whether or not the time is really right to make the big push to some kind of theocracy, they have left themselves little choice. Either end martial law before the end of Palin's second term or use it to create the Christian Nation."

Of course even Sanjay, with all his foresight, didn't call that one exactly right.

"And Greg," Sanjay continued, "as to the cognitive dissonance, with respect, this is an example of how 'thinking like a lawyer' can get you into terrible trouble. People are endowed with reason, but it rarely rules their minds. They have access to logic, but they use it sparingly. One of the most remarkable things about the human brain is its ability to embrace contradictions."

"San, dear," Emilie interrupted, "if you are going to protect us from Christian extremist knuckleheads, you are going to need to speak more plainly. No one knows or cares about 'cognitive dissonance.' Just say what you mean. Most Americans will believe almost anything—golden tablets from God buried under a hill in upstate New York, alien souls bouncing around the universe and inhabiting our bodies, getting to fuck seventy-two virgins as a welcome present when you arrive in heaven—it's all the same crap. If you are raised to believe it, or are dumb enough and desperate enough, then you'll believe anything."

Sanjay, unusually, seemed both amused and annoyed. "You, Emilie, will not be writing my speeches. And my comments were targeted at tonight's particular audience, who I assumed to be sufficiently intelligent and educated to handle a bit of philosophical digression. But since I apparently was wrong, let me give you a specific easy-to-understand example. Remember Terri Schiavo? I think history will record the

Terri Schiavo affair as one of the seminal events of our modern history, a singular watershed for the evangelical movement and for conservatives. The reconstructionists, previously somewhat at the margins, were propelled to the center of a fight that galvanized the entire Christian right. And what was at the heart of it? You had a question—whether to let the doctors remove life support from a brain-dead woman as authorized by her husband and opposed by her parents. This is and always has been a question solely for the states. There is absolutely nothing in the Constitution that makes any part of this a federal question. Think of it this way: If the Florida court had ordered that the feeding tube *not* be removed, then any federal intervention would have been anathema to the Christian right—yet another in the long line of grievances where federal courts frustrate the will of the people on federal or constitutional grounds. But this time, the *state* court ordered the feeding tube removed. So, was their response consistent with their own fundamental political belief—that is, to defer to the state and keep the federal government out of it? No. When federal courts properly declined to intervene, George Bush flew back from Texas, Tom DeLay recalled Congress, and the Congress of the United States attempted, by federal law, to prevent the doctors of a brain-dead woman in Florida from removing her feeding tube because, in the particular belief system of a single sect of a single religion, this is seen as euthanasia and contrary to the law of the Old Testament. A few brave Republicans at the time saw the monumental hypocrisy. You know what Chris Shays, the congressman from Connecticut, said?"

"I haven't a clue," said Emilie, "and I'm not really sure that I care." Sanjay was not deterred.

"He said, 'My party is demonstrating that they are for states' rights unless they don't like what states are doing. This couldn't be a more classic case of a state responsibility. This Republican Party of Lincoln has become a party of theocracy.'"

"Of course," said Emilie, oozing sarcasm. "Theocracy. It's where all roads lead. Our karma."

"Not necessarily. But do you not see? The imposition of Christian values by the federal government violates fundamentally the conservative principles of individual liberty, states' rights, and limited government. You could be forgiven for thinking that this is an absolute barrier to a conservative embrace of theocracy. But it is not. These values, what some conservatives call 'process conservatism,' will always be thrown under the bus if they conflict with 'substantive values,' such as the right to life. Mike Huckabee, the governor of Arkansas, was at least frank about it. He just shrugged and said, 'There's a larger issue in play, and that is the whole issue of the definition of life.' So there you have it. Personal freedom, states' rights, and limited government—all pushed aside in a moment when there is a 'larger issue.'"

"Sanjay, you seem as preoccupied with this Terri Schiavo person as the knuckleheads are," said Emilie. "For God's sake, it was seven years ago. That's an eternity."

"You are right. I am preoccupied. I think this incident is incredibly revealing of what we can expect from the fundamentalists. And it's not just the casualness with which personal liberty, states' rights, and the rest were thrown aside. This was a manufactured 'crisis.' Millions of good people around the country were manipulated into really caring about the woman. They cried when she died. And so the movement gained a martyr—a symbol that the puppet masters, when it suits their purposes, can use to reconnect the faithful with that emotion."

Emilie looked thoughtful. "That's a pretty cynical reading, San."

"And one last thing: The movement flirted with violent resistance. Jeb Bush actually dispatched armed state agents to forcibly remove Terri Schiavo from the hospice in violation of court orders, but those state agents were stopped by the local police who upheld the law. Jeb Bush should have been impeached and jailed for that stunt. But instead he became one of the heroes. I was really surprised to learn that a large plurality of Americans would have approved the use of violence to 'save' Terry Schiavo."

Emilie yawned. "Come to bed, Greg." I did.

★   ★   ★

PRESIDENT PALIN kept her promise. Through November 6 she never spoke publicly about a single topic other than ridding the American "homeland" of Islamist terrorists. Palin was renominated by acclamation at the Republican convention, held only four weeks after 7/22. In her acceptance speech, not a word was spoken about the economy or about the Christian Nation. The campaign plan, brilliantly conceived by Steve Jordan, was simple: all 7/22, all the time. The terrorist outrage gave them a blank slate. Everything before was trivial except as it related to whether and how the attack could have been prevented. It put even the still-disastrous economy in perspective—hundreds of thousands of Americans lost spouses, children, siblings, and friends, and you are complaining because your mortgage is underwater? And spoken of in only the subtlest way, the almost subliminal message that they hate us because we are Christian.

Despite 7/22, I managed to close the rare-earths project in August. We mobilized $8 billion of capital for one of the poorest countries on earth, prevented the Chinese from obtaining a monopoly position in a strategic commodity, created billions in value for our clients' shareholders, and earned a fee in excess of US $10 million for RCD&S. The timing could not have been better. The firm's elections for partnership were held in early November. The odds start out pretty long, with over a hundred lawyers starting in a class and typically fewer than ten of them becoming partners eight years later. Moreover, the process and criteria were opaque to the associates, and the results seemed to us to be unpredictable. It was, one of the partners reminded me cryptically, "an election" where the dynamics of decision making were prone to sudden shifts in view. There were, I was told at every performance review, "no guarantees." Nonetheless, I felt quite confident about my chances. Rationally, I told myself to be philosophical about the outcome. After all, if RCD&S didn't want me as a partner, I could walk into a partnership at a number of other firms only very slightly down the pecking order from RCD&S. But in moments of honesty with myself, I admitted that I would take rejection by the firm badly.

When I admitted to Emilie that I was nervous about the outcome, she looked incredulous.

"For God's sake, grow a pair, Greg. If you want to be a winner, you have to believe you're a winner. A whiff of doubt and they'll crucify you."

It continued to alarm and annoy me that, each year, Emilie's language became increasingly vulgar. She knew how to "behave" when we were with older people in social situations, but she brought home with her the casually foul language of the trading desk. I wonder now why I didn't tell her more often how much it bothered me.

Seeking a sympathetic ear, I had a late dinner the next night with Sanjay, who listened attentively to my angst about partnership. And I listened to an energized Sanjay, who was now deeply convinced that Palin would get a second term and that it was inevitable that she would use her martial law powers to advance the only agenda about which she, Steve Jordan, and Sam Brownback really cared. Not surprisingly, the imposition of martial law had given Theocracy Watch a boost. Millions of Americans were farsighted enough to be deeply scared by how martial law might be used by the Palin administration. Sanjay once again emerged as a prominent spokesman, one of the few who publicly linked the martial law powers with the long-standing agenda of the Christian right.

I did not see it that way. 7/22 was real, not some Terry Schiavo–like controversy cooked up to mobilize the movement. And whatever ulterior motives Palin and Jordan may have had in crafting their response, they were right about one thing. We didn't get it right the first time, and no one would be safe until the Islamist threat was somehow eradicated.

In late October, Sanjay gave a speech at the New School in New York that was advertised as "How to Take Over the USA." I kidded him about the title. "They'll think you're some sort of anarchist. Some anti-globalization crusader. They'll be tapping the phones of all your friends. What were you thinking?"

"I was thinking that I need to think like *them*. The evangelicals have said their goal is to acquire political control and use that control to implement their agenda. About this they are entirely transparent. There is no need for analysis or speculation regarding what they would *do* with political control should they achieve it. But *how* will they achieve it? That is the question. Implementing their stated agenda requires casting aside the constitutional mandate for separation of church and state. It requires changing the nature of our republic from one governed by the laws of men to one governed by the ancient laws of a single religion. It would be, really, nothing less than a takeover of the country. That is certainly what *they* would call it if it were communists or socialists or Islamic fundamentalists pursuing their agenda through the consolidation of political power."

"You're right," I replied. "This is the question—and maybe, San, the answer. After all, how can you take control in a sustainable way when less than half the population is with you? And with all the protections built into the Constitution?"

"Right. So I have read everything their leaders have ever said on the subject. I have studied Steve Jordan and the way he thinks, pretended I am he, and then outlined the strategy he must be following. A strategy for how to take over the country. That is what my talk is about. Why mince words?"

★　　★　　★

I HAVE LOOKED long and hard in Adam's files to find a copy of the speech. It's not there. Before the Holy War, scholars were already labeling it as "historic." I remember an opinion piece in the *Times* during the siege that called it one of the most prescient works of political and cultural analysis in American history. For the five hundred of us packed in the Tishman Auditorium at the New School that night, it was a riveting experience. Sanjay was a compelling speaker. After only a few minutes, the audience intuited that he was an utterly sincere man, and scrupulously honest. He did not play with their emotions. He did not dumb down his speech, nor did he indulge in unnecessary jargon or convoluted analysis. He laid out the facts, thoroughly and methodically.

Sanjay started by reminding his audience about the path followed by most revolutionary movements, starting from the fringes and proceeding to the legitimate mainstream and then insinuating themselves into the very power structures they seek to overthrow. This of course had already been accomplished. But the Christian fundamentalists, according to Sanjay, had four other, more unusual strategies, each of which, he argued, had the potential to be successful. These included moving the Christian religion itself from its moderate Protestant roots to the fundamentalist beliefs in biblical literalism and godly authority, the reinvention of American history to establish the origin myth of America as a Christian Nation, the inculcation in all Christians of a strong sense of victimization and threat, and preparing the ground for the inevitable necessity to use violent means to achieve the final transition to the theocratic utopia. I remember that he closed by reminding his audience of Hannah Arendt's conclusion regarding the driving motive behind all totalitarian revolutions: "unwavering faith in an ideological fictitious world, rather than lust for power."

His audience was shocked but at the same time motivated. For the first time I saw the sort of visceral fear and determination to act that would later come to unify New York and power its resistance.

After San's speech, we went back to his apartment for a drink. I thought that the speech had been truly brilliant and told him so.

"Greg, I wish to ask you something. I know it will cause you distress, and for that I apologize in advance. But I must ask."

"Jesus, San. You don't have to apologize. You can ask me anything."

"Thanks. Greg, I want you to come and work with me at TW. I have decided that I cannot shoulder this burden alone. 7/22 and a second term for Palin changes everything. We are now in the final stages, and what we do in the next year could mean everything. I do not wish to sound presumptuous. But for the first time I have a clear vision of how this can play out. I also now know what needs to be done, what needs to be said. And I also know my limitations. You know them better than I do. And we complement each other, G. You know the law and you know Wall Street. You know how to get things done. We will need lots of money. We will need powerful allies. I need a partner who can talk to these people. I need someone to watch my back. In short, and to be blunt, I need you to leave RCD&S and join me as co-head of TW. And I need you to do it now. That is what I am asking."

I felt I had been punched in the stomach. He saw this on my face.

"G, I am sorry. I should not have asked."

For a few moments I could not speak. I realized it was the decision I most wished to avoid, the choice I most wished to be spared. I flushed with anger at having to confront it.

"You bastard. I mean, Sanjay, I've killed myself for eight years. I'm up for partner *next month*. What are you thinking? You cannot, you just cannot lay this on me now. Not now." I couldn't think of anything else to say.

"I know you," Sanjay said.

My initial anger passed, and I started to regain some control.

"San, I'm sorry. I know you mean well. You're a fucking saint. It's hard to have a best friend who's a saint."

"I am no saint," he said.

"Look," I continued, "I'm not like you. I am not a person of passion. I'm practical. I have made choices in life. I chose to pursue a career in the law. I chose to try to make partner. I am a person who makes choices and then lives with them. I am reliable, steady, and predictable. And I've got to tell you, San, I respect your work. I hear your arguments; I respect your conviction. Even though what you said tonight was awesome, really scary stuff, everything inside me, everything I've learned, everything I know about the world and how it works, every instinct and belief and calculation tells me the same thing: You're wrong. You're wrong because it can't happen here. It's America in the twenty-first century and it cannot happen here. I should have told you before, San. I'm sorry. But I believe you're wrong. It just can't happen here."

Sanjay laughed out loud and the tension instantly broke. I laughed with him.

"What's so funny?"

"Have you read Sinclair Lewis?" he asked.

"Sinclair Lewis? In high school, I think. *Main Street* or *Babbit*, I get them confused. What . . ."

Sanjay was rooting around one of the many bookshelves that lined the walls of his tiny apartment.

"Here. Here's a Sinclair Lewis I bet you never read."

He handed me a small volume. *It Can't Happen Here.*

"He wrote this for you. Yes, really. I insist. You must read it."

As was the case with most of Sanjay's books, the upper right-hand corners of dozens of pages were folded over, and the text was heavily annotated with circles, underlines, exclamation points, and question marks. I flipped open to one of the turned-down pages and read out loud the underlined bits:

"Why, there's no country in the world that can get more hysterical —yes, or more obsequious!—than America. Look how Huey Long became absolute monarch over Louisiana, and how the Right Honorable Mr. Senator Berzelius Windrip—"

I interrupted myself, "Who was Senator Windrip?"

"It's a novel. He's the demagogic character who suspends the Constitution."

I continued,

"Senator Windrip owns his State . . . Remember the Ku Klux Klan? Remember our war hysteria, when we called sauerkraut "Liberty Cabbage" and somebody actually proposed calling German measles "Liberty measles"? And wartime censorship of honest papers? Bad as Russia! . . . Remember when the hick legislators in certain states, in obedience to William Jennings Bryan, who learned his biology from his pious old grandma, set up shop as scientific experts and made the whole world laugh itself sick by forbidding the teaching of evolution? . . . Remember how trainloads of people have gone to enjoy lynchings? Not happen here? Prohibition—shooting down people just because they might be transporting liquor—no,

*that couldn't happen in America! Why, where in all history has
there ever been a people so ripe for dictatorship as ours!"*

I had nothing to say.

"You," Sanjay said, "studied history."

"Lewis was a socialist, wasn't he? I mean, it was the mid-1930s . . .
This is different." I trailed off lamely.

"All I ask is that you use your skills as an historian. Your perspective.
This is what is required here. A serious historian could never say 'it
can't happen here.' A serious historian would ask what were the conditions under which fascism prospers, and ask—"

"Fascism," I interrupted. "Give me a break."

Sanjay looked out the window.

When I got home, I did not tell Emilie what Sanjay had asked me
to do. Let's just say I did not sleep very well that night.

★   ★   ★

On November 6, 2012, Sarah Palin was reelected with 56 percent
of the popular vote and an even stronger majority in the electoral college. Riding the wave of 7/22, the election would doubtless have broken
the same way had the Houses of Worship Free Speech Restoration
Act not been passed early in Palin's first term and ultimately survived
constitutional review in a 5–4 decision by the Supreme Court. But the
election was notable for being the first where the evangelical churches,
the threat to their tax exemption removed, spent heavily on political
advertising. The mega-churches themselves became centers for partisan
political action by conducting elaborate get-out-the-vote and phone-
bank efforts and other political activities. The full consequences of this
legislation would not be generally recognized until four years later. The
other thing driving the 2012 results was the remarkable success by Steve
Jordan in forging such a close alignment between the Tea Party and the
Christian right that the media had started to call it the Teavangelical
movement. During the campaign, Ralph Reed boasted that he had the
cell phone numbers of 13 million Teavangelical voters.

In addition to the reelection of the Palin/Brownback ticket, the House and Senate both returned to Republican control, and the new Congress included a large number of new members who had ridden an ugly wave of post-7/22 anti-immigrant Christian nationalism.

*   *   *

A WEEK AFTER the national election, I received a phone call from the law firm's chairman at two o'clock on a Wednesday afternoon. As soon as I saw his number flash on the screen of my phone, I knew I had been elected partner. We all knew that the chairman had the happy job of informing the lawyers who made it. Had the head of my practice group appeared in my doorway, I would have known instantly that it was bad news. The rest of the afternoon, a parade of partners called and dropped by the office to congratulate me. I was startled just now to remember how euphoric I felt that afternoon and to realize how devastated I would have been had the result been different. Sanjay used to say that attaining a thing ardently sought usually results in disappointment. In this case he was wrong. It was even better than I had imagined. My only dilemma that afternoon was about two friends who were up for partner and did not make it. I debated whether to go see them to offer condolences or whether my presence might cause them pain by letting them see my happiness. I decided to wait a day or so. At 5 p.m. I was dragged off to Harry's Bar with a group of younger partners and other associates for a celebratory drink. Emilie came downtown to join us. That night in the black car driving home to our apartment, in a throwback to the first year of our relationship, she snuggled up, kissed me warmly, and said, "You're a rock star and I really do love you." I told her that it was her victory as well and I couldn't have done it without her. I meant it. That night I did not think once about Sanjay or the theocratic peril that held him in its thrall.

CHAPTER TEN

The End of Law

2013

In time of war the law falls silent.
—Marcus Tullius Cicero, 52 BC

WHEN I ARRIVED AT THE OFFICE on January 3, all my things
had been installed in a partner's office about the size of the tenement
in which my Irish grandfather had raised his five children. It had a
spectacular view over New York harbor to Governors Island, and
a massive antique partner's desk. Otherwise, things were the same:
the same backlog of "pink slip" telephone messages from clients with
urgent problems, the same queue of junior lawyers looking for a few
moments of my time, the same parade of e-mails flashing on the screen
and demanding attention, and the same stack of documents waiting to
be read and marked up.

Later that day one of the senior partners invited me to his office to
sign the partnership agreement; he handed it to me folded open to the
signature page. Thinking this could perhaps be one last test of my diligence, I demurred, suggesting that it was unprofessional for a lawyer
to sign a contract that he had not read. The older man laughed and
noted that for 126 years every new partner had signed the agreement
without reading it first, but if I wished to be the first to decline to do
so, that was my prerogative. I signed.

The main moment of ritual for new partners occurred at the first weekly partners' lunch of the new year. The chairman greeted each new partner by name, and each was welcomed by genuinely warm applause. Every person there understood what each new partner had gone through to reach that moment. The real thrill for me, I admit, was the year-end financial report delivered at the lunch. Although the trade press was full of rumors about how much the partners of RCD&S earned in a year, the associates really didn't know. After lunch, those of us who had just made partner knew. Let's just say we were not disappointed. I remember wishing that afternoon that there was someone I could tell. My parents, my father in particular, would have been awestruck and enormously proud. Under the terms of our confidentiality obligations, I couldn't tell Emilie unless I married her.

Three weeks later, Sanjay came over to the apartment to watch Sarah Palin's inauguration with Emilie and me. Palin mounted the steps of the Capitol building as one of the most powerful presidents in US history. She enjoyed a filibuster-proof sixty-eight Republicans in the Senate, and a large majority in the House. Martial law had been in effect for over five months, and not since the Civil War had the federal government wielded as much power with as little legal restraint.

The former newsreader who mounted the podium that day could only rarely craft a coherent sentence on her own, but she was very good at reading words written by others:

Six months ago, our nation endured the worst attack in its proud history, far worse than Pearl Harbor, far worse than 9/11. Almost seven thousand godfearing innocents were slaughtered right here in the homeland. Seven thousand Americans going about their daily activities—working, eating, praying—obliterated in an instant by radical Islamic foreigners, most of whom had been welcomed to this country and invited to share our freedoms. Like so many of you, I have prayed long and hard about this tragedy. How did our Lord, who so loves America and its people—who established this Christian Nation to do His will on Earth—how did He allow this terrible thing to happen? What did we do wrong? We know His justice is perfect and His mercy is without limit. So we know this was a punishment we deserved. But for what?

I think, my fellow Americans, we all, deep in our hearts, know the answer. The Bible tells us of so many instances where God's people have strayed from His path, where the people have lived godless lives, and where His retribution is swift and just. God's justice is an eternal truth. Do we think because the pages of the calendar have turned, because we live in a twenty-first-century age of technological wonders, that somehow these eternal and universal truths do not apply?

Emilie interrupted, "Wait a minute, is she saying that we got 9/11 and 7/22 because we deserved it? That it was God's just punishment for gays and abortion and all the stuff they don't like?"

"Yes, exactly," answered Sanjay. "That's nothing new. Remember Columbine? The Speaker of the House, Tom DeLay, suggested that one of the causes of the Columbine massacre was the teaching of the theory of evolution."

Palin continued.

My fellow Americans, the fact is that some of you did fall into the illusion that God's eternal truths no longer apply. Yes, many of us did indeed believe that we could ignore God, turn our backs on Jesus His only son, disobey His commandments and somehow escape His justice. Well, those who believed these things have been proved wrong. With 9/11 God in His mercy gave this great country a call—a call to turn back from the mass slaughter of innocent children in the womb, to turn back from adultery and sexual license, to turn back from tolerating the terrible sin of sodomy, to turn back from the illusion that a culture could be built on a foundation of human desires and laws made without reference to the one and only eternal lawgiver. And what did we do? Did we heed His warning?

We did nothing. We not only failed to answer God's call, but our federal courts prevented us from doing God's will. They decided that the commandments of God could not even be displayed in public. They decided that our citizens could not pray in schools and other public places. They decided that practicing evil was a right, nothing more than an "alternative lifestyle." They decided that our leaders and public officials could not follow the dictates of their faith in performing their public service.

A few brave citizens foresaw the peril to the nation. They preached that God's justice would follow. They begged their fellow citizens to study our history and to reconnect with the essence of this country as a nation born in godliness and dedicated to establishing on this Earth a commonwealth governed by His laws. They cried out against the savagery of abortion, the horrifying attack on the fundamental institution of marriage, the tolerance—even the celebration—of deviant sexuality. But like the prophets of old, their words were not heeded. In retrospect, the result was inevitable.

So this I pledge to you. My administration will fight the terrorist threat with all the means at our disposal. But we will also attack the root cause of our present peril by answering your call to return this nation to a godly path.

At this point the usual decorum associated with an inaugural ceremony was cast aside as scores of congressmen leapt to their feet, hooting and hollering as if their team had just scored a touchdown. The vast crowd on the mall erupted and refused to quiet down for a full five minutes. Palin assumed what the press called her Joan of Arc face, a carefully practiced blend of stoic determination mixed with the smug satisfaction of a woman remembering moments of intimacy with the divine. The television focused in on the more liberal members of the Supreme Court squirming uneasily in their seats as the ovation refused to abate. Palin made no effort to interrupt. Only when the crowd went completely silent did the president continue.

Now, my friends, the remarkable thing is that this does not require a revolution. No. It does not require anything remarkable or radical or new. For just over 220 years ago God gave us our beloved Constitution containing the perfect recipe to build a nation under God. So all we need, my fellow Americans, is to return to our roots. We need to embrace our Constitution and restore it to its place as the foundation for all our laws. That is why, tomorrow, my administration will send up here, to Capitol Hill, the Constitution Restoration Act, which came so near to passage in 2004 and 2005 and was originally conceived by one of our most brilliant jurists, Roy Moore.

The crowd that was gathered on the mall roared its approval. I could not believe my ears. Roy Moore was a state court judge from Alabama who had become a hero to the evangelical movement by refusing to obey a federal court order to remove a stone carving of the Ten Commandments from his courtroom. He had been described as many things but never before as a "brilliant jurist." Sanjay looked grim.

This legislation will restore God to His rightful place as the sole and sovereign source of law, liberty, and government in America. Any federal judge who acts contrary to this truth will be impeached. And no one will again surrender the sovereignty of America—no international organization, no UN, no bizarre group of atheist dictators—will again dictate to the people of America what they can or cannot do. We answer to God and to the Constitution and not to the UN.

Again the crowd erupted. "The fucking black helicopter crowd," said Emilie.

And finally, this brilliant piece of legislation will fulfill the promise of Article III of the Constitution by exercising Congress's right to deny the Supreme Court the power to review laws that liberal judges just don't like. In America, under America's Constitution, the states are sovereign.

She looked up, departing from the script, adding helpfully, "That means they're in charge."

And if a state in this Union wants to allow prayer in its schools, wants to recognize and embrace its Christian heritage, wants to save the lives of innocent babies, wants to protect the sanctity of marriage—well, that's what the state will do, and after next week, after our new Congress acts, no liberal judge will again defeat the will of the people.

The president was interrupted by another ten minutes of tumultuous applause and cheering. It took me some time to absorb what she had said.

"San, do you know what's she talking about?"

"Yes. It's not complicated. The bill purports to deny jurisdiction to the federal courts on all separation of church and state issues. Denying God as the source of "law, liberty, and government" is an impeachable offense. And there is the oddly xenophobic provision prohibiting federal courts from considering or enforcing treaties or 'foreign laws.'"

"They can't do that."

"You are the lawyer, G, but I think perhaps they can. They argue that Article III of the Constitution allows Congress to make exceptions to the Supreme Court's appellate jurisdiction, which is true, and that by extension this means that Congress can deny jurisdiction to federal district courts for any matter as to which the Supreme Court lacks appellate jurisdiction. If this argument is accepted by the current Supreme Court, then it will be the law of the land."

I was incredulous. "That's ridiculous. The Constitution specifically grants to the federal courts original jurisdiction on all matters arising under the Constitution. If it didn't, it would mean, in effect, that on church-state separation issues the individual states are not subject to the Bill of Rights. They could pass laws abridging freedom of speech. There would be no enforcement of the establishment clause or of privacy rights. It might mean that states could require school prayer, criminalize homosexuality, outlaw abortion—all of it."

"I think," said San, "that is precisely the idea."

"Where did this come from?" asked Emilie. "I've never heard of such a thing. I mean, why didn't someone do something?"

Sanjay allowed himself a raised eyebrow. "This very same law was introduced to Congress in both 2004 and 2005. The 2004 national platform of the Republican Party pledged support for it. It is nothing new."

"Fuck," said Emilie.

The speech only got worse.

My fellow Americans, we are a nation at war. And many other times when our nation has been at war, we have done what we needed to do to protect our people. Well, my friends, I swear that this president will do nothing less. I will do what our Founding Fathers did in time of peril, what Abraham Lincoln did when faced with the breakup of our sacred union, what our leaders did in 1917 when faced with the dangers of world war. We are introducing tomorrow the Defense of Freedom Act, modeled on legislation enacted by the Founding Fathers in 1798 and the variations on those laws that protected the country in the Civil War and First World War. It sounds complicated, but it's just common sense. If an alien—that means someone who is not an American—is suspected of terrorism or other activities that pose a threat to our great country, then the president will have the power to imprison or deport the person. Common sense. If someone publishes scandalous or malicious lies designed to hurt our nation and help our terrorist enemies, or advocates treason or insurrection against our sacred Constitution, it's a crime. Common sense. And nothing that hasn't been done before. I repeat, nothing that hasn't been done before. My fellow Americans—you are going to hear a lot of talk from the liberal elites about civil liberties. You will hear lies and taunts about dictatorship. Well, just remember this. What we are doing is no more than our Founding Fathers did, than Abraham Lincoln did, than Woodrow Wilson did. If you think they were dictators, well then—go ahead and believe our critics. But if you think they were patriots, then have confidence that what we are doing is right, is Constitutional, and is necessary to protect you and your families.

I will not record the rest of the speech. It's here in Adam's file, and I am suddenly seized by curiosity about whether the version now carried on the Purity Web is the same. I doubt it. Very few historical documents appear on the Web unedited. History has been scrubbed clean of the awkward, the untidy, and the un-Christian. I know that the Constitution Restoration Act is now taught as a seminal moment in the development of the Christian Nation, but I wonder about Sarah Palin's modern version of the Alien and Sedition Acts. I suspect that that is viewed as a nasty bit of history completely unnecessary to an understanding of the Christian Nation movement.

President Palin's legislative agenda was enacted within weeks of the inauguration. The opposition party launched a spirited but fruitless fight, but when it became clear that the Constitution Restoration Act and the Defense of Freedom Act were going to become law, the national mood turned to accommodation. No one wanted to hear, and certainly did not want to believe, that these two pieces of legislation put the country on the road to some kind of authoritarianism. The price of civic illiteracy was now being paid in full. Few Americans understood the basic features of the Constitution or had the patience to follow arguments about the meaning and effect of these bills. If they trusted President Palin, if they were afraid of another terrorist attack, or if they took their lead from their preacher on Sunday morning, then they most likely accepted that these new laws were in the national interest. Even many people distrustful of Palin and her ultimate intentions were inclined to dismiss the critics as alarmist and simply hope for the best.

Sanjay saw clearly what was happening. He knew that the proponents of theocracy were patient. Their strategy was incremental, and it embraced both the ebb and flow of popular sentiment. They used each ebb in support, like the 2010 midterm elections, to undermine critics like Sanjay who saw the big picture and to reinforce the view of those like Emilie, who saw each setback as the final retreat from a moment of temporary insanity. Sanjay often quoted the brilliant journalist Michelle Goldberg, who wrote, "It's kind of like being a lobster in a pot, with the water heating up so slowly that you don't notice the moment at which it starts to kill you." In retrospect, 2013 was that moment.

After President Palin's inaugural address, I could not concentrate on my work. As a lawyer, I understood the Fourteenth Amendment, the Bill of Rights, and the sad history of America's previous flirtations with the criminalization of dissent. I understood that the president's program threatened to severely weaken, if not completely undermine, the foundation of our liberties. I could see the "setup." These laws did not establish a state religion, nor did they constitute a full frontal attack on tolerance. But they sought to disable the laws and courts that would be our front line of defense against future attempts to do just that. Whether this effort would succeed was up to the Supreme Court.

Justice John Paul Stevens, then ninety-one years old and a stalwart of the liberal wing of the court, had steadfastly refused to consider resignation during the first Palin administration, knowing that his vote would almost certainly be replaced with that of a radical conservative appointed by Sarah Palin and confirmed by the still-Republican Senate. He remained in good health, swimming in the ocean daily during the summers. But it was unrealistic to think Stevens could hang on for another four years, and following the election most Supreme Court watchers expected that he would bow to the inevitable and tender his resignation. But the old man, horrified by the legislation so hastily passed by Congress and knowing that the constitutional challenges that followed would soon wend their way to the Supreme Court, issued a terse two-sentence press release stating that he had no intention to resign in the face of the critical and historic work facing the court.

One month later Stevens was killed in a car crash on the way to work, his limousine broadsided by a Hummer only blocks from his town house near Capitol Hill. The security camera at that intersection was out of order and thus did not record the driver, who fled the scene of the accident and was never found. The Hummer had been stolen from the driveway of an army colonel seconded to the State Department. Although the investigation was not completed, the official view was clear: a stolen car, the thief fleeing the scene, and bad luck for Justice Stevens. There was no specific evidence of foul play, but millions of Americans felt intuitively that this had been no accident. For many Americans, the death of Justice Stevens was a moment where cold creeping fear supplanted anger and ridicule as their reaction to the administration's insistence on a "Christian Nation."

President Palin was elaborate in her praise for the deceased justice and surprised everyone by sending to the Senate a nominee who was reliably conservative but not as radical as anyone, including her own supporters, had expected. Often described as an Ivy League Tea Partier, Ted Cruz was the son of Cuban immigrants, a graduate of Princeton and Harvard Law School, former attorney general of Texas, clerk for Justice Rehnquist, and prominent Supreme Court litigator with a major firm. His pro-gun, pro-prayer, anti-separation, and anti-abortion credentials were impeccable, but the left could not claim he was unqualified. With the filibuster-proof majority in the Senate, Cruz was quickly confirmed.

Justice Souter, appointed by the first President Bush but more often aligned with the liberal wing of the court, had long wished to resign and return to his native New Hampshire. But he was a younger man, only seventy-three, and he too shelved his retirement plans when Justice Stevens was killed.

The US Supreme Court, even with its new solid majority of five judicial conservatives, still gave only a mixed verdict to the president's signature legislation. The Defense of Freedom provisions essentially criminalizing criticism of the government as "sedition" were struck down on First Amendment grounds, but the alien deportation portion of the legislation was upheld. The Constitution Restoration Act provisions attempting to prevent courts from giving effect to treaties to which the United States was a party were also struck down, given the specific constitutional sanction accorded to treaties signed by the president and ratified by the Senate. But the far more troubling parts of the act were those purporting to reverse decades of Fourteenth Amendment "substantive due process" jurisprudence, which is what prevented individual states from acting to limit individual rights and freedoms, whether specifically mentioned in the Constitution, such as those in the Bill of Rights, or those derived from other parts of the Constitution or fundamental concepts of personal liberty (such as the right to privacy). These parts of the act the Court upheld on the highly controversial basis that Article III of the Constitution allows the Congress to make exceptions to the Supreme Court's appellate jurisdiction and thus that by extension the lower federal courts have no jurisdiction on any matter as to which Congress has denied the Supreme Court appellate jurisdiction. I did not know a single lawyer at RCD&S or elsewhere, no matter how conservative their politics, who agreed with this part of the decision. The deans of the top twenty law schools signed a public letter protesting both the result and reasoning of the decision. It was now the law of the land that any federal judge could be impeached for attempting to exercise jurisdiction on any matter "concerning [any governmental] entity's, officer's, or agent's acknowledgment of God as the sovereign source of law, liberty, or government." The long history of the federal courts as the enforcers of separation of church and state was at an end.

The consequences were immediate. Oklahoma, Wyoming, and Alabama declared themselves Christian states. And in a frenzy of legislative activity, freed from the constraint of constitutional review, states throughout the South and West adopted scores of laws that had been languishing at the fringes of their state capitals for years. The most popular included "banning" Islamic law, making it illegal to extend spousal benefits to gays, banning the teaching of evolution unless as one of several possible theories including both creationism and intelligent design, re-criminalization of sodomy and adultery, making school prayer mandatory, banning from use in schools any book by a gay author or with a gay character, and dozens of other hugely popular pieces of legislation that the evangelical-controlled state legislatures believed would be protected by the Constitution Restoration Act from scrutiny by the federal courts.

Although federal jurisprudence on abortion was based on an implied constitutional right of privacy and had nothing to do with the separation clause, the state legislatures, under the coordination of Tony Perkins's Family Research Council, nonetheless soon passed scores of anti-abortion bills. Each of the new laws was designed differently, with the idea that at least one type of anti-abortion law was bound to survive federal scrutiny under the new Supreme Court even though *Roe v. Wade* was still the law of the land. A Family Research Council "score card" from 2013 in Adam's file showed four hundred anti-abortion bills working their way through the state legislatures. Alabama passed five. The legislative tactics were varied: abolishing all family planning services (so as not to single out abortion and contraception), requiring all women to have an ultrasound prior to an abortion, banning (again) use of all taxpayer money for abortion services, banning (again) public insurance coverage for contraception and abortion and extending the ban to all private insurers, as well as the more straightforward criminalization of both the giving and receipt of an abortion. All were challenged in federal court, but the number and variety of legislative approaches at the state level were such that the ACLU declared itself "overwhelmed." The right case on which to reverse *Roe v. Wade* had not yet made its way to the Supreme Court, but with the death of Justice Stevens, observers of the court believed that it was now just a matter of time.

Within a year of the inauguration, we had in effect become two countries, with the legal norms of one antithetical to the other. A few pessimists said this was the beginning of the end of the United States and predicted the gradual erosion of the country into a loose confederation of convenience between the two blocks—a view that was dismissed as extreme by even the avowedly liberal press.

During 2013 and 2014, legal challenges to the social and religious legislation by the states started to be decided by both state and federal courts. The results were startlingly incoherent, with some federal district courts and circuits construing the Constitution Restoration Act narrowly to allow only those state laws dealing with traditional "separation" issues (such as the display of religious symbols on government property) while others construed it broadly, disclaiming judicial review for virtually any state legislation premised on religious or moral grounds. State court decisions cited state constitutions and various legal theories in addition to the Constitution Restoration Act as the basis for failing to give effect to federal preemption of the newly enacted state laws. Courts issued orders to stay the enforcement of decisions by other courts, and enormous uncertainty followed regarding what the law was at any particular time and place.

Toward the end of 2013, the Fox Faith & Freedom Network announced a national movement to ensure that the Constitution Restoration Act was fully enforced, with nightly exhortations for citizens to report to F3 any public official who appeared to be resisting the mandate to put God back at the center of our national life. Within weeks, any red state federal, state, or municipal judge without a Ten Commandments plaque in his or her courtroom was at risk of becoming the target of noisy public protest and attempted impeachment. No small-town mayor dared resist a call for a Christmas crèche outside of town hall, and no school principal dared discipline a teacher who insisted on starting each day with his or her children on their knees in prayer to Jesus Christ. And without reliable intervention from the federal courts, evangelical activists pushed for enforcement of other state initiatives on evolution and gays in education. The country and world watched with fascination as elected attorneys general in Oklahoma, Kansas, and Alabama prosecuted science teachers refusing to follow state mandates to give equal time to creationism and intelligent design. Sanjay pointed out to the national media that each of those teachers was also openly homosexual.

F3 led a relentless campaign to diffuse popular anger and doubt about these developments. Scholars and historians appeared daily to lecture on America's constitutional design, with the states—being closest to the people—remaining sovereign. We had lost our way, they argued, due to the influence of socialism in the twentieth century, which envisioned a federal government that was big and all-powerful. Discarding this discredited notion took us back to our historical roots and ensured more perfect freedom.

"What's free," the dean of Oral Roberts University Law School asked, "about a little girl not being able to pray in school to her God for strength when her mother is sick? What's free about a small town in the South not being able to enjoy the crèche in front of town hall that was there for their parents and grandparents? What's free about a couple in Oklahoma, faithfully married for thirty years, now being told that their marriage means something else entirely? Why should big-city folks tell rural Americans how to live? I don't know about you, but I think we now finally have regained what our grandparents had—real freedom. I just don't understand how all these liberal elites think it's freedom to tell other folks how to live and to try to destroy their religion."

This live and let live feint was surprisingly successful. Blue state people of ordinary intelligence were not inclined to accept the really big lie—that the growth of a secular and tolerant society constituted the tyrannical suppression of Christianity. But they *were* inclined to accept that those folks out in Oklahoma could live how they wished, including teaching their children whatever crazy nonsense they wanted. After all—this strain of thinking went—no one has to live in Oklahoma, and if they don't like it they can leave. Not my problem.

This was Emilie's view. Looking back, I can see a strong current of fear behind her anger. This was not how she had planned to see her world unfold. Her plans required the financial services–led economic boom to continue without interruption from the stupidity of politics and politicians. She would make managing director at Credit Suisse, leave with one of her clients to found a private equity firm, then make more money than could be spent in a lifetime on her first deal. Only then would she marry me (or perhaps someone even more suitable) and have children. The rest of her life would be spent decorating fabulous houses and raising perfect children.

That summer for the first time, Emilie and I rented a small house about an hour's drive north of New York in the charming hamlet of Cold Spring-on-Hudson. At least I thought it was charming. Emilie would have preferred Bedford or East Hampton, but she allowed me to persuade her to pick the Hudson Valley only because a senior Credit Suisse partner, whom she idolized, spent the weekends in a fabulous house on the river in nearby Garrison and had offered to introduce her to "everyone." She was somewhat surprised when "everyone" turned out to encompass not only bankers and lawyers but musicians, authors, environmentalists, and the local building contractor. But it endeared me to the place even more.

One weekend in July, Sanjay came for a visit. Our small house, which sat up behind the village, was perched on the lower slope of a steep hill. My favorite part of the house was a simple screened porch that faced the river. After dinner, Sanjay, Emilie, and I sat in old-fashioned rocking chairs positioned to take advantage of the spectacular view to the west, where the distinctive bulky profile of Storm King Mountain rose without prelude from the narrow river, creating a dramatic gorge. The featherweight disk of the moon had positioned itself in artful counterpoint to the hulking mountain, illuminating both the water and the granitic façade of the ridge.

"For God's sake, San, why can't we leave them alone?" Emilie broke the silence. "Why do you have to ruin my life just so you can keep them from ruining theirs?"

And by ruining her life I think she meant both stirring up the sort of fear and uncertainty that is unconducive to economic growth and, perhaps, luring me off a path that she considered suitable for a mate. Emilie knew that, despite my burst of enthusiasm upon becoming a partner, I had become dangerously distracted by the public drama that was playing out every day. After all, my making partner was not the limit of her ambition. Only a few weeks after I became a partner, she said in the jesting voice that she used only when she regarded the topic as very serious, that she hoped I had now turned my sights on becoming head of my practice group and then, eventually, chairman. She knew this required a single-minded focus on my work that permitted no distractions, and Emilie feared that I was being distracted. Being married to a B-list partner, even of the city's best firm, would have been difficult for her. A cheating spouse would have been better than a professionally mediocre one. Thus her fear of my increasing interest in current events. But she didn't fear—and couldn't imagine—what I was soon to do.

In early August 2013, less than nine months after I had become a partner of RCD&S, it was an ordinary day in the office. I was supposed to be marking up a prospectus for the initial public offering of a South American paper company. Looking up, I saw a CNN e-mail news alert and read that the federal Department of Education and the National Science Foundation had jointly released for comment rules setting new conditions for participation by colleges and universities in federal grants and funding. Almost every American college depended on its students continuing to be eligible for federal loan programs, and eligibility for federal grant funding was vital to any top-tier scientific program. As a result, although presented as conditions to a federal benefit, they would, if adopted, become de facto requirements. The first of the new conditions was that the university must not maintain any rule or practice that prevented university libraries from acquiring books dealing with creationism or intelligent design as legitimate theories. The second condition was that the supported institution must not maintain any rule or practice preventing the display of Christian symbols in public places on campus. Such a rule prohibiting Islamic, Hindu, or Wiccan symbols, the commentary explained, would be acceptable but was not required. The final condition was that the supported university would be required to adopt a policy forbidding the further acquisition into any university library of any book "celebrating or promoting" a "homosexual lifestyle."

I went to the Federal Register website and read the proposed rule in its entirety. The first two conditions—merely requirements that a

college *not prohibit* creationist texts or religious symbols—would doubtless be viewed by much of the general public as trivial or perhaps even
fair. But that view was profoundly in error. To say that you cannot
deny or exclude the patently false (creationism) is only a small step away
from requiring you to believe it. And for our greatest universities to ban
from their collections any new work acknowledging homosexuality or
dealing with its implications would require them to acquiesce in and
enforce a sexual taboo, thus failing their core missions to be custodians
of civilization and clear-eyed proponents of reason.

As tempting as it was to see this as more symbolic pandering to the
religious right, and far less serious than the other parts of Palin's legislative program, it affected me more strongly. Our elite universities were
the stewards of our true national history, our temples of reason and the
keepers of our collective memory. They, more than the Supreme Court,
are the ultimate guardians of the enlightenment. To me, a door had
opened that could lead only to a single destination: a new dark age of
ignorance and superstition. This was about far more than politics and
power.

It seems strange in retrospect that it was this relatively minor regulatory initiative in the field of education, and not the broad frontal
attack on the Constitution, that finally triggered one of my moments of
situational awareness. Just like that day long ago before my first middle
school football game, I seemed to rise above the noise and complexi-
ties of the moment and look down on the field of play. I saw neither
ambiguity nor uncertainty but a society tumbling toward the most
conventional type of religious authoritarianism. They would tell us
what to think and believe, and those beliefs were primitive, ignorant,
and dangerous. They would systematically eliminate from society any
potentially contradictory voice. Their efforts were relentless and gain-
ing traction and speed. I saw that Sanjay was right.

Since the night before the election when Sanjay asked me to join
him at TW, he had not raised the subject again. We had adopted one
of those comfortable fictions, each behaving as if the question had not
been asked and as if the answer were not outstanding.

The very next day I walked into the office of the partner who had been my longtime mentor, who had become a friend, and who had been instrumental, I was sure, in having me elected as a partner. I sat down and decided to dispense with the pleasantries.

"John, I think you know how much I appreciate all you've done for me. I couldn't have imagined that I would ever do something to let you down."

He interrupted.

"Greg, if you've screwed up in some way, we can work through it. We've all made mistakes."

"No, it's not that. I'm resigning from the firm and going to work with Sanjay at Theocracy Watch. Given what's happened, I feel I have no choice."

He stared at the papers on his desk, and then he looked up.

"You always have a choice."

"You're right. I'm sorry. To be more precise, I have made a choice. Not because I don't owe everything to you and the firm. Not because I'm unhappy in my work. Not because I don't think I'm a damn fine lawyer. I have chosen something . . . well, something more important."

"Sanctimonious doesn't become you, Greg. And you know better. You sell your judgment to the brightest people in the country for thousands of dollars an hour. You know that it makes no sense to throw away your career to help people who . . . well, who don't know the world as it really is and don't know how to make things happen. They have no standing. No power. People like you, people like us, Greg, if we want to save the world, we do it from the inside."

"I don't want to save the world. John, think of World War II. What did the partners here do? Did they say the war was for others and their place was with their clients? No, they jumped, and jumped first. Think of Roger Leman."

He was an RCD&S partner who was the first American killed in action in World War II when he was helping evacuate the British army at Dunkirk. I knew that John admired him.

"Where's the war, Greg?"

"It's here, John. It's all around you. *They* call it a war, why shouldn't we? What do you think will happen to RCD&S in a Christian fundamentalist state?"

"I find it all as distasteful as you do. But I find most politicians distasteful. You think I don't cringe having to listen to that idiot night after night on TV? But you have to learn not to overreact. The economy goes on. Companies get bought and sold. Capital needs to flow. RCD&S will be fine."

"Is that all that matters?" I asked, instantly regretting it.

"Don't be insulting. If I thought there was any possibility that fascism was around the corner or that a real religious authoritarianism could take root in this country, then of course I'd be with you. But it can't happen here."

I wondered if he'd read Sinclair Lewis, but I decided not to go there.

"I hope you're right, John. I will do everything possible so that the firm is not embarrassed."

"Do you understand what you're leaving behind?" he asked.

"I do."

His face was passive, revealing neither annoyance nor sympathy.

"Thank you for telling me."

And that, after eight and a half years of striving and sacrifice, was that.

CHAPTER ELEVEN

Not So Bad

2015

> For true blissed-out and vacant servitude . . . you need
> an otherwise sophisticated society where no serious his-
> tory is taught at all.
>
> —Christopher Hitchens,
> "Why Americans Are Not Taught History,"
> Harper's magazine, June 1999

> I hope I live to see the day, when, as in the early days
> of our country, we won't have any public schools. The
> churches will have taken them over again, and Chris-
> tians will be running them.
>
> —Jerry Falwell,
> America Can Be Saved (1979)

FOR THE ENTIRETY OF MY WORKING LIFE, I had only one
job. For almost nine years I entered the same lobby, rode the same
elevators, and passed through the same double mahogany doors into
the offices of RCD&S. I had focused relentlessly on the single goal of
becoming a partner, and I had achieved it. And then, one Monday
morning, I pulled on jeans, took the subway to Chambers Street, and
arrived at the third-floor loft space that housed the staff of Theocracy
Watch.

They say humans are creatures of habit, but for me the habits of those nine years were set aside in a day. Within only a week or so, the years I spent at the firm had assumed a dreamlike quality. In contrast, other memories were fresh, harsh, and hurtful. At some level I must have known that my decision to leave the law was a decision to end things with Emilie. But although we had been together for eight years, I did not consult with her about my decision or even tell her what I intended to do.

The night after my meeting with John, Emilie was there when I arrived home. I looked her in the eye and told her that I had resigned from the firm and was going to help Sanjay at TW. For a moment she held her breath. Then, slowly, she started gulping air with sharp hiccup-like inhalations. Her arms reached across her chest, and she embraced herself. I remember watching the bare skin on her upper arm turning white from the strength of her grip. Within moments, her staccato exhales evolved into loud sobs. She sat on the couch, rocking back and forth. I stood perfectly still. Her crying continued wordlessly for what seemed to me to be a long time. When it abated, she raised her head and showed a face contorted with a mixture of humiliation and rage.

"Out. Get . . . out. Now."

I didn't answer.

"Now," she screamed.

I turned and left and have not seen her since.

As I write this, I again feel a dull tightness in my gut, as I have every single time during the past fourteen years that this scene has replayed itself in my mind. I make no excuses. It is one of the two things in my life about which I still feel a deep sense of shame. Looking out at the lake, I see that it is perfectly still, a featureless mirror. There is no current, no ripple connecting one point with another.

In an effort to distract myself from the disaster of my personal life, I threw myself into work at TW. Sanjay had surrounded himself with young people who were bright and motivated, but none had my ability to get things done. Of the $400 million from the sale of *You and I*, little had been spent on the organization. Sanjay wasn't cheap; he certainly wasn't spending it on himself, nor did he have any desire to grow or even maintain his wealth. Instead, he believed that TW's credibility depended on a wide base of support, and he was determined that its successes should not be perceived as having been "bought" by his fortune.

I managed to persuade him that now was the time to let a bit of his money do some good. We hired a recently retired reporter, Walter Evans, who had spent his career at the *Wall Street Journal* and resented enormously the loss of that paper's independence as under Rupert Murdoch's ownership it eventually became yet another vehicle for the F3 movement. Walt was tough, well connected, and mad as hell. We had our new communications director. I also realized that our online footprint needed to be reinvented from the ground up. I hired a tech entrepreneur from California on the rebound from founding a clever but failed shopping co-op online social network. He understood middle America and was gay, horrified by the direction of the country, highly motivated, wonderfully creative, and much more tuned in to the rising generation than either Sanjay or I.

About a week later I found Sharon Heller, a middle-aged woman who had spent a career doing professional fund-raising for charities, most recently for the Topeka Symphony. That orchestra had been disbanded when the Kansas state legislature suddenly withdrew all support for cultural institutions in the state, banned National Public Radio, and conditioned the state tax deduction for charitable giving on an annual certification that the charity was not involved in "the promotion of abortion, homosexuality, secularism, or other evil." Within months, she said, the vibrant cultural scene in Topeka—once a bastion of enlightenment against the retrograde politics of Kansas—was lost. Thousands of artists, musicians, writers, and liberal academics left the state. She too was motivated and really knew how to raise money. My final hire was a director of security. We had kept it quiet, but a few months before, someone had fired a shot through TW's third-floor windows. The bullet lodged harmlessly in the ceiling, but I did not believe it to be an accident. We catalogued dozens of threats against Sanjay's life on social networks and blogs, and—despite his disregard for his own security—I convinced him he owed it to me and all his other employees to take security more seriously.

Two weeks after I arrived, Walter Evans came to my desk.

"So, Greg, guess what I got. It's too brilliant. Nah, you'll never guess."

"Well then, I won't. Tell me."

"Stewart. Jon Stewart. *The Daily Show.* Where our target demo gets their news and laughs. Average of one and a half million of them every day. He's in love with Sanjay. Bloodly hopeless love. Thinks he's a prophet. Wants to help. I mean really. Not take cheap shots. Really help."

And so Sanjay had his first appearance on *The Daily Show,* and it was brilliant. The extroverted wisecracking Stewart had met his match and didn't mind one bit. Like everyone else, he could not avoid Sanjay's penetrating gaze. And many of Stewart's fans listened to what Sanjay had to say simply because they were captivated by the way he looked. After our first appearance on the show, our daily website hits went from about twenty thousand to eight hundred thousand. We had truly gone national, and proven there was an audience for Sanjay's message.

Shortly thereafter, President Palin made her first comment about Sanjay. She had delivered her prepared remarks at the morning service at the giant New Life Church in Colorado Springs, the epicenter of mega-church evangelism, and was taking questions afterward from the audience, her polished face looming on jumbo video screens all around the twelve thousand parishioners.

"Madam President," asked a stout woman with big hair, "there are some people saying that you do not believe in democracy. People actually complaining that we want to have a God-centered country. What's wrong with that? Isn't that democracy? Isn't that exactly what we want? Isn't it what Jesus came for?"

"God bless you," the president responded. "You got it exactly. You're right, and some people are more determined than ever to stop it. I mean, if you want to stop God, which is everything good, then doesn't that have to mean also that you're, well, the opposite of good, which is evil? I'm no genius, but it seems right to me. I mean, also, have you heard this new guy, this foreign guy who is organizing a movement against our Lord? Theology Watch, I think it's called. Well, have you seen him?"

She turned to the pastor standing next to her. "What does the Bible say about the Antichrist, Reverend? That you shall know him as a young man with a handsome face and the tongue of a serpent. Something like that? And, from what I hear, a . . . you know . . . well, a grievous sinner. Well, have you *seen* him? The Bible warns us that just when the Kingdom is closest, an Antichrist will come to try to reclaim America for the devil. As usual, if it's in the Holy Book, it happens. So yes, there are dark forces gathering. But really, my friends. Also, really, this is really, you know, a cause for joy. Because it means we are close. Really close. Thank God. Thank you, Jesus."

That night, the service, including this exchange, was seen by millions of evangelical Americans on CBN, the Christian Broadcasting Network. Palin's remarks about Sanjay were picked up by CNN and eventually the networks other than F3.

The next day, arriving back in Washington, the reporters shouted questions: "Madam President, are you saying that Sanjay Sharma is the Antichrist?" "Madam President, do you know what the word 'theocracy' means; do you know the difference between 'theology' and 'theocracy'?" "Do you think he's cute?" "Do you know that Mr. Sharma is an American citizen?" "Do you think all Americans of Indian descent are foreigners?"

Her aides, once again in control, ushered her along, and the questions were answered only with a small-mouthed "God bless you."

Walt and I were delighted by this unexpected development, but Sanjay was not so sure.

"It's not supposed to be about me," he said.

But it was. Sanjay's picture hit all the papers, tabloids, and news magazines. Suddenly his face was ubiquitous. "*The face of evil?*" was the caption on the cover of *Time*. Christian blogs and websites overflowed with biblical analysis mostly pointing to overwhelming evidence that he was indeed the Antichrist (replacing Prince William and Barack Obama as previous Internet favorites). Ironically, one of the factors most often cited was Sanjay's obvious gentleness and goodness. Many evangelical pastors cited a well-known early church sermon on the subject:

> *. . . while a youth, the crafty dragon appears under the appearance of righteousness, before he takes the Kingdom. Because he will be craftily gentle to all people, not receiving gifts, not placed before another person, loving to all people, quiet to everyone, not desiring gifts, appearing friendly among close friends, so that men may bless him, saying—he is a just man, not knowing that a wolf lies concealed under the appearance of a lamb, and that a greedy man is inside under the skin of a sheep.*

At press conferences, reporters from the Christian media tried to connect Sanjay with biblical prophecy regarding the Antichrist, asking, for example, whether he would support a seven-year treaty guaranteeing peace with Israel, the rebuilding of the Temple in Jerusalem, a socialist "New World Order," or one-world religion (all signs of the end times familiar to the millions of devotees of the *Left Behind* series of books and films). He was even asked if he had ever visited Babylon, to which he replied in a typically light but respectful way, "If you mean the location of the ancient Mesopotamian city, the ruins of which are currently located in modern Iraq, the answer is no. If you mean the town on Long Island, yes, I confess I attended a friend's wedding there. A Christian wedding."

F3's attack against Sanjay was more sophisticated and began with a multipart "exposé" of TW, focusing not on the biblical case for belief in Sanjay as the Antichrist but making an astonishing array of spurious allegations about Sanjay and the staff, board, and funders of TW, all based on "informed sources" and not a single one backed by any evidence. These included accusations that TW was funded by radical Islamic groups, that new staff members underwent bizarre homosexual induction rituals, that I had been fired from RCD&S for embezzlement that was then covered up so as not to embarrass the firm, and that Sanjay subscribed to an obscure Hindu pagan yoga cult whose rituals required aborted fetuses. It would have been farcical had most of the enormous F3 audience not simply accepted it all as true.

The liberal and mainstream press again fell into the trap of ridiculing the president's ignorance and superstition as opposed to taking her words at face value. But at least Sanjay and TW now had a platform. When we held a press conference, all the media showed up. When Sanjay traveled and lectured, he was treated as a celebrity.

After the burst of legislation in the first months of Palin's second term, the considerable drama of Justice Steven's death, the Supreme Court's dramatic reversal of a century of constitutional jurisprudence, and the resulting tsunami of social legislation in the red state capitals, the second year of the Palin administration was relatively quiet, and the East and West Coasts of the country seemed to draw a collective sigh of relief. But Sanjay knew that the pacing was deliberate. Jordan and the other evangelical leaders allowed the fear to abate and the non-evangelical population to adjust to the new reality. After a year, the prevailing view, expressed both by pundits and the man on the street, was "It's not so bad."

While things became relatively quiet in the Congress, the administration was busy imposing its agenda on the executive branch of the federal government. In early 2014 President Palin appointed Michael Farris as the new secretary of education. Farris was the founder and chancellor of Patrick Henry College, a four-year Christian college founded in 2000 whose motto is "For Christ and for Liberty." But Farris was no ordinary Christian educator. A lawyer, Farris in 1983 founded the Home School Legal Defense Association and was the leading force persuading evangelicals to remove their children from the public schools and all the distractions of a modern education. Instead, he promoted a curriculum of Christ-centered homeschooling texts to ensure that the children emerged into adulthood with a wholly fundamentalist Christian worldview and prepared, as Generation Joshua, to assume their places in the battle to retake America for Jesus. He was remarkably successful. And these evangelical homeschoolers— estimated to number somewhere between one and two million—were in addition to the 15 percent of all private school students in the country who were enrolled in conservative Christian academies.

All faculty and students at Patrick Henry were required to sign a Statement of Faith, and all teaching was strictly required to adhere to the literal truth of the Bible as its core principle. The college had been denied accreditation in the normal way due to its exclusive teaching of creation science, although it did receive an alternative accreditation from something called the Transnational Association of Christian Colleges and Schools. In a widely aired radio interview, Farris had explained his contempt for the concepts of religious and social toleration. No other religion could be tolerated, he explained, because it was "error." His comment that "tolerance cannot coexist with liberty" had been widely reported. This was the core theocratic principle: True liberty meant the liberty of the Christian to exist in a Christian Nation free of competing faiths or tolerance of practices at odds with his fundamentalist theology. As a result, in a perversion of ordinary meaning and common sense, the pursuit of liberty became the pursuit of a society in which there was no freedom to believe or live in any way that was at odds with the evangelical faith.

In any other period of American history, Farris's appointment to any position in the cabinet would have been unthinkable, but in the second year of President Palin's second term, it hardly seemed surprising that such a man would assume a high position. The second Bush administration provided over $1 billion in federal funding to subsidize fundamentalist Christian homeschooling texts, so it was hard to argue that Farris's obsession with homeschooling was something new to government. But the rigor and purity of his evangelical beliefs would be a potent force at the highest levels of the administration.

At the Farris confirmation hearing, Senator Charles Schumer from New York read one of the Patrick Henry "credos"—professions of belief that were required of all students and faculty:

"Satan exists as a personal malevolent being who acts as tempter and accuser, for whom Hell, the place of eternal punishment, was

prepared, where all who die outside of Christ shall be confined in conscious torment for eternity."

The senator then asked, "So, Mr. Farris, in your capacity as a future secretary of education, does this mean that every child in America should be taught to believe that every Hindu or Muslim in India, every Buddhist or Confucian or atheist in China, every Jew, every Roman Catholic, every person everywhere in the world who has the bad luck to be born to parents who are not born-again evangelical or Pentecostal Christians, that every one of those other people, when he or she dies, faces conscious torment for eternity—that this is the fate chosen for all these people by their creator? Do I have that right?"

"Yes, Senator," Farris replied, "that is what the Bible says, but only if they die outside of Christ, without having accepted Christ as their redeemer, which of course is their choice. With respect, sir, you may think it strange, but who are you to question the wisdom of God? I don't second-guess my creator."

F3, by now the principal source of news and views for almost half the population, hyped the purported achievements of Patrick Henry students and Farris's own academic and legal credentials, and the appointment was approved by the Senate over the vociferous objections of the minority Democrats.

Only a few weeks after the Farris confirmation, Walt conceived of a platform for Sanjay that proved remarkably effective. The National Prayer Breakfast was an event that had been held in Washington every February since 1953. The breakfast itself was safely anodyne, and the US president, together with three thousand other politicians and movers and shakers from around the world, could usually attend the event at the DC Hilton Hotel without fear of embarrassment. Walt's idea was that Sanjay should use his new celebrity status to shine a spotlight on the more sinister aspect of the gathering. Sanjay called a press conference on the street outside the Hilton and, while the breakfast was proceeding in the ballroom inside, opened with a short statement:

I am sure most Americans think that having our president—and members of Congress, judges, diplomats, and other leaders—come together for an annual moment of spiritual reflection and prayer, a moment of unity, is not a bad thing—indeed, that it should be commended. I agree completely. But since 1953 those same good Americans have been deceived by the people inside this building. Yes, that is right. Deceived. *They have been deceived because this breakfast is sponsored by, and is one of the rare public manifestations of, a long-standing secret political movement that calls itself The Family. This organization, led by the man—Doug Coe—whom our national leaders are inside applauding as I speak, has only a single purpose: to recruit politically powerful people to the cause of dominionist theology—that is, rule by God's law, or theocracy. There can be no confusion; The Family exists to acquire power. Doug Coe has said, in a perversion of everything I know about Jesus Christ, that Jesus "prefers power to piety."*

Once you realize what its goals are, then it should be no surprise that The Family operates on the basis of strict secrecy. They describe themselves as "an invisible organization," and they want to hide their methods and goals from the American people. They deliberately emulate the structures and practices of the old Communist Party, organizing themselves as a system of "cells" without traditional hierarchies and with few if any members having sight of the whole organization. Did you know, my friends, that these cells, sometimes simply referred to as "prayer groups," have existed for years within the White House, the Supreme Court, the Senate, the Pentagon—in virtually every department of our federal government? Did you know that The Family tries to impose its fundamentalist policies on impoverished foreign countries, like Uganda, where they prevented our country from supporting programs promoting condom use, causing a doubling of AIDS infections, which was followed by The Family's urging that the country adopt the death penalty for homosexuality? It is true.

So I ask the media and the American people to ask themselves, and to ask President Palin and the representatives and senators who attend this event every year, whether they are members of The Family and support its goals. Please ask them if they believe that biblical law and not the Constitution should be the ultimate rule in this nation. If so, please ask them why are they not honest with you about this. Please ask them when they come out of this building whether they are members of a prayer group that meets in government offices. Please ask them why they hold those meetings in secret. And please, please ask them whether or not they are committed to tolerating the beliefs of their fellow Americans who are not born-again evangelical Christians.

It was a brilliant move. The press did just that. For the first time ever, the politicians leaving the National Prayer Breakfast were accosted by reporters and asked most of the awkward questions suggested by Sanjay. Many admitted with pride to participating in long-standing Family-sponsored prayer groups, and said they had never hidden their conviction that God's law was supreme. Others denied any knowledge of something called The Family. All stumbled over the question of tolerance. In an act of breathtaking double-speak, Congresswoman Michele Bachmann, whose husband had called gays "barbarians" and ran a Christian counseling clinic that advised youngsters to "pray away the gay," answered, "Of course I'm not for intolerance, because it is against freedom and un-American. But let me be perfectly clear, I am against, and the Lord tells us we must take a stand against, evil in all its forms. That I cannot tolerate and will not tolerate. So if that's what you mean by intolerance, well then, that's something different. That's what America is all about."

The Palin White House was not pleased, and F3, backed now by a perfectly coordinated Christian broadcasting industry, launched a strident campaign against the "coastal media elite." I found a clipping in Adam's file that was typical of the F3 editorial view:

These Ivy League egghead intellectual so-called journalists are noth-ing but frustrated radical liberal professors mounting a rearguard

*action against the American people. The American people have
spoken, but they do not hear. Instead, they take the public for idiots,
repeating and spreading every lie and slander anyone can think up
to embarrass President Palin, Steve Jordan, and religious people
everywhere. They hate God—you can hear it in their voices. They
hate ordinary Americans—they hate how we live, how we look,
how we eat, how we raise our children, and they hate our religion.
It is completely outrageous, and unacceptable, that these people—so
out of touch, and with such an extreme agenda—command most
of the airwaves and talk time and newspapers in this great country.
We call on President Palin and the Congress to do something about
it. The use of the airwaves and bandwidth in America is a public
trust, and they have breached this trust. Do something, Madam
President. We just cannot take it anymore.*

But it was not that easy. The Supreme Court was still functioning,
the Constitution was still in effect, and Jordan knew that overt censorship would alienate the undecided Americans who still didn't know
whether to support the Christian Nation as an overdue restoration of
traditional values or to fear it as an authoritarian movement fundamentally at odds with personal freedom. He knew that overt censorship
would suggest the latter. Nor could they resort to the old mantra of
"fair and balanced," as F3 itself was universally understood to be a partisan advocate for the Christian Nation project. So the media initiative
in the last year of President Palin's administration was more nuanced,
but still oddly misconceived and ultimately unsuccessful. Their first
step was to have the Internal Revenue Service promulgate a regulation
providing that no media company could deduct as a business expense
the costs of a newspaper or news program that consistently demonstrated "extreme liberal bias." This would have resulted in all related
gross revenues being taxed as profit, making continuation of news programming by the targeted companies impossible on other than a not-
for-profit basis. This was a rare stumble by Steve Jordan, as the clumsy
regulation contravened a host of administrative law and constitutional

principles and was widely opposed by the business community. A federal court overturned it within months of its adoption.

The second initiative was equally unsuccessful. In retribution for Jim Lehrer's PBS program, *NewsHour*, devoting an entire show to an interview with Jeff Sharlet, a journalist who years before had written a brilliant but underappreciated exposé of The Family, the Corporation for Public Broadcasting (whose board had been highjacked by Palin/Jordan partisans) cut off all funding for the program. The next night, Lehrer was able to announce on the program that its various charitable foundation "underwriters" had agreed to step up and replace the funding pulled by the government. PBS responded by announcing that it was dropping *NewsHour* from the network's schedule. After missing only a single night, the *NewsHour* crew reassembled at the CNN studios in New York and carried on as before—without commercial sponsorship and with increased visibility and stature as a fiercely independent and fiercely intelligent source for old-fashioned nonpartisan journalism.

About a week later, everyone in the TW office was startled when the receptionist called across the room to Sanjay, "Sanjay, Steve Jordan is on the phone." Sanjay raised an eyebrow, returned to his office, and closed the door. Only about a minute later, he emerged.

"Steve Jordan has agreed to meet me. I sent a letter asking if he would. He asked if I would come down to DC next week. I said yes."

Sanjay took me to his only meeting with Steve Jordan. The meeting was at F3's headquarters in Washington, not the White House. We were ushered into an ordinary corporate-looking conference room that smelled of stale cigarette smoke. Jordan did not behave as if he was meeting the Antichrist. He entered alone, greeted both of us cordially, and made Sanjay a cup of tea.

"I thought," said Sanjay, "that we should meet."

"I welcome the opportunity. What would you like to discuss?"

"May I ask you a question?" Sanjay asked.

"Sure," Jordan replied, apparently completely relaxed.

"The core message of your religion is love. So why do you hate me?"

"I don't. I hate your sin. You, Mr. Sharma, might still experience God's love. All you need to do is to accept what He has offered, which is Jesus Christ as savior. Your sin can be redeemed."

"You believe that God created me?"

"Of course."

"Then how can it be a sin to be who I am? He made my skin brown. He made me a homosexual."

"You are mistaken. You have free will and your creator has told you clearly that homosexuality is a serious sin. It is no more a defense to say that God made you a homosexual than it would be for a murderer to say that murder is not a sin because God made him a murderer."

Sanjay looked thoughtful, then continued. "You say my creator has told me. With respect, my creator has not spoken to me. The Bible was written and assembled by men. I understand completely that, following prayer and meditation, an individual person may have insights that take the form of answers. But when you take these individual answers and give them a privileged and authoritative position, this is very dangerous. Claiming the authority of God can justify any ambition and absolve you of personal responsibility for any act. What about your murderer? What if he simply asserted that it was God's will?"

Jordan ignored the question. "May I ask you something?"

"Go ahead."

"Do you believe that the essence of the human condition is ignorance? That the gift of reason properly tells us that most of what is important is not understood or understandable?"

"Man is a deeply spiritual animal," Sanjay replied, "aware of the great mysteries and questing always for answers."

"And doesn't this imply the moral imperative of humility?" Jordan continued. "Humility, Mr. Sharma, is what allows us to submit to authority. And that is what you and every man must do, and in it you will find great joy. That is what God is: authority. God said sodomy is a sin. You don't ask why; it is because He said so. God made the speed of light 186,000 miles per second. You don't ask why, do you? It just is."

"I understand authority. I understand it in parents, bosses, and generals. All are given a type of authority by society that is not only limited but can be taken from them if they abuse it. And, with the exception of children before they are emancipated, we submit to that authority by choice. But your God gives us no choice and is not account-able. And the purported expression of His authority is an old, imper-fect, and conflicting set of texts. As a practical matter, this means that the real authority is vested in those, like you Mr. Jordan, who boldly claim to speak for God."

"Then you just don't understand faith. Faith is a type of knowledge, and it is the means by which we accept the authority of God and His word."

"I understand what faith is. I have no problem with faith; it is a very human thing and can be a good thing. But faith should never demand credence in the face of demonstrated contradiction. Faith maintained in the face of manifest contradiction is not a type of knowledge; it is a type of ignorance. There was a tribe in Papua New Guinea whose faith stipulated that the people of their tribe were the only people on earth. Then, after thousands of years, a bunch of Australians hiked over the mountain and presented a new fact. The tribe adjusted. The faith that you promote precludes the possibility of adjustment. It demands cre-dence in the face of contradiction on matters ranging from evolution to whether people are born homosexual or choose it."

"You should understand, Mr. Sharma, that one of the reasons I believe you are a dangerous person is that you promote sin and dis-obedience and actually make possible sins by others, like abortion. It is one thing to engage in individual sinful behavior; it is another thing to lead a movement that opposes God. As Christians, we have a duty to deal with that very harshly."

"If that is what you think, Mr. Jordan," Sanjay replied, "then I am glad we are having this meeting. I defy you to present one bit of evi-dence that I oppose God. I do not believe in the existence of a personal God in the same way as Muslims, Jews, and Christians do, but I do not oppose those who choose an omnipotent being as their model for the great mystery. As for what I promote, it is laws and a society in which every person's freedom to do just that has our highest protection. Do you not see, sir, that by being so certain in the infallibility of your own beliefs, that it is you who oppose the God of others?"

"You have, Mr. Sharma, fundamentally misunderstood what religion is. The essence of every religion is the exclusivity of its truth claim. Either Mohammed is God's prophet or he is not. Either Jesus is the life and the way to eternal salvation or he is not. More than one religion cannot be true. Ecumenicalism is an impossible dream; the beliefs of the major religions are simply not consistent. Torture them into some sort of mush where one can live alongside the other, and they lose all their coherence."

"On that," Sanjay said, "we may agree. But that doesn't mean that human destiny is for all religions to war with one another until one triumphs. The other alternative is that no religion triumphs, that mankind as a whole recognizes that all religious stories are best understood as parables and properly celebrates and respects the wisdom in all of them."

They continued in this fashion for two hours. Jordan ended the meeting saying, "Mr. Sharma, I'm glad you asked for this meeting. It's been useful—extremely useful, actually—for me to understand you better."

As fascinated as I was by being present at this exchange, it simply confirmed my view that religious zealotry was ultimately tautological. Sanjay was deeply committed to discussion. To me, the meeting demonstrated that discussion would get us nowhere. Sanjay was abnormally quiet and thoughtful for the next couple of weeks. He did not want to talk about it.

★   ★   ★

During the final part of President Palin's second term, the administration went quiet. No new Christian Nation initiatives were announced, and Congress and the president focused on improving the economy in advance of the 2016 elections. But during this period Steve Jordan emerged from his self-imposed obscurity and gradually assumed the de facto role of a co-president. The president rarely appeared in public without him, and when she did, Jordan's telegenic confidence, articulateness, and intelligence tended to overwhelm her own uncertainty and complete reliance on scripted statements and responses. In a strange way, the media and public were relieved that someone capable appeared to be with the president at the helm. In a process I believe to be unprecedented in American history, an unelected person—other than a presidential spouse—was accepted as performing many of the duties of the presidency and, by doing so, became an obvious and accepted candidate to replace the president he was assisting. President Palin took to referring to him as "our next president" and "my successor." Not a single serious candidate emerged to challenge Jordan in the Republican primaries. As a result, all his political speeches during the primary campaign were aimed at the political center, designed to appeal to the non-evangelical electorate that needed to be convinced that Jordan should be welcomed and not feared. The God-centered rhetoric was suddenly gone, and Jordan's speeches from those months could have been made by any conservative Republican primary candidate from ten years before. Showing again a tendency for wishful thinking that ultimately proved fatal, many Americans indulged the hope that this Christian Nation business had been taken as far as it would go and that this intelligent and competent man would stabilize things after the embarrassments and traumas of the Palin years.

I watched Steve Jordan's acceptance speech at the Republican convention from the TW office with Sanjay and most of the rest of the staff. After a few minutes we relaxed a bit, as Jordan largely followed the stump speech from his primary campaign and stuck to safe subjects like defeating terrorism, small government, deficit reduction, and no tax increases.

"Thank God," said one of the TW political strategists, "I was right. He knew he needed to tack to the center to get elected. The Teavangelicals won't like it, but they'll still vote for him."

But then Jordan paused dramatically, took a deep breath, and looked right at the camera, seemingly ignoring the nineteen thousand delegates and others packed into the Tampa Bay Times Forum.

"While I talk about saving, yes literally saving, this country by returning it to its moral foundation, my critics talk about civil rights. But I ask you—the law, the so-called rights of man, even our beloved Constitution—what are they compared to the word of the eternal and almighty God?"

The crowd went silent.

"They are nothing. Bubbles in the river of time, real only for a moment, then forgotten. Brief illusions born of man's imagination, without real power or substance. I promise you—I promise you as my most solemn duty as a man, my most solemn duty as a Christian—I promise you that as a candidate and as president I am going to talk to this country about something real. Something important. Indeed, the only real and important thing there is—the word of God our Father, the message of His son and our redeemer, our Lord Jesus Christ, and the truth of His revelation."

The crowd erupted in a visceral roar. Old ladies clasped their hands in prayer. Young men wept. A sea of attractive blond women raised their arms in ecstatic prayer, eyes closed, shouting. The cheering continued for fifteen minutes.

Later that night Sanjay made the rounds of the network television booths cantilevered over the convention floor. He appeared on every network other than F3. Most of the interviews followed approximately the same course.

"Mr. Sharma, you run an organization called Theocracy Watch. What does that mean? Please explain to our viewers what a theocracy is."

"Well, Jane, it just means a country where those who govern claim to act with divine authority and where law and policy are based on the sacred texts of a single religion. The easiest thing for your listeners to think about is Iran under the Islamic Revolution or Afghanistan under the Taliban. They were both theocracies, countries where the requirements of a single religion—in those cases Islam—trumped democracy or law. So, for example, if the religious text said that the penalty for theft was cutting off the right hand, then the people, the legislators, and the ordinary judges were powerless to decide that the penalty should be something else. The whole society is based on an ancient religious text. And because God is not available to tell us how these texts should be applied to contemporary problems, the law is based on those texts as interpreted by the religious leaders who have assumed civil authority. Needless to say, this gives the religious leaders a great deal of power—very nearly the absolute power of a dictator."

"Mr. Sharma, you keep talking about theocracy, but Steve Jordan, and indeed all the major evangelical leaders around the country, deny it. They say it is a total overreaction and misunderstanding of what they want—that true theocrats are only a tiny minority within the evangelical movement."

"You know, Jane, I am so glad you asked that, because in one sense they are right. Many of our fellow Americans who are evangelical or Christian conservatives really believe that what they want is not a theocracy. But here's the thing: When they talk about democracy, they focus on the part of democracy that is about rule by the majority. If the majority of Americans are Christians, they say, then it can be a Christian Nation. If the majority thinks homosexuality is evil, they say, then it should not be allowed. That, they say, *is* democracy, not theocracy. But Jane, that is not *constitutional democracy*. Our democracy here in America protects the rights of *minorities*. It does not matter how many people are offended by what you are saying, the Bill of Rights guarantees your right of free speech. It does not matter how many people think homosexuality is evil; as a homosexual citizen I am guaranteed equal rights under the law. The revolution Mr. Jordan is leading may ultimately be a majoritarian revolution. But just because he gets over half the vote, it does not mean he can do what he wants. And the proponents of a so-called Christian Nation have been absolutely clear what they want to do with power if they get it, which is nothing less than a total transformation of society at the cost of the freedom of non-Christians, including freedom of speech, privacy, and all sorts of other rights. This is a big change. In the old days, they wanted to save souls. Now they want to reinvent America as what they call a Godly Kingdom, and that's exactly what they will do if Mr. Jordan wins this election, no matter what the Constitution says."

"So you are saying, sir, that the system that Steve Jordan is advocating is a dictatorship?"

"I do not think Steve Jordan is being very honest about *what* his vision of a so-called Chrsitian Nation really means. But yes, what he wants *is* a type of dictatorship. An Iranian journalist who lived through the Islamic Republic in Iran was asked once what a theocrat was. He answered in a way that I think all of us can understand. He said 'a theocrat is someone who wants to take full control of your lives, dictate every single move you make 'round the clock, and, if you dare resist, he will feel it his divine duty to kill you.' That about sums it up. It does not sound very American to me, even though President Palin, Mr. Jordan, and their supporters try to wrap it up in the flag and the Constitution."

Jordan's dramatic admission that proselytizing for evangelical Christianity and establishing the legal primacy of God's law would be the central goals for his presidency should have given an opening for the Democratic candidate to put the theocratic question at the center of the campaign. Sanjay and I, together with millions of others, understood that the election would be a fundamental turning point in American history, a choice between the republic that our founders had given us and an authoritarian Christian state where our core liberties would be redefined in theocratic terms. But the Democratic Party was deeply demoralized by sixteen years out of the White House and eight years of frustration and failure in opposing the Palin administration's legislative program. Moreover, the Democrats were divided over the type of candidate to field against Jordan. The most progressive wing of the party, and many coastal and urban Democrats, felt an historic calling to field a candidate who would offer the clearest and most stark alternative to Jordan and his program, running on a commitment to strict separation of church and state, the unwinding of the Constitution Restoration Act and the rest of Palin's legislative legacy, termination of martial law, and a fierce defense of the rights of gays and religious minorities. Their candidate was a smart, passionate, telegenic, and independently wealthy thirty-five-year-old man named Sam Newbridge. He had been the co-founder of a hugely successful technology company, a key advisor to the Obama campaign eight years before, and a strong and effective supporter of progressive causes ever since. He was one of TW's main financial backers. He was also gay and married to a man.

The other wing of the party was supporting Hillary Clinton. Hillary had not run for national office since her 2008 primary contest against Barack Obama, but she served continuously as US senator from New York and, from that perch, maintained her powerful national network within the party. Her decision not to run in 2012 had proved lucky, as, following the terrorist attack on 7/22, Sarah Palin was unbeatable. So now, in 2016, at sixty-eight years of age, she finally had her chance. The case for Hillary was compelling. Her ex-president husband had died the year before, and the sympathy factor was strong. The political pros who ran the party believed that women would again be the swing demographic. And Hillary would play the role that Sam Newbridge could not: the centrist elder statesperson, a devoted moderate Christian and healer of the national divide. And besides, they whispered at first but finally said out loud, giving the people a married gay candidate would play right into Jordan's hands. His base would truly see the election as an apocalyptic struggle, and even moderate conservatives might still have qualms about a gay president and a feeling of discomfort with one who was married.

Only historians, if we ever have serious historians again, will be able to speculate whether the party's choice could have changed the outcome. After all, the Houses of Worship Free Speech Restoration Act had changed fundamentally the dynamics of American politics. The churches became the top sources—over political action committees, corporations, and individuals—of political advertising. Partisan endorsements from evangelical pulpits virtually guaranteed the votes of those congregations; there was little that any candidate could do to change the mind of a voter whose trusted pastor had informed him or her that one of the candidates was backed by God. And perhaps most importantly, the pastors ensured that their congregations would vote. There's an old adage that to win an election, the first step is to have your supporters show up. For several decades, the *lowest* percentage of Americans polled describing themselves as "born again" or "evangelical" was 33 percent (and the high was 47 percent). That translated roughly to 70 to 100 million evangelicals of voting age. I remember one pollster estimating that election turnout in 2016 among the home-schooled, the graduates of Christian academies and colleges, and those self-describing as "born-again" or "evangelical" was over 85 percent. You can do the math—just remember that it took only 50 million popular votes to elect George Bush in 2000 (and I was one of them). So perhaps the choice of the Democratic candidate in 2016 would not have changed the result. But thinking about it all day, in a long walk around the lake, I'll tell you how it looks to me. I believe the choice of Hillary Clinton was a catastrophic mistake.

The cumulative effect of the eight-year recession had been devastating to the average American family. Many had fallen from the middle class. Many were fearful about how they would survive pending retirements. It looked as if the American century may have ended with the millennium. China was the rising empire, and Americans felt inferior for the first time since the Civil War. They did not like the feeling. The dream—the American dream as their parents had understood it—seemed to be an illusion. Hard work and a mortgage had not proven to be the ticket to a good life. Many people struggled without the support networks of close-by family and community that had gotten the country through the 1930s.

When passion meets pragmatism, passion usually wins. Jordan had a vision and defended it with passion. His vision was a path to renewed national greatness, to honor, to community. He called on the idealism of the American people. And he packaged it all in a comforting fantasy that the people were ill equipped to resist. Hillary, in contrast, offered a defense of the traditional political and economic system. She tried to call on memories of happier days under the Clinton presidency. She offered legalistic arguments about the unconstitutionality of the Palin/Jordan program. She was sixty-eight years old in a country whose youth culture was then the most extreme in history. She was the establishment in a moment where anti-establishment sentiment was at a fever pitch.

CNN called the election at 8:00 p.m., not bothering to wait for the polls on the West Coast to close. The people had chosen Jordan as their forty-sixth president and given him a comfortable but close majority in the House of Representatives, and a Senate with sixty-nine Republicans —enough to defeat a filibuster by the opposing party and to carry votes with a constitutional requirement for two-thirds of the Senate.

★   ★   ★

I HAD A talk today with Adam about the memoir project.

"You've finished two hundred pages," he said.

"Yeah."

"And . . . ?"

"And what?" I was annoyed by the question. It's true that I was totally engaged in the project, rising every morning with eager antici-pation to get to work. But I was not doing it for me. I was doing it for them. "So what more do you want? I've been here almost a month. Am I not doing what you asked? It's all I do. I'm not thinking of the future, of what will happen when I return. I live each day in the past completely. As you asked."

"I'm not here to complain. You are doing what we asked. I hope you also now know it's the right thing to do." He paused to give me a chance to reply, which I did not. He continued, "So here's something I just came across that you may find interesting. When Hannah Arendt tried to understand the rise of totalitarianism in Germany and Russia, she finished her book only four years after the end of the war. In 1967, looking back on the writing of her book, she said the following: 'It was, at any rate, the first possible moment to articulate and elaborate the questions with which my generation had been forced to live for the better part of its adult life: *What happened? Why did it happen? How could it have happened?*' Isn't that interesting?"

He walked out of the room. For the first time, I fully understood the questions that I was being asked to answer in this book.

CHAPTER TWELVE

New Freedom

2016–2017

The national government will preserve and defend those basic principles on which our nation has been built up. It regards Christianity as the foundation of our national morality and the family as the basis of national life.
> —Speech by Adolf Hitler, February 1, 1933

Today, not only in peasant homes but also in the city skyscrapers, there lives alongside of the twentieth century the tenth or the thirteenth. A hundred million people use electricity and still believe in the magic power of signs and exorcism. . . . What inexhaustible reserves they possess of darkness, ignorance and savagery! Despair has raised them to their feet; fascism has given them a banner. Everything that should have been eliminated from the national organism in the . . . course of normal development of society has now come gushing out from the throat; capitalist society is puking up the undigested barbarism.
> —Leon Trotsky,
> *What Is National Socialism?* (June 1933)

"I SUBMIT AMERICA TO CHRIST."
With those words, Steve Jordan began his inaugural address. Within

moments, the rain promised all morning by the gray skies began to fall gently and did not stop.

For the twenty years prior to that rainy day when Steve Jordan finally mounted the steps of the Capitol, Christian fundamentalism had been the largest mass cultural and political movement in America, and the fortunes of each side in the ongoing "culture war" had ebbed and flowed. For the eight years following the election of McCain/Palin and Sarah Palin's unexpected ascension to the highest office in the land, the nation had headed slowly and unsteadily down the path envisioned by its evangelical leaders. But the year 2017 was entirely different. With the long-sought goal in sight, a popular mandate for Jordan, both houses of Congress solidly in control of the Christian right, martial law still in place, and a Christian Militia in almost every state ready to do their bidding, Jordan and his team now sprinted toward victory.

In an Orwellian twist, Jordan chose in his inaugural address to call his program New Freedom. It encompassed neither more nor less than the Christian right had promised were it to obtain unrestrained power.

In the speech, Jordan claimed the mantle of "our great devout, Bible-believing twenty-eighth president, Woodrow Wilson," quoting Wilson, correctly, as saying, "My life would not be worth living if it were not for the driving power of religion, for faith, pure and simple." It was left for Sanjay to point out that Wilson, although no doubt devout, would have found the evangelicals' biblical literalism to be abhorrent, and that Wilson's program to *increase* economic and political liberty bore no resemblance to Jordan's attempt to limit personal freedom in the name of religion.

Jordan said that the New Freedom would be a blessing to the nation and a foundation for finally creating the Godly republic that America's founders had envisioned. The New Freedom program, he explained, had seven principal planks. First and foremost, the touchstone of all his policies would be obedience to the will of God. Second, he would protect the sovereignty of the United States so it was entirely free to fulfill its destiny. Next, the federal government, he promised, would officially recognize the authority and laws of Jesus Christ, would enforce the law in a manner consistent with biblical authority, and would remove any federal judge who stood in its way. Fourth, he would dedicate his administration to freeing the small and large businesses in America to enjoy the blessing of "biblical capitalism," the only path to the prosperity promised to America by the Lord. Fifth, he would protect and defend marriage and the family from every single slight and assault. Next, he said he would work within the Constitution toward the goal of eradicating abortion, homosexuality, adultery, and all other practices similarly abhorrent in the sight of God. And finally, he would ensure that each and every American child was free to enjoy the blessing of a Christian education.

Given the constitutional barriers standing between Jordan and the implementation of the New Freedom program, he did not immediately introduce implementing legislation but instead fell back to the age-old refuge of Washington politicians, and appointed a commission charged with developing, within ninety days, a specific legislative program to implement each of the seven planks of the New Freedom. Its chair was President Palin's education secretary, Michael Farris, the lawyer, homeschooling advocate, and former president of Patrick Henry College. The members included Senators Coburn, DeMint, and Santorum; former vice president Brownback; former Bush attorney general John Ashcroft; Texas governor Rick Perry; evangelical leaders Gary North, James Dobson, Tony Perkins, Howard Ahmanson, Jr., Rick Warren, Doug Coe, Ralph Reed, David Barton, Charles Colson, Luis Cortes, and Gary Bauer; and a group of legal and constitutional "scholars" from Christian colleges.

When the speech was over, Sanjay was interviewed on the steps of the Capitol building holding a black umbrella and surrounded by a crowd of Jordan campaign workers who had attended the inauguration. His bodyguards shifted nervously from foot to foot. The interviewer asked, "So, Mr. Sharma, you heard the president. Can he do what he wants?" Sanjay did not give a false smile, nor did he look grim. His answer was unequivocal.

"It cannot be done," he said. "The Supreme Court stands as the guarantor of our liberties. The Founding Fathers were prescient in understanding that the day might come when the citizens of the country would need to be protected against the religious yearnings of a majority. That's the difference between pure democracy and constitutional democracy. Even the conservatives on the court will not permit it. They are scholars and serious men and women. They will not let the United States of America join with the likes of Iran and Saudi Arabia in embracing intolerance as a core principle of the state. The essence of this country is diversity and tolerance, not fidelity to a single faith enforced by authoritarian rule. The whole point of having constitutional rights is that they cannot be overridden by the majority. The president is seeking to save face with the Farris Commission, but there is no legislative program that can fulfill his objectives that will be found constitutional by the Supreme Court."

Sanjay was wrong. Shortly after the inauguration in January 2017, Associate Justice Ruth Bader Ginsberg, one of the four remaining justices who consistently opposed the conservative approach of Justices Roberts, Scalia, Thomas, Alito, and Cruz, died of a recurrence of pancreatic cancer. At eighty-four, she had overcome the death of her husband, colon cancer, and a previous bout of pancreatic cancer and was the court's most ardent defender of civil liberty. Ginsberg said repeatedly that only death could take her from the court while Sarah Palin was president. Friends said she had become deeply depressed by the Jordan victory in November and seemingly lost the will to live.

Jordan's response to Justice Ginsberg's death set the tone for his presidency. Three days later, at a press conference in the Rose Garden, with his nominee standing by his side, the president nominated the deposed former chief justice of the Alabama Supreme Court, Roy Moore, to the highest court in the land.

Roy Moore was one of the great heroes of the evangelical movement but was only vaguely known to the rest of the country. The rest of us learned quickly. Moore was a fundamentalist Christian of the more robust sort, having worked as a cowboy and kickboxer, attributing his pugilistic successes to divine favor and intervention. As a state judge in Alabama, he displayed wooden Ten Commandments plaques in his courtrooms and opened his judicial sessions with prayers, sometimes calling on a clergyman to lead the jury members in conversation with God prior to the start of jury deliberations. He was then elected by the people of Alabama to the position of chief justice of that state's supreme court.

To drive home his fundamentalist belief that God was the sole legit-imate source of law, and that all civil institutions must be subservient to God's will, in 2001 he arranged for a five-thousand-pound granite monument to the Ten Commandments to be placed in the rotunda of the state courthouse. The federal courts ordered its removal, and Moore responded that the orders of the federal courts on such a matter had no legitimacy and that he obeyed only the orders of God and the great state of Alabama. The great state of Alabama responded by establishing a judicial commission that proceeded to remove him from office. It is sobering to remember that in 2003, when the federal courts ordered the removal of the monument, 78 percent of Americans polled objected to the federally ordered removal, expressing the view that Judge Moore was entitled to have the Ten Commandments in his courthouse. Seventy-eight percent is a high number and should have been seen by all of us as a foreshadowing of how the non-evangelical middle would tip when it came to questions of separation of church and state.

"Roy's Rock" then began its peripatetic travels in the American heartland, appearing at hundreds of Christian conventions and state fairs, including appearances in thirty-one different states in one year alone. Moore became a folk hero to the Christian right, and in 2003 drafted the Constitution Restoration Act, which was finally passed in the early days of President Palin's second term, opening the door to the theocratic legislative program of the states whose legislatures were already dominated by evangelical forces.

The response to Jordan's nomination of Moore was powerful. An ad hoc group of several hundred law professors and federal judges of every political persuasion took out full-page ads in the country's major newspapers and petitioned the Senate Judiciary Committee to reject Moore. Chief Justice Roberts and Justice Kennedy broke protocol and leaked to a trusted reporter their views that the nomination, if confirmed by the Senate, could "destroy the Court." "Maybe," said a leak from the White House in response, "the Court needs a little bit of 'creative destruction.'"

The nomination proved wildly popular with the nation's evangelicals. F3 orchestrated a day of national "outrage" at the "snide, sniping, liberal whining about a true American hero." Senators were deluged with petitions, calls, and e-mails in support of Judge Moore. The day the Senate Judiciary Committee started its hearings, a crowd estimated at 750,000 gathered on the national mall chanting "Take Back the Court," "Get Out of Our Way," and "The Time Is Now."

When the Senate confirmed Moore, every Democrat and six brave Republicans opposed it. Four of those Republicans failed to achieve their party's nomination at the end of their terms. The two others were dead by the start of President Jordan's second term.

Moore's tenure on the court had a rocky start. Chief Justice Roberts, who would traditionally administer the two oaths required of an associate justice, reported to the chief administrative officer of the court that he was indisposed, and he instructed the officer to poll the associate justices in order of seniority to see if one of them would be willing to do the job. Justice Thomas administered the oath with no other justice or federal judge of any seniority in attendance. The president responded to this slight by hosting another oath ceremony at the White House the following day. It was, I think, the first time that a wooden cross joined the row of American flags as the backdrop for a White House event. From that day forward, it was how we always saw the president on television and in photographs: the top of the cross over his right shoulder and an American flag over his left.

The ceremony opened with the president himself administering the oath to Moore a second time and presenting him with a small model of Roy's Rock. This was a sweet moment for tens of millions of Americans, a symbolic righting of what they regarded as a monstrous wrong.

A succession of evangelical senators then delivered speeches in praise of Moore, reminding the nation that the jurisdiction of the federal courts had been limited by Congress as expressly permitted by the Constitution and that the days of the will of the sovereign states, the will of the people, and the will of God being thwarted by an overly active federal judiciary were well and truly over. But Moore's real job, of course, was to ensure an ideologically pure vote to ensure a sympathetic majority even when, as was feared, one of Justices Alito, Kennedy, Roberts, or Cruz, would join the remaining liberal jurists to overturn the legislation necessary to implement Jordan's "New Freedom."

★   ★   ★

SOON AFTER JUSTICE GINSBURG's timely (for Jordan) death, things continued to break in favor of the new administration. Just one week following Justice Moore joining the Supreme Court, the court heard a petition for a writ of certiorari in the case of *Gonzales v. Nebraska.* The case had been winding its way through the federal judiciary for nearly four years since the Nebraska legislature, during the frenzy of state legislation following President Palin's signing of the Constitution Restoration Act, had adopted a law constituting a full frontal assault on *Roe v. Wade.* The Nebraska statute simply outlawed abortion outright regardless of the time during pregnancy or other circumstances. With *Roe* still the law of the land, this seemed like an empty political gesture. The Nebraska statute, as expected, was promptly stayed by a federal district court and declared unconstitutional following a short trial. A year later, the Eighth Circuit Court of Appeals upheld that decision. Had the cert petition been received two weeks earlier, it would almost certainly have been denied, but with Moore added to the court, acceptance of the cert petition signaled to the world that at least four of the justices were prepared to overturn *Roe* (this was because the informal "rule of four" ensures that a hostile majority cannot prevent cases from being brought before the court). When word leaked out from one of Justice Moore's new clerks that five justices had voted to accept cert, abortion foes around the nation were overjoyed, believing that the era of legalized abortion in America was coming to an end. They were right. The case was heard and decided on an accelerated basis, and during a sitting in early June, the court's decision in *Gonzales v. Nebraska* was released. The day both dreaded and longed for by millions of Americans had come. The court, with Justices Scalia, Thomas, Alito, Cruz, and Moore creating the majority, simply reversed its 1973 finding of a right of privacy under the Fourteenth Amendment or otherwise and held that there was no constitutional bar to the Nebraska statute.

After the *Gonzales* decision, President Jordan released a short statement expressing his gratification that the dreams and prayers of millions of Americans had been answered. He called the short forty-four-year period during which abortion services had been widely available "our national nightmare." He noted correctly that since 2009 more Americans had self-identified as pro-life than pro-choice and that finally the federal judiciary had stood aside and acquiesced to the will of the people. "This is a landmark day in America's history," he said. "We have in one day taken a first step in creating a more perfect democracy and at the same time removed one of the greatest sources of God's displeasure with America."

Later that night, in one of the first signs that the governor of New York, former New York City mayor Mike Bloomberg, would emerge as a national leader in opposition to the Jordan administration, the governor announced that the Supreme Court's decision was wrong and "unacceptable," although he refused then to be baited into stating what that meant. Instead, he reported that New York National Guard troops had been dispatched to provide physical security at every family planning and abortion clinic in the state and he had signed an executive order that day making women from any other state eligible to receive such services in the state of New York. He said that abortion doctors and family planning professionals fleeing other states would be welcomed in New York. He also announced that his charitable foundation had set aside $300 million to provide funding to any woman in the country who could not afford to travel to New York for family planning, counseling, or abortion services.

In a carefully planned move, the relatively subdued statement from the president contrasted with a frenzy of excitement from F3. We had the first of many demonstrations of the consequences of having a president who personally controlled the nation's largest and most influential media conglomerate. This was quite different from the nationalization of media we had seen in other countries or even the alignment between newspapers and political parties that had long been the practice in the United Kingdom. Although F3 was often aligned with the Republican Party, it was not under its control. It did, however, act at the direction of the president, who together with Ralph Reed controlled the Faith & Freedom Coalition and who, after the merger with Fox, maintained, together with the Murdochs, a controlling position in the company. As a result, the White House communications director, for the first time in history, was not only orchestrating use of the media platform provided by the presidency but also determining the coverage provided to that president by America's largest and most influential family of media outlets. This allowed President Jordan to be "presidential" and for F3 to play the role of agent provocateur, urging the people into the streets to show their "intolerance" for baby killers and calling for law enforcement—or, should they fail to act, the Christian militias—to stand on guard to prevent the murder of unborn children.

The results were predictable. In every state that did not join New York in dispatching National Guard troops to provide security for clinics, the clinics were subjected to vociferous around-the-clock demonstrations and overt threats of violence by armed Christian militias. Many were burned. Within a week, without state legislatures even having to act, providers of abortion and other family planning services had abandoned great swaths of the middle of the country.

* * *

IT WAS THE *Gonzales* decision that thrust me, personally, into a public role. Sanjay and Walt argued that it was strategically desirable for TW to have a second spokesman. Sanjay, they argued, should continue to speak on political and moral issues. He would continue to be the face, voice, and emotional center of the opposition. But legal matters were different. What was needed there was credibility and authority. I would be promoted as an establishment figure, a lawyer with unimpeachable credentials as a former partner of one of the country's most prestigious law firms. I would serve as an expert, outside of politics, interpreting for the people the technical implications of the New Freedom legislative program and the actions of the Supreme Court. "Just be yourself," advised Walt. "Don't try to be Sanjay."

Surprisingly, it was easy. When I stood in front of the cameras, I just pretended that I was briefing a client. One thing a corporate lawyer learns to do well is to take complex legal issues and translate them for a corporate executive—the decision maker—in a way that he or she can understand. My first press conference, with Sanjay and Walt standing at my side, was on the subject of *Gonzales*. My message was simple. Although the independent press had correctly interpreted the case as allowing the state legislatures to criminalize abortion at any time, including from the point of conception, they had failed to focus on the implications of the manner in which *Roe* was overturned. The Supreme Court's decision in *Roe* was built on decades of Supreme Court jurisprudence that established a constitutional "right to privacy." This "right" is not listed in the Bill of Rights. The word "privacy" does not appear in the Constitution. Instead, the court developed the concept of a "right to privacy" to capture the overarching constitutional presumption in favor of personal liberty that needed to be taken into account when judging whether laws infringing those liberties were constitutional. The right to choose to have an abortion before the fetus is viable was not the only "right" implied in the Constitution based on the right to privacy. The others included the right to engage in whatever private sexual acts you choose in the privacy of your bedroom, the right to read or view pornography in the privacy of your residence, the right to choose to terminate medical treatment, the right to marry the person you choose, the right to procreate or withhold from procreation, and the right to rear your children as you see fit, including to select the schools they attend. None of these rights is enumerated in the Constitution. But the

Supreme Court had held for many years prior to *Roe v. Wade* that this right to privacy is there: there because the Ninth Amendment makes clear that the list of rights in the Bill of Rights is *not* exclusive; there because the Bill of Rights itself should be read expansively; and there because the substantive due process rights established by the Fourteenth Amendment extend to protect our personal "liberty." Take away this "right to privacy," I pointed out, and the constitutional door was once again open for federal and state governments to legislate in the sphere of sex, family, and personal behavior. Our liberties were in grave danger. No serious scholar disagreed with me, but none of us had a constitutional answer. The president was duly elected, Moore had been duly appointed and confirmed by the Senate, and the Supreme Court had spoken. This was now the law of the land.

The great irony here was that for decades the far right had argued that when constitutional processes failed us and our personal liberties were at stake, the founders had wisely ensured an armed population to prevent tyranny from again taking root in the New World. But now, without irony, and showing the hypocrisy demonstrated in the Terri Schiavo affair, F3 assured the nation that the only true freedom, the only freedom consistent with the views of our Founding Fathers and our national destiny, was the New Freedom. The law of the land, they said, was clear, and we had no higher duty as citizens than to submit to the rule of law even when we disagreed with the result.

I do not recollect this in an immodest way, but from that moment on, TW—and not the Democratic Party, the ACLU, or any other political organization—became the primary voice of opposition. And we got their attention. F3 and the president were not amused when I published a paper demonstrating that the right to homeschooling and the right to send your child to a religious, and not public, school were both based on the right to privacy, and that the Supreme Court's decision opened the way for states to legislate away these parental prerogatives. We had a lively debate at TW about whether we should urge the remaining blue states to do just that.

For the superstitiously minded, it was tempting at the time to accept that Jordan had benefitted from some sort of divine intervention or, at the least, extraordinary good luck. Had Justice Ginsberg not died at exactly the moment she did, and had *Gonzales* not become ripe for cert just after Justice Moore's arrival, the Farris Commission would have had neither the courage nor the legal basis to formulate The Blessing in the way that it did, and American history would have been very different.

Adam disapproves of this line of thought. He tells me to stick to the story and not waste energy with "what ifs." I disagree. Didn't he tell me my job was *"What happened? Why did it happen? How could it have happened?"* Don't the "what-ifs" help us to answer the why? Don't they illuminate the truth about history, the truth that is so deeply unsatisfying to the human mind—that human choices interact uncertainly with random events to determine the course of the story? What if John McCain had not risked America's future for political advantage and had rejected Sarah Palin as his running mate? He had a choice. What if the cellular membrane holding in the tiny bulge in President McCain's cerebral artery had not failed that day in Moscow? A random event. What if I, and only a few hundred more like me, had joined Sanjay six years earlier? A choice. What if Justice Ginsberg had survived for another twelve months? A random event. So how could it have happened? Well, it seems to me that you needed to have both. Without the bad choices, the random events would not have mattered. Without the random events, the bad choices would not have led to disaster.

The report of the Farris Commission was released by the president in a national address on July 4, and for the first time Americans learned about the fifty Blessings that would come to control every aspect of their lives. The fifty Blessings were unlike any other legislative program in the history of the republic. The president explained:

> *My fellow Americans, for over five months a group of our most experienced and distinguished legislators, this country's finest legal scholars, our leading historians, experts on the Constitution, our best theologians and the most trusted Christian leaders in the land have*

worked together day and night to understand to what great purpose this nation is called and how to restore this nation to grace and greatness. Not since the Continental Congress assembled in Philadelphia to boldly dedicate their lives to establishing a nation under God have wiser or better men pondered the future course of our republic.

And yes, he was being accurate. Not a single woman served on the Farris Commission.

They prayed together and they prayed separately; they prayed day and night for the Lord to guide them and were overwhelmed and humbled at the wisdom with which God filled them. I am told that when the Commission members assembled in the morning, one would tell the group that he had prayed all night on the question before them and been given the answer by our Lord—and the others around the table would fall to their knees in wonder and thanks, as each had received exactly the same answer to his own prayers. The Lord was truly with them.

The president bowed his head, as if momentarily overcome, and then looked up and continued.

So what was revealed to these men by the Lord? I assembled the Commission led by Michael Farris to formulate a legislative program to implement the New Freedom program announced at my inauguration. Proving once again that God does always know best, they have come back to me with something different: not a series of regular laws but a covenant. My fellow Americans, by the grace of God, what I have the honor to give to you today is a final covenant with our Lord, a covenant to put this nation on the path of virtue, grace, and obedience, and to secure for all Americans the gift of eternal salvation through Jesus.

Most Americans know their Bible well, but I remind you that the first covenant was made by Abraham, and then later God sent His son, Jesus, and made a new covenant with mankind—a covenant that if we believe in Him and accept Jesus as our savior, then in the eyes of God the death of Jesus will atone for our sins.

And now, a new and final covenant—the last before the second coming of Jesus—is offered to us by God to restore America to its true purpose and former greatness. This new covenant is a magnificent blessing, the greatest blessing bestowed by God on any nation or people. It seals for us God's favor and protection; if we accept it, it will once again make this land God's shining city on a hill, a holy and sacred place that He will henceforth protect from all evil. This is why our new American covenant with the Lord is called The Blessing.

The Blessing is an offer from God. I submit it today, on the nation's birthday—which will also henceforth be the date of our nation's rebirth in Christ—to the Congress and to the American people. God offers us this new covenant, and you, through your chosen representatives, must decide whether to accept it. Later today the full text of The Blessing will be e-mailed to every American with an e-mail address. I ask you to read it, to study it, to pray about it. I ask every congregation in America to devote this Sunday to prayer and discussion. Then, please communicate with your representatives and senators. In two weeks' time, Congress will take a simple yes or no vote. If they accept The Blessing on behalf of the American people, I will sign it immediately, and it will become a binding covenant between this nation and God, with the status of a law that prevails over all other laws of the land. Over time, our laws and regulations and procedures will be conformed to it. I trust this momentous decision to our great democracy and to our God-given Constitution. I know these great institutions will not fail us. God bless you, and God bless America.

Every American alive today knows The Blessing by heart. But not knowing for whom this memoir is intended, I asked Adam whether I should include it in the book. His answer was interesting, and I could not fall asleep last night pondering his words.

"We dream," Adam said, "that your book will be read not only by those alive today—many of whom know very little about how they came to live as they do now—but also those who live in a future America where the Christian Nation is a distant nightmare. Assume nothing. Tell the whole story."

Last night was the first time I ever allowed myself to consider a future different from the present. Can I conceive of a "future America where the Christian Nation is a distant nightmare"? It has been wrenching enough to relive the past. Do I have the strength yet to think about the future?

We were all quite amazed when, within an hour of the president completing his Independence Day speech to the nation, each of us received an e-mail from the federal government with the text of The Blessing. It was, I believe, the first time the federal government had sent a mass e-mail to the entire citizenry. The e-mail each American received read as follows. Each of the fifty specific rules, called Blessings, was organized under ten general assertions, which were called Covenants:

The Blessing

I. There is no power but God, and the powers that are ordained by God.

1. *As the fate of the nation depends entirely on unbending obedience to the will of God, it shall be treasonous to deny the existence of God, to question the Word of God, or to advocate disobedience to the will of God.*

II. The Lord created America that His will may reign on earth.

2. *The sovereignty of the United States of America is absolute. Accordingly, the United States shall not join or support any international organization.*

3. *The United Nations is hereby expelled from the territory of the United States. Its operations shall be relocated within one year.*

4. *Any treaty that abrogates the absolute sovereignty of the United States is hereby repudiated and declared null and void.*

5. *No US citizen shall be extradited to face criminal or civil proceedings in another country.*

III. This nation devoutly recognizes the authority and law of our Lord Jesus Christ.

6. *The most important task of man is to accept, embrace, and obey God's law.*

7. *God's law, as set forth in the Bible, shall be the supreme law of the land, prevailing over any imperfect human law.*

8. *The American Constitution is a divine gift and shall be strictly construed. The Constitution shall be interpreted in accordance with the higher law of the Bible.*

9. *The purpose of the federal and state court systems shall be to do God's will and to faithfully interpret and enforce the law of the land in accordance with the Word of God.*

10. *No judge shall interpret the law or render any judgment that is contrary to the will of God as evidenced by the Bible.*

11. *Only persons who have accepted the Lord Jesus Christ as their savior shall serve as federal judges.*

12. *The Constitution wisely limits the role of government, and such limitations shall be deemed to prohibit involvement by the federal government in education and social welfare, which shall remain the exclusive domain of the people, their churches, and, if permitted by state constitutions and state law, the states.*

13. *No state or local government may enact any law prohibiting so-called "hate crimes," which can too easily be used to persecute or abuse those faithful to the Word and laws of God.*

IV. The Lord gave America the biblical capitalist system for our material comfort; He reigns over our economy and demands obedience to His will in return for our prosperity.

14. *Only one economic system, the free enterprise system, is consistent with God's will and God's law.*

15. *No economic system other than the free enterprise system shall be taught or practiced within the United States.*

16. *The advocacy of socialism in any form is treasonous.*

17. *Poverty is due to disobedience to God's will.*

18. *In a Christian Nation, where obedience to God is the measure of equity, "labor unions" are unnecessary and illegal.*

V. The Lord gave us marriage for our pleasure and for procreation.

19. *Marriage shall be the sole form of civil union or partnership recognized for any purpose within the United States.*

20. *Marriage means marriage between one man and one woman.*

21. *No other form of "marriage" consummated in or recognized by any other jurisdiction shall be recognized or valid for any purpose whatsoever within the United States.*

22. *Adulterous behavior by either husband or wife is a crime.*

23. *Homosexual behavior of any kind is a crime.*

24. *Sexual relations outside of marriage are a crime.*

25. *Sexual perversion, even between husband and wife, is a crime (provided that a wife may pleasure her husband in any way her husband desires and to which she consents).*

26. *No person shall participate in the creation, distribution, or use of pornography, all of which shall be crimes.*

27. *Abstinence from all sex (including masturbation) outside of marriage shall be the only form of sex education permitted.*

28. *No foreign national who is homosexual shall be eligible for immigration to, or resident alien status in, the United States.*

VI. The Lord created the male, who shall reign in headship over the family.

29. *Upon marriage, a wife shall be obligated to obey her husband.*

30. *A child shall obey his or her father.*

31. *The primary responsibility of a husband and father shall be to align the family with the will and Word of Jesus Christ.*

VII. The family is the basis of American life and the fundamental unit of American society.

32. *The discipline of children is in the sole discretion of parents. No unit of government shall outlaw or regulate the discipline of children, or prosecute any parent or teacher for the disciplining of a child.*

33. *It shall be unlawful for a child to strike a parent.*

34. *Incorrigible juvenile delinquency shall be a crime.*

VIII. Only the Lord may determine when life shall begin and end.

35. *For all purposes of the law, life begins at conception.*

36. *Abortion, meaning any act that terminates life following conception, shall be illegal.*

37. *Killing an unborn child through abortion shall be a capital offense.*

38. *A woman who permits her child to be aborted shall be guilty of a felony.*

39. *Euthanasia, meaning any act that terminates life prior to its natural end, shall be illegal.*

IX. The Lord loves our children, and gave His Word and His will as the basis for educating our children.

40. *Children shall be instructed that God's Word is the only reliable path to the truth.*

41. *Reason unguided by God's Word is an illusion, often perverted by Satan to divert us from obedience to God's will. It shall be a crime to teach that philosophical investigation or the so-called "scientific method" are the sole or primary paths to knowledge.*

42. *There shall be no tolerance of lies, falsehoods, and illusions. The primary task of all teachers is to protect children from falsehood.*

43. *A principal task of public education shall be to teach obedience to God's will.*

44. *A principal task of public education shall be to teach sexual purity.*

45. *No atheist, homosexual, or single woman shall be permitted to teach or play any role in a public or private school, at any level. For this purpose, (i) any person over the age of thirty who has never been married shall be presumed to be a homosexual, and (ii) any person not registered with and certified in good standing by a recognized church shall be presumed to be an atheist.*

46. *Each classroom in America, public or private, shall, at the commencement of each school day, recite the Pledge of Allegiance, and join in a prayer of thanks to God for America. The prayer may, but is not required to, mention our Lord Jesus Christ (but shall not mention any other purported deity, prophet, saint, or other figure from a specific religious tradition other than Christianity).*

X. **Although a Christian Nation and its Christian citizens have a duty to open the eyes of all its citizens to the Word and light of Christ, the right of non-Christian citizens to believe and practice, in the private sphere of their families and places of worship, religions other than Christianity shall be protected.**

47. *Religions other than Christianity are permitted. Witchcraft, Wicca, astrology, the worship of Satan, any violent sect of Islam, and other cults are not recognized as religions.*

48. *All places of worship and other property, real and personal, present and future, of superstitions and cults that are not recognized as religions shall be forfeit to the state in which they are located.*

49. *Non-Christian religions shall be entitled to maintain places of worship but shall not be permitted to make public displays of the symbols of their religions in any place other than the premises of such places of worship.*

50. *The promotion of non-Christian religion through advertisement or missionary or proselytizing activity shall be prohibited within the territory of the United States of America.*

The next two weeks were among the most extraordinary in American history. Many of the 70 million or so Americans who called themselves evangelical or born again stopped work, school, and every aspect of their daily routine and devoted each waking hour to persuading their friends, neighbors, and congressional representatives to accept the ten "covenants" and the individual Blessings associated with each of them. The owners of many professional sports teams cancelled games and instead hosted huge choreographed rallies at their stadiums. Stadium rallies had been part of the fundamentalist subculture for decades, but in these circumstances the echoes of Nuremberg were hard to ignore. I remember watching on television, with a combination of awe and horror, an event at Reliant Stadium in Houston. The rally unfolded in the manner of an Olympics opening ceremony. At the beginning, all lights were extinguished to create complete darkness representing the "dark age of sin and disobedience" from which we were about to emerge. Then a single white spotlight followed a young boy who walked alone onto the enormous field clutching a copy of The Blessing. When he reached the center he knelt and raised his face to heaven. The silence was broken by his voice saying only "Thank you, Lord." At that moment, the whole stadium was brilliantly illuminated, revealing the combined choirs of fifty Texas churches (one for each Blessing) arrayed across the field in the form of a giant cross. The massed choirs began singing a gospel version of "The Battle Hymn of the Republic" complemented by fifty trumpeters. From all around the stadium, long gold banners unfurled, one by one, revealing fifty crosses, each a hundred feet high. The production continued in this fashion for an hour and left the seventy thousand faithful in attendance exhilarated and exhausted.

The members of the Farris Commission worked the media nonstop, telling gripping stories of how their prayers had been answered miraculously by direct and detailed revelations from God. They argued that there was a broad and long-standing consensus from all Christian denominations in support of the ten Covenants. They detailed the specific and indisputable biblical bases for each of the Blessings. The so-called "constitutional scholars" argued that The Blessing was not only consistent with the Constitution as properly construed but was based on the laws, traditions, and values of the country from the time of its founding until the moment it lost its way around the time of the New Deal. To that part of the population already attuned to the alternative Christian narrative of American history—and bereft of the perspective, historical facts, or the skills needed to consider the document critically—the case for The Blessing seemed strong.

What was not seen on F3 but was covered by the independent media was the chaotic reaction from the moderate and liberal corners of the country. It was as if the entire non-evangelical community awoke at a single moment from a long slumber. Upon their awakening they professed complete shock that the nation stood on the brink of a theocratic revolution. To hear the sputtering outrage, you would have thought that Bush and his born-again allies had not ruled for eight years and revolutionized federal policy on everything from stem cell research to abstinence education to faith-based social services. You would have thought that the Christian Nation resolution and first-term legislation sponsored by Sarah Palin had not occurred, that martial law had not been declared, and that the Constitution Restoration and Defense of Freedom Acts had not already fundamentally undermined their civil liberties. You would have thought that Justice Stevens had not been killed, that the Supreme Court had not been neutered, and that the most extreme fundamentalists, serving as cabinet secretaries, had not begun implementing their theocratic program department by executive department. You would have thought that the heartland was not already overrun by armed Christian militias sanctioned by the states, that books had not been burned, and that gays and abortion doctors had not already been run out of countless towns. To hear their shock and outrage, you would have thought that for the last twenty years the proponents of the Christian Nation had not said exactly what they would do and now were simply doing it.

Most opposition rhetoric was an undirected brew of blame and confusion as to how the situation had come to pass. Despite our best efforts, the public and political campaign during the two weeks allowed by Jordan was, for the most part, ineffective. In those weeks TW received nearly $600 million of donations and pledges. Dozens of business and Wall Street leaders called TW and promised unlimited funding—"whatever it takes," they said, "just don't let it happen." Despite an enormous public education campaign and media spend, TW could not spend all the money that had come its way. Jordan had the votes, and however shrill or well funded the opposition, we knew that The Blessing would become the law of the land at the end of two weeks.

I was relentless in forcing our team to focus on what we would do after the inevitable happened. Our strategy was simple. The Blessing would be completely impotent if each and every of its fifty elements was litigated in federal court and the courts of each of the states. The Blessing read like no federal statue (or any statue in any country) and was not only unconstitutional on numerous grounds but also completely deficient as a law due to its vagueness and uncertainty. As long as we had a functioning court system in the country, we figured we could delay its implementation for years—at least four years in any case, following which the country would have the opportunity to replace the House and restore to the White House a president who would take seriously his or her oath to uphold the Constitution. It was on this that we pinned our hopes.

I do not want you to underestimate our effort during those two weeks. The Catholic archbishop of New York, with the sanction of the Vatican, convened a summit of all the non-evangelical religious leaders in the country. The entire conference of American Catholic bishops, the apostles of the Mormon Church, the leaders of Orthodox and Reform Judaism, the most respected American imams, the Episcopal bishops, the presidents of the great Presbyterian seminaries and leaders of each other mainstream Protestant denomination all gathered at St. Patrick's Cathedral to consider The Blessing. It was the idea of New York's mayor, Christine Quinn, to turn the event into a major spectacle that would capture the attention of the country and illustrate to those waffling on the edges of the fundamentalist movement that this was not a battle between God and the godless but between this peculiarly American strain of fundamentalist Christianity and all the other Abrahamic religions that worshiped the same God. Delegations of religious leaders arriving at the city's airports were treated like visiting heads of state and escorted into Manhattan by impressive motorcades led by scores of NYPD motorcycle cops. Fifth Avenue was closed to traffic, and crowds lined the sidewalks to witness the arriving religious leaders. Each group was greeted on the street in front of the cathedral by the mayor and governor with symbolic keys to the city. The archbishop stood at the top of the steps to Saint Patrick's and made short remarks of welcome to each delegation. These remarks, more than anything else about that day, gave great swaths of the country momentary cause for optimism. The archbishop, a jovial Irishman who was also a learned religious scholar conversant with all the denominations represented, spoke movingly of the traditions and teachings of each other denomination, emphasizing all that it held in common with other faiths and assuring the leaders of the profound respect of the Roman Catholic Church. This was followed in each case by a warm bear hug from the archbishop. The first time it happened, I saw a tear leak from the governor's eye. Christine Quinn beamed with joy. Part of me wanted to believe this would be a redemptive moment, pulling the country gently away from the precipice by reminding it of its better self. But the other part of my brain could only ask why they had waited so long. Why hadn't this happened immediately after 9/11? Or after Sarah Palin's Christian Nation resolution in 2009?

At the end of the day, the delegations reappeared on the steps of the cathedral and issued a forceful joint condemnation of The Blessing. They even asked their own faithful to take to the streets and oppose the law, but they fell short of a call for violence. Jordan and F3 stridently contested the part of the religious leaders' statement claiming that The Blessing threatened their own religious freedom, pointing to the Tenth Covenant guarantee of "the right of non-Christian citizens to believe and practice, in the private sphere of their families and places of worship." Many Americans took this at face value and believed that their own rights of belief and religious practice would be protected.

After the summit of religious leaders, the Mormons, never easy bedfellows with the evangelicals, worried that they alone among the other Christian denominations in the country would be considered a "cult" whose property would be forfeit to the states. They immediately began moving their financial assets to Canada in secret, an error that eventually made their worst fear a self-fulfilling prophecy.

The United Nations Security Council met in emergency session and adopted a resolution warning the United States that implementation of the theocratic system contemplated by The Blessing would breach the Universal Declaration of Human Rights and that it and its members would take all actions available to them under international law to enforce America's obligations under the United Nations Treaty, the UN Headquarters Agreement, and America's many other multilateral and bilateral treaties. All the NATO allies warned that abrogation of the NATO treaty would be illegal and fundamentally destabilizing to world peace. China and Russia, however, said repeatedly that it was "an internal matter" for the United States.

The country stood still for two weeks, transfixed by the situation in which it found itself. The stock market tumbled by 40 percent in the days following Jordan's speech, to which the Securities and Exchange Commission responded by suspending trading until after the vote, which itself dealt a devastating blow to Wall Street and other financial markets. Mainstream college campuses were gripped by violence, with noisy clashes between right and left rendering most of them unable to maintain a secure environment for the continuation of classes. So many evangelicals had poured into Washington on church buses from around the country that non-evangelical constituents could not break through the crowds to lobby their legislators on Capitol Hill.

Two days before the vote, TW recruited virtually all mainstream American popular entertainers to participate in the Real Freedom mega-concert in New York's Central Park, televised and streamed live on every media outlet other than F3. If reason could not win the argument, we hoped to turn popular culture—a tool that the other side had used with such great effect—against them. Under a clear sky and a full moon, three generations of pop, rock, rap, and blues stars stepped to the stage, performed their all-time hit songs, and then entreated their fans to stand up for their rights and prevent the introduction of a religious state. Many wept and cried and begged America to come to its senses. Millions were moved by the event. But virtually none of Jordan's political base watched the concert, for at the same time all the leading country and Christian music stars had assembled on the mall in Washington for a competing Thanks for The Blessing concert.

It is hard for me to think in an orderly way about that time. Sanjay and I hardly slept. TW had trebled its staff, and law professors, scholars, historians, and journalists from around the country signed up to volunteer. What they wanted from us were assignments. We dispatched them to interviews, to rallies in the coastal cities, and to interface with congressional staffs. We were in a mode of hyperactivity, but at the same time we were watching a slow-motion train wreck because we knew the outcome of the vote.

We toyed with the idea of sending Sanjay to the House gallery to be present for that vote but decided against it, fearing that he might be arrested before he could leave Washington. Sanjay and I were invited to New York governor Bloomberg's Manhattan town house to watch the vote on television with Mayor Quinn and some of the governor's close friends. The House voted first, followed immediately by the Senate. When it was over, Mayor Quinn was in tears, holding the hand of her partner and sobbing on her shoulder. I looked at Sanjay, who was staring at his hands. I remember wanting to give him a hug. I didn't. The governor let loose a string of expletives and left the room.

★   ★   ★

AT THE END, only five Republican representatives and two Republican senators broke with the administration and opposed the bill. The strangest piece of legislation in American history passed with overwhelming majorities. What they voted on became, after the president's signature, a federal law, but its opening words were the following: "An Act to Accept a Covenant With God and the Blessings Thereunder. The United States of America hereby humbly and gratefully enters into a covenant with the Lord our God and protector, accepting each of the following as His Blessings, and as the supreme law of the land." The text of The Blessing, with its strange combination of vague generalities and specific normative standards, thus entered the US Code as federal law.

Within hours of the vote and presidential signature, in a strategy orchestrated by TW, every possible class of plaintiff with a legal complaint against The Blessing—non-evangelical Christian groups, non-Christian churches, states and municipalities, judges, unions, businesses, and individuals—filed more than 2,500 lawsuits in every state and in every federal district court in the country, challenging each one of the fifty Blessings on multiple grounds. It was a massive effort to pull together and execute in two weeks. This had been my job. I persuaded the most prominent lawyers and firms in the country to appear as counsel of record, including every living former head of the American Bar Association and the deans and senior faculty of every major law school. Together, the various lawsuits sought immediate stays of the effectiveness of, and any action predicated on, The Blessing as well as seeking eventual determinations that the purported federal law should be invalidated. My job was to be sure that every possible legal basis for challenge was being advanced and that every relevant jurisdiction and court was engaged.

True to the pattern set by Jordan from the day he first walked in the side door of Sarah Palin's White House, he allowed the nation to revert to a strained calm following the tumultuous two weeks preceding the vote on The Blessing. The stays we requested from the courts had in almost every instance been granted, so The Blessing had no legal effect and, for the moment, people's lives were not changed.

During this lull, Sanjay made a close study of Jordan's cabinet and subcabinet-level appointments to better understand the administration's most likely next moves. Jordan had appointed the globally popular evangelical preacher and author Rick Warren (author of *The Purpose Driven Life* and its many spin-offs and franchises) to be the secretary of Health and Human Services. It was one of a number of celebrity appointments made by the new President. *Time* magazine noted that it was the most media-savvy cabinet ever assembled, with the great majority having risen to prominence through media-centric careers in the now nearly unified realms of journalism, entertainment, and politics. Each of these cabinet appointees had compelling personal narratives, an uncanny knack for pandering to the narcissism of the American public, a deep knowledge of how to peddle the fantasies for which America thirsted, and a profound mastery of celebrity style. Five cabinet secretaries, *Time* reported, had appeared on reality television shows. I remember the comment by another journalist that I thought particularly revealing at the time. She said that the Jordan cabinet marked the triumph of personality over character.

A few days into his study of Jordan's appointments, Sanjay made a strange and disturbing discovery. A federal office for the promotion and coordination of "faith-based initiatives" had been established under President Bush and, although not eliminated, was strangely inactive during both of Sarah Palin's two terms. President Jordan, during the transition, chose the evangelical preacher and popular revisionist historian David Barton to head the Office of Faith-Based Initiatives. Sanjay was one of the few people to focus on the Jordan administration's lower-ranking appointments to that agency. He discovered, to his surprise, not the usual group of evangelical pastors who had delivered key precincts for the party but a strange mix of MIT-trained computer scientists, Chinese software engineers, and web consultants who had worked for the governments of Iran and Saudi Arabia. Most of the Palin appointees to the faith-based office had been summarily dismissed following the transition, and the two most disgruntled of them spoke to Sanjay's sources. Over a period of two months, Sanjay pieced together the story, discovering that Barton had assembled a team of the world's leading experts on Internet censorship. The credentials and experience of these new employees of the faith-based office included the development of efatwa.com (a site for obtaining Islamic religious rulings online); the invention of the algorithms for China's famously sensitive and flexible web censorship; and the development, for the infamous Saudi religious police, of the software for the monitoring and integration of all security cameras in the kingdom (this software allowed for the automated detection of activities—such as single women driving cars or couples kissing in public—that were forbidden under the kingdom's version of sharia). This project, dubbed by the code name Purity Web, was under the personal supervision of the president, with Barton as his chief lieutenant. What exactly the goal of the project was, Sanjay could not say, but when he revealed all he had found out, there was a firestorm in the media, and the president himself had to appear on F3 to explain.

"This," said President Jordan, with the customary cross over one shoulder and flag over the other, "will be a wholly modern presidency. I just cannot understand the fuss. What do they think—that religious people are stuck in the Middle Ages? God commands us to use all the tools at our disposal, and I have always been completely transparent about that. In 2008, when Ralph Reed and I were growing the Faith & Freedom Coalition, we were absolutely clear that we were not going to cede web-based organizing, web-based fund-raising, and techno-savvy political action to the liberals. You may remember that all of our original Faith & Freedom chapters were virtual. Ralph said then that the Internet's first wave was e-mail, that the next wave was social networking, and that there was going to be a third wave. Well, that's what we said in 2008, and that's what we are doing today. We are figuring out that third wave—how to use technology to perfect our democracy, to ensure more perfect freedom, and to advance our country toward its destiny as Christ's Kingdom on Earth."

The F3 interviewer of course neglected to ask why the architects of Chinese web censorship and surveillance by the Saudi religious police were appropriate choices "to ensure more perfect freedom." But Sanjay and I did ask. We asked loudly and persistently. We pointed out that as a result of 9/11 and 7/22, the federal government had access to an almost comprehensive video surveillance infrastructure. Without it having been announced, debated, or budgeted, fifteen years after 9/11 we found ourselves with web-linked cameras covering all our major city streets, factories, offices, schools, shopping centers, and virtually all other places of public assembly. Moreover, our traditional distaste as Americans for any kind of surveillance seemed to have evaporated. Reality television shows like *Big Brother* and *Survivor* had glamorized the idea of life under the unblinking eye of the camera.

Our campaign succeeded in causing vague disquiet among many people, but without more of an understanding of what the Purity Web was really all about, we were unable to use it as an effective tool against the administration. By the time Jordan went public with the Purity Web during the Holy War, it was of course too late. Jordan's long-promised Internet third wave now seems so obvious and so inevitable that I find it difficult to understand how we failed to figure it out in 2016.

After a lull of about six weeks, with The Blessing still completely tied up in court, the administration announced the first of a series of "implementing regulations" under The Blessing, this one under Covenant V dealing with marriage. The regulation was titled "On Sexual Deviancy." We understood later that, following extensive debate, the administration was persuaded not to refer publicly to the "homosexual problem" because of its deep and disturbing echoes of the use by the Nazis of the phrase "Jewish problem." The "regulation," which was promulgated as a presidential order without compliance with the public hearing and other procedures normally required for a federal regulation, was straightforward. All homosexuals would be required to register with the federal government within 90 days and, for their own protection, to be tested for AIDS: "a long-overdue public health measure for the good of those who choose the homosexual lifestyle," explained President Jordan. Although The Blessing stated that "Homosexual behavior of any sort is a crime," the "regulation" did not set forth the penalties for homosexual behavior, noting that determination of appropriate punishment would be up to each of the states. The Farris Commission, however, simultaneously promulgated a paper from biblical scholars stating that the second covenant, recognizing the higher authority of biblical law, ought to be read to require states to re-impose the death penalty for the crime of sodomy.

The balance of the "regulation" was remarkable for its insidious cruelty to the gay population. First, no benefits, such as pension rights or health benefits, could be extended by employers to the partners of homosexuals, even those purported to be married, and any such benefits already vested were forfeit. Second, all gay adoptions were summarily voided, with special panels of pastors and Christian doctors set up to review each situation, with a strong presumption that the children of single men and male couples must be returned to social services. There was an exemption for children over age five living with female couples *if* the family were living as Christians and willing to submit to the ongoing supervision of the panel. Finally, no will, contract, health care proxy, or power of attorney would be enforceable if it afforded one gay person rights or discretion in relation to another.

Although this regulation was also immediately challenged in the courts, gay people, especially those with children, were terrified. Gays with children felt they couldn't risk even the coastal sanctuaries of San Francisco, Boston, and New York and began a gradual exodus to Canada and Europe, marking the beginning of the debates there about the granting of refugee status to gays fleeing America.

Gays without families had been steadily leaving the heartland since the raft of state anti-gay laws at the beginning of Palin's second term, but after the Deviancy Regulation, the exodus of gays from middle America accelerated sharply. Many of those states were amazed to discover the number of gay households in their midst, and shocked that home prices fell sharply as large numbers of residences, sometimes up to 10 percent of the housing units in an area, flooded onto the market. Sanjay and I figured out what had happened. By requiring all homosexuals to register with the federal government, the option of remaining a closeted homosexual disappeared. The presumption that single people over a certain age must be gay, as well as wild rumors about tests that had been developed to determine sexual orientation, led many to conclude that they inevitably would be "outed" under the new regime. Men and women who had given no indication of homosexuality— some in heterosexual marriages and others masquerading as divorced or separated from heterosexual partners—feared for the first time that discretion would be no protection from the wave of anti-gay violence and persecution coming their way.

Again taking New York's lead, eight state governors immediately affirmed their own state's statutes permitting all that the federal Deviancy Regulation purportedly prohibited, and they promised to recognize and honor marriages, adoptions, health care proxies, wills, powers of attorney, and contracts entered into by gays under the laws of other states if brought to their states for enforcement. The US Chamber of Commerce tersely noted that for its members to deny employees vested benefits would expose them to litigation and liability and thus refused to do so until the legal situation was clarified.

The week after the Deviancy Regulation took effect, the country was shocked when an eighteen-year-old gay man, a quiet Buddhist monk who had come to America as a refugee from Myanmar, immolated himself on Pennsylvania Avenue in front of the White House. Or, to be more accurate, only that part of the country was shocked that had access to television, web, or newspapers not controlled by F3. The millions of Americans for whom F3-controlled media outlets were their sole or primary source of news never knew that it happened.

*   *   *

I STOPPED WRITING this afternoon, haunted by the image of the young monk who burned himself alive on a quiet summer day in the capital. Suddenly, I could see again the horrifying video clip. I remembered his beautiful name, Banya Vamsa. I remembered his story. He was a quiet and earnest young man, persecuted by the military regime in Myanmar for his politics, his religion, and his sexual orientation. His whole short life had revolved around a seemingly impossible dream, the dream of America, a place of sanctuary and freedom. And then, thanks to a small community of Buddhist nuns outside Atlanta, the impossible dream became real. I cried today, thinking of his anguish when the America of his dreams betrayed him. For a moment this afternoon, it seemed to me sadder than the collective anguish of the country in the decade that followed.

Remembering the young monk, it suddenly occurred to me to wonder what Sanjay had felt while all this was happening. I never asked him. Was *he* afraid? How could he not have been? I realize now that we never talked about it. What was he thinking when we were watching the video of the young man burning alive? No one in the country had less reason for guilt, but I imagine that Sanjay would have felt some sense of responsibility. I imagine him now, comparing himself to the young man and wondering whether the monk had more foresight, more courage, or more goodness than he did. I can easily see him having some inchoate sense that he, Sanjay, should have stood in the monk's place. And what did I do or say? I remember the conversation.

"Awful," I said. "Can we use it? How will it poll? San, what do you think, will it matter?"

"It has to matter," he said. And that was all we said. I should have said more.

Although TW's main hope was to stall the implementation of The Blessing through a massive onslaught of litigation, we never gave up trying to help all Americans to understand what was happening. One of our strategies during this year was to let the American people see themselves through the eyes of those outside the United States. Americans always have had enormous pride in their country and tend to become anxious and unhappy when the country is criticized or derided by others. During the two terms of Sarah Palin, the position of America in the eyes of the world had deteriorated steadily. As a result of the McCain corpse debacle during the first moments of her presidency, Palin had lost any claim to being taken seriously as a leader on the world stage. The leaders of our allies and foes alike were coldly proper when meeting the US president on international occasions, but she had been completely frozen out of those parts of meetings like the G8 and the G20, where the leaders hammered out economic and political deals. The president did not mind. On more than one occasion, usually mis-citing one of the Founding Fathers, she argued that her place was at home and that she was merely obeying George Washington's famous injunction to avoid misguided foreign entanglements. She had, she said repeatedly, finally and firmly stopped our slow, steady slide toward a global currency and the maturation of the United Nations into a world government—strange claims that seemed to constitute the entirety of her administration's foreign policy apart from its steadfast support of Israel, or, as she usually put it, "the necessity of a biblical Israel." The leaders of Israel returned the favor but always looked a bit uncomfortable when the president let slip, as she often did, that the sole reason for America's defense of Israel was to fulfill the biblical conditions for the rapture of the Christian church and the apocalypse to follow.

But America after Jordan's New Freedom was viewed as something else altogether. The leaders of Europe, and of our allies in Japan, South Korea, and Taiwan, were profoundly alarmed. The people of Europe had finally lost their long-standing cultural affinity with Americans, due primarily to religious differences. As early as 2011, when 60 percent of Americans said that God "played an important part in their lives," only 20 percent of Europeans held this view. Could the United States under President Jordan really sustain its "special relationship" with Britain, where 45 percent of those polled positively denied the existence of a God? Fashionable books in Britain and the rest of Europe spoke now of the threat of religious fundamentalism in America in the same breath as the Islamofascism that was being embraced by so many of the Muslim minorities scattered throughout the continent. TW streamed these views into the US market, hoping that moderate Christians would be alarmed by the gradual isolation of the country from all its traditional friends and allies other than Israel. It didn't seem to help.

Looking ahead to various possible outcomes of the fight over implementation of The Blessing, and concerned about the authoritarian flavor of the president's still inchoate Purity Web project, Sanjay and I thought it was time to tackle the issue of violence and the potential use of violent force head-on. If we won in the courts, Jordan might well choose to deploy the Christian militias to foment chaos and violence, thus provoking an excuse to use martial law and do an end run around the ordinary judiciary. So on Labor Day weekend in 2017, Sanjay and I—this time with a large team from TW and a pool of reporters from the national press—visited Oklahoma, where, eight years before, Sanjay had been among the first to publicize the rise of a violent and aggressive strain of conservative Christianity. We thought that the holiday weekend would be an appropriate time to try to get the entire nation focused on the rapid development of a domestic army sworn to implement the theocratic vision. For years the militias in Oklahoma had failed to persuade the state legislature to formally recognize them as an "unorganized militia" under the Second Amendment. But in March of that year, the Oklahoma legislature finally acted. The state sanctioned something now called simply the Christian Militia (a change from only eight years before, when they were called Liberty Boys or Freedom Fighters). When asked what was the mission of the newly recognized "unorganized" militia, the sponsor of the Oklahoma bill replied, "to eradicate evil."

Dozens of red states quickly followed suit, and by summer hundreds of thousands of men (there were no women) were spending every weekend marching, drilling, training, displaying their weapons, and preparing to defend the Christian Nation and The Blessing from gays, abortion doctors, communists, Muslims, liberals, immigrants, and elites. The militia exercises usually started with a loud pledge to the "Christian flag," which first became popular after Dan Quayle was reported to have recited it in 1994: "I pledge allegiance to the Christian flag, and to the Savior, for whose Kingdom it stands. One savior, crucified, risen and coming again, with life and liberty for all who believe."

Rallying in Oklahoma City with a ragtag collection of secularists, humanists, lawyers, and other opponents of The Blessing, we asked the media to focus on the fact that "liberty" and "freedom" had been dropped from the names of these militias and all these armed men were now simply "Christians," sworn not to protect our liberty or even the Constitution but now sworn officially to "defend the Christian Nation and the covenants of The Blessing" and, unofficially, to "eradicate evil." We asked everyone to listen closely to the pledge to the Christian flag, which substitutes "life and liberty *for all who believe*" for the traditional "liberty and justice for all." Could it be more clear, we asked, that Jordan and his supporters had now turned their backs on the Constitution they long claimed to venerate? Could it be more clear that they were betraying the conservative and American values of personal freedom and limited government? Could not everyone see the sort of hypocrisy foreshadowed by the Terri Schiavo affair, with the proper scope and role of government depending entirely on who controlled it and on the ends for which it was being deployed? Limited government was all well and good when liberal elites were in control and pursuing a liberal agenda; but look at how quickly the federal government ceased to be a target for disdain once it was firmly in fundamentalist control and dedicated to the implementation of their theocratic vision.

We asked every American of good faith to consider the implications of having an armed national militia outside the control of our professional military and law enforcement, a militia dedicated to ending the freedoms of conscience, worship, speech, and privacy for all who did not embrace their fundamentalist views. Where, we asked, would this be stopped and how and by whom? There was only one answer, we argued. It could be stopped only if each and every American of good will rose up and proclaimed that intolerance would not be tolerated, and defended our constitutional democracy with the same vigor that they would defend their families from physical assault. And yes, if you want to know if by "vigor" we meant necessary violence, yes. This was a large and difficult step for Sanjay, who by nature was entirely nonviolent.

When Sanjay and I returned to New York with the TW team, we received a vivid reminder that martial law was still in effect. All the Oklahoma-based organizers of the rally at which we spoke were arrested by federal troops the next day, without explanation to their families except that they were being detained under martial law powers and that military tribunals would hear their cases. This was a first. During the second Palin administration, the federal military was slow to employ its martial law powers. Initially, troops made some high-profile detentions of illegal immigrants, who were generally deported without hearings or other legal nicety. Then Muslims, including US citizens, began to be arrested on grounds of "national security" and detained in special Guantanamo-like facilities established for domestic terrorism suspects in Alabama and Wyoming. Shamefully, the legacy of 7/22 was such that there was little public outcry against this practice. But, to our knowledge, neither administration had before used its martial law powers against political opponents or outspoken critics of the Christian Nation. And now, when Sanjay and I were safely home in New York, all the dissidents whom we had put in the national spotlight were arrested and, effectively, "disappeared." Sanjay held another press conference denouncing the arrests, as did the governors of a dozen other states and every remaining independent member of Congress. But these protests had no impact. Shortly after we returned to New York, I said to Sanjay, for the first time, that I feared that the situation might be irreversible. Tonight I remembered exactly what he said in reply.

"Just remember, G, there are battles and there are wars. And even nations that win wars do not stay on top forever. Nothing is irreversible."

CHAPTER THIRTEEN

Secession

2017

> *The central conservative truth is that it is culture, not politics, that determines the success of a society. The central liberal truth is that politics can change a culture and save it from itself.*
>
> —Senator Daniel Patrick Moynihan

IT WAS A SHORT AND PLEASANT WALK from TW's offices near the World Trade Center, up Broadway and through City Hall Park to the Daniel Patrick Moynihan Federal Courthouse on Pearl Street. The sky was that spectacularly clear September blue that New Yorkers who were there in 2001 will forever associate with 9/11. In addition to the sky, what I most remember about our walk is the superficial impression of profound normality. Wall Streeters queued at their favorite coffee carts, and bike messengers weaved in and out of traffic. Female bankers in expensive shoes climbed the steps from the subway with young Indian software engineers and Jamaican secretaries. We watched an angry Russian limo driver scream profanities at a Sikh cabby while the Russian's passenger sat in the backseat reading the *Times*, unperturbed. Normal. And yet there we were, on our way to hear a federal judge deliver the first decision arising out of our many challenges to a statute whose existence—only ten years before—would have been unimaginable. This unimaginable thing had happened, and yet everyone was acting normally.

Of course, I remember thinking, the unimaginable happens. I in particular knew that. I was a person with two parents and a sister and, suddenly, I was an orphan without siblings. Unimaginable. I thought of those who had walked up this stretch of Broadway before me. Could the Native Americans whose ancestors reaped the riches of Mannahatta for forty generations have imagined the smelly, disease-ridden white men who sailed into the harbor on great floating birds with white wings and put an end to their civilization? Could the Dutch citizens of this island have imagined that overnight, without a shot fired, the burghers of New Amsterdam would become subjects of the British crown? Could the crowd watching George Washington's inauguration as the republic's first president have imagined that in a little more than a century, the ragtag collection of colonies would surpass the great historic global empires of England, France, and Spain as the world's new superpower? Could the commuters in Lower Manhattan on the morning of September 10, 2001, have possibly imagined that a day later the Twin Towers would be gone, three thousand of their neighbors dead, Lower Manhattan in flames, not a plane in the sky, and the world again changed forever? Nothing seems more inevitable than the status quo, and yet nothing is more certain than that it will—eventually—end suddenly and that we will need to make our lives in a new, unfamiliar and unexpected landscape.

★   ★   ★

HEADING TO COURT that morning, we were both exasperated and comforted by the relentless, reckless normality all around us on the street.

"You worried?" I asked Sanjay.

"Not unless you are," he replied. "You told me that this was one we really could not lose. You told me that Denny Chin was the right judge. You told me that we were fantastically lucky that the first challenge on the merits was Blessing One. So no, I am not worried."

I was worried. It was true that the best lawyers in the country were responsible for the tsunami of litigation that we had unleashed in the federal and state courts. And we were relieved that most courts promptly issued a "stay"—an order preventing the challenged legislation from coming into effect pending resolution of the challenge on its merits. But the real test would come when the courts addressed the substantive question of whether or not the law should be invalidated due to its conflict with the Constitution, or some other deficiency.

We were on our way that morning to hear the first of those substantive decisions on the "merits." The case dealt with the first Blessing: "As the fate of the nation depends entirely on unbending obedience to the will of God, it shall be treasonous to deny the existence of God, to question the Word of God, or to advocate disobedience to the will of God." This first Blessing was, from a constitutional and legal perspective, particularly egregious. Of course making it treasonous to deny the existence of God violated the separation clause, the Bill of Rights, the Ninth and Fourteenth Amendments, and a raft of other constitutional protections. The Supreme Court's elimination of the right of privacy in its *Gonzales* decision made the constitutional challenge more complicated but still easy to establish. In addition, as a federal statute, its form was deficient in almost every respect in which a law could be deficient. Although evangelicals believed that the Word of God and will of God were somehow objectively ascertainable, presumably through reference to the Bible, as the basis for criminal treason, the concepts were fatally vague and uncertain. Moreover—putting aside the issues of whether God is a real or an imaginary being, and which "God" is being referred to—a crime consisting of "questioning" God's "Word" and "advocating disobedience" to His "will" would be impossible to apply and adjudicate consistently and equitably. The US solicitor general obviously had struggled with his defense of the legislation. The government's brief, among other things, had argued that The Blessing did not specify which "God" was being referred to and therefore could not be viewed as establishing any particular religion.

It was my former partners at RCD&S whom I chose to bring this particular case. There were no smarter, more thorough, or more strategic litigators in the country. I suspected they would come up with a brief that wove together dozens of grounds for objection, virtually ensuring that even if the court rejected some of our arguments, a dozen more would survive, and survive appellate review. I was right. The case they developed was brilliantly tactical—relying not only on the best arguments from a legal perspective but the principles and lines of authority that were most deeply embedded in constitutional jurisprudence, with the result that an appellate judge or a hostile Supreme Court tempted to reject the principle or overturn the line of authority would be forced to undermine dozens of other Supreme Court decisions vital or convenient to the fundamentalist Christian cause.

The street outside the courthouse was packed with media and a large group of protestors bussed in from a Pennsylvania mega-church, who knelt in prayer and held signs with crudely painted messages, including "Judges who reject Christ will Burn in Hell Forever," "Give us Real Freedom," "Christians will not be victims anymore," and "The people have spoken, get out of the way." As Sanjay approached, the crowd first quieted, and then the pastor rose from his knees, pointed dramatically at Sanjay, and yelled "Antichrist!" The congregation joined in with yells of "Satan." Sanjay's bodyguards scanned the crowd nervously, their hands hovering near their hidden holsters. Sanjay stopped and paused for a moment, and then turned to walk directly toward the preacher. The flustered minister lowered his pointing arm and went silent. Surrounded by TV cameras and microphones, Sanjay extended his hand and the man, out of reflex, shook it.

"Pastor," Sanjay said, "countless Americans have died to defend your right and my right to believe what we wish to believe, to worship in the manner we desire, and to practice our religions freely. Will you join me in a prayer of thanks?" The pastor was speechless. "Thank you, Pastor," Sanjay continued after the briefest pause. "Let us pray." Like a deer caught in headlights, the pastor had no choice but to bow his head. His previously rowdy congregation became silent. "Let us remember the dark days when our forefathers in the Old World were forced to conform to the religion and beliefs of their monarch. Let us remember the thirst for freedom that drove them across the ocean. Let us remember and give thanks for the brave men and women who have defended our republic and its freedoms against every assault. Let us give thanks that our fathers and mothers in the last century were prepared to give all they had to defeat fascism and communism, systems that tried to tell us what to believe and what to think and to control every aspect of our behavior and lives. We give thanks for having been delivered from these great evils. And may we meet today and go forward from this place in the spirit of Jesus, whose radical commandments to love our enemies, to love the sinner, and to turn the other cheek have shown us the only path to peace and justice in this world. Amen."

A smattering of uncertain "Amens" echoed from the congregation. Sanjay gave the pastor his warmest smile, shook his hand again, turned, and walked into the courthouse.

I was nearly as thunderstruck as were the pastor, his flock, and the press. I had never heard Sanjay utter a prayer, and thought that his scruples would have prevented him from addressing a supplication to God, which, so far as I could tell, he regarded as a wholly imaginary being. It took me only moments to realize that the prayer, though it took the form of a supplication, was not expressly addressed to the deity or anyone in particular. Instead, it was a simple invocation of collective memory and of collective gratitude. Prayer, Sanjay later told an interviewer, was a singularly important and powerful thing, and something on which Christianity had no monopoly. Like meditation, it caused us to pause, focus, and turn inward and to organize and express our thoughts and desires. It was a meditation on desire and happiness and our relationship to the world, fate, time, and one another. When done in a group, it defined community. It was cathartic, energizing, and calming. All these benefits, he noted, were fully realized whether or not the prayer was addressed to, heard, or answered by a supernatural being.

His gesture to the Pennsylvania pastor captured the daily news cycle and initially threw F3 into a rare state of confusion. F3 first cycled through a series of explanations: the prayer was a cynical exploitation of people's faith that was typical of the Antichrist; the prayer was a staged event where the purported pastor and congregation were really fronts for TW; the prayer and reference to Jesus were evidence of the Holy Spirit having descended for a brief moment, overcoming the power of Satan and illuminating Sanjay's mind with the power of Christ. But when a couple of ministers giving unscripted interviews said they thought Sanjay's prayer was a useful reminder that those building the Christian Nation must not overstep their bounds and interfere with the freedom of conscience and freedom of worship of other faiths, F3 simply dropped the entire episode and pretended that it had never happened.

The other networks, in their coverage of the incident, decided they needed to explain to their audiences Sanjay's references to "fascism" and "communism" and why Sanjay was implying similarities between those movements and the Christian Nation. This was in response to a flash poll by Pew that revealed that only 8 percent of those Americans polled that afternoon could even vaguely define the word "fascism" and only about 30 percent gave a satisfactory account of communism. I just remembered something that really shocked me that evening. As part of the coverage of Sanjay's prayer, CNN reporters interviewed high school students across the country about the cataclysmic events of the twentieth century. A polite, well-spoken girl from Iowa was introduced as a "straight-A" student and asked whom America had fought in the Second World War. "Uh, I'm pretty sure it was the Jews, right?" she answered. And there you had it. Only seventy-two years after the end of World War II, the identity of the enemy, the phenomenon of fascism, and even the Holocaust itself all had been erased from the cultural memory of the new generation of America's middle class. All the confused straight-A student knew is that it all had something to do with the Jews.

This confrontation with the Pennsylvania pastor was typical of Sanjay at the height of his power. Had it been conceived and planned in advance, it would have been a brilliantly strategic move, well designed to advance our cause. But it wasn't. It was even stronger by virtue of being completely spontaneous and authentic. Viewers could tell, when Sanjay paused before turning, that he was acting on instinct. They knew that his desire to reach out and connect was genuine. They saw that Sanjay truly believed that he had more in common with the pastor than differences. And, importantly, they accepted that his admiration for Jesus and his message was real. This was the Sanjay whom the country saw in action almost daily during that year. He was disarming, charming, authentic, earnest, modest, and compelling. And—unlike any politician and most other charismatic public figures—his motivation was completely free of ambition or greed. Charisma when turned to the good is a powerful thing. And yes, had he really been the Antichrist, he would have been a superb one.

Inside the courthouse, Sanjay and I sat behind the RCD&S legal team, who greeted us cordially. I have to say that all awkwardness with my former firm had disappeared. I had become the alumnus of whom they were most proud, and my association with the firm and its resulting leading role in pro bono support of the anti-Blessing movement now made it the firm of choice for law students anxious to have the chance to do something to avert the disaster.

Judge Denny Chin mounted the bench. He was an enormously respected jurist who was widely expected to have been elevated to the Court of Appeals but was bypassed during both terms of the Palin administration. Judge Chin read his decision from the bench. Within moments I realized he had adopted the arguments in the plaintiffs' brief almost as written. It was a complete victory on every front. He was scathing in his denunciation of The Blessing as a strange beast, wholly decoupled from our long tradition of common law, jurisprudence, and civics; he said it was ignorant of and in violent conflict with the Constitution; and he stated that he considered it to be a thing whose very structure and substance betrayed a deliberate and broad authoritarian program, anathema not only to the Constitution and the law but to Western civilization itself.

This afternoon at my desk, the feelings of that day—not the memory of them but the actual feelings—seemed to replay themselves from a recording buried deep in my gut. I felt again feelings of jubilation and vindication so profound that I could not stay seated in front of the typewriter. I paced up and down the edge of the lake, realizing that it had been one of the happiest days in my life and reveling in the feelings of accomplishment that the memory had unleashed.

Although we had dared to hope for this type of decision, we had underestimated the impact it would have. A respected federal judge had not only analyzed the myriad legal shortcomings of The Blessing in learned detail but also called out the administration and Congress on their motives and predicted the inevitable political outcome were The Blessing allowed to stand. All the mainstream media's carefully measured rhetoric, respectful speech when talking about the president and Congress, and dedication to covering "both sides" now evaporated, and the independent media conveyed the sense of historic urgency that TW had promoted since the election. From that day on, the media and coastal public treated Sanjay as a prophet whose lone voice had suddenly been vindicated and validated and to whose predictions they now accorded a presumption of truth. It was a privileged but dangerous position.

No historians, of course, have been able to look inside the Jordan White House, analyze the original source materials, and illuminate the decision making that then occurred. I have no idea whether they considered other courses, whether more moderate Republicans urged caution or whether brave men and women refused to go along with the plan ultimately adopted and paid with their careers and/or their lives. All this I don't know. What I do know is that the two weeks following Judge Chin's decision were the only good weeks in the year 2017. During those weeks, two additional federal judges, one in Illinois and one in California, released equally favorable decisions. We were ecstatic, and once again a number of pundits began to declare The Blessing "dead on arrival," and to predict that the House would be retaken by a non-evangelical majority the next year, and that the Jordan administration would be seen by history as one of those strange quirks of American culture that was quickly overwhelmed by the strength and soundness of America's constitutional architecture, rule of law, and judiciary.

But instead the story took a very different turn. Two weeks to the day following Judge Chin's decision, with no media present but F3, the chairman of the House Committee on the Judiciary tabled resolutions of impeachment against the three federal judges whose decisions against The Blessing already had been released. The minority members of the committee and staff scrambled for their phones to alert the media and their leadership. The majority counsel outlined the case in about ten minutes. Despite numerous motions and protests, the chairman called for a vote. The minority rose from their seats and walked out of the room as the chairman called the roll and obtained the required majority to report the articles of impeachment to the full House. Later that afternoon, with the minority having exhausted its parliamentary options, the articles were approved by the full House and "managers" of the impeachments appointed to present the case to the Senate.

Jim Lehrer opened his *NewsHour* that night with the report that the United States had experienced the first stages of a "constitutional coup d'état." The Senate majority leader referred the article to a special Impeachment Trial Committee and allowed the three judges exactly one week to prepare for their trial. Since the matters in contention were of a legal and not factual nature, each trial was short, and all three proceedings had been decided by the following week. The committee recommended conviction to the full Senate. Exactly four weeks after Sanjay and I sat in the Moynihan Courthouse and listened to Judge Chin's decision, he was convicted by the required two-thirds vote in the full Senate, whereupon he immediately and automatically forfeited his office. Impeachment convictions by the Senate are not justiciable matters, and thus no review by the Supreme Court was possible. It was done and could not be undone.

Not only was it done, but the Speaker of the House and the majority leader of the Senate appeared together and made clear that any other district or appellate judge similarly overturning The Blessing or its implementing law or regulations on purportedly constitutional grounds would suffer the same fate. The impeachable offense of which Chin and the others had been convicted was acting beyond the scope of their authority and thus having treasonously attempted to usurp power committed by the Constitution to the people and their representatives in Congress. Therefore, the congressional leaders explained, any judge doing the same would be impeached and convicted in expedited proceedings as the basic legal issue—whether or not blocking The Blessing on constitutional grounds was improper—had already been decided by the Congress. They had no interest, they said, in continuing the impeachments, and noted that in other cases impeachment had been an effective deterrent to similar errors by an overactive judiciary.

I was mortified that I had not seen this coming, and I could not forgive myself for having failed to do something proactive to preempt the impeachment strategy. After all, the far right, and the Christian right in particular, had advocated impeachment of "activist" and "liberal" judges for decades. The idea gained a significant popular following after the *Romer v. Evans* decision in 1996 (overturning a Colorado referendum conflicting with gay rights) and a similar case in California. And the idea moved from Christian blogs to mainstream Republican policy when the then-House majority whip Tom DeLay had called for impeachment of "left-leaning" federal judges.

Back in 1997, this overt threat of impeachment, intended as a deterrent, had deeply alarmed the legal establishment. Seventy-five bar association presidents and 104 law school deans wrote an open letter to House Speaker Newt Gingrich protesting "proposals to initiate impeachment proceedings against federal judges who have rendered politically unpopular decisions in cases or controversies properly before them." The American Bar Association (ABA) set up a special commission, and in his farewell letter to the bar, ABA President N. Lee Cooper noted:

> *[DeLay] was clear on his reasons in seeking these judges' impeachment. It was not corruption; it was not that the judges were involved in illegal or unethical activities; it was not that the judges committed*

treason, accepted bribes, committed "high crimes and misdemeanors" as required by the Constitution as grounds for impeachment. No, the reason the Majority Whip targeted these specific judges for impeachment was because he and other members of Congress disagreed with one decision rendered by each of the judges.

In response, the Christian right establishment was unrepentant and became firm in its belief that only impeachment could remove the judicial impediments to implementation of their highest priority social and cultural agenda. The Christian law schools devoted themselves to exhaustive studies of the history of impeachment. They cited seventeenth-century precedents under which usurpation of authority (through upholding constitutional challenges to popular legislation) was found to be "treasonous." They selectively cited the Federalist Papers to establish that the Founding Fathers intended "high crimes and misdemeanors" to include "disregard of the public interest," "affronting the will of the people," and "seizing the role of policy-maker." They argued that under Article III of the Constitution, a federal judge served only "during good Behaviour," thus providing a broad alternative basis for removal. To a public unschooled in the Constitution and constitutional jurisprudence, this all seemed to have logic and common sense on its side. If the people decided in a fair referendum that no government entity in Colorado should treat gays as a "protected class," then who but some out-of-touch elitist from the coast could think it was democracy to have an unelected judge say they were wrong?

But even with all the groundwork laid over decades by the Christian right, it is not clear to me that the Senate—even with the conservative Republicans holding the necessary two-thirds majority—would have had the courage to cross this line and impeach honest and respected federal judges had the Constitution Restoration Act not specifically provided that it was an impeachable offense for a federal court to hear any case concerning a government's or official's "acknowledgment of God as the sovereign source of law, liberty, or government." No reasonable lawyer believed that considering the constitutionality of The Blessing in a case properly brought before the court constituted "treason, bribery, or other High Crimes or misdemeanors" (the standard for impeachment in Article II, Section 4 of the Constitution). But that is exactly what the Senate decided in its conviction of all three judges. That the Senate's decision was erroneous did not matter. There was one thing that the fundamentalist lawyers got right: under the Constitution, the correctness or incorrectness of conviction by the Senate was a "political question" not subject to review by the courts. There was no appeal.

The euphoria in the red states at the long-sought "reining-in" of "activist judges" was exceeded only by the gloom in New York. There were only two possibilities: Either the threat of impeachment would cause a significant number of judges to rule against us, or, if a judge bravely stayed the course and rejected one of the planks of The Blessing, he or she promptly would be removed from office and replaced with a reliable Christian conservative. Either way, we lost. Only a month following the euphoria of our initial success, we knew our legal attack against The Blessing was bound to fail.

After the collapse of our litigation strategy, there was little for me to do other than to monitor developments and advise Sanjay and, increasingly, the ad hoc group of governors opposed to The Blessing about what it all meant. At my suggestion, we started hosting weekly phone calls with the gubernatorial staffs from ten influential states with sympathetic governors: Massachusetts, New York, Vermont, Maryland, Illinois, Connecticut, California, Maine, Washington, and Minnesota. After the impeachments, most of the Governors themselves participated in the conference calls. It was through those calls that I became better acquainted with Mike Bloomberg, the longtime mayor of New York City to whom the state's voters turned in 2016, instinctively understanding that a man of proven competence was required to navigate what clearly were going to be myriad challenges for New York under a Jordan presidency.

They were prescient. In addition to competence, experience, and a first-class team around him, the governor had two things that no other state governor did. First was money. The governor's personal fortune had increased during his return to the private sector, and despite hyper-active philanthropy his foundation had billions of dollars from which to provide funding to public initiatives that would otherwise have strained the state's chronically overextended budget. The second was his own media base. It wasn't the broad and ubiquitous behemoth that F3 had become, but Bloomberg LLP was a major global media company with savvy professional journalists and a team of sophisticated web techni-cians and engineers.

Just before Thanksgiving, the governor called me on my cell phone. He asked if I could meet him that evening at his town house on 72nd Street. I asked if I should bring Sanjay, and he told me that it was me he wanted to see.

A formally dressed butler opened the door to the governor's town house and directed me upstairs. I was amused that, instead of having an English, pseudo-English, or otherwise posh or affected accent, the but-ler spoke in the thickest Brooklynese. The governor was seventy-four years old, but he looked younger and seemed to me as vigorous as when he had stepped down as mayor of the city. The governor skipped the pleasantries and asked me to leave TW and come work for him. He said he needed a lawyer, but someone who was an experienced and committed foe of the theocratic effort. He said there was no other candidate and that he would pay me whatever I wanted. I surprised myself by saying yes immediately. We talked long into the night, and I was impressed at the deep consideration he had given to the various possible outcomes of the current struggle. He was a man who was thinking ahead. He was also a man who was highly motivated.

"Greg, these fuckers are monsters . . . Nazis," the governor said at one point during the evening. "You gotta understand this is not about religion or rights or law, this is about people. Yesterday I sent the jet to Topeka. You know why? My cousin Maude has a son who lives there. He's a music teacher, gay, been with his partner for ten years, and they had a little girl together. He's the nicest young man in the world, and they adore the little girl. Maude's son is the biological father. A week ago some official from the Kansas Department for Children and

Families came to the house with the local sheriff and took the child away. The sheriff and some militia thug said that if they complained or came after the girl, they'd both disappear. It's the fucking same thing, Greg. Just like what the Jews went through in Germany. Maude was hysterical. So yesterday I sent the jet with five of my bodyguards. They got the boys safely on board first and then went to the DCF and took the little girl at gunpoint."

I must have looked astonished.

"That's right, just walked in, drew their weapons, and said they were taking the child. I never thought I'd see the day in America. But I'll tell you, it's the single best thing I ever did with my money. They're all back in Fort Washington now with Maude. So we're drawing the line here, Greg. You understand? Make it legal if you can, but one way or another, it's not going to happen again, not on my watch."

I did not call Sanjay when I left the governor's. I did not call him that night. I knew I had done the right thing, but part of me felt I was letting Sanjay down. In bed that night, I thought about my decision to leave RCD&S and Emilie's reaction. This was different, of course, but still I could not shake a bad feeling.

As soon as I arrived at the office the next morning, I told Sanjay what Bloomberg had asked and what I had decided.

"I agree," he said. "There really was no choice. Of course you have to do this. New York and Bloomberg will naturally assume a leadership position among the states in opposition. You can make an enormous difference. You can leverage your skills there in a way that you just cannot do here."

I waited for more, which seemed to puzzle him. He resumed, but this seemed more in response to some expectation of mine as opposed to having something he wanted to say.

"G, you and I have worked so well together because we are some-what different. You know the world and engage with it. You are hap-piest when you have a plan. For me, that sort of engagement is . . . an effort. I am a contemplative person who prefers action that is not directly confrontational. I would rather inspire by personal example.

Unlike me, you are a fighter, and the final stage of this fight will be played out in your arena and not mine."

He stopped talking.

"That's it?" I asked, betraying some annoyance.

He looked confused, mentally checking whether he had missed something.

"It seems clear enough to me, G. You have the chance to advise the man who may be our last chance to stop them. Do you disagree?"

"No . . . but I did think you might at least try to talk me out of it, you know, to keep me with you at TW."

"Ah. Of course I should have said that I *want* you to stay. I need you, G. I hope you know that I will always need you. Do you know that?" he asked, as if it just occurred to him for the first time that I might not. I was too surprised to answer. He continued. "Shall we perhaps start this conversation over?"

I could not help but laugh at his suggestion of a do-over. Almost twenty years and I should know better than to expect the conventional niceties from Sanjay. Two decades of his loyal friendship and I should have been well rid of all the old insecurities. I was San's best friend. Perhaps, come to think of it, his only close friend. Of course he would miss me. And of course he wouldn't, and shouldn't, have to say it.

"San, I'm sorry. Not necessary. Can you imagine, thirty-six years old and an ego still so fragile? Fuck." I rarely used profanities.

"G, this is a big moment. I am sorry to treat it as an easy decision." He paused. "Can I tell you something stupid? Something completely irrational? Sometimes I remember my dreams. I had a dream about us. It was simple. You and I were fireworks, two shells launched at the same time. At first the shell that was me arced higher and burned brighter. Then our trajectories crossed. Yours ascended even higher, and it became clear to me that it would travel much much further. I think, G, that this may be the point where our trajectories cross."

I laughed. "San, the world is in big trouble if you are starting to believe in dreams and portents. In the fireworks department, I can assure you that you may be the shell burning brightly, but I'll never be more than the guy who sets things up and helps light the fuse. But that's fine with me. And if that's what Bloomberg wants, then I'm in."

*   *   *

ONE OF MY first assignments for the governor was to outline all possible legal theories on which New York and other dissenting states could refuse to recognize and apply The Blessing. On my first day at the governor's New York City office on Third Avenue, he called me into his room.

"Greg, you need to understand that the goddamned Blessing will never be enforced in this state as long as I am alive," said the governor. "You understand? It just won't. So what I'm asking you is to find me the best legal face to put on it. I don't care whether it's perfect, or even right, as a legal matter. But when I say to the world that New York and ten to twenty other states simply refuse to recognize the goddamned thing, I will turn to you to tell the world *why* I can do that."

It was richly ironic that much of the work I needed to do for the governor already had been done by our opponents. A succession of conservative Christian scholars had studied over the past decade the knotty problem of how to ignore or disapply federal laws that they did not like. They, of course, had assumed that federal legislation would be liberal and secular and that evangelical-controlled states would be seeking the means to resist its reach into their jurisdictions. The legal solution that they developed was drawn from the old doctrines of "nullification" and "interposition." These two related concepts had been much discussed and debated from the earliest days of the republic. Both doctrines held that if the federal government exceeded its authority and enacted unconstitutional laws, then each state—as a free agent that had entered in the federal compact delegating to the federal government only those powers set forth in the Constitution—has a fundamental right to declare the federal action unconstitutional and prevent its enforcement in that state. Nullification was the fairly straightforward purported right to declare the offending law unconstitutional and thus to nullify its effect in that state. Interposition was a slightly more complicated version of the same theory, in which a state, or multiple states acting together, had the right to interpose a right they had—such as reserved states' rights under the Tenth Amendment, the right to petition Congress, or the right to originate a constitutional amendment—in order to prevent the enforcement of an unconstitutional law. Federal laws disliked by the Christian right, such as laws concerning immigration, education, gun control, discrimination, separation of church and state, hate crimes, and privacy—had been the subject of red state nullification and interposition campaigns for years.

The only problem was that neither one was a valid constitutional doctrine. It had been settled law since the nineteenth century that only the federal courts, and not the state legislatures, were entitled to determine the constitutionality or unconstitutionality of federal legislation. Each of the assertions of nullification or interposition attempted by the southern states prior to the Civil War had failed legally, and the Civil War was thought for many years to have finally put an end to the matter. But the doctrines were revived in the 1950s when ten southern states adopted various versions of nullification and interposition in response to federal civil rights statutes and Supreme Court decisions. The Supreme Court again rejected each such attempt. During the festering decades of the culture wars, these doctrines—repeatedly held to be invalid—were revived with particular energy by the emerging network of evangelical legal "scholars." Remarkably, in 2010 the old theory of nullification emerged from the shadowy world of the more extreme fundamentalist blogs into mainstream legitimacy when Rob Bishop, a Republican from Utah, with the full support of the House Republican leadership, introduced a bill commonly referred to as the "Repeal Amendment." This proposed amendment to the Constitution read, "Any provision of law or regulation of the United States may be repealed by the several states, and such repeal shall be effective when the legislatures of two-thirds of the several states approve resolutions for this purpose that particularly describe the same provision or provisions of law or regulation to be repealed." The amendment, of course, was quietly dropped at the beginning of President Palin's second term, when the movement had already completed the mental shift from seeing the federal government as the liberal and secular enemy to realizing that the federal government would be the instrument for the realization of their dream of a Christian Nation.

It was tempting to cite the doctrines of nullification and interposition in rejecting The Blessing and then to brush aside any objections by referring to decades of arguments in support of those doctrines by those now in power. But I couldn't do that. I was still a lawyer, and I could not advise the governor to act on the basis of a theory that was so clearly invalid. I recoiled at descending to their level. However worthy our ends, they could not justify the means.

Several days later, Governor Bloomberg, surrounded by the governors of twenty-two other states, stood at the base of the Statue of Liberty in New York harbor and announced that each of their respective state legislatures had passed, and the governors had each signed into law, legislation suspending the application and enforcement of The Blessing in their states. The explanation he gave reflected my solution to the conundrum.

"For decades," the governor said, "President Jordan, Justice Moore, most of the members of the Farris Commission, and all the scholars associated with the Christian colleges and law schools proclaimed that each state had the fundamental right to nullify federal legislation that it deemed unconstitutional or improper. They were wrong. They were wrong because it was settled law from the earliest days of the republic, it was settled law after the Civil War, and it was settled law again after the civil rights movement that only the federal courts have the power to determine whether federal legislation is unconstitutional. So instead of following the unlawful path charted by our opponents, we did what the Constitution required. We turned to the federal courts to decide the matter. And, as has been the case so many times before, our federal judges stood firm in favor of the fundamental rights and freedoms of our Constitution, which do and must prevail, no matter how popular, convenient, or compelling the case for overriding them in the name of a purportedly greater good.

"But then," he continued, "for the first time in our national life, the other two branches of our federal government refused to recognize and accept the judgment of their third and co-equal branch, the judiciary. Congress turned to its constitutional power of impeachment to remove those judges, even though it was clear to everyone that the judges' conduct did not constitute 'treason, bribery, or other high crimes or misdemeanors' as required by the Constitution. For that particular misdeed by Congress, our Constitution provides no remedy.

"So," the governor asked, "where does that leave our states and the majority of the American people whom we represent? It is one of the oldest maxims in law that each right must have a remedy. The principle is so ancient and so fundamental that every law student still learns a bit of legal Latin: *Ubi jus ibi remedium*—where there is a right, there is a remedy. It is the cornerstone of what lawyers call equity—the doing of the just or fair thing even if strict application of the law itself does not produce a just or fair result. So when the Constitution provides a preferred remedy that is unavailable, then we have the right to an alternative remedy. In this case the preferred remedy—declaration of unconstitutionality by the federal judiciary—has been rendered unavailable by the improper impeachments and threatened impeachments by Congress. So in these circumstances, and these circumstances only, we turn to an alternative remedy, in this case the doctrine called interposition.

"I know it sounds complicated, but let me give a simple explanation. When an unconstitutional law—in this case the so-called Blessing—threatens to deprive the people of a state of their constitutionally protected rights, and none of the preferred remedies is available, then the state has the right to interpose various protections between the unconstitutional law and the rights that are threatened. The fact that twenty-two state legislatures from all parts of the country have come to exactly the same conclusion provides powerful validation of the justice and fairness of our course of action. Each of the twenty-two states whose governors are standing here with me has declared—based on the decisions of the federal courts rendered *prior to* the commencement of the administration's campaign of impeachment and intimidation of federal judges—that the so-called Blessing is invalid and thus has no legal force or effect in any of our states. Second, it shall be a violation of state law in each of our states for any person, including any federal or state law enforcement personnel, to take any action in furtherance of enforcing the so-called Blessing.

"So," he concluded, "what does this mean for the citizens of our twenty-two states? It means that non-evangelical Christians and people of all religions can be confident in their right to worship as they please. It means that homosexual men and women and their families can be confident not only that we recognize and respect their civil rights but that we will act vigorously to protect them. It means that your personal sexual behavior in the privacy of your own home is of no interest to our governments. And it means that in this part of America, we still proudly pledge 'liberty and justice for all' and not, as the theocrats would have it, 'liberty and justice for all *who believe.*'

"Finally, my fellow governors have asked me to address specifically our fellow Americans residing in the states whose governors are not standing with us here today. We are one country, and we are all confident that the day will come when this attack on our federal court system ceases, when the theocratic program of the current administration is rejected and reversed, and America returns to its proud role as a beacon of freedom in the world. But in the meantime, each of you in Kansas and Texas, and Oklahoma and Alabama, and all those other states—each of you is our brother or sister, and we pledge that you will find sanctuary with us if needed. No woman threated with prosecution for adultery, no doctor or family-planning counselor whose life is at risk, no gay couple who lives in dread that their children will be taken from them, no Catholic or Jew or Muslim or Hindu—none of you will be turned away at our borders. You will find sanctuary in each of our states, and all of us here are sworn to do everything possible to attend to your material needs until this madness stops."

The press immediately dubbed the twenty-two states opting out of The Blessing as the Secular Bloc, which quickly was shortened to "Sec Bloc." Most citizens of the Sec Bloc states felt an enormous sense of relief. They wanted to believe that Jordan would be content with the status quo. After all, if the other states wanted to live by The Blessing, they could; perhaps they would just leave the Sec Bloc alone. Moreover, the display of political will demonstrated by the governors and legislatures of the Sec Bloc was the first political success—indeed the first political act of any scale—in opposition to the Christian Nation program since the death of John McCain. It was tempting to believe that the political establishment had woken up and erected for the first time a serious speed bump, and that the limits of the theocratic effort finally had been reached.

Tempting, but wrong. At first, the White House simply announced that the attorney general and Department of Justice were studying the actions by the dissenting states and that the president would speak when the legal review had been concluded. One week later, the president called a press conference and started with a statement. His treatment of the interposition issue was almost casual in tone, even dismissive. The president said the Justice Department had reported back to him that the purported "interposition" was of no legal effect. Accordingly, as far as the federal government was concerned, The Blessing was in full force in every state, and all federal law enforcement personnel had been instructed to act accordingly. Any federal law enforcement officer not doing his or her duty would be dismissed, and any person interfering with federal law enforcement would be prosecuted. At the end, almost as an afterthought, Jordan mentioned that the attorney general had advised him that he had concluded that there were substantial grounds to believe that various state officials, in attempting interposition, had violated the Defense of Freedom Act, and he was convening a grand jury to consider indictments.

The Defense of Freedom Act, the updated version of the infamous Alien and Sedition Acts from the early days of the Union, was passed by Congress at President Palin's behest following the 7/22 attacks. Its martial law provisions survived judicial review, but the "sedition" part, which initially had been struck down by the Supreme Court on First Amendment grounds, had entered into force earlier in the year when the post-Moore court reversed its position. The sedition provisions, similar to those that also had been in effect during parts of the First World War, provided that no use of the mails or other instruments of interstate commerce (including telephone, fax, or Internet) could be used for the transmission of "any material urging treason, insurrection, or forcible resistance to any law." The president's casual concluding remark was explosive: the administration was considering prosecuting the Sec Bloc governors and legislators for "sedition" due to their actions in "resisting" The Blessing.

We had not anticipated this move, and Jordan's response was a major disappointment. I asked Sanjay to come in to share his views with the governor. Sanjay's advice was clear:

"Jordan's casualness, Governor, was not an affectation. Your interposition response was fully anticipated by the feds. Their only uncertainty was how many states would go along. The days allotted to the purported review of interposition by Justice was a fiction; my sources tell me that the response to interposition had been ready to go before you began the speech at the Statue of Liberty. Their main strategy now is most likely to be a show of force designed to intimidate Sec Bloc states from pursuing secession. They will find a few Sec Bloc states with loyal FBI bureaus and where the National Guard will accept a call to federal duty. They will then proceed in these states with high-profile arrests and prosecutions of governors, Democratic leaders in the legislature, newspaper publishers, and others."

"Will they try that here?" the governor asked.

"Highly unlikely, Governor," Sanjay answered. "I think they will be more tactical. I have found five states where, by arresting the governor, lieutenant governor, and the head of one branch of the legislature, the governorship will pass to a Republican. This is not one of them. Also, I doubt they can count on the Guard and other federal law enforcement here in New York."

"OK. Good. Go on."

"After the arrests, I am quite sure that the proceedings will be martial law proceedings in military tribunals. With missing governors, or new leadership loyal to Jordan, a number of the states that stood with you at the statue will be knocked out of the secession movement. But in addition to those, I fear that governors and legislative leaders of a number of other states simply will be intimidated by the threat of arrest and disappearance. For the rest, I believe they have a plan for the Christian militias to instigate violent confrontations in the state capitals, to which the administration will respond by federalizing the National Guard in that state and establishing military security. That "security" will either intimidate or outright prevent the state legislatures from convening. That will make a secession vote impossible. That, sir, is what I believe you face. You had twenty-one other states with you for interposition. I believe that number could drop to fifteen or, in the worst case, as few as eight, for secession."

"Can they really take over the New York Guard?" the governor asked. I answered.

"Yes. Since 2007, a governor's consent is not required for the president to assume command of the Guard in a state. What we need to do is ensure that all the senior officers are loyal to you, sir. If they are not, we must replace them while we can. I'll go see each of them. OK?"

"Take the jet." There were benefits to working for Mike Bloomberg.

We needed to replace only about a half dozen Guard senior officers in New York State. Within two weeks I had sworn written statements from all the senior officers that they would refuse orders from Washington and answer only to the governor, notwithstanding any order to the contrary. This was a brave thing for these men and women to do. If we lost, it would be treason. I had similar meetings with each of the FBI, Homeland Security, and other federal law enforcement agencies in the state. They were in a difficult place, but most of them were New Yorkers, many were Catholics and Jews who felt personally threatened, and most were opposed to the Christian Nation idea. I simply asked if they would recognize the state's interposition statute and decline orders to enforce The Blessing. Most said yes. And New York—unlike many other Sec Bloc states, such as California—was not home to large regular military bases close to urban areas. With the Guard and law enforcement on our side, it would be difficult for Jordan to mount the sort of direct intimidation and intervention that Sanjay predicted.

The day I came to work for the governor, he asked me to start work on secession, but he emphasized that the word was not to be uttered in meetings and that no one—not even other senior staff—was to know that it was an option that he was actively analyzing. Once again it was our opponents who provided the template for the move that we were now considering. Secession scenarios had been analyzed and promoted by the fringe groups on the right, many of them fundamentalist, for decades. By 2011 there were six active secessionist organizations in the state of Texas alone, groups like Texas Nationalist Movement and Texas Secede. Although some had been simply nutty, others had pursued a sophisticated investigation of the legal, moral, and philosophical arguments that would have supported a split from the United States. For most of this time, the notion of secession had been a fringe idea, a powerful taboo that required mainstream politicians to avoid any hint of association or sympathy with these groups. But early in the Palin administration, following revelations of her husband's flirtations with a secessionist group in Alaska, Governor Rick Perry in Texas had broken the taboo and publicly acknowledged the movement, implying there might be circumstances where secession would be legitimate.

The law on secession here in the United States is completely straightforward. Under the Constitution, unilateral secession is prohibited. In the 1869 case of *Texas v. White*, Chief Justice Chase wrote, "What can be indissoluble if a perpetual Union [established under the Articles of Confederation], made more perfect [the express goal of the Constitution], is not?" Notwithstanding the obsession of some Christian fundamentalists with compacts and covenants, their view of the American union as a voluntary compact that could be exited at will was simply incorrect. As the chief justice explained, "The act which consummated [Texas's] admission into the Union was something more than a compact; it was the incorporation of a new member into the political body.

And it was final. The union between Texas and the other states was as complete, as perpetual, and as indissoluble as the union between the original states. There was no place for reconsideration or revocation except through revolution or through consent of the states." As a result, I was clear with the governor from our earliest discussions of the subject that talk of secession was talk of revolution. And for that he didn't need a lawyer, but he would have to call on the considerable body of moral and political philosophy regarding the justification of illegal and violent resistance to the established order.

In the case of interposition, we took care to have a sound legal basis for disapplication of The Blessing. But secession was a completely different matter. We were indifferent as to whether our purported secession from the Union was or was not valid. This is because none of the governors actually wanted their states to leave the Union. Secession was a purely tactical move designed to again raise the stakes for Jordan and the Congress and provide them with a powerful incentive to come to some sort of settlement or accommodation with that part of the country that was resisting the theocratic project. We calculated that the seceding states might account for up to 43 percent of the country's gross domestic product. By withdrawing, the members of the Sec Bloc would deprive the federal government of 47 percent of its tax revenues. New York alone accounted for nearly 10 percent of the federal government's revenue base. Put simply, without the more liberal coastal states and other large economies like Illinois, the federal government would not be viable.

During the last month of 2017, arrests and civil violence unfolded around the country largely as predicted by Sanjay. Following arrests on sedition charges of state leaders in New Hampshire, Iowa, Wisconsin, and New Mexico, new conservative Republican governors took office. National Guard troops and Christian militia shut down the smaller state capitals, including Olympia, Washington; Salem, Oregon; and Lansing, Michigan, preventing the legislatures there from convening. At the end, secession legislation became law in fourteen states: New York, Massachusetts, California, Maine, Connecticut, Vermont,

Maryland, Rhode Island, Hawaii, Illinois, Delaware, New Jersey, Minnesota, and Pennsylvania.

The governor had asked me to draft some sort of declaration or joint statement that could be made by the seceding states. At the outset of the Civil War, the southern states took similar approaches to secession. Each adopted an Ordinance of Secession, typically providing that the acts taken to join the Union were repealed and that the union of their state with the other states accordingly was dissolved. But a number of southern states also issued a Declaration of Causes, and these I studied carefully. One night in early December, I sat down at my desk in the governor's midtown office to start drafting our version of a Declaration of Causes, which would take the form of a statement by the governor on behalf of the seceding states.

My fingers hovered over the keyboard for many minutes. I stared out the window up Third Avenue toward 42nd Street, unable to start. It was 10 p.m., and yet the traffic was as dense as that in most American cities at rush hour. Suddenly I saw myself from above, sitting at the desk, and realized that this person was about to draft a document that would rank among the most important in American history. But sitting at the desk wasn't a Jefferson or a Lincoln, a Webster or a Clay—it was me. It must be a mistake, I thought. Sitting there was a lawyer, a technician, and an advisor to others; a person who saw both sides of every argument rather than embracing one side with passion. Surely this was not the person to write the words that would tear apart a great nation that had endured for nearly a quarter millennium.

But honestly, there was another reason altogether that I hesitated. I was scared. I knew that I was committing treason. I am a person who is uncomfortable jaywalking, who gets fidgety if exceeding the speed limit, and who is burdened with a bourgeois respect for authority. I knew that secession is unlawful and that treason is a crime rarely judged kindly by history. We will probably lose this fight, and then what, I wondered. I will be arrested, convicted in a martial law court, and what—shot? I couldn't blame the evangelicals for this one. Treason is a capital crime almost everywhere. Tap those keys and die.

As insights go, this was one I could have done without. I called Sanjay and asked if I could come over. After a couple of Brooklyn lagers,
I explained my problem.

Sanjay laughed.

"I hardly think it funny that I've discovered that I'm a coward."

"You are not a coward. You are a human being. Everyone is afraid.
Fear is a gift. Sometimes fear is a salutary warning to step away from
the precipice. Sometimes fear is simply a call to courage and action. You
must decide which, but I think you already know that."

The next morning I went to the office and finished the statement.
When the fourteenth state had passed and signed its Act of Secession,
the governor called a press conference that was carried live throughout
the country. He read the short statement I had drafted on behalf of the
fourteen governors:

> *Fourteen states have today suspended their participation in our
> federal Union. We do so with heavy hearts but with a strong con-
> viction that we have acted in the best interests of our great nation
> and its people. Even the greatest country can lose its way. A stri-
> dent minority has seized the instruments of federal power intent
> on implementing a theocratic society completely at odds with our
> Constitution, our values, and our traditions. This is not merely a
> debate about politics or policy. The freedoms and lives of millions
> of Americans are at grave risk. Neither the fourteen states stepping
> out of the Union today, nor the thirty-six remaining states, can
> prosper or endure on their own. We have taken with us nearly half
> of the federal government's revenues and over 40 percent of our
> national economy. Know this and take courage from it—deprived
> of these resources, President Jordan and all those who serve him can-
> not govern. They cannot succeed and they cannot implement their
> theocratic vision. Take courage and stand against them because they
> can be defeated. Our nation must and will again be whole. When
> the voters return to power people committed to the restoration of
> constitutional government, we will rejoin the Union. When the*

so-called Blessing is withdrawn, we will return. When martial law is lifted and our fundamental freedoms are restored, we will return. We will return. My fellow governors, our brave legislators and millions of our citizens join with me in making this promise: We will dedicate our lives, and make any sacrifice required, so that America will be whole, free, and great again.

CHAPTER FOURTEEN

Holy War

2018

If your brother, the son of your father or of your mother, or your son or daughter, or the spouse whom you embrace, or your most intimate friend, tries to secretly seduce you, saying, "Let us go and serve other gods," unknown to you, whether near you or far away, anywhere throughout the world, you must not consent, you must not listen to him; you must show him no pity, you must not spare him or conceal his guilt. No, you must kill him, your hand must strike the first blow in putting him to death and the lands of the rest of the people following.

—Deuteronomy 13:7–11

"Yes, march against Babylon, the land of rebels, a land that I will judge! Pursue, kill, and completely destroy them, as I have commanded you," says the Lord. "Let the battle cry be heard in the land, a shout of great destruction."

—Jeremiah 50:21–22

You can't make an omelet without breaking eggs.

—Napoleon

THE START OF THE HOLY WAR was anticlimactic. Everyone knew the inevitable consequences of secession, and the only question was how and when Jordan would react. He chose a presidential address on Christmas Day. It is worth quoting:

My fellow Americans. Today is Christmas Day, a day which America, as a Christian Nation, has solemnly celebrated for all of its national life. So to each of you and your families, I wish you a happy and joyous Christmas, filled with the light and grace of Christ. 2018 years ago last night, an angel told a simple shepherd the greatest news that has ever been communicated to a human being—that our loving Father had sent us a redeemer, our Lord Jesus Christ. Today, I share with you similarly joyous news. America, God's shining city on a hill, the consummation of all He desired and planned for His children, has itself nearly completed its own redemption as a Christian Nation. The Lord never said it would be easy. For nearly 250 years He has tested us with the challenge of establishing human dominion over a vast wilderness, and most recently the challenge of casting off a thoroughly corrupt and disobedient culture that brought down upon us the grave weight of God's displeasure. Our Lord Jesus Christ, who was crucified for us at Calvary, taught us to shoulder the burdens of the Lord joyfully, and so I tell you today the good news that we are now prepared to shoulder—with joy and determination—the last burden set for us on the path of God's plan for man. I hereby declare that the United States of America is at war—a Holy War for the Union—with the states that have purported to secede from our great and God-given nation. Our Union is a holy and indissoluble one, like holy matrimony, and only the hand of Satan would dare attempt to rip it asunder. So with reverence, I pray that God will accept this national sacrifice on the day of Christ's birth. I know that you join me in committing our nation to this course. By the Lord's birthday next year, our national redemption will be complete, our nation will be whole and finally truly free, and all Americans will live in peace until the joyous time when we ascend to eternal life by the grace of Jesus. Thank God for the Blessing of His Word and His law, God bless each of you, and God bless America.

It was an odd feeling, during that winter, to hit the gym and go through my familiar routine; to ride the subway where I often sat near the same large Jamaican woman reading *Guideposts* who always gave me a friendly smile that made me feel good about my morning; to queue up at the same coffee cart where Abdul didn't need to be told my order; to pass through the metal detector sternly operated by the largest state trooper I had ever seen; and to enter the governor's midtown office and sit down in front of a computer like millions of other New Yorkers, all doing what we always had done, as if nothing had changed. And then, when you least expected it during the day, you would look out the window and suddenly remember that we were at war. Something called a Holy War, no less, which somehow felt infinitely worse. But we knew it only because Jordan had said so, and a compliant Congress, with all Sec Bloc representatives and senators absent, had agreed.

But what did it mean? Was a twenty-six-year-old lieutenant sitting in the humming electronic control room of a US Navy destroyer in the Atlantic far over the horizon beyond Brooklyn preparing to dispatch a laser-guided missile so F3 could play a video over and over showing how the president had taken out the entire executive leadership of New York while impressively limiting "collateral damage"? Would we see tanks rolling up Third Avenue late some afternoon? Were snipers lounging in a rented office across the street just waiting for the governor or me to step in front of a window? What exactly did this "war" mean?

In college I read a book about Paris during the two weeks before German troops entered the city. The author interviewed a baker who, that morning in June 1940, had risen early, baked his baguettes, sold them as usual, and then meticulously cleaned his store as the first rank of Nazi troops marched past his *boulangerie* to occupy the city. "How could you do it," the author had asked him, "when the world you knew was ending?" "How could I not?" the baker had replied. So each of us pressed on like the baker, pressed on with our daily routines, and for the time being, life in New York, and in most of the Sec Bloc, appeared normal.

What I knew, but most others did not, was that New York was

woefully unprepared for any type of physical confrontation with the federal forces, which most of the Sec Bloc population now referred to simply as "the Holies." Had Jordan chosen to launch an assault in January or February of that year, promptly following the declaration of Holy War, I believe that the result would have been swift and certain. But civil war was one contingency for which the US military had not planned. And full-blown civil war is a tricky business. A regular army knows what its resources are. But at first the Pentagon could not predict which Guard units, reservists, and other troops would respond to federal direction and which would choose to defy orders and defend their home states. Planners could not know which hardware located within the Sec Bloc would remain available to commanders and what equipment would be commandeered or sequestered by forces loyal to the Secs. And perhaps most difficult for our opponents, Jordan's advisors needed to make some assumptions about what the troops would and would not do. It was far from clear that even the most disciplined naval aviator would follow orders in the customary way when the bomb he has been told to drop is destined for Beacon Hill or Harvard Yard, or the strafing run is to disperse a crowd from Times Square. In conventional wars, troops manage to dehumanize the enemy, a psychological defense mechanism that is vital to having good young people engage in horrific violence against a political (as opposed to personal) enemy. But this is more difficult in a civil war where the enemy may include your niece or nephew, your college roommate, or your sister's boyfriend. It is more difficult when the place being attacked is where you went on your eighth-grade trip, your honeymoon, or your last vacation. America then was a mobile society. You grew up in Iowa, went to college in Florida, had your first job in Atlanta, and married a woman from Colorado. All this explains why regimes fighting long-standing wars against their own people rely mostly on special forces distinguished by their fanatical commitment to the cause, such as the Republican Guards in Iraq or the Revolutionary Guards in Iran. As far as we knew, Jordan didn't yet have a reliable force of holy warriors who would follow orders to kill their fellow Americans and obliterate the coastal cities of their own country. This, we speculated, was one of the reasons why the Holy War, once declared, did not actually commence.

Sanjay's celebrity and moral leadership of the secular opposition brought him e-mails, letters, and phone calls from sources within the Christian Nation Bloc of states, including the few remaining secularists in positions of authority in Washington. Quite soon we were able to piece together the administration's military strategy. Evangelicals had been deeply embedded within all branches of the military for many years. They had dominated the chaplaincy since the beginning of the Iraq War, and for at least two decades born-again commanders had preferentially promoted fellow evangelicals within the ranks. The only remaining task was to create special units and squads in all the relevant commands that had been purged of any but the most fervent and fundamentalist evangelical troops and thoroughly screened for family ties to the Sec Bloc. This process took about four months. The resulting units were cohesive, with each soldier sharing a worldview that included deeply rooted disdain for the godless coastal elites, whom they believed had for decades scorned, ridiculed, and victimized true Christians. For them, this was now about payback. These special units were called Joshua Brigades.

So while those of us at TW and in the governor's inner circle understood the reason for our peaceful winter, the prevailing view within the Sec Bloc population was that the declaration of Holy War was a final desperate gambit to pressure the Sec Bloc states to back down and rejoin the Union. Those holding this view believed that Jordan needed to declare war to call the bluff of secession, but that real civil war was a line the theocrats would not cross.

Sanjay worked relentlessly to ensure that the Sec leadership did not embrace this fallacy. On the weekly conference call of the Sec Bloc State governors, the governor of Delaware said she had received assurances from those close to Jordan that actual war, violent war—tanks-in-the-street kind of war—just would not happen. Sanjay was always patient and methodical in his replies:

"Governor, I very much doubt this. Interposition gave Jordan the perfect opportunity to slow down in a face-saving way. He had the chance to preserve—for that part of the country that could tolerate it—The Blessing and everything else the Christian Nation project has achieved over the past ten years. This would have allowed him to keep the Union together and thus consolidate his control of all the instruments of federal power. Martial law would have stayed in effect. He would have been in the best possible position to contest the 2018 and 2020 elections. It was the best possible choice for him. But he walked away from this opportunity. So we need to ask ourselves why."

"Is he reasonable, even sane?" Bloomberg asked.

"My opinion," replied Sanjay, "is that he is entirely sane, quite brilliant, and extremely strategic. But you must understand that when these people say they believe, they believe. People who do not have religious beliefs too often fall into the trap of failing to accept the professed beliefs of others at face value. Don't think of faith as belief; think of faith as a type of *knowledge*. They *know* that God exists, they *know* that the Bible is the revealed word of God, they *know* that their highest calling in life is to obey God's will, and they *know* that if they do not, they will suffer unbearable torment for all eternity. How does this compare with the things that motivate you, Governor?"

Those in the room shifted uncomfortably in their seats.

"The closest analogy," Sanjay continued, "might be your knowledge that you love your children, and always will, no matter what happens. Any other condition is unimaginable. Is that unreasonable? Is that insane? The key here is never to indulge in the hope or assumption that they do not really believe what they say they believe."

Bloomberg looked grim, and the Delaware governor on the phone was silent.

I interrupted Sanjay. "I agree with that, but you must understand that their faith does *not* mean that they are unable to think reasonably, only that there are real limits to the way reason and strategy will determine their behavior. If your child is threatened, you'll use all your stores of reason and strategy to help her. But when none of that works, you don't give up. You keep trying; you do something manifestly unreasonable, bold, or rash. A mother runs suicidally into a burning building to save her child. This sort of unreasonable behavior happens every day all around us. So the Holies will calmly and rationally continue to plot to achieve their objectives. But when they meet a hopeless roadblock, they'll abandon reason and do whatever they can."

"Greg is right," Sanjay said, "because on the other side of the road-block stands the most important thing in the universe ever to happen—the most important thing that *can* ever happen, which is the second coming of Christ. And they know that America must be a godly king-dom in order for that to occur. And they know that we are now in the end times and that the rapture and Armageddon are near. So no, they are not bluffing about war. For two decades they have been educating their children and preparing their parents to use violence. Gen Josh, Joshua's Army, Warrior Christ, making Christians the victims and sec-ularism the aggressor, inuring popular culture to violence—these are the things they have done to prepare. Violence is what is now required. So, I am sorry, violence is what we will see."

"OK," Bloomberg replied. "I get it. But still, let's remember we never pretended that we could win a war. Secession was an *economic* strategy. Cut off their money; show them that the United States is not a viable country without half the GDP, without Wall Street and the banking system, without Hollywood, without the ports of Long Beach and New York. We cut the heart out of the country, and if that doesn't bring them to the table, then God help us."

"I understand," Sanjay replied. "It was the right thing to do. The only thing to do. And it might work. But it might not. And if it does not, you need to decide whether or not to fight. If you decide to fight, then now is the time to prepare."

I interrupted. "But, San, I know they will fight. The question is will *our* people really fight? The Guard perhaps, some of the troops loyal to the Sec states, maybe law enforcement. But ordinary people taking to the streets for a full-blown civil war? Fighting professional soldiers? I don't know. We don't have guns. It would be suicide for a bunch of ordinary New Yorkers to stand up in front of charging marines. Isn't it over if they can get the regular military to come in?"

"Let's not worry about that now," the governor said, interrupting. "Everything we do, every single little thing, should raise the stakes, raise the cost of a real war. If it puts them off for a month, a week, even a day, we should do it. If they send in the US Air Force and Marines as if this were Grenada, well, we know how that story ends. Nothing I can do about that. But I can do lots of things so history says we tried our best to ensure that that day never comes."

And so, during the winter and early spring of 2018, what people were calling the "phony war" simmered on with a gradual escalation of violence. In places like rural central California, upstate New York, and western Pennsylvania, the Christian militias engaged in periodic harassment of institutions such as universities, public schools, and local television stations that were disrespectful of The Blessing. Two liberal federal judges were assassinated near Harrisburg, and the president of Cornell University was briefly kidnapped and then released after the trustees agreed to shut down the college radio station, which had acquired a national following for its spirited sophomoric mockery of The Blessing. Outside Albany, arsonists burned the houses of the Democratic leadership of the assembly and senate, who were not home at the time but thereafter prudently left to stay with relatives in Brooklyn.

Only weeks later, the simmering violence was brought home to New Yorkers in a shocking way. On a Saturday afternoon in late April, Mayor Quinn and her wife attended a wedding in Queens. The groom was the most senior officer in the New York City Fire Department who was openly gay and one of the department's most decorated heroes. The *Daily News* coverage of the wedding included a photomontage of all the children and others he had carried out of burning buildings under the headline "*Mazel tov!*" After a decade with his partner, they were getting married. Any mayor would have attended this wedding, but it had special meaning for Quinn, who was also gay. Only moments after the ceremony was completed, five gunmen in commando fatigues appeared from behind the altar. A brief staccato

burst from military-issue automatic rifles followed, and the commandoes disappeared as suddenly as they had arrived. A security camera
captured two black SUVs in the rear parking lot, but these were never
traced. Inside, the wedding party and a dozen guests in the front rows,
including the mayor and her wife, were killed instantly. A score of others were injured. New York Police Department security officers never
had the chance to draw their weapons. "Terror" is a word cheapened
by two decades of abuse. Although a wedding is a joyous occasion
and a funeral a sad one, both are moments where we feel fragile and
exposed. The undercurrent of a wedding is that happiness is transitory,
and this fact is affirmed by a funeral. So the Taliban knew what it was
doing in targeting weddings and funerals. This was a day when New
Yorkers felt real terror.

Due to the events that unfolded over the course of that year, the city
was unable to hold an election to replace Mayor Quinn. Although a
deputy mayor became the acting mayor under the city's charter, from
that point on Governor Bloomberg in effect performed both jobs.

During this period, our principal strategy was to do everything possible to starve the federal government of resources and prevent it from
functioning in the normal way. The day the secession laws were passed,
each Sec Bloc state required its corporate and individual taxpayers to
pay all federal taxes to a special escrow account in New York. The fourteen Sec Bloc states that seceded—though only 28 percent in number
of the states—provided the federal government with nearly 50 percent
of its tax revenue, and a day after secession the US Treasury was cut
off from that portion of its normal cash flow. Moreover, US Treasury
borrowing operations were dependent on New York City: Manhattan-
based primary dealers bought the bulk of the treasury bonds, notes,
and bills at auction; those trades cleared through New York; and New
York financial institutions handled custody, payment, and numerous
other functions necessary to sustain the deficit funding to which the
federal government was addicted. The entire board and staff of the
Federal Reserve Bank of New York "defected" to the Sec Bloc and
cooperated with the financial strategy being run out of the governor's

office, effectively disabling the usual operations of the Washington-based Fed.

Jordan and Congress had an interesting dilemma. Although the revenue sources of the government had been decimated, the federal budget was in some sense self-correcting. Forty-three percent of federal expenses were for entitlements, including Social Security, Medicare, and Medicaid. The administration immediately cut off all payments and transfers to the Sec Bloc states, at once eliminating almost 25 percent of their customary expenses. They suspended servicing of interest owing on treasury securities to persons resident in the United States, but, afraid of the Chinese, they kept paying interest to foreigners. This move cut another 3 percent of expenditures. But this still left a severe gap in funds available to run the federal government and plan a civil war. Federal employees were paid only sporadically, and entitlement payments to citizens left in the Christian Nation Bloc were often late or reduced. The disruption to the nation's financial, trading, and transportation systems had again thrown the economy back into recession, and as a result the tax revenues of the federal government further eroded over the balance of the year.

Although business outside the Sec Bloc was cut off from the normal means of raising capital domestically, China continued to fund—at shockingly high rates—both the federal government and American corporations. Although the disruption was as severe as any since the Civil War, businesses on both sides of the Holy War divide showed enormous adaptability and resilience. Somehow goods moved around, energy sources remained reliable, consumers consumed, employment stabilized, and the impact on ordinary families was far less than we had predicted.

In mid-March, with financial pressures on the federal government escalating, Jordan again showed his strategic prowess and his determination to keep building the new Christian Nation while simultaneously dealing with the coming war. The president called a press conference to say that the temporary loss of tax revenue from the Sec Bloc states was part of God's plan and a great blessing, as it would at long last precipitate a reshaping of the federal government to a sustainable size. He tabled legislation, passed by Congress within a week, that eliminated hundreds of federal departments, agencies, boards, and commissions ranging from enormous organizations, such as the Department of Education, Department of Energy, Department of Housing and Urban Development, and the Environmental Protection Agency, to perennial right-wing targets such as the National Endowments for the Arts and Humanities, the Federal Emergency Management Agency (FEMA), National Institutes for Health, and the National Science Foundation. The savings, he announced, would nearly close the federal budget gap, and it would free American business to grow and prosper. The hundreds of thousands of DC-based federal workers thus cut off from their jobs mostly fled north, further taxing the social services in New York and other big cities. But in an instant, Jordan had achieved the right-wing dream of disassembling much of the post–New Deal federal governmental apparatus.

Having unleashed the spirit of total revolution, the controlling "Teavangelical" bloc in Congress promptly seized the social agenda from the administration and—free of any meaningful parliamentary, judicial, or other restraint—proceeded to pass almost every bill introduced by any individual member, however ill conceived. These included an anti-blasphemy statute, under which "taking the name of the Lord in vain" became a federal felony. The text was modeled on a United Nations resolution promoted for years by the fundamentalist Muslim countries, but the scope of its protection was limited to "the true God and His son Jesus Christ," and it provided expressly that no speech about "Allah, Mohammed, Buddha, Satan, Hindu deities, yoga, false secular values, or any other purported deity" would be considered blasphemous. The United States thus joined Iran, Pakistan, Saudi Arabia, Yemen, and a few others as countries whose gods were so thin skinned that they demanded retribution for disrespectful speech. Soon thereafter, the statute of limitations for abortion crimes was abolished, and prosecutions began for abortions committed prior to the time that all abortion became illegal, in clear violation of the Constitution's protection against ex post facto laws. This result was justified based on the long-standing rule that there is no statute of limitations for murder and the argument that abortion always was murder, regardless of the failure of corrupt and satanic federal judges to recognize that fact. Long-retired abortion doctors who had failed to flee to the Sec Bloc were executed in Kansas, Oklahoma, Alabama, and Texas within two months of President Jordan signing this law.

Another bill, introduced by Senator Inhofe, who entered the Senate in 1994 following a campaign based on "God, guns, and gays," invalidated all state or municipal hate crime legislation, a long-standing objective of the evangelical community, which believed that hate crime legislation "victimized" Christians by potentially criminalizing their campaign against the evils of homosexuality. Even before The Blessing, many states had abolished their individual hate crime laws. Tony Perkins's Family Research Council had been clear for years: Defining hate crimes to include crimes against gays would lead, inexorably, to the criminalization of Christ. On this theory, it was still murder, they conceded, if a lesbian woman was murdered, but if she was murdered because of her sexuality, it was unacceptable for that crime to be treated any differently from any other murder, for to do so could restrict religious speech, like the common slogans at evangelical rallies, "Kill the Faggots," "God Hates Faggots," and "Gays Must Die." Besides, senators argued on the floor of the Senate, since states were now free to execute people for the crime of sodomy, it seemed anomalous to be providing that those who killed gays because they were sodomites should be guilty of some special crime.

Another piece of legislation, cynically titled the Jewish Homeland Act, galvanized the nation's religious Jews, who before this moment were deeply divided between those who admired the administration's religiosity and steadfast support for Israel and those who recognized the incipient threat to their own religious freedom. But after the Jewish Homeland Act, that divide disappeared, and Jewish activists belatedly mobilized in support of the secular cause. The convoluted legislation, which was premised on "second coming readiness" and the necessity for a strong "biblical Israel" as the homeland for the Jewish people worldwide, was ultimately clear in its implications: Jews in America had five years to accept Jesus Christ as the Messiah or to relocate to Israel. Jordan vetoed a similar piece of legislation that called for a Shia Islamic Caliphate to which all American Muslims would be required to relocate.

The last straw, and a sign of things to follow, was a burst of new federal laws dealing with education. The Christian far right had for decades studied and admired an Islamic movement in Nigeria called Boko Haram. Literally translated, the phrase meant "education is prohibited," but the principle as implemented in parts of Nigeria prohibited all but strictly Islamic learning. The evangelical version adopted for American purposes prohibited any curriculum or teaching that could reasonably be expected to "undermine respect and reverence for the Bible as the Word of God." Its proponents argued that affirmative Christian education was not required but that intolerance for Christian teachings and values was inconsistent with, and unacceptable in, a Christian Nation. And then, late in the month, the Congress of the United States passed legislation invalidating the charters of each of the hated Ivy League universities on the purported grounds of sedition, treason, and a long catalog of illegal anti-Christian activities. The statute provided that their property was forfeit to the federal government. Of the eight Ivy League universities, only Dartmouth was located in a state that had failed to secede and was thus then controlled by federal forces. The nation was transfixed when regular army troops secured the campus, arrested senior members of the Dartmouth administration, and installed a new president, who immediately demanded the resignation of every member of the faculty. A committee, he announced, would screen the tendered resignations and accept those from professors whose work was seditious, socialist, blasphemous, or promoted the homosexual lifestyle or other types of sexual deviancy. When students clashed violently with army troops controlling the campus, most parents withdrew their children, and the new administration suspended classes and announced that operations would recommence the following September.

This unfiltered spew of federal legislation did more than even The Blessing itself to energize the citizens of the Sec Bloc. Even those who didn't have the vocabulary to describe it now understood that what they faced under the Christian Nation was not simply the loss of religious freedom but a comprehensive authoritarianism that would affect every element of their lives. Ordinary people became angry, scared, and determined to resist. Across the big cities and suburbs of the Sec states, community boards, block associations, condos, schools, non-evangelical churches, unions—almost every element of civil society—started to organize itself for armed resistance. And then, almost immediately, the Holy War began in earnest.

Jordan's patience and planning paid off. Just after midnight on the last Friday of the month, Joshua Brigades from the army and marines gathered in staging areas outside Dover, Delaware, and Annapolis, Maryland. By dawn, they had occupied and sealed the capitol buildings, state government executive offices, the offices of local newspapers, and all radio and television stations. By noon, the governors, lieutenant governors, and noncompliant legislators had been arrested and removed from their states. The entire operation was bloodless with the exception of a single state trooper guarding the governor of Maryland, who opened fire as the governor, in her nightgown, was dragged from her residence. Marines killed the state trooper instantly. When crowds started to gather in Baltimore and Wilmington, tanks moved in to clear the streets. Schools and offices were ordered closed and a curfew was declared. Theocracy Watch sources in both states reported that all broadcast, cable, and Internet had been blocked, and only F3 network programming now streamed through media devices of every sort. The US attorney general appeared at a news conference that afternoon and announced that new governors had taken office in each state, and each had promptly signed legislation passed by the rump legislatures rescinding the prior acts of secession. He reminded the country that secession was an illegal act and was being dealt with as a law enforcement matter, with the assistance of federal troops as contemplated by the continuing congressionally mandated martial law regime. He said that President Jordan had ordered that the replacement of each rogue state government was to be carefully planned and surgically executed to minimize violence, and that he was particularly gratified that our brave and skilled soldiers had carried out his orders with virtually no violence or collateral damage. The attorney general reminded the leaders of the remaining twelve states that any bloodshed that resulted from their continued resistance to federal authority would be on their hands. The door was open for them to rejoin the Union peaceably, but if they refused, then force would be used. If their citizens suffered as a result of the deployment of military force, they would have only themselves to blame.

The atmosphere at the governor's Third Avenue office that Friday evening was subdued. We spent the morning glued to coverage of the military actions in the two mid-Atlantic capitals, sobered by the ease with which the two secular state administrations were removed. Tanks were on the streets, and although sullen groups of citizens shouted profanities at passing tanks, larger gatherings were skillfully prevented. New York was more complicated, but we realized that what we had seen that day would be methodically repeated, one or two at a time, and that New York's time would come.

Late in the afternoon, Sanjay came uptown. The governor opened a bottle of Dalwhinnie twenty-nine-year-old single malt Highland whisky, his favorite.

"Where do you think Lucy Ingram is now? She's a delightful lady. Tough, smart, and a great governor. A popular governor. My God, do you think they've already killed her? I can't believe they actually did it."

Sanjay seemed almost as dispirited as the governor. "I think California is next. Someplace that matters. Delaware and Maryland were too easy. My bet is California."

I was annoyed with both of them.

"Governor, we've got to act," I said. "We've got to do something tonight. The country is looking to you."

"What? What can I do?"

The ideas were forming in my head faster than I could articulate them. "Call the Sec governors tonight, right away. Tell them each to get on all local media tonight, right now, to declare a public holiday tomorrow, and ask every single citizen—every family with their children—to turn out on the street and stay there all day. The whole Sec population should rise up to tell Jordan that they will not allow what happened in Delaware and Maryland to happen in their states. That they will fight. Today Jordan showed the country he would fight. Now, immediately, we must tell him that we'll fight back. Each governor should explain to their people that no army will come to their aid—that they will need to defend their homes and families and freedom by themselves. Each governor must say that he or she will fight in the streets with the people. Stand in front of their tanks. This is the Churchill moment, Governor . . . right now."

Sanjay looked thoughtful and read to us quietly from his iPad. "June 4, 1940. The Nazi invasion of France was on the verge of complete success, France about to fall, a day after the miracle of Dunkirk. Everyone knows, 'We shall fight on the beaches . . . we shall fight in the fields and in the streets' and so on. But this is the best part, I think. Churchill said:

> '[I]f the best arrangements are made, as they are being made, we shall prove ourselves once more able to defend our island home, to ride out the storm of the war, and to outlive the menace of tyranny, if necessary for years, if necessary alone. At any rate, that is what we are going to try to do. This is the resolve of His Majesty's Government.' "

The governor was visibly moved. Our island home was Manhattan. We would fight, if necessary for years, if necessary alone. That would be our resolve.

★   ★   ★

IT HAS BEEN hard for me to write about Saturday, March 31, 2018. I took a swim, walked around the lake, and then sat on the dock for an hour, staring at the large rock on the opposite shore, trying to calculate how many March 31s had passed since the last glacier had randomly deposited the gray-green granite boulder in its most fortuitous resting place at the edge of Indian Lake. I wanted to do anything but remember that day. Why is it that memories of past happiness are far more painful than memories of loss, exclusion, and other types of sorrow? I swam again. The lake water was so soft that it hardly felt like water. Gravity seemed to have dimmed. I was supported, floating without effort. Breathing. And then the door opened and I was again in that day. I wept easily, my tears joining the soft sweet waters of the lake.

Saturday, March 31, 2018, is one of the great days in American history, yet you will find no mention of it in any text or account of the Holy Wars available in America today. It was a day when no one could have wished for more from the American people. It was a day that finally proved that our national reserves of courage, independence, and common sense were intact. It was the day that Sanjay had been working and waiting for ever since our fateful visit to a mega-church in Pennsylvania thirteen years before. By noon on Saturday, over 100 million Americans in every Sec state left their houses and gravitated to those places that were the traditional hearts of their communities. In New England, it was the town squares. In Boston, millions crowded the Common and Public Garden, packed the entire length of the Commonwealth Avenue Mall, and spilled into the field and bleachers at Fenway. In New York, 1.5 million came into Central Park, with millions more assembled in parks and squares in every borough and neighborhood. In San Francisco, people streamed south across the Golden Gate Bridge on foot, filling the Presidio and all of Golden Gate Park. Chicago's entire Lake Shore was covered with crowds estimated to grow to 2 million by midday. In the suburbs, people by instinct left their cars at home and walked down highways and gathered in whatever green and open spaces had survived sprawling development. Although none of the gatherings turned violent, the tone was one of anger and defiance.

In the afternoon, something most remarkable happened. The crowds thinned, divided into groups, and went to work. They parked cars and buses to make a defensive cordon around state legislatures and other buildings. Contractors moved concrete barriers from highway work sites to block tank access to main streets. Ground-level entrances to local television and radio stations were boarded up. All around the Sec states, people prepared for the coming Joshua Brigade attacks as they would for a hurricane. The spirit of unity and cooperation was unprecedented. Yes, people were shocked at what was happening, and driven by anger, defiance, and patriotism. But there was also an overwhelmingly pragmatic determination not just to express their anger but to *do* something. Over and over, when interviewed, ordinary people shrugged off the question of whether their preparations really could be expected to stop or deter the US military. That didn't matter. Over and over, they simply said they had no choice but to do something, to do their best.

In that one day, Sec America had been transformed. No one speculated that Jordan would stop with Maryland and Delaware. There was no more talk of "phony war." People accepted that, one way or another, their lives would be completely changed. And they were prepared to fight. Mayors announced that tanks would be met with bulldozers. Weekend pilots promised kamikaze-style raids on local air force bases if the planes there took to the air against the Sec forces or local populations. The National Guards, almost uniformly loyal to the Sec state governors, set up their own tanks and defensive positions around government buildings and media centers. Barriers and checkpoints were built on the main roads into major cities. And weapon stockpiles were widely distributed to prevent capture by invading Holies and to allow a sustained guerrilla-style campaign even if the state governments fell. America woke up that day from a decades-long slumber and found to its surprise that it still possessed the courage, can-do pragmatism, inventiveness, idealism, and teamwork that had made the nation the envy of the world.

The official history of what else happened during the balance of that summer and autumn is, unfortunately, mostly true. Sanjay was correct: Jordan tackled one of the big states next. California hosted thirty-seven military bases, and the majority of active-duty personnel on those bases were conservative Christians from the old red states. He calculated that they would follow orders, and he was correct. Although Democrats had a substantial lead over Republicans in voter registration statewide, the inland areas of the north, the Central Valley, and Southern California outside Los Angeles all were heavily conservative and would not require a substantial dedication of resources to secure. The difficulty for Jordan was the cities.

The "liberation" of California, as it is now called, took only a week and signaled a tougher approach by the administration. It started when the state Capitol building and main state office buildings in Sacramento were obliterated in nighttime bombing runs, which not only effectively disabled the opposition administration but terrified the half million people of the city, who largely remained inside as Army units secured the city and captured the governor and nearly all opposition members of the legislature. The large California National Guard was already split, with some units remaining loyal to the governor and others accepting the call to federal service. With the governor and state-level command structure removed, even loyal commanders had difficulty coordinating their actions, and the California Guard failed to mount an effective defense anyplace in the state.

What followed the next day in San Francisco shocked the nation. Marines landed at San Francisco International Airport and quickly established a perimeter across the peninsula from the airport to Pacifica. The Golden Gate and Bay Bridges were closed. As a result, there was no way on or off the peninsula. That night, at 2:00 a.m., a single air force plane dropped a dozen MK-77 incendiary bombs on the Castro. In the resulting conflagration, the historic neighborhood burned to the ground within an hour. Given the time of night, we estimated that about twelve thousand people, mostly gay men, died in their beds. More people were murdered that night in San Francisco than were killed in the attacks of 9/11 and 7/22 combined.

This single act had profound repercussions. The people of San Francisco, horrified and feeling trapped and vulnerable, acquiesced to the inevitable. F3 and other evangelical leaders, freed from even the minimum degree of restraint that had previously governed their remarks about homosexuals, celebrated the attack as an act of divine justice. The rest of the world reeled in disbelief as a United States senator justified the incineration by the United States of twelve thousand of its citizens as an act of "sanitation." Others referred to it as a "cleansing fire" unleashed by God.

The bombing of the Castro was the act that fully and finally turned this country into a pariah in the eyes of the world. Many nations recalled their ambassadors in protest. Canada, Australia, New Zealand, Norway, Sweden, Denmark, Finland, and a dozen other countries offered refugee status to any homosexual or transgender American. Few gays outside New York risked remaining in the country. Many traveled to Vermont, and then fled north on foot and by car across the open border between Vermont and Canada. The Canadian people were particularly generous in welcoming these refugees into their homes and giving them support, medical care, and shelter pending relocation to the country of their choice. In one of TW's last acts, Sanjay issued a report estimating that 4 percent of the US population had accepted refugee status in various countries before the borders were closed.

★   ★   ★

I WILL NOT recount the many Holy War battles that followed, most of which are now studied by schoolchildren as highlights of modern American history. Jordan and the military were methodical, carefully consolidating their position in each state or region before proceeding to the next. Resistance to troops on the ground was fierce, with many thousands of Sec militiamen and -women dying as they bravely attacked tanks and armored personnel carriers with bulldozers, trucks, and buses. But federal air power proved irresistible.

After Hawaii, Minnesota, and Illinois fell, there was a hiatus before the government attempted to take the Northeast. It became increasingly difficult to obtain reliable news from the West. We knew that in San Francisco and Los Angeles, as much as 40 percent of the adult population participated in guerrilla-style attacks on the centers and symbols of federal power. Sympathetic nations and citizens around the world offered to re-arm the resistance, but federal control of sea and air was such that very few weapons found their way into the occupied cities. When weapons and ammunition were exhausted, the guerrilla attacks died off. Tens of thousands of citizens in California alone were killed in violent confrontation with the Joshua Brigades sent to maintain order in the principal cities.

By mid-autumn, the feds took Boston from the water and began an overland march to the north and south, slowly securing Vermont and Maine, and then Rhode Island and eastern Connecticut. By October, they drove north through Philadelphia, pausing along the Raritan River in New Brunswick. Most people thought the Holy War was nearly over.

CHAPTER FIFTEEN

Siege

2019–2020

10. When thou comest nigh unto a city to fight against it, then proclaim peace unto it.

11. And it shall be, if it make thee answer of peace, and open unto thee, then it shall be, that all the people that is found therein shall be tributaries unto thee, and they shall serve thee.

12. And if it will make no peace with thee, but will make war against thee, then thou shalt besiege it.

—Deuteronomy 20

WE ALWAYS BELIEVED THAT, one way or another, the Sec resistance in America would make its last stand on the island of Manhattan. But eighteen months before, working late in the office on the interposition strategy, I was genuinely startled when the governor pulled me aside and asked me a strange question.

"Greg," he said, "you studied history. What do you know about the Siege of Leningrad during World War II?"

I was silent for more than a few moments, struggling to remember something interesting or useful. In a war filled with so many dark moments and impossible horrors, I knew that the Siege of Leningrad was one of the worst.

"All I know, sir, is that there was terrible suffering, including mass starvation. And also, of course, heroism. Do you know the famous story about the seed guy?"

"Seed guy? Nope."

"Before the war," I explained, "a renowned Russian botanist had made discoveries that revolutionized agriculture and the ability of Russia to feed its people. He was a hero to all of Russia. I can't remember his name. But, there in Leningrad, he had amassed the largest collection of seeds in the world. The collection was carefully protected during the siege, as they believed that it was the key to avoiding starvation once the war was over. During the siege his staff died of starvation one by one. Finally, the last scientist sat in the laboratory surrounded by these seeds—all edible. All he needed to do to survive was to start eating the seeds. He didn't. He starved to death rather than eat a single one. Can you imagine? Sitting surrounded by food and having the willpower to starve. Funny, it's the only specific thing I remember about the Siege of Leningrad. Sieges, I think, are all about food."

The governor then asked me to undertake some research—discreetly—about the history and conduct of sieges. He wanted to know what we might expect should the Holies decide to blockade New York, and what we could do to prepare.

I turned first to the Bible and was soon gripped by the notion that a siege of Manhattan might be too tempting for the Holies—obsessed as they were with the Old Testament—to resist. Siege was one of the main punishments that the Hebrew god Yahweh would use against His people as punishment for their disobedience; and disobedience, in evangelical eyes, was the main characteristic of our city. I soon discovered that the Old Testament was filled with examples of siege and contained detailed instructions about how to conduct them and how to defend against them.

We believed that Jordan and the feds would understand that an outright assault on Manhattan would come at a very high cost to the nation. The high-rise nature of the island and the extraordinary density of building would make conventional attack strategies difficult.

And then there was the symbolic and political aspect. Would even the most ardent fundamentalist believe that the American people would tolerate the US government *itself* reducing the new World Trade Center building or other New York landmarks to rubble? We also hoped that the feds would realize that the United States was simply too dependent on New York—financially, economically, and culturally—to destroy it. And so, even without the biblical mandate, a siege seemed to us to be the preferred military strategy: surround Manhattan, blockade all goods and travel on and off the island, and wait. Starve the decadent city folks into submission. And if submission never comes, then a conventional amphibious assault, to subdue the city without destroying it, would be far easier against a weakened population. The Bible, in this case, really did have all the answers.

Within two weeks of my first conversation with the governor about the Siege of Leningrad, he had appointed a clandestine working group dedicated to siege preparation. Our first insight was that the outer boroughs of the city could easily be taken by ground troops employing conventional methods, and a blockade or siege, were it imposed, would almost certainly be limited to Manhattan. Then, to our great relief, our engineers advised that short of dynamiting the three massive tunnels that fed the city's water system—a step that would render New York uninhabitable for decades—there was no practical way to cut off all the water inputs to Manhattan.

Electricity was a bit less clear. We had only one small power plant on the island, but multiple cables supplied the city from the north, east, and west. The good news was that the grid supplying Manhattan was complex and interconnected and not designed to be switched off from a location outside Manhattan. As a result, shutting off all power to the island was not a simple matter of flipping a few switches. But with effort, it could be done. We settled on two steps to make this more difficult. It turned out there were only five engineers capable of executing a deliberate shutdown of large portions of the grid in Manhattan. Each of these men was brought into our planning and moved with their families into Manhattan. The grid diagrams, shutdown procedures, and other materials necessary for others to figure it out were quietly lost and erased from the Con Ed computers.

Our second strategy was far riskier and more expensive. Using Bloomberg Foundation money, in only five months of work three new super-conducting cables were installed in unusued conduits under the Hudson and East Rivers. They appeared on no system map or diagram and were unknown to the rest of Con Ed's personnel. Unless they were found and physically destroyed, these new cables would automatically route power from Westchester, the outer boroughs, and New Jersey into Manhattan if the existing feeder cables were disconnected. We were not completely certain they would work. Nor could we be sure that this major piece of engineering had escaped the notice of the federal authorities. But it was the best we could do under the circumstances.

In a biblical siege, if the wells could not be poisoned or fouled, the principal purpose of troops surrounding the besieged city was to deny it supplies of food, and starve the citizens into submission. My study of Leningrad and other modern sieges yielded key strategic guidance for our preparations. First, we would attempt to stockpile as much food as possible before the siege commenced. I learned that virtually all the food stockpiles in Leningrad became targets for German bombing and arson, so we decided that ours needed to be made as secure as possible. We chose the largely empty workrooms and storage facilities adjacent to almost every subway station in Manhattan, and they were quietly adapted for food storage. But stockpiles alone would not feed Manhattan.

At my recommendation, the governor hired the charismatic doyenne of urban agriculture, Annie Novak, who ten years before had pioneered large-scale, for-profit vegetable farming on the rooftops of Brooklyn. Her job was to develop plans to quickly convert every available patch of land in Manhattan—and every rooftop that could take the weight—to the production of vegetables and other food should a siege be commenced. Under her guidance, hundreds of thousands of yards of green-roof soil mix began to be stockpiled at every sanitation garage in Manhattan. No one except a few bemused sanitation workers noticed that the sanitation trucks that usually hauled road salt were now loaded with a custom mixture of sterile light soils and pure compost. Annie also established extensive collections of vegetable seeds and seedlings at every public library branch in Manhattan and organized a small army of community organizers and urban farmers who would be ready—at the governor's signal—to fan out across the island and teach the population of the world's most densely populated place to become self-sufficient in food. As far as we could tell, the federal authorities never learned of these efforts.

But even if Manhattan managed to feed itself for some time, other supplies, such as medicines, would be critical. Close observers at the time noted that the governor's jet logged multiple trips to London, Stockholm, Oslo, and Helsinki. The goodwill of northern Europe, and the governor's money, resulted in substantial commitments from foreign governments and companies to step up and provide New York, if necessary, with the essential goods that it normally procured domestically. But how to bring supplies into a blockaded Manhattan remained a vexing question, right up to that week in November 2018 when we watched with alarm the advance of the federal forces, represented on F3 by little lines of gold crusader crosses marching across the electronic map.

By the time the federal troops reached the Raritan River in New Jersey, a strange calm had settled over the city. The normal throng of tourists and business travellers left town, all commuters returned to the suburbs, and trains and airlines suspended service. Anyone left in New York assumed they would be here for the duration. State Guard troops were stationed at places where major highways entered the city, but with few tanks and no effective antiaircraft defenses, we realized these checkpoints would fall quickly against any regular military force determined to proceed. We had little hope of keeping federal troops out of the Bronx, Queens, Brooklyn, or Staten Island should they choose to advance from the north and east. But Manhattan itself was heavily and effectively fortified, with each potential landing point around the island defended by multiple rows of barbed wire, concrete barriers, and Guard and volunteer Sec troops manning well-protected defensive positions.

On the Tuesday before Thanksgiving, the feds advanced up through New Jersey, and the formidable Joshua Brigades from Oklahoma, Kansas, Alabama, and Colorado took up positions up and down the west shore of the Hudson from the George Washington Bridge in the north down to Bayonne. Manhattanites lined the east bank of the Hudson staring across at the alarming sight of tanks and artillery all poised to shoot across the river at the full length of the island. In a symbolic gesture, the Holies occupied Liberty Island from the Jersey side and draped the base of the Statue of Liberty with the "Christian flag." At the same time, a small unit of marines landed at Stony Brook, on the North Shore of Long Island, and proceeded south to secure McArthur Airport in Islip. We watched nervously as huge air force C-17 transports streamed continuously in and out of MacArthur Airport all afternoon, discharging troops, tanks, vehicles, and supplies. The next morning, the city was transfixed by TV images of tanks and armored personnel carriers streaming west along the otherwise empty Long Island Expressway and Southern State Parkway. The defense perimeters at the city's eastern edge were pierced following a brief skirmish. A brave unit of Guards briefly halted the advance around Kennedy Airport using only three old tanks, brought down from Camp Smith in Peekskill, until helicopter-fired missiles destroyed each tank. The governor pulled all our forces back to Manhattan and deployed them at the bridge and tunnel exits, which were relatively easy to defend, and reinforced the troops at the most obvious spots for amphibious assault around the island's perimeter. By the end of the day, the same formidable line of tanks, artillery, and troops lined the east bank of the East River all the way up to the South Bronx.

The governor and all the senior staff spent the night in our command center on Third Avenue, most of us believing that it might be our last night alive or at least our last as free men and women. Well after midnight, we received reports of guerrilla-style attacks on the rear and side flanks of the Joshua Brigades arrayed along the river in Brooklyn on a large flat area just south of Newtown Creek that included the Greenpoint Playground. The gunfire continued for well over an hour, and when it ended we did not know whether the citizen soldiers of Brooklyn had been killed or had staged a tactical retreat.

Around 4 a.m. we were again summoned to the roof as a single US Air Force bomber flew low and slow over Greenpoint, blanketing the neighborhood behind the harassed troops with bombs, presumably in retribution for the attack. We did have antiaircraft weapons mounted on the tops of some of the taller buildings in Manhattan, and several of those shot unsuccessfully at the slow bomber. After only a few minutes, the plane departed. Although the bombs did not appear to be the incendiary type used on the Castro, the effect was equally devastating. From Newtown Creek down to Greenpoint Avenue, the entire area west of McGuiness Boulevard, almost thirty square blocks, was leveled by violent explosions. Not a single building was left intact. We stood on the roof on Third Avenue and gazed silently to the east. Thick black smoke obscured the stars and drifted on the wind to the north. But under the smoke, yellow flames enveloped the ruins of collapsed buildings and illuminated the surface of the East River. For the sixteen thousand households living in the neighborhood of old brick and wooden structures, there was no escape. No one knows how many died that night, but it cannot have been less than half of the neighborhood's population of about forty thousand Poles, South Asians, North Africans, artists, rooftop farmers, foodies, and other young people who had been attracted in the years before to one of New York's most affordable and dynamic communities. When we came down from the roof, the governor was in shock.

"Not in New York. I really didn't think they would do it. Not here. It's my fault. We should not have let the people think they could fight and win this battle. How many . . ." Sitting on the couch in his corner office, he covered his face with his hands, elbows on his knees. After a minute, he sat up straight, wiped his eyes with the monogrammed sleeve of a day-old shirt, and seemed determined.

"That's it," he said. "No more. We're going to surrender. I'm going to call Jordan."

"Don't, Governor," I said abruptly. "Please, sir. They will not come after Manhattan tomorrow. I'm sure of it. It will be a siege. Go ahead and make a statement for the outer boroughs. If you want, tell the militias there to give up. Tell them the price is too high, that they cannot win. Tell them the price for continuing the fight is their neighbors dying in their sleep as they did in Greenpoint. But not Manhattan. We must try to hold Manhattan." I paused.

"Mike"—I almost never called the governor by his first name—"think of the gays. To give up now is a death sentence for them. And we have to think of the millions in the rest of the country who don't go along with this madness. As long as secular rule continues somewhere in the country, even if it's just Manhattan Island, they all will have at least some hope. They need us to hang on, sir. If we lose, all those people out there will give up. The siege will give us time. Anything can happen. The world may come to our rescue. Jordan could die or lose the next election. We have time; we've got to take it. Please—"

I stopped talking abruptly. The governor stood at the window looking out at Third Avenue. He asked the others for their advice.

A few hours later, at six o'clock on Thanksgiving morning, the governor summoned the media. It was the first time I ever saw him meet the press without shaving. Deep purple creases under his eyes made him look old. He honored the troops who had perished trying to stop the advances against the city from the north and east. He said simply that November 24, although celebrated by the fundamentalists as a triumph, would instead, ultimately, be seen as a day of infamy. No true Christian, no American, no person of goodwill could possibly condone the murder of sixteen thousand innocents in their beds. History would judge it to be a crime against humanity, the horrible fruits of fanatical belief. The governor then begged the people of Brooklyn, the Bronx, Queens, and Staten Island to stop fighting. He said they should continue to resist in every way available to them other than violence. He said seeing the city ripped into two broke his heart, but violence in the

occupied parts of the city would bring only overwhelming and dispro-
portionate retribution against which we had no defense. The other boroughs had been occupied by federal forces and must acquiesce for the
moment to the inevitable. He then addressed President Jordan directly:

*Mr. Jordan—for I am too much of a patriot to call you president—
Mr. Jordan, hear this clearly. We draw the line at Manhattan. Yes,
you have the power to destroy us. But think a moment. This island
is the capital of the world and a microcosm of the whole world. Our
people are the best and brightest who have come from all corners of
the earth drawn by the promise of America. Our diversity, and the
energy and creativity it drives, are a model for what the world can
be. Our dozens of great museums and private collections hold the
most important art, sculpture, and artifacts of all human civilization. Here on this island live some of the world's most accomplished
musicians, dancers, actors, and artists. Here are the headquarters of
dozens of the world's largest enterprises, providing jobs for tens of
millions of Americans and people around the world. Here lies the
heart of the world's financial system. You cannot take Manhattan
without destroying all these things. If you do, your name will be
recorded by history alongside the likes of Pol Pot, Saddam Hussein,
and Adolf Hitler—you will be regarded by history as a genocidal
maniac and vandal of civilization. So I tell you this. Not one federal
soldier will set foot on this island. The 1.7 million New Yorkers
who live here will fight you in every neighborhood, every street,
every building, every alley. This is a promise and a fact. What do
we have to lose? We who have come from all over the world for
the promise of American freedom and the American dream—we
have nothing to lose, because losing that dream is to us like death.
Our brothers and sisters whom you want to slaughter for their God-
given sexuality—they have nothing to lose because they fight for
their lives. So think well, Mr. Jordan, what you do next. And I ask
the governments of the world to do everything they can to help us,
and I ask the people of the world for their prayers.*

It was not a great speech. I wrote it without having slept for two nights, and the governor, who was also exhausted, extemporized freely. But it worked. The violence in the outer boroughs subsided, and the world watched and waited to see what Jordan would do next.

Later that day, when families around the country rose from their Thanksgiving meals, President Jordan addressed the nation. I watched the address from a conference room and could barely contain my anger upon seeing his carefully coifed contentment, that slick telegenic face masking a lurid cruelty. Behind him, the triumphant image of the cross in the White House, now on a par with the American flag, reminding us what they had really meant when they said this was a Christian Nation.

My fellow Americans. Almost one year ago I promised you that by Christmas this year our nation would again be whole and free. It is thus appropriate that on this Thanksgiving Day, the day when the whole nation thanks God, its patron and protector, for all His many Blessings, I can ask you to join me in thanking the Lord and His son Jesus Christ, who have once again shown their divine favor by granting us victory in the Holy War we waged in their name. All fifty states are once again together in this sacred Union. All the state capitals are free. Senators and representatives from all the states once again work together in Congress for the people. By any measure, the battle should not have been so easy. With God's grace and favor, with His miraculous intervention on more than one occasion, our brave Joshua Brigades—consisting of our finest federal men and women in uniform—retook the rebellious states with a minimum of bloodshed. We thank each of those men and women for their service. And even today, in their finest hour, our troops proceeded to the very shore of Manhattan Island, awaiting only my order to take the last bit of American soil under the control of the rebels.

My fellow Americans, like you, when I face a tough decision, I turn to the only advisor a man needs, to our Lord Jesus Christ, and to the good book he gave us. And lo and behold, my Bible opened right to Deuteronomy 20, and this is what I read:

> 10. When thou comest nigh unto a city to fight against it, then proclaim peace unto it. 11. And it shall be, if it make thee answer of peace, and open unto thee, then it shall be, that all the people that is found therein shall be tributaries unto thee, and they shall serve thee. 12. And if it will make no peace with thee, but will make war against thee, then thou shalt besiege it.

My fellow Americans, I am no longer surprised, but always grateful, when the Bible has a direct answer for every question.

And so tonight, on this day of Thanksgiving to the Lord, I do what I have done my entire life and career, and seek humbly to follow the will of God. For the last year, I have said over and over to Governor Bloomberg and each resident of Manhattan, peace be unto you. I have come at the behest of the Lord to fight you, but I have offered you peace as the Lord instructed. If you had responded in peace, and offered us peace, then you would have been returned to the bosom of your country in the peace of the Lord. It's not too late. But you have not made peace with us. You have made war. So the Bible is clear. We shall besiege your island. Effective immediately, I announce to the people of America and the nations of the world that the island of Manhattan is quarantined. Its waters have been blockaded by our navy. Every connection between the island and the outside world is under the control of US forces. No one may enter and no one may leave. No food or other goods shall be allowed in or out. Manhattan is surrounded, just like Jericho was when under siege by Joshua and the armies of God. The prophets, thanks be to God, were right, and it all ends now with a siege against the godless and disobedient. I don't know whether it will take seven days, like Jericho, or seven months, but I tell you this.

Just as the indestructible walls of Jericho tumbled to the ground, everything yields eventually to the power of God's intervention and God's favor. Good night, and may God bless America.

In remarks to the people of Manhattan the next morning, the governor, who had a good sleep and a shave, was in high spirits:

My fellow New Yorkers. Well, now we know. We know their limits. For the moment, they will not destroy Manhattan. I don't know whether they are planning on having the arc of the covenant and trumpeters march around Manhattan for six days. I don't know what their endgame is. But we will prepare and we will resist and we will not surrender. New Yorkers are the toughest people in the world. We will learn how to live in isolation, how to survive—how to be the seed from which this great country will be reborn. It is possible that a friendly nation will come to our rescue. It is possible that America will rise up and defeat Jordan and the theocrats, or dispatch them at the next election. Time is on our side. The president cited the Bible. But, you know, the Old Testament is the territory of my people, the Jews—and I know my Old Testament. What Jordan didn't tell you is what comes next in Deuteronomy. When the siege is ended, what does the Bible tell them to do? It says,

> And when the Lord thy God hath delivered it into thine hands, thou shalt smite every male thereof with the edge of the sword; But the women, and the little ones, and the cattle, and all that is in the city, even all the spoil thereof, shalt thou take unto thyself.

And don't believe that they will do anything else. I have no doubt that every male New Yorker will be smitten. Or that they will take the women and the little ones unto themselves. This is exactly what they will do. So, my friends, it's clear that we fight not only for our country and our Constitution, but for our lives and for our families.

The governor set us two priorities. First, survive. Do everything necessary to permit the besieged island to feed itself and carry on through the coming winter and beyond. Second, prepare for the inevitable. The Holies might be hoping for a miracle like the falling of the walls of Jericho, but we knew that if the Jordan administration survived eventually they would need to retake Manhattan in a more conventional way, probably an amphibious attack and street-by-street urban battle. The governor asked Annie Novak, who had led our urban agriculture preparations, to lead the team dealing with food, and I was in the unlikely position of supervising, with a retired Marine Corps colonel, our attempt to prepare an island of office workers to be combatants in an urban war.

I studied some of the great conflicts of the twentieth century that had played out in the crowded streets of European cities, not unlike the canyons of Manhattan. Most intriguing to me was the Battle of Madrid during the Spanish Civil War because of its many parallels to our situation. The Spanish Republicans entrenched in Madrid saw it as a battle for civilization and promised that Madrid would be the "graveyard of fascism." On the other side, Franco's troops were heavily supplemented with criminals and thugs from all corners of the continent. With rich irony, the key battles played out around the faculty buildings at Madrid's University City. The improbable battle cry of the fascists: "Down with Intelligence." This wasn't the Christian Nation slogan, but it might have been had they been more honest. After his victory, Franco controlled Spain for nearly the next forty years. Franco called himself *Caudillo de España, por la gracia de Dios*, claiming the mantle of divine authority to justify over a hundred thousand summary executions of intelligentsia, atheists, and republicans, *by the grace of God*. This is what we could be facing, and the end result could very well be the same.

The long-standing urban agriculture movement in New York gave us the experience and knowledge necessary to grow food for 1.7 million New Yorkers on our small island largely covered by concrete. The day after the siege began, city parks department workers started plowing up all the lawns in Manhattan parks and covered that ground with metal hoop houses—curved pipe covered with clear plastic—creating large shelters for the growing of winter vegetables. The stockpiled soil supplies were hauled to the roofs of larger buildings and also covered with various types of ad hoc cold frames. Every day Annie Novak was on television and radio, as well as present all around the island, coaching tens of thousands of urbanites in the art of sowing and growing food crops. She was assisted by Manhattan's many community gardeners, men and women who for years had coaxed vegetables and flowers out of abandoned and vacant lots in Harlem, Spanish Harlem, and the Lower East Side, now retooled as civil servants, teaching nurses, lawyers, and architects how to grow food for their own survival.

The city's food stockpiles, available with the ration coupons that we had printed and distributed nearly six months before, were supposed to be just enough to keep us going through the coldest months of winter. But we were counting on these stockpiles to be supplemented with fresh winter vegetables, including turnips, radishes, cabbage, spinach and other winter greens, short carrots, sunchokes, kale, leeks, and whatever else could grow under the hoops in New York's cold winter weather. Henhouses became a feature in every schoolyard, park, and green space, and schoolchildren delighted in their daily assignment of collecting the eggs. When late March arrived, every inch of ground— the median of Park Avenue, the bases of street trees, the edges of every playground and dog run—all were topped with supplemental soil and densely planted by brigades of local farmers. Each community board was responsible for coordinating the planting and harvesting in its area, and these famously fractious civic institutions became models of cooperation in allocating public land, assigning farmers, and ensuring an equitable distribution of the resulting produce.

One day in late April, I walked with Sanjay down Broadway to Bowling Green. It was a warm spring day; the city had persevered through three long months of winter, and we were both in a good mood.

"Have you noticed," I asked, "how quickly you adjust to the new look of the city? I mean, it's been only four months without cars or taxis or buses, and yet I find it hard to conjure up the look of the streets without people on them. I know that Bowling Green used to have a lawn, but now the rows of vegetables look, well, just right."

"Yes," said Sanjay, "and of course there is a certain temporal echo, or historical symmetry, that is pleasing." Sanjay had learned to speak plainly and simply when addressing the public and the media in his role as spokesman for TW. But with me, he reverted to the more complex locutions that were natural to him. "New Amsterdam was a fort, walled off to the north against the sometimes hostile native peoples. Is it not ironic that this part of the city was originally designed for siege? For self-sufficiency? I cannot remember exactly, but I think that long before it was a place of recreation, Bowling Green was the site of the public well and a food market. And now, after three hundred years, it again serves the same purpose. You know, G, anything that suggests that time is not completely linear has a lot of deep resonance with us Indians."

Suddenly it occurred to me to ask him a question I had never asked before. "San, are you saying you believe in reincarnation?"

Sanjay smiled. "I am glad you are not a reporter."

"Well?"

"'No' is the simple answer. But there is a great deal of wisdom in the idea. You know how physicists now think that space consists of ten or eleven tightly rolled up spatial dimensions? It would not surprise me to find that time is also not completely linear. I've always thought of time as a bit loopy, in the sense of patterns repeating themselves, the future influencing the past, and other connections between events that defy linear time."

"So when we are dead we are dead?" I asked.

"Are you not content with the wonderful gift of a single life? Yes, our bodies and our minds are dead, but our actions and words bounce around time for eternity. That is something. It is enough for me."

We paused to look at the teardrop-shaped park, the hoop houses now gone, revealing neat berms of soil behind the famous Wall Street bull. A few young women were sowing seeds by hand. The atmosphere— without the usual city sounds of traffic—was almost pastoral despite the looming stone-clad office buildings on all sides. Bowling Green was nestled into a notch of large buildings that hid the rolls of barbed wire at the water's edge and the long line of tanks and guns pointed at us from the other side of the river. It was one of those places in Manhattan where, for an hour, New Yorkers could forget the reality that was just out of view.

San seemed to be thinking a lot about history. "All citizens of New Amsterdam," he said, "grew food. Although it is true that the rise of cities required advances in agriculture and transportation, the idea of city as consumer and countryside as producer was a false dichotomy. I wonder whether what we have accomplished here will be noticed and studied. Whether it will change the way other cities feed their people. I wonder, G, if that will be part of our legacy."

I had noticed a melancholic streak in San as we emerged from the winter. His mind seemed to be someplace far in the future, looking back. I couldn't tell whether it was a future where we had won or lost. In any case, Sanjay's mood probably resulted in part from the fact that there remained little for him to do at TW, and he was constantly looking for outlets for his prodigious energy.

I remember the day in early December that Sanjay arrived at an office the governor sometimes used in City Hall accompanied by a rather disheveled unshaven man with long blond hair and wearing high-top sneakers, dirty cargo pants, and a black T-shirt. The man stared at the large Joseph Chambers painting of New York harbor that hung in the conference room, and ignored the governor.

"Governor," said Sanjay, "please permit me to introduce you to Steve Duncan."

Duncan looked up and the governor looked skeptical.

"Steve Duncan, *PhD*," Sanjay added. "From Columbia. PhD in urban history. He specializes in, I suppose you would say, things under the city. Tunnels, for example."

"What can I do for you, Mr. Duncan?" the governor asked.

"I think it's what I can do for you, Governor."

"OK. What's that?" the governor answered patiently.

"Well, sir. We have a problem. Yes. Yes. I suppose you know that. I mean not just the siege, but the problem of how to smuggle things into Manhattan. I assume there are people who would send us medicines, parts, food, other things, if they could."

"Absolutely."

"Yes, well, I know a great deal that the Holies do not. This is a city of tunnels, Governor. We've been digging them, using them, abandoning them, losing them, and forgetting about them for a few hundred years. But I've been poking around in them—sometimes illegally, I have to say—for all my life. It's not just urban legend. We live on top of a maze. Beautiful double-barreled brick sewer tunnels; abandoned subway lines; pedestrian tunnels between buildings; half-built railway tunnels; old pneumatic tunnels; ventilation tunnels; water, electric, and steam tunnels—and off to the side of many of them, forgotten access and service tunnels. But you know who didn't forget about these? The Underground Railroad before the Civil War. Confederate sympathizers during the Civil War. Bootleggers during Prohibition. Smugglers and drug runners. And the mole people. Yes, sir, they're real. Not an urban legend. And I'm the only one they trust."

Sanjay noticed that the governor looked distracted.

"Governor," Sanjay said, "we need to think like bootleggers. How do we smuggle product onto the island? We can't do it by boat. We've established that. The navy patrols are continuous, and they have radar, video, and sonar covering every inch of water around Manhattan. But Steve tells me there are thirteen tunnels under the East River alone. And as far as I can tell, the feds don't know about three of them. Dr. Duncan here has volunteered to coordinate a major operation to bring supplies in through these abandoned tunnels. Our idea is to signal our friends on the outside every night with a different location. There are enough connected access points in Brooklyn, Queens, the Bronx, and New Jersey that we can use a different one every night."

"And the best part," Duncan added, "is the mole people. They not only know underground New York better than anyone else, they're pros at evasion. The police have been after them for years. From spending most of their time underground, they've developed a sixth sense. They can tell when someone else enters a tunnel blocks away."

"You're kidding me, right?" said Bloomberg. "You're telling me there are people in Manhattan who actually live underground?"

"Absolutely. I know dozens of them. They've been my guides and mentors in my work on underground New York. And they're on board for this project. If you want to meet one of them, I can arrange it."

"And there is even better news," interrupted Sanjay. "Do you remember, Governor, the repair of the Rondout–West Branch tunnel—the diving crew that lived for a month in a pressurized tube to get at the valve?"

"Of course. One repair cost the city $500 million, with a 100 percent overrun. It was a nightmare."

"Yes. But do you remember what part of that $500 million bought us? Diving bells and so-called pigs—pressurized vessels capable of passing through the water tunnels."

"Pigs?" the governor asked.

"Pigs are like little submarines designed to pass through pipelines. They are used for inspection and repair. We checked. They are all on the Manhattan side now. They will work in water Tunnels One and Three. We can put in under Central Park and ascend at any of the valve chambers in the rest of the city and some in Westchester—the best probably being the valve complex at Van Cortlandt Park. We can do it; we can bring in critical supplies through the water tunnels."

The governor looked impressed. "Do it. Medical supplies and spare parts for the electric grid and subway have priority. But let's be cautious. If they catch our people on the outside, they'll quickly figure out what we're up to. Start slow. And Dr. Duncan, thank you. If we survive this thing, a major grant from the foundation is headed to Columbia for anything you want."

★   ★   ★

STEVE DUNCAN TURNED out to be a brilliant organizer and natural guerrilla. The mole people were fearless and effective. Together, they quickly grew a dusk-to-dawn operation, creating a continuous flow of products and materials onto the blockaded island. We established in City Hall an office code-named Amazon, which prioritized orders from Manhattan hospitals and public services, routed those orders to active Sec supporters on the outside, and, through Steve Duncan, coordinated our clandestine system for delivery into Manhattan. A few couriers were shot for breaking curfew, but others promptly took their places.

By the end of the winter, we realized that we could not have endured the siege without this network. I checked once at the archives to see if there was any record of Steve Duncan on the Purity Web. It was a foolish thing to do, as each search is recorded, analyzed, and added to my profile. Duncan had, as I suspected, been removed from history. There was no record of his birth, his dissertation, his tenure at Columbia, his books, or his role during the siege. I don't know whether he is alive or dead. I realize now that once those of us who were there during the siege are dead, no future historian will know he existed or what he did for New York. Steve Duncan was one of the great heroes of the siege of New York, and I hope some copy of this memoir survives, if for no other reason than to carry that message to a future historian.

The spring of 2020 was a joyful time in Manhattan. The 1.7 million citizens of this twenty-four-square-mile island had survived the winter without, frankly, terrible hardship. Yes, we were sick of protein shakes, turnips, and apples, but suddenly every horizontal surface of the city burst with spring vegetables. We feasted on fresh sweet greens, snap peas, asparagus, and spinach. The hospitals somehow managed to carry on, the subways still ran, electricity flowed, children went to school, and a certain rhythm had settled over this new and strange form of urban life. People reported to offices, even if little work needed to be, or could be, done. With the dramatic increase in leisure time, the libraries, museums, and gyms were full all the time. There was virtually no crime. At first it seemed as if we could carry on this way indefinitely.

But the relief and jubilation of early spring proved to be only a temporary distraction from the underlying peril of our situation. In early June we became nervous that the seven-month anniversary of the siege might be a symbolically potent time for the Holies to end it. Joshua brought down the walls of the besieged city of Jericho in seven days, following a parade of seven circuits around the city walls, and so a triumphant occupation of Manhattan after seven months of siege would have a satisfying biblical resonance. So literal were our foes in their beliefs that we posted special lookouts around the island for the sole purpose of detecting the beginning of any kind of processional circumnavigation of Manhattan that might signal that an attack would follow within seven days.

At that point I had spent over a year considering how to defend Manhattan against an amphibious assault. Thanks to the density of skyscrapers and small scale of open spaces, the use of airborne troops in quantity would be difficult. We knew they couldn't use the bridges or tunnels. This left a seaborne invasion as their only practical choice. Since there were no beaches on Manhattan, this would require open spaces with low edges in which amphibious assault vessels could discharge their troops. If these water's-edge spaces abutted open seas as opposed to narrow rivers, this would increase room for maneuver and the rapidity with which subsequent waves of assault vessels could pull up to the land, unload, and retreat.

The strategy I proposed was counterintuitive. Battery Park, with its long gently curving low seawall, the expansive waters of the harbor beyond, and the open lawns of the park on the land side, was by far the best spot for an amphibious assault. It thus might have been logical to erect all the physical barriers we could to block a landing at that spot. But in my view, what we needed was a virtual guarantee that the Battery would be irresistible as the place of attack for the simple reason that our shortage of trained troops and very limited supply of weapons made it impossible to defend all the potential landing spots along the thirty-two-mile perimeter of Manhattan Island. If we were not confident of where the attack would come, we could not mount a resistance even remotely likely to repulse it. When I convinced the governor of my logic in early December, we decided to use the last of our precious fuel stores to position all city buses, trucks, and private vehicles then in Manhattan to create physical barriers to landing at all the potential landing spots around the island *other than* Battery Park. We posted highly visible gun and Guard units at a number of these other places, so it was not totally obvious that we were indifferent to their defense. And we added all remaining stores of razor wire to the edge of the Battery so it did not appear too obviously inviting.

When the seven-month anniversary approached in June, the governor ordered our forces to a state of high alert. The bulk of the Sec fighters and virtually all our artillery and automatic weapons were placed in defensive positions around the Battery. Our Sec fighting force comprised roughly twenty thousand men and women of all ages, most of whom entirely lacked military experience. They were led by officers consisting of the few National Guard commanders left in the city when the siege commenced, about a hundred veterans, and a handful of senior brass from the NYPD. The squads were assembled in a totally ad hoc way. One, for example, consisted exclusively of sanitation workers led by a union officer who had been a master sergeant in Vietnam. Another squad was staffed primarily with Chinese American male nurses from New York Downtown Hospital. The lack of weaponry was our major problem. During our siege preparations—and frankly in the smuggling operations over the winter—we had concentrated on food, medicines, and other essentials, affording low priority to weapons and ammunition. This was a choice that we regretted when faced with the prospect of trying to repulse an actual military invasion.

I was surprised when the seven-month anniversary at the end of June passed without any visible activity on the part of the feds. They had failed to starve Manhattan into submission, but they had succeeded in laying the groundwork for an invasion. The people remaining in Manhattan, whose energies and aspirations had been focused on surviving the winter, and who were jubilant in early spring at having succeeded, were now again facing the grim reality that they were living on a twenty-four-square-mile island surrounded by overwhelming force and any day or night could end with a violent invasion. As the spring progressed, fear and impatience transcended hope as the prevailing sentiment. The talk among increasingly bored New Yorkers turned more and more to the probable fate of the city following the end of the siege. Would its male inhabitants be slaughtered, as seemingly authorized by the Bible? Would residents be allowed to remain or be transported to other locations? Would the governor call for surrender, as he did for the outer boroughs, when further resistance was futile?

I was convinced that the day we all feared would dawn sometime soon, and certainly before the one-year anniversary in late November. We never demobilized the Sec fighters who had been placed on alert to resist the expected invasion in June, so all our defensive positions were staffed around the clock. But as long as there was no visible sign of activity on the part of the blockading forces, half the troops left Lower Manhattan each night and returned home to sleep. During the days, we drilled in an organized but increasingly desultory manner. By early August, when the weather turned hot and muggy, even the slightly salty sea breezes blowing across the Battery could not revive the troubled spirits of the men and women assembled there.

My patrol partner on the night of Tuesday, August 19, was Matthew McManus, a happily married thirty-something who before the siege had been a personal trainer ministering to a diverse roster of private clients who had in common only stress, money, and Matthew. Matthew relieved the tedium of many a night standing watch in the Battery with entertaining accounts of confidences shared by his clients, such as the Citigroup mergers banker and mother of two who revealed that she moonlighted as a dominatrix specializing in latex, which she assured Matthew was the fetish of the moment among thirty-somethings working in private equity.

★　　★　　★

"GREG, WAKE UP," Matthew said at about four in the morning.

"What?"

"It's starting," he said. "Fuck."

Our company was arrayed in forward positions behind the

twenty-foot-high concrete and marble slabs of the Battery Park East Coast World War II memorial, two rows of four each, lined up like gigantic dominos and engraved with the names of the dead. Our mission was to cover the central part of the Battery seawall with thick fire and grenades to prevent the first wave of commandoes from blasting down the railing, cutting through the razor wire, and opening the way for amphibious landing craft. Our positions were well shielded from forward fire and located only yards from the water's edge.

There was no hint of dawn over Brooklyn, but we could just make out a smudge of dark gray arcing across the water. Through the night-vision binoculars, the smudge was revealed to consist of scores of landing craft, side by side, each with their ramp bows aimed at the seawall. At least six identical rows of the small ships appeared behind the vanguard and wrapped ominously around the west side of Governors Island.

Moments later, through the channel between Governors Island and Brooklyn, where for years I had watched with fascination the Queen Mary 2 turn and dock, two navy destroyers emerged at high speed, their big guns ominously lowered for the close-range target. An almost grotesquely fat robin, doubtless having feasted on the unusual abundance of worms aerating our urban food gardens, landed heavily on the oakleaf hydrangea bush just a few feet to my right and set about greeting the dawn. The next moment the big guns opened fire and four shells exploded on the lawn behind us. We heard screams. Moments later, two helicopters swept in from the west and attempted to take the air just in front of the tall buildings along Battery Place, and from that position to strafe our defensive positions from the rear. The antiaircraft batteries arrayed along the tops of those buildings opened fire, and one helicopter plunged dramatically to the street, careening off the reflective glass façade of an office building.

The cacophony and chaos were almost instantaneous. In one moment, the robin's song occupied the deep silence of early morning. In the next, I was surrounded by percussive violence so extreme that I lost my balance and bearings. The combination of the destroyer fire, antiaircraft guns, crashing helicopter, and strafing from the remaining helicopter was overwhelming. We had not trained with live fire.

One of the Guard officers in charge of our position ran up the center of the memorial shouting "Twelve o'clock. Twelve o'clock. Give 'em all you've got."

Straight ahead, on axis with the center of the memorial and the Statue of Liberty in the distance, two almost comically small boats—they might even have been Zodiacs—pulled next to the seawall. With astonishing courage and calmness, a group of commandoes, with only the cover provided by machines guns mounted on the bows of the small craft, placed explosive charges at the bases of about ten posts support-ing the railing atop the seawall. Then they retreated only a few yards, blew the charges, and returned to cut the top rail with a saw and pull a large section of rail into the harbor. A second team of commandoes emerged with long-handled wire cutters and started to cut through the tangle of razor wire along the water's edge. Finally one of our forward teams threw two grenades, and one of the boats and her crew were obliterated. A moment later I saw a disembodied hand, still gripping wire cutters, floating on a fragment of wood. I felt the bile rise in my throat and swallowed hard. The second crew was momentarily dis-oriented, and our machine gunners peeked around the corner of the massive walls and killed all the second crew. At the same time, the Sec antiaircraft team on the top of One Battery Place scored a direct hit on the second helicopter, which had been only moments away from being in position to strafe us from the rear. There was only a brief pause in the action when the navy ships again started their barrage of the park from the water.

Two new Zodiacs took up the position, and a second wave of com-mandoes attacked the razor wire with urgency. Their gunners, hav-ing observed the fate of the first crews from only yards behind them, pinned our forward gunners behind the memorial pylons with unre-lenting fire. I was close enough to see the arm patch that identified the Joshua Brigades, the stylized city wall and battlement image now of course well known to all and a favorite motif for teenagers to wear on the back pocket of their jeans. Within less than a couple of minutes—which seemed to me, and must have seemed to them, an eternity—the second team of commandoes had opened a hole in the razor wire that was at least forty feet wide. Two of the amphibious ships, with their broad ramps up and presenting a formidable shield, advanced on the opening. When they were only sixty yards offshore, the Sec fighters nearer the water again managed to take out the two Zodiac machine gunners with grenades. For the moment, we were free to blanket the opening with fire, which we did the moment the first boat lowered its ramp. It struck me as completely suicidal for the marines in these ships to attempt to come ashore.

But come ashore they did. Low and weaving, maintaining the shelter of the partially raised ramp for as long as possible, the first wave of marines leapt onto the lower promenade of the park with a blaze of offensive fire. At least half of them were hit by our fire and dropped to the ground. But more marines kept coming. There was no hesitation. I admired the bravery of these men, but I needed to remind myself that they were the enemy, here to kill me if I did not kill them first. In the next wave, one marine who moved laterally to the west and was not hit swung around our right flank. Matthew, who was standing on the outside shooting around the west edge of our slab, took the first bullet. Matthew dropped to his knees and turned to face me. The top right side of his head was gone, as was his right eye and his face down to his mid-cheek. His left eye was active and very much alive. He stared at me hard, eye to eyes, in a look of confusion that hardened almost instantly to desperate imploring. I remember speaking the words, "What, Matt, what do you want?" Before my question was complete, the light in the remaining eye faded and he fell facedown. I looked beyond him to the west and saw a young man, red hair visible below his helmet. He had thick freckles on a pale face, which twisted with anger and hate. He charged in from the right, firing, but at an angle from which I was protected by the wall. He was screaming. I heard "Die faggot." I realized that even before Matthew had hit the ground, I had taken a grenade from my belt and pulled the pin. I had no idea how long before. I swung my arm in a lazy underhand loop, and the grenade landed right at his feet. He paused, and then disappeared in a fine red mist.

I turned to my left and peeked around the east side of the wall. A unit of marines leapt over the end of the ramp, landed on the inside of the Battery seawall, and charged up the center of the memorial plaza. Without thought, I stepped to the outside of the wall, knelt, and fired into the group of running soldiers. I remember counting out loud the ones who dropped. The last thing I remember was softly saying to myself the word "three."

CHAPTER SIXTEEN

Camp Purity

2020

> *It is not by one way alone that we can arrive at so sublime a mystery.*
>
> —Quintus Aurelius Symmachus, 384

THE DAY I ARRIVED AT GOVERNORS ISLAND unfolded so strangely that I have replayed it over and over in my mind to assure myself that these memories are accurate and not part of the delirium we all suffered during the two days we spent tied on the ground in Battery Park. Months before the amphibious assault on the Battery, the feds had planned meticulously for the end of the siege. The centerpiece of their plan was the conversion of Governors Island, the 172-acre former military base in the heart of New York harbor, into a "re-education camp" for male Sec fighters. The female Sec fighters were taken to a converted summer camp on Staten Island.

After an intake procedure that seemed familiar from every prison movie ever made, thousands of male prisoners, dressed identically in orange jumpsuits, were ushered into a large auditorium. We had not been permitted to speak with one another since leaving the staging area in Battery Park. We were still shocked from the suddenness of the assault on the Battery, the savagery of the fighting, and speed with which it ended. The left side of my head, which was still covered by a large bandage, ached and throbbed from the wound to my skull. I was still trying to adjust to the fact that I was alive.

A clergyman strode to the lectern on the stage in the front of the room. An elaborate carved plaque affixed to the front of the lectern showed a sword and crucifix crossed against the background of a gold shield.

"Let us pray," he said. "Oh God our father, the giver of life and giver of law; oh Lord Jesus Christ, Your son and our redeemer. These men, your children, have sinned against You most abominably. The illusions of Satan have penetrated their hearts, and they have taken up arms against their father and their brothers. The eternal torments of hell are their just rewards. And yet, merciful God, You still hold out the redemption of Christ, the possibility of eternal life in Christ, to *all* Your children. So I pray, oh Lord, that these children confess their sins and open their hearts to the light of Your Word. I pray, oh Lord, for the judges and the officers of this place, that they may do Your will. In the name of Jesus Christ, our Lord, Amen."

A few muffled "Amens" rose from the room.

Three men in army uniforms—colonels, I believe—walked to the center of the stage.

"Thank you, Reverend," one of them opened. "The special military tribunal convened by order of the president to deal with domestic enemy combatants in the Holy War for the Union has reached a judgment in your case. Although Executive Order No. 424 gives the military tribunal exclusive jurisdiction, the president asked that our finding be reviewed by the United States Court of Appeals for the District of Columbia Circuit, which also sits as a special court to advise the federal judiciary on questions of biblical law. The commission has instructed us to come before you to read its decision." He looked up and then continued.

"In the matter of *The People of the United States of America v. Enemy Combatants in the State of New York,* this tribunal finds said enemy combatants guilty of sedition, treason, armed insurrection, and conversion of federal property. You are hereby sentenced to death." He again paused to let this sink in. I heard only a few gasps and quiet groans in the large room.

"However, the sentence of death is hereby suspended for three years, or until such earlier time as you indicate by your words or deeds that you have closed your heart to the saving grace of Jesus Christ. Each of you is ordered confined to the federal Faith & Freedom Rehabilitation Facility, Governors Island, until such time as you are born again in Christ's love and you have demonstrated for six months thereafter the sincerity and total conviction with which you have accepted Jesus as your savior, following which time you shall be released and your death sentence commuted. May God bless you and forgive you for your sins."

The three colonels left the stage, and a murmur erupted among the men until the guards brusquely demanded silence.

A blond man in his late thirties in civilian dress came to the front of the room. His large boyish face presented a picture of corn-fed innocence, but the head sat atop a body that exuded danger. It was a body that suggested vanity, pride, and obsession with physical prowess. Half of a crucifix tattoo peeked out from the arm of a T-shirt, the sleeves of which seemed to me to be unnecessarily tight. He moved with an awkward self-consciousness. His expression tended toward a sneer. This is a person, I imagined darkly, who likes watching others suffer.

"Welcome," he said, "to Camp Purity. I am Joe Jones, superintendent of the Faith & Freedom Rehabilitation Facility, Governors Island, better known among those who will be your . . . your . . . hosts here as Camp Purity. In case there was any doubt about your sentence, let me make it clear. You are criminals who have been convicted of multiple capital offenses and sentenced to death. That sentence has been temporarily suspended. You now have a choice. You will accept Jesus as your savior and be born again in Christ, or you will be executed. If you cease to work in good faith on your rehabilitation in Christ's love, you will be executed. If you falsely claim to have accepted Jesus Christ as your savior, a heinous sin and crime, you will be executed. If you are not born again within three years, you will be executed. Are you getting the picture?"

He paused for dramatic effect, his gaze fixed on a large crucifix, with a Christ figure that was at least fifteen feet tall, mounted on the side wall of the large hall. His gaze drew mine and others. This was not the lanky Jesus mild of countless medieval and Renaissance depictions. This was Jesus the warrior, with the musculature of a marine and a fierce gaze that spoke of defiance to his torturers, not submission and suffering. His crucifixion was grotesque, with splayed skin and bone fragments hanging from the nail wounds in his ankles, and tendons and blood vessels spilling from a large tear in his right wrist. The dirty cloth that was supposed to maintain the modesty of the crucified Christ instead suggested his virility. As a sculptural object, the crucifix was literal, empty, and entirely without art. I could not imagine how it could inspire devotion.

"On the other hand," Superintendent Jones continued, "if you look honestly at your lives, if you are truly contrite for the terrible sins you have committed, if you open your hearts to Christ, if you study the Bible and pray, if you maintain your purity, and if you hand over your life to Jesus, then you will experience the most wonderful thing that can happen to a mortal man. Your old selves—your grasping, dark, sinful, satanic selves—will suddenly melt away. The lies of Satan will disappear in a moment when they're exposed as the illusions they are, and you'll be filled with the light of Christ and know that you have gained eternal life through his grace. For six months after this wonderful epiphany, you will stay here with your brothers so the strength and integrity of your second birth can be tested. When we know it to be real, you'll be released to take your places as devout and useful citizens of our Christian Nation. Any questions?"

As a lawyer, I had to admire the clever construction of our sentence. Our death sentences were suspended for three years (meaning we died if we had not converted in thirty-six months). But the suspension also lapsed (that is, we would be executed) *before* the three years were up if we indicated by our words or deeds that we have *closed* our heart "to the saving grace of Jesus Christ." So, if at *any time* they thought we were not trying hard enough to be saved, then they had license to kill us at will. I could imagine President Jordan explaining to the people how his government had shown the mercy of Christ to the rebels on Manhattan, sparing our lives and giving us every chance to find the peace of the Lord and emerge as free men. No one would know that each of us stood under the sword of Damocles, hanging by a thread, facing death every minute of every day, if by word or deed or bad luck one of our captors decided that our heart was irredeemably closed to the light of the Lord.

Having scanned the room, the superintendent suddenly looked more animated than he had at any other stage of the proceedings.

"Now that you understand your sentence, and the gracious mercy of Christ that has been extended to you by your fellow citizens, I will turn to the next topic. This is masturbation."

I thought at first that I had not heard right and looked to the person to my right for affirmation. He arched an eyebrow. Seeing the confusion in the room, the superintendent repeated himself.

"Yes, that's right, masturbation."

For ten months they had laid siege to Manhattan. Tens of thousands of Americans all around the country had died in the Holy War. And now that victory was finally theirs, now that they had the most committed Secs within their control, theirs to reshape in accordance with their holy vision, now that their moment had come . . . I didn't know whether to laugh or cry. In my confusion, I remembered a comment Sanjay had made—that all authoritarian regimes, were they not so tragic, tended toward the farcical. Superintendent Jones continued.

"Look within yourselves. Somewhere deep down you knew this day would come. From the first day you pleasured yourself you knew it was wrong. Ugly. Unclean. A perversion of the purpose of sex. An abomination in the sight of God."

He glanced dramatically at the crucifix.

"A terrible violation of His temple, your body. Impurity—the corruption of your bodies—is what opened your souls to Satan. Impurity literally cracked open the door to evil, and evil flowed through that crack and filled up the work with corruption, like water flowing through the crack in a dam. So you see, impurity is what lies at the root of every social and political evil. And, what's worse, you and your culture were blind to impurity; instead, you tolerated, even celebrated, the corruption. And this tolerance of impurity is what caused God to punish us on 9/11 and then again on 7/22."

We had heard this part before. The moment that President Palin publicly endorsed the idea that America's disobedience to God caused both 9/11 and 7/22 is the moment that so many of us first awakened to the danger we faced. Many in the room shifted in their seats.

"Do you understand? Everything, everything that was wrong with you and with the wicked culture you built was based on the black foundation of sexual violation. Thus, it is obvious that to create the conditions where you can enjoy the redemption of Christ's love, we must pull down that foul foundation. The place to start on the road to your second births is simple. You will cease to masturbate. This is the first and most important rule of Camp Purity." He gazed around the room as if looking for someone, then continued.

"This is so much more than a rule. This is a covenant you will make with yourselves, with one another and with God. Knowing how to make and keep covenants is the first step to knowing God. When you get to your rooms, you will find a contract on each bunk. It's a binding agreement among the six of you in the room. Your five roommates are your brothers. They are your new family. Their role is the same as your brothers in your first life—to love and support you, to keep you strong and pure. You will agree to do this for one another and for God, and you will sign this contract. If you break your word, you are betraying yourself and your brothers and God. If one of you fails, all fail."

Superintendent Jones continued with his hands on his hips, his right bicep flexing so that the tattooed cross on his arm distractingly emerged from below his sleeve.

"You will be monitored at all times. If you attempt to masturbate, you and all your brothers will be punished . . . punished severely. If you observe someone else attempting to masturbate and you do not report it, you and all your brothers will be punished, severely. This is the nature of your covenant with one another—a sin by one is a sin by all. There is no such thing as punishment of one of you, for the failure by one is a failure by all."

He again paused for effect, but this time he kept his eyes on us.

"And in case you continue to think we are idiots, I will tell you that you are being watched at all times. Privacy is a liberal conceit and an illusion. Do you seriously think that you can hide anything from God? Privacy is an invitation to corruption. Privacy is the refuge of the pervert and the criminal. There is no privacy at Camp Purity. Just because you don't see a camera doesn't mean that one is not there."

"But let me be clear," he said in a brighter tone. "Submission to the will of God under threat of punishment is not what we're after. Submission to the Lord and His law is a choice. And this decision happens first in the heart. If you don't decide in your heart to submit to God and live a pure life, then you haven't really submitted at all. It's your decision—but with God's grace all of you have the capacity to make the right decision. That is all. You are dismissed."

★   ★   ★

DURING THE COURSE of the first year, we came to understand this surprising start to our "rehabilitation." After all, most religious texts encompassed sexual taboos, and the evangelical movement had been preoccupied with sex since its inception. From the 1990s on, the movement was almost defined by its insistence on abstinence with the Abstinence Clearinghouse, the Southern Baptists' celibacy program called True Love Waits, and a blizzard of other initiatives aimed at youth of high school and college age. "Purity balls" and "abstinence teas" entered the lexicon of red state students. An evangelical speakers' bureau of beautiful male and female "power virgins" spread the word on college campuses across the South and West. What most people didn't realize at the time was that "abstinence" included not only abstaining from sexual intercourse but also abstaining from masturbation. I became aware of that only by accident when, sometime around 2011, I was walking through Atlanta airport with a colleague and noticed black plastic arm bracelets on a significant number of young men. I had assumed the bands represented a disease, as in pink for breast cancer. But the younger lawyer with whom I was traveling set me straight.

"They're masturbands," he said.

"What?"

"Masturbands, as in masturbation."

"What? I mean, why? Like what—as if it's a disease?" I asked.

"Not exactly. It started about six years ago. You wear it as long as you've stayed pure. If you're weak and you beat off, then you have to take it off. And everyone knows and won't shake your hand. "

"But . . . why?"

He had no answer. During our first months at GI, the theology behind the preoccupation with masturbation became clear. One of our purity courses at Governors Island included videotaped lectures from Christine O'Donnell, a protégé of Sarah Palin who was elected as US senator from Delaware in 2012 and was one of the few members of Congress who felt it was consistent with the dignity of that office to lecture publicly about the dangers of masturbation. Her explanation was at first difficult to decipher:

> *It is not enough to be abstinent with other people, you have to be abstinent alone. . . . The Bible says that lust in your heart is committing adultery, so you can't masturbate without lust. The reason that you don't tell [people] that masturbation is the answer to AIDS and all these other problems that come with sex outside of marriage is because, again, it is not addressing the issue . . .*

Although she couldn't get it quite right, it was reasonably clear to me. The Bible says that to masturbate is to have lust in your heart; it says that to have lust in your heart is adultery; and it says that adultery is forbidden—*ergo*, masturbation is forbidden. Not only is all sex other than marital sex forbidden, but all sex, to be permitted, must be sacred. As one of our instructors put it, "The only acceptable sex is a threesome, between man, wife, and God. Without God in the picture, it's just fucking, like animals."

So in the first days of our incarceration, when we expected interrogation, abuse, and even torture, we met our roommates and signed our no-masturbation contract with much ribald comment. After all, most of us were wounded, exhausted, devastated at our failure to defend the last outpost of tolerant democracy in the country, and still apprehensive that our lives could be taken at any moment. Moreover, we were living in a setting that did not offer much in the way of either sexual stimulation or privacy. Let's just say that few of us found obeying the first commandment of Camp Purity to be much of a sacrifice.

CHAPTER SEVENTEEN

Assembly

2020–2022

> *. . . Christocentrism is inevitably a religion of suffering, of agony and death. The emblem of Christ nailed to the Cross that is set up everywhere is a vision of horror . . . The story of Jesus is full of crying, weeping and sudden dramas. . . .*
>
> *[In contrast] serenity, when it wears a human face— seems to me, in fact, to be the fundamental value of Eastern religion and philosophy.*
>
> —Michel Tournier,
> *Gemini*

OUR PROGRAM AT GI WAS BUILT around a four-step method to second birth that our captors called the Four Graces. The first step was to see that we were vile sinners, disgusting in the sight of God. The second was to understand that, nonetheless, God loved us. Third was accepting that God, out of his love for the sinner, sent us His son Jesus to redeem our sins. The final step was to accept Jesus as our savior and be born again. Each prisoner wore a colored name tag that included the number of his current phase in the Four Graces program. The badges of the born again were gold and in the shape of a five-pointed star.

As cynics and, for the most part, atheists, most of us found it hard to take the Four Graces program seriously. We furtively referred to it as SLURS (sin, love, redemption, and second birth). A morning in

SLURS class had the intellectual content of a late-night infomercial. Our instructors spoke in a language that bore little relation to the English we used in Manhattan. Their sentences were peppered with the clichés of game shows and reality television and leavened with the cadences of the southern preacher. The inventor of SLURS must have been an earnest student of a twelve-step addiction program or, more precisely, a dumbed-down Jenny Craig–like version of the twelve-step idea. Eternal salvation was mapped out in four easy steps, with much group encouragement and upbeat coaching along the way. Unlike Alcoholics Anonymous or Weight Watchers, however, the SLURS program came with the significant additional motivational tool of execution as the penalty for failure or inadequate effort. This tension between the farcical absurdity of our training in purity and religion and the realities of prison life, with its incipient threat of violence, created a bizarre and unsettling atmosphere at the camp.

During the first few months, as the horror of the invasion receded and our physical wounds healed, we adjusted to the rhythm of life at GI. The threat of violence remained an undercurrent that had not yet erupted, and many of us optimistically created a mental narrative in which we were to endure a sort of extended religious summer camp, go through the motions of being saved, and then return to our lives. We gathered in a large mess hall for breakfast and prayer. Morning Bible study was conducted in neat classrooms. Midday we did welcome physical labor and chores around the island. We were not in chains. SLURS training and Bible study again in the afternoon. After dinner, they rang a bell and we were required to sit quietly for two hours and read the Bible verses that were the subject of the next day's class.

Our growing sense of routine was also facilitated by the familiarity of our location. We were not in the American equivalent of Siberia. Our 172-acre island stood only a half mile from the tip of Manhattan. Each time we looked out, we took comfort from familiar landmarks: Brooklyn Heights; the Brooklyn and Manhattan bridges; the Verrazano-Narrows Bridge off to the south; the Statue of Liberty, Battery Park, and the familiar skyline of Lower Manhattan. In the center of that skyline was the building in which I had worked for nearly nine years, close enough to see at night which of the office lights were on or off. Close enough to see the office that used to be mine. Close enough to be reminded, every day, that but for a single choice, the person at that desk—giving a thought, or not, to the Sec fighters imprisoned outside his window—would be me. I wondered who else has been imprisoned with a mirror in which he sees, every day, the alternative universe in which he is a free man? I could not decide whether it was a comfort or a cruelty.

GI was remarkably well suited to our rehabilitation program and was a smart choice by the Jordan administration. As an island, it was highly secure, both from escape and uninvited visitation. Most of the large barracks had been built before World War II, during which troops from all over the country were assembled on the island before boarding transport ships for Europe. Liggett Hall, the main barracks building, was the first single structure big enough to house all the facilities of an entire army regiment. It was huge, spanning nearly the entire width of the island, with an imposing arch and tower at the center. Designed by McKim, Mead & White, architects of the gilded age, Liggett was certainly one of the classiest buildings ever to serve as a prison. With his well-known sense of theater, Stanford White gave the building an enormous courtyard designed as a dramatic setting for the ceremonies of regimental life. It proved equally suitable for the ritual needs of Camp Purity.

Equally useful to the eventual needs of Camp Purity was Castle Williams, an early nineteenth-century fort used by the federal government as a prison for Confederate troops during the Civil War and thereafter maintained as a military stockade. The castle was the New York counterpart to Fort Leavenworth in Kansas. Some called it the Alcatraz of New York harbor. Its small stone cells remained largely unimproved for two hundred years. For the first few months, we did not know that Castle Williams was anything other than an historical monument. Indeed, for the first few months, some of us simply pretended that we were not in prison. Yes, the edges of the island were wrapped in double rows of coiled razor wire. And yes, guards with guns were everywhere. But you see what you want to see.

Each morning, after breakfast and before morning Bible study, the entire company of prisoners, guards, and workers gathered in the impressive courtyard behind Liggett Hall for "assembly." Superintendent Joe Jones, whom we quickly nicknamed Super JJ, the other federal civilian administrators, the military officers, and the clergy sat on a raised platform with their backs to the building. A small stone obelisk-like structure dating from the nineteenth century marked the center of the courtyard, and all 3,500 prisoners stood in an arc around it and faced the leadership on the platform. The guards were arrayed in a larger-radius arc in back of the prisoners. We never saw Super JJ or the other administrators wearing a tie. Instead, they all dressed in mid-American "business casual"—khakis, brown loafers, and short-sleeve button-down shirts. Super JJ, whose buzz-cut hair and fondness for tight T-shirts gave him a more military look, was the exception. The guards were all in military uniforms, and the prisoners wore standard-issue orange jumpsuits.

Assembly followed the same pattern every day. The chief chaplain, referred to by Super JJ only as "padre," opened with a prayer. Super JJ's adjutant then made announcements regarding things like mess hall hours and the posting of Bible class and work assignments. Super JJ then gave a brief summary of what he described as the "news" but that we believed was a carefully programmed series of lies dripped out to convince us of the finality of their victory and the hopelessness of the secular cause. We later learned that his description of events—the immediate capitulation of Manhattan following our loss at the Battery, the return of New York to the Union, and the gradual cessation of violent resistance throughout the country—was largely accurate.

Toward the end of the second month, the assembly program changed for the first time. The chief deacon reported each morning on inmates who had advanced to a new step in the SLURS program. The first time he appeared at assembly, he introduced about a score of prisoners who had progressed to step one (understanding that they were vile sinners), who were then invited to come forward to an area in front reserved for those in the first stage of grace. Within another week, about the same number had advanced to step two (understanding that, notwithstanding their sin, they were loved by God). When a prisoner progressed, his badge also changed color, allowing guards and prisoners to know at a glance his progress. Over the first months the ranks of those in step one swelled to hundreds, scores reached step two, and a couple even stood alone in the quadrant reserved for prisoners attaining step three.

Although we indulged in the minor disobedience of using nicknames for the staff, and sometimes referred disrespectfully to the Four Graces as SLURS, we did so with circumspection, believing—correctly as it turned out—that all interior spaces on GI were closely monitored by video. We eventually discovered many of the pinhole cameras, which were ubiquitous. For example, there was not only a single camera in the hall bathroom used by my brothers and me but one in every shower and toilet stall. The food line in the mess hall was miked, as was each table. After a couple of months, we all felt the considerable strain of not being able to discuss our situation freely. With little more than glances, we shared with trusted acquaintances our skepticism about the growing band of prisoners advancing to step two, but we were unable to discuss it further.

For me, the apparent progress by hundreds of prisoners through the Four Graces program was truly puzzling. Yes, I knew about the Stockholm syndrome, and the natural tendency to want to please those who control your life. But the 3,500 men in that courtyard were New York's most committed secularists. All had chosen to risk their lives to resist the Christian Nation. They were mostly committed atheists, with many observant Jews and the occasional Muslim. My fellow prisoners were cynical journalists, tough-minded lawyers, foul-mouthed cabdrivers, and liberal professors—hardly the ideal candidates for conversion, much less full-on second birth. And though we had been through a period of enormous stress, and rose every morning under threat of execution, it seemed improbable to me that capitulation would start to occur so quickly. I was preoccupied with the question of how and why a new group, every morning, transitioned publicly to steps two and three. Was it an escape strategy? Had they learned how to fool our captors? Were they plants intended to inspire the real prisoners? Or had the mental strain of the war and imprisonment unbalanced their minds sufficiently that they were in fact open to religious conversion?

"So you made step two," I said with complete neutrality to a stranger following assembly. We were outdoors, where we all hoped the risk of being overheard or recorded was lower.

"Yes," he answered.

"I'm interested. How did it happen?"

"Think about it. Aren't we all sinners?" he said, walking away and revealing nothing.

I did not dare to pursue him.

★　★　★

THE MORNING OF the first flogging changed everything. We assembled and the program proceeded as usual. Super JJ, who usually had the last word, ascended to the podium.

"A reading from the Book of Deuteronomy, chapter 25, verse 2:

Then it shall be if the wicked man deserves to be beaten, the judge shall then make him lie down and be beaten in the presence with the number of stripes according to his guilt.

"That is the infallible word of God. You are all wicked men, and with justice and fidelity to God's word we could beat each of you every day. But in the Christian Nation we have a mandate to live our lives according to the model of our Lord Jesus Christ and his mercy. I have been clear with you about the rules, and clear about the consequences if you break the rules. Prisoner Number 4587, come forward with your brothers."

A prisoner whom I did not know was brought in front of the podium by two guards, and behind him two guards similarly held each of his five brothers. The guards looked nervous.

"Yesterday evening Prisoner Number 4587 was observed engaging in sexual intercourse with one of the assistant cooks behind the kitchen. She has been sent off island and will be dealt with by the civilian authorities. The prisoner has been sentenced to twenty-four lashes. Each of his brothers, accordingly, will also receive twenty-four lashes. As you know, the Bible permits a maximum of forty lashes, so this sentence is a merciful one. Each of the brothers will be punished first so that the miscreant can observe the consequences of his own sin. Only when all his brothers have suffered will he be permitted to join them. Guards, do not hesitate to do God's will."

The stone pole that I had always thought of as an obelisk had old iron rings mounted about seven feet off the ground on each face. I now recognized that it was a nineteenth-century whipping post. The guards took the youngest of the five brothers, a scrawny redhead who looked to be about twenty-five, and roughly unzipped and removed his jumpsuit. Trying not to look scared, he gave the guards a cocky look of defiance as they looped a rope around each wrist, snaked the ropes through the rings on the right and left sides of the post, pulled his arms above his head, and secured the rope on cleats lower down the post. I could no longer see his face. They then attached a stiff wide belt around his waist, a device to protect the kidneys and lower back that I recognized from the extensive media coverage given to "judicial caning" in Singapore. I was sure that in their eyes it gave the ancient barbaric punishment a modern clinical veneer. One of the guards then unfurled a whip. The single-tail black bullwhip was about eight feet in length.

The first stroke produced a loud cracking sound that no one was expecting. A red welt rose from the upper right shoulder to midback. The young man threw back his head in wordless pain.

"One," said the other guard.

On the third stroke a loud "oh" escaped from the man, the breath expelled in a blast from the force of the whip on his back. The fourth stroke was the first to cross another, and blood began to trickle from the places where the stripes crossed.

"Six," said the first guard, handing over the whip to the other guard, who recommenced the flogging from the other side.

With this stroke a long sob welled up from the man's gut. The only sounds in the large courtyard were the sickening crack of the whip, and sobbing that became increasingly convulsive and desperate with each stroke.

By the time the second guard handed back off to the first guard following the twelfth stroke, the prisoner whose indiscretion had given rise to the flogging, had lost all color and looked to be on the verge of collapse. His mouth was open and his eyes were blank. Two of his four other brothers were crying softly. Two looked outraged.

Only months before, I had killed men and seen men killed. I saw horrible suffering. But that suffering was incidental to a violent battle. The point of that violence was to kill the enemy, not to inflict pain. It was far different from deliberate physical torture. I had never seen anything like this. I had never seen one man look into the suffering eyes of another and calmly count out further torment. I had never seen a torturer steel himself to the sounds of desperation and carry on. At eighteen strokes the victim's back was a single blue and purple bruise decorated with a crazy crisscross of red lines oozing blood. The soft touch of a single finger would have been unendurable on such a back, and yet he would receive six more lashes. It did not seem survivable.

An angry murmur rose from the prisoners. A few guards shouldered their weapons, and others shifted their weight uneasily.

By the time the guard shouted "twenty-four," the young man hung limply from the ropes. When they took him down I saw he was conscious, his eyes partially rolled back into his head, his breathing shallow. The guards who had administered the flogging took one arm over each shoulder and dragged him upright in the direction of the infirmary.

The eyes of his brothers and all the other prisoners turned expectantly to Super JJ. I longed to believe that he would be satisfied with the horror we had just witnessed and suspend the other punishments. The guards holding the next brother looked similarly hopeful. The Super disabused these hopes with a barely discernible nod to the guards to proceed.

The second brother, terrified, panicked and struggled against his guards. Two others rushed forward to hold his arms while the ropes were looped over his wrists. Even secured to the post, he continued to struggle like a wounded animal, moaning over and over "no, no, no." They tied his feet and waist so he could not turn around. After the first stroke, he let out a scream. It was more the sound of terror than of pain, but as the strokes went on, the pain overwhelmed the terror, and he too was reduced to gasping sobs, sobs that eventually abated as he sank into shock during the final strokes.

By the time the final prisoner was secured to the post, both he and the assembled company seemed to be in a daze. Disoriented. More uncomprehending than scared or angry. JJ and his thugs had committed the crime, but it was the other prisoners and I who felt guilty. We had stood and watched a monstrous evil and done nothing.

At the end, the superintendent resumed his place at the podium.

"Remember this. What you saw this morning is nothing compared with the suffering of our Lord. Nothing. Each flogging should remind you of the terrible suffering that Jesus endured for you. He suffered to redeem your sins. And with his stripes, we are healed. Think on this. You are dismissed."

After this first flogging, the atmosphere at GI changed considerably. The summer camp illusion was shattered. The prisoners became sullen and the guards more aggressive. It was as if the genie of latent violence had been released. In our private metaphoric language, certain prisoners started to allude to rebellion and escape. Others accelerated their progress on the four-step program, focused only on escape through the path that had been laid out for them. The vast majority was simply at sea. Being born again was not something they could do honestly, and to do so dishonestly was both repulsive and risky. And yet, somehow having survived the Holy War, our determination to live seemed to have grown. We did not want to die.

The first floggings led inevitably to a spiral of disobedience, fear, and further violence. Prisoners were caught speaking out against the authority of the administration. Small acts of resistance proliferated.

The guards became more cautious in their dealings with inmates, and they took offense more easily. The next flogging occurred only three days after the first and thereafter became a regular feature of morning assembly. Super JJ had reduced the standard sentence from twenty-four to twelve lashes because, as rumor had it, the initial victims of twenty-four strokes had yet to leave the infirmary.

It would not be exactly correct to say that we became accustomed to the morning violence. We no longer suffered the shock of the first day, but the weight of observed suffering accumulated differently within each man. All of us, I think, felt a gradual sense of emasculation and helplessness as, day after day, through our inaction we became complicit in their crimes.

Time passed slowly, marked by the larger and larger numbers of inmates clustered at assembly in the spots designated for those who had reached steps two, three, and four. At the first anniversary of our incarceration, more than two dozen men wore the gold badges of the born again and had commenced the six-month trial designed to test the authenticity of their second-birth experiences. Scores of others had reached step three.

As for me, after the first year I had read the Bible front to back three times. We were permitted no other reading material, so I devoted all my intellectual energy and analytic skill to that single anthology. I regretted not knowing Greek, as some prisoners were allowed to read the gospels in their original language. I was a diligent student and an active participant in Bible study, but I needed to be exceedingly careful not to stray too far into the mode of literary criticism, thus indirectly challenging the only approved manner of engaging with the text, which was as revelation received directly from the omnipotent being. We were permitted to debate what God meant and how to apply the lessons and the mandates of the Bible to everyday life. We were not permitted to note the inconsistencies among the gospels and the wonderfully different voices of their human authors, or to acknowledge the existence of the non-canonical gospels.

I gave little thought to the endgame. I had managed a sophistic confession of sin and moved to step one, but I remained stuck there for many months. To profess knowledge of God's love was to admit to the existence of God, a line I saw no way to cross. But the third anniversary was still a long way off, and I did not allow myself to think ahead.

Oddly, I was not miserable. My brothers and I had avoided the whipping post, and I found myself much strengthened in body and mind from the regime of regular food, sleep, study, and fresh air. After all, the years before my incarceration were years of unparalleled stress and uncertainty. In contrast, at GI, there seemed during this period to be little uncertainty about what the next day would bring.

CHAPTER EIGHTEEN

October 9, 2022

Men never do evil so completely and cheerfully as when they do it from religious conviction.

—Blaise Pascal,
Pensées

OCTOBER 9, 2022, STARTED LIKE each other day. My brothers and I rose, showered, shaved, dressed, and cleaned our room. At GI, purity included a quaint emphasis on cleanliness and grooming. Facial hair was not permitted.

It was one of those rare early October days with the clarity and cleanliness of autumn but the lingering warmth of summer. The leaves were still on the trees and had not yet turned color. The harbor reflected the hard blue of the cloudless sky and slightly cooled the warm breeze out of the south. It was, in some ways, a paradise. The assembly area was shaded by 250-year-old white oaks, straight-trunked passive observers of the long-running human drama played out beneath their crowns. The trees inspired confidence. Behind them, the great McKim, Mead & White barracks were an exemplar of the classical revival style—visible testimony to the Enlightenment, an architecture of reason and civilization. Surely, I thought, the species that computed the entasis of the column and took joy in its perfection would return to its senses. It started out as a very good morning.

When Super JJ entered assembly, I was surprised to see two men with video cameras following behind. Our morning program had never before been televised. I tried to imagine what propaganda end might be served by recording our normally pedestrian proceedings. If there was to be a whipping, that hardly seemed like something to advertise to the outside world.

My good morning turned to a spectacular one when, a few seconds later, I was amazed to see Sanjay, dressed like the rest of us in an orange jumpsuit, escorted by two guards to stand at the edge of the platform. I had last seen Sanjay on the evening before the invasion of the Battery. I was busy listening to the instructions of our sergeant, a retired marine from the Bronx. I had understood that Sanjay was with the rest of the civilian leadership at City Hall, so I was surprised to see him walk into the park carrying a small machine gun. Sanjay had not accepted military training. I left my unit and walked over to him.

"You know how to use that thing?" I asked.

He looked exhausted but managed a weak smile. "I am learning quickly."

We stared at each other in silence.

"I have come to fight with you," he said simply, and then turned to follow a turbaned Sikh to a position about thirty yards to my south.

Hours later during the chaos of the marine landing, I looked over at Sanjay's position, but I could see nothing. I did not see him on the ground after the fight, or anytime thereafter at Governors. I assumed that he had either been killed in the invasion or captured and killed afterward. And now he stood before me. Within seconds, his eyes found mine in the crowd. My face broke into a broad grin, which his eyes told me was not a good idea. But no one seemed to notice.

I heard nothing of the assembly program that followed. We both reveled in our wordless connection, and the time passed slowly.

After the business of the assembly was complete, the camp chaplain mounted the platform and turned to face the born-again group. The gold-star crowd in Zone Four had grown slowly over the first eighteen months but then increased rapidly over the course of the summer. None had yet been released, although we understood that the genuineness of their second births would be tested over a six-month period, following which they would return to civilian life. For the first time, the chaplain addressed the gold stars directly:

"Beloved in Jesus. We are brothers and sisters. You and I have accepted a new father, our Lord Jesus, and become united as a single family in his love. We are, thanks be to God, saved. Redeemed. Granted eternal life and spared an eternity of torment. Our old lives are gone, and in their place is a life with Christ at its center. Christ who is everything. For Christ we live and for Christ we would do anything. Anything. We do not question his word. We do not question his law. We do not question his justice. For we know nothing, and he knows everything. Our human instincts and judgments, like the human beings who make them, are flawed. Only in Christ's love are we perfected. Today is the time to show us that perfection. To show us that you have indeed been born again in God's love, for if you have, you will do his will, joyfully and without question. Look inside yourselves. Recapture that light and faith and love that you felt the day you were born again. Make it burn bright within, this I pray, in the name of our Lord Jesus Christ. Amen."

"Thank you, Padre." Super JJ strode to the podium looking, it seemed to me, uncharacteristically nervous. Perhaps it was the cameras.

"Gold stars, make a semicircle around the front of the post. Guards, clear the area."

A murmur arose from the crowd. The general company of prisoners was moved back, and the gold stars were arrayed in a single row arcing in a semicircle around the post. Guards stood behind them, one for every four or five gold-star prisoners. My mind seemed to move slowly, reluctantly, not wanting to connect the dots.

With a nod by JJ to the guards, Sanjay was brought forward to the post. One of the guards roughly pulled up his orange jumpsuit and two others tied his wrists in front of him. He was shoved with his back against the post, so he faced the semicircle of born agains, and his arms were pulled up and stretched tightly above his head. This in turn stretched his torso, revealing each rib. His feet were spread and pulled back, each tied slightly behind the post. This position left his smooth brown body grotesquely exposed. I had never seen anyone look so completely naked or so vulnerable. Sanjay's breath remained deep and steady. I, in contrast, could not breathe, and dreaded the whipping that I assumed would follow.

Super JJ looked carefully at Sanjay and nodded his satisfaction to the detail of guards, who then stepped away.

"A reading from the book of Leviticus: 'And he that blasphemeth the name of the Lord, he shall surely be put to death, and all the congregation shall certainly stone him.' A reading from the book of Deuteronomy: 'If there be found among you . . . that . . . hath gone and served other gods, and worshipped them . . . Then shalt thou . . . stone them with stones, till they die . . . If thy brother, the son of thy mother, or thy son, or thy daughter, or the wife of thy bosom, or thy friend, which is as thine own soul, entice thee secretly, saying, Let us go and serve other gods, which thou hast not known, thou, nor thy fathers . . . thou shalt stone him with stones, that he die.' Thanks be to God."

As JJ had been reading, four puzzled-looking men from the maintenance crew had entered the courtyard with wheelbarrows and dumped small loads of stones, each ranging in size between a golf ball and a baseball, at the feet of the gold stars.

"You, my brothers born again in Christ. This man you see before you has been Christ's greatest enemy in this world. He is an agent of Satan. He is an atheist, a pagan, and a sodomite. He not only turned his heart from God, but he harnessed Satan's power of illusion to turn millions of others from Christ. He reeks with the blood of infants, the dark stain of sin most vile. And God calls out for vengeance, for justice. So for you, our first class of sinners born again in Christ's love—for you we have reserved the unique privilege of showing your devotion to Jesus by doing this just thing. The Bible calls us to justice, and to you we extend the special privilege of doing God's will. If you falter, we know that Christ's light does not truly burn in your heart and that you have deceived us. And you know the consequence.

Brothers in Christ, pick up the stones and do as the Bible tells you. You may proceed."

There was no sound in the courtyard. I remember hearing the sound of a ferry engine and the faint echo of a taxi blowing its horn in Red Hook. My eyes were locked with Sanjay's, paralyzed. I was terrified. His eyes were calm. Resigned. Not a person in the semicircle moved. To a man, their eyes were cast down, staring at the stones. Eyes trying to make invisible the bodies to which they were attached.

Super JJ walked down the stairs and into the space between the gold stars and Sanjay. He scanned the faces and walked up to a man who must have reminded him of himself. A balding man who was large and muscular, with receding hair and a buzz cut. Perhaps ex-military. He raised his eyes. JJ stood in front of him.

"You will pick up a stone and start," JJ said.

"I will not," the man replied. In an instant, JJ drew his sidearm and shot the man in the middle of his forehead. He dropped in place.

The Super stepped back and again scanned the circle. He walked up to a younger man, probably a student when Manhattan fell, with curly red hair and acne scars. His face was pale and he was too scared to look up. "You will start," said JJ. The redhead looked up at Sanjay and started to stammer, "I . . . I . . . No, I . . ." The back of his skull and half his brain exploded backward from the shot to his head, splattering a guard behind him.

Again, JJ stepped back and scanned the circle. As he approached the next man, the man dove to the stone pile, picked up a small stone, and hurled it at Sanjay. I heard the crack of a rib and stared at the purple bruise on the side of Sanjay's chest.

"Everyone. Now," said JJ.

The stones started to thud against Sanjay's body in a regular rhythm. Some men threw them frantically, some methodically, and many laconically. A few wept.

It seemed to me that I had breathed only a single breath since JJ stepped off the stage. I had not moved. I can remember observation but no conscious thought. But the instant I understood what was happening, I darted from my place in assembly, around the side of the gold-star circle and through a hail of stones, to Sanjay. I wrapped myself around the exposed side of his body and grasped my hands together behind the post, intending never to let go.

My body now shielded his from the stone throwers. Some of the prisoners stopped throwing, but others continued. A few stones hit my back and the back of my legs, but I felt no pain. Sanjay was conscious. I felt his breath on my neck, and for a few moments I heard only the sound of his breathing, now labored.

"San," I said. "I'm here."

The guards rushed forward and the stoning stopped. The first two to arrive grabbed my shoulders and tried to pull me away. I held my left wrist with my right hand. I had never felt stronger. A third guard arrived and wrapped his forearm around my neck and gave a stiff kick to the back of my knees. I did not let go.

Sanjay turned his head and whispered in my ear, "G, you must remember."

Two more guards arrived, and with four arms pulling each of mine, they succeeded in breaking my grip. They yanked me away and dragged me back to the edge of the circle. I was held down by the guards.

All stoning had stopped, and each gold star was staring at me in shock.

"No," I begged them. "Don't do it. You know it's wrong."

JJ raised his gun. I remember wondering what it would feel like. Instead, he pointed it in the general direction of the forty born-again prisoners.

"You will now show me how much you love Jesus. Again."

A dozen prisoners instantly resumed the stoning, and within moments all had joined in. Sanjay's body now twitched and jerked from the force of the blows. The stones from the throwers at the ends of the arc landed on his sides, and most of his ribs soon had fractures that penetrated the skin. When a large stone fractured a kneecap, he cried out in pain for the first time. Blood streamed from a wound in his throat. Agonizing minutes later I saw a prisoner heft one of the larger stones and, with the deliberation and strength of a professional pitcher, land a blow on Sanjay's left temple. Sanjay instantly lost consciousness. It was, I choose to believe, an act of mercy. The stoning continued for another few minutes. Although the sight was unbearable, I was determined not to avert my eyes. I did not blink. All I could do for Sanjay was to witness.

Then JJ held up his hand silently, and within moments the throwing stopped. With a nod he summoned the doctor, whose starched white coat was already stained with a misty spattering of Sanjay's blood. The doctor's step faltered when he approached the pillar. His outstretched fingers had trouble finding the carotid artery beneath Sanjay's purple and bloated neck. He pulled a small flashlight from his pocket and raised one of Sanjay's eyelids. The other eyelid was missing. He turned and nodded to the Super and mouthed, silently, the word "dead."

CHAPTER NINETEEN

Born Again

2022

*Very truly I tell you, no one can see the Kingdom of God
without being born again.*

—John 3:3

I STILL HAVE NO IDEA HOW LONG I was unconscious. It could
have been an hour, it could have been days. When wakefulness lapped
gently but insistently at my unconsciousness, I resisted. Eventually my
eyes opened, but confusingly no images came to replace those of my
dreams. My brain signaled my arms to stretch, but they remained in a
tight embrace across my chest.

My conscious brain was numb, indifferent to my situation. But the
intensely practical programming in my primitive brain was insistent
and slowly unraveled the mystery of my situation. The punishment
cells were windowless and thus completely dark. The doorjambs were
thoughtfully cushioned with black rubber lest even a few photons stray
through the crack to comfort the occupant. The ceilings were high
enough for standing, and the room was large enough to take two paces
in one direction and three in the other. A small hole in the floor allowed
the prisoner to evacuate his waste to the vaulted cistern below. The
floor was concrete, the back wall was stone, and the other walls were
roughly stuccoed. I knew all this because my brothers and I had spent
two days in the cells of Castle Williams when my "brother" Jamie
unwisely flirted with one of the girls in the serving line at the mess hall.

When told we were going to the castle for two days, we joked about it. There were no jokes when we returned. It does not take physical torture to drive a man to despair. It is a sad irony that a technique so cruel to the tortured requires so little effort and occasions so little guilt on the part of the torturer. As virtually every authoritarian regime has discovered, a couple of days of solitude in total darkness leads to nasty hallucinations and, in a few more days, many people experience a complete mental breakdown akin to psychosis. After our previous visit of two days, we were highly motivated to enforce strict discipline among the brothers.

This time was different. I soon realized where I was and the reason for the darkness. But my arms worked strangely, and for some time—minutes or hours, I really don't know—I thought perhaps I was injured or paralyzed. But eventually the picture emerged. I was lying on my side, secured in a canvas straightjacket, arms across the chest—loose enough so that I could move my arms slightly in all directions but not so loose that I could pull my arms out. The first time I tried to stand, I discovered that the back of the straightjacket was attached to a metal ring in the floor by a chain too short to permit me to stand upright. I could stand with legs straight and torso bent over, or kneel or squat on the floor with torso upright and straight. The chain was just short enough to prevent me from walking or crawling to the latrine hole.

It was so typical of GI. Superficially the veneer of twenty-first-century civilization was preserved. Would any of this shock the conscience of the American public? I was not beaten; there was no sexual humiliation, no grotesque tortures. After all, before the Christian Nation hundreds of American prisoners and mental patients were kept in solitary confinement and secured in straightjackets for their own protection. I had no doubt that the meticulous records of GI would faithfully record that the prisoner was secured in a lightweight canvas straightjacket for his own protection, the doctor having advised of a risk that he was a danger to himself.

I occupied myself the first few days becoming accustomed to the routine: the way in which food and water would be delivered without allowing any light into the room; the way to piss and shit as far as possible from the place where I could lie down; the way to stand and squat given the short chain; how to keep my arms from seizing up and keep the blood flowing; how to scratch using the wall.

Soon, however, everything changed. In a world of darkness and silence, time becomes flat, constrained, like a physical world of two dimensions. The passage of time is not marked by events in the empirical world, for there are none. Instead, the landmarks on the map of time are purely mental. Looking back, distance is impossible to judge, and even sequence is uncertain. I do know I went through a welcome phase of vivid hallucinations. They were terrifying but welcome. When they ended, the real torture began. For during most waking moments I felt nothing other than the cold terror that this could last forever. I slowly became obsessed with the thought that I would be left here for the rest of my natural life, and eventually convinced myself that this was their plan. At some point I came to believe that I had already been in the cell for two years and that, at age forty-two, I could be here for another thirty to forty.

I learned that insanity can be sensed as an event just over the horizon, a feeling not unlike the sense that you are coming down with a cold. We call it a mental breakdown, but those who live out their lives in sanity have no idea how aptly the phrase captures what it purports to describe. The mental processes we take for granted—perception, logic, deduction, short-term memory—all start to falter. Like an ominous rattle in the depths of your car. A momentary shimmy. A shudder. A skip. There's that moment when an accumulation of ominous symptoms makes you lose confidence in your vehicle. You start to wonder if you'll make it home.

At first I welcomed this development. After all, it was something. Something happening. A change. A mystery. A destination. What would happen? How would it feel? Finally, like normal people, I would have an answer to the question "What did you do today?" I could answer, "Today I lost my mind."

I believe I was within moments of surrendering to this temptation.

But instead I decided to die. The plan formed itself in an instant, and in an instant I decided. As I rocked slowly back and forth on the floor, the allure of allowing myself to sink into insanity receded, and I decided to stop eating. Like so many prisoners before me, I realized that the only path of resistance, the only path to preservation of autonomy, was to end my own life on my own terms. The only discretionary act left to me was the choice of whether or not to kneel before the plate of food and bowl of water shoved through a hatch at the bottom of the door at irregular intervals. I had other choices: whether to lie on my right side, left side, or back; whether to squat or stand. Where to piss. But these decisions were of no consequence because *they* were indifferent to my choices. But the choice not to eat was a choice that would have consequences. It showed them that I was still ultimately master of my own life. It would frustrate whatever plans they had for me. It was all I had, and it filled me with a sense of purpose and determination.

It may seem strange, but the weeks I spent on my hunger strike were some of the most satisfying of my life. My hellish sentence of decades in the cell had been commuted. I had stepped away from the brink of an irretrievable psychotic breakdown. Every time I woke, there was a purpose to my waking. Something to do. Something to achieve. And best of all, I joyfully imagined the frustration and difficulty I must be causing Super JJ and his gang of thugs. Every physical symptom of starvation was a welcome affirmation of my autonomy. I was fascinated that hunger persisted for what seemed like only a few days. I celebrated the first time I could not rise to a squatting position, triumphant at the strange and unexpected failure of the quadriceps to perform the function they had reliably performed for forty years. My wrapped hands, now completely at home in their position on the sides of the ribs, probed in wonder as my flesh seemly melted and the ribs emerged proudly, shrouded only by the skin's thin sheath. In contrast, my feet and ankles swelled to a bizarre size. This cornucopia of events filled my days with new things to experience and a happy validation of my plan. When I was a lawyer, I was never happier than when I had a plan.

I don't remember when they took me from the cell. I remember going to sleep in the cell and then, suddenly, a waking that was not gentle. With a single injection to my intravenous tube, the medically induced coma was ended and I was jolted back to consciousness. I dimly saw a nurse smiling warmly and noticed that she was holding my hand. My hand, strangely, was down next to my knee, and not in its customary position wrapped around the opposite side of my chest. I was wearing dark sunglasses. The bed was soft and clean. My skin was clean. My beard was gone. I bent my knees and elbows, and each extremity moved until it was gently stopped by a canvas loop, luxuriously lined with sheepskin, that attached each limb to rails along the side of the bed. I looked down to see an intravenous drip to my left arm, and I felt the strange sensation of urine being drained through a catheter.

"Welcome, back, Sweetheart," the nurse said. "How do you feel?"

It took days for me to answer that question. I know that, as I could once again tell day from night. My private room had a high ceiling and six-foot-tall windows overlooking a leafy courtyard. During the day, the shadows of the oaks danced on the wall, a show I found more riveting than any film.

I never spoke to a doctor. My hunger strike was never discussed. I never saw a guard. A cheerful blond physical therapist came twice a day. The restraints were removed from a single limb, and she would skillfully work the limb, stimulating the muscles, stretching the tendons. It was not the same as going for a run, but my muscles started to grow back, and the stiffness in the joints disappeared in a few days.

"How do you feel, Sweetheart?" the nurse asked every morning.

The only question I ever asked her, after about a week, was the date. When she told me, I became angry. "Please, why are you lying?"

She looked genuinely startled. "What? Lying? Why would I lie about the date?"

"It cannot be," I said. "I was at the castle for over two years."

She held my hand. "Greg, you were in the castle for five weeks. You didn't eat for the last two weeks. You've been here for ten days."

When I looked distressed, she went into the hallway and came back with the *New York Times*. "See," she said, "November 26, 2022."

Until that moment, I had been floating in a dull stupor, my body enjoying the nutrition and comfort, my mind reveling in the light, company, and stimulation. I had no interest in thinking about anything. How did I feel? Like a dog, content with the gifts dispensed by a benign and responsible owner. There was only a comfortable present. After the chain and straightjacket, the padded restraints were a luxurious caress. Until that moment, I felt gratitude. But now this peaceful interlude was at an end as my mind struggled with the implications of the fact that the period of my dark self-embrace in the cell at Castle Williams had been only five weeks.

What happened next seems sufficiently ordinary as to hardly merit reminiscence. During the entire time at the castle, I had not thought once about Sanjay. Now I dreamed every night about the stoning. In most dreams I managed to hang on and endure the stoning, usually waking at the moment I lost consciousness in the dream. Sometimes I told him jokes. Sometimes he comforted me. Sometimes I swore vengeance. Sometimes I lost my grip and was dragged away by the guards. In my waking hours, I thought obsessively about the hunger strike, ridiculing my plan and chiding myself for the childish illusion that I was engaged in something meaningful.

Within a few days I had sunk into the most conventional of depressions. The pretty nurse and therapist, the animated oak shadows on the wall—all the ornaments of my little world lost their appeal. I was unable to make the simplest decision, and not, strangely, merely from lack of caring (although it is true that I didn't care) but from some distinct mental disability.

"Orange juice this morning, Sugar? Or grapefruit?"

I actually struggled with the decision, straining to figure out the answer. When I gave up, it became another failure with which to torment myself. Despite Adam's urgings, I don't think I have anything to add to the rich literature of clinical depression. My fatigue was continuous. I was consumed by feelings of worthlessness and self-loathing.

More than anything else, I believed with utter conviction that the days and nights of lurching from hurt to hurt was my new and permanent normal. Even suicide, the last refuge of the depressed, was cruelly denied to me. I could stop eating, but they would feed me intravenously. Yes, it was a lighted room with a soft bed, but it was much worse than being strapped and chained in the darkness. Finally, I knew the true meaning of despair. My condition must have been obvious to the nurses and whoever monitored the video feed from my room. But I was left, strapped to the bed, to sink deeper and deeper into despondency.

One morning in April, with no apparent precipitating factor, I had an idea that quickly became an idée fixe: hell. My God, I thought, they were right. There is a hell. I know because I am in it. And it is something completely supernatural, something surely not of this world. My lawyer's mind ran with the idea. Never-ending torment, my new reality, was something impossible for any man to cause. I didn't choose it or make it, nor did they. It was, simply, something outside nature and outside human nature. Therefore, there must be a God or at least something like a God. If there was, and if this God had created this hell for me, then this God could end it. End it. The seemingly impossible notion that there could be an end to my suffering floated there miraculously. The impossible suddenly seemed possible.

I asked the nurse to send a chaplain. Fifteen minutes later, one of the camp clergy, whom I knew from daily prayers and Bible study, entered my room and sat by the side of the bed. He was the first person, other than the nurse and physical therapist, I had seen or spoken to since leaving the castle. He waited for me to speak.

"Reverend," I said, weeping, "it happened. This morning. I finally understood. My God, it's true. There is a God. There is a heaven and a hell. I can see it now. So clearly. Why? Why couldn't I see it before?"

"What do you mean, son? What do you see?"

"I see that I am, am . . . nothing. I am worthless. A speck of dust. I mean nothing apart from Him—apart from creation, apart from the creator, apart from God. And I don't know what, what I have done or been or said, but He has punished me. And I *am* in hell. A hell only

He could conjure. A hell so terrible, so hopeless that I cannot bear it. And there, right in front of me—right inside me, was my redemption. He sent me this hell. He can take it away. That's what I have figured out. That's what I now know. I pray to God with all my heart to take away my suffering."

"Are you a sinner?" he asked.

"Yes, yes, a sinner," I said. "How else, why else would I be in this hell? I must be a sinner. I *am* a sinner."

"And do you repent your sins?"

"Repent? My God, if that's what brought me to this place, then I regret them more than anything. Would that I could undo whatever I did to offend God and never have experienced this pain. I would give anything, everything." My sobs flowed from the gut, nearly choking me. I had never wept like this in my life. I was practically hysterical.

"Is your heart open to God and His son, Jesus? Do you want the redemption of Jesus Christ?"

"Yes, yes," I cried, "I want it more than anything else I have ever wanted." And I had never spoke a truer word. My whole being was an open wound. My soul was empty and crying out to be taken and filled.

"Pray with me, son. 'I believe in you, Jesus. I accept you. Please come into my life. I commit it to you.'"

"Lord Jesus, I believe in you. I accept you. Please come into my life. I commit it to you," I stammered.

"Son, you repeat that prayer. You keep that feeling. You open your heart to Jesus and, if you truly repent your sins, and if your heart is truly open to the Lord, he will come in and you will experience the most wonderful thing a man can experience, the taking of your life by Jesus, the certainty of eternal salvation, and your rebirth in Christ. Keep praying, son. I will come see you tomorrow."

For three days I lived as an open wound. Inside out. My whole being nothing more than a desperate hollowness longing to be filled. I begged and begged, and cried and cajoled for Jesus to enter my heart. I begged the Lord to end my pain. I promised I would do, say, believe, and be anything if he would lift the hell.

The pastor sat by my bed each day and did his best to give me strength.

"If Jesus has not entered your heart," he said, "it is because some corner, some part of your being remains closed to his love. Some part of your repentance is imperfect. Some pride remains."

Sometime on the third sleepless night, a startling calm took hold of my troubled mind. For the first time since the stoning, my conscious self felt familiar. And then I seemed to float to the ceiling, look down at my pale body strapped to the hospital bed, and see everything clearly. In a single insightful flash, I understood it all: In the depths of depression and despair, I had opened my heart. I was as ready for redemption as any man could be. I had never wanted anything more completely or more genuinely. But no one was home. No redemption came because there was no redeemer. I had, like a child, longed for a miracle to put an end to my troubles, but the miracle hadn't come, and I was, again, on my own. And that was fine. It was how I was born and how I would die. It was the human condition and it was OK.

I was stunned but alert. I felt that peculiar ease of thinking that follows restorative oblivion. By morning I had a plan. During the hour before the nurse arrived to take my blood pressure, I did *ujjayi* breathing exercises—long, slow, slightly constrained inhales and exhales taught to me by Sanjay to lower my blood pressure and lock in the calmness in my mind. I carefully remembered and organized everything I knew about the born-again experience, developed my script, and rehearsed it over and over in my head. When the pastor arrived, I was both the physical and mental picture of equanimity.

"My son, what's happened?"

"Just as you said, Reverend. Last night, just when I thought I could go no lower, I was filled with a strange peace. I felt—well, free—for the first time in my life. Where only a moment before there was a most terrible emptiness, there was a fullness, a . . ."

At this point I teared up and choked, and for the first time I smiled faintly.

". . . a joy. And he was here. Just as surely as you are there. Jesus was in my heart. I didn't have to ask or beg or grasp or try. The moment I was fully open, there he was. And he was pure light, and perfection, and love and grace and . . . I just cannot describe . . ."

"Thanks be to God."

During the next two weeks, a series of camp chaplains and doctors came to interview me. My appetite returned, and I had no physical symptoms. When the room was empty and my only audience was the video camera that I knew must be somewhere, I moved my mouth in silent, and sometimes whispered, prayer. I did not complain, and when the restraints were removed I asked for nothing other than a Bible.

During the balance of my time at GI, I never indicated to a single one of my fellow prisoners, by so much as a wink or grin or raised eyebrow, that I harbored the least bit of skepticism or discontent with the Christian Nation program. I led Bible study and was a model prisoner. I was released two months before the three-year deadline, my death sentence commuted.

Until the last hour, when my fingers tapped out the truth for any reader of these words to discover, I have lived this lie to perfection. My actions and words became automatic. I taught myself to believe that I was saved, to ease the burden of dissembling. For five years I have lived the lie, not half-heartedly, not incompletely, but so thoroughly as to call into question what really happened that night. All the evidence in the world points to the fact that I was born again that Easter Sunday 2023, six months to the day after Sanjay Sharma's death. Only I, and now you, know it to be untrue.

CHAPTER TWENTY

Christian Nation

2024–2029

"Ordinary," said Aunt Lydia, "is what you are used to. This may not seem ordinary to you now, but after a time it will. It will become ordinary."

—Margaret Atwood,
The Handmaid's Tale

Under a tyranny, most friends are a liability. One quarter of them turn "reasonable" and become your enemies, one quarter are afraid to stop and speak, and one quarter are killed and you die with them. But the blessed final quarter keep you alive.

—Doremus Jessup,
in *It Can't Happen Here*, by Sinclair Lewis

AT THE END OF MY OUTPLACEMENT appointment in a small office next to the ferry waiting room, my counselor opened the familiar white box with the embossed Apple logo. "This is an i20 Device. Only the best for our graduates," he said, attempting a joke.

The top of the thing looked a bit like the iPhone that had been taken from me three years previously, upon arriving at GI. But it was thin and much smaller, like an overscaled wristwatch. And I was surprised to see when he took it out of the box that it was somewhat flexible.

"Is it a phone or a little iPad or what?" I asked.

"I still find it funny that you guys don't know. Everyone in the country has one now. And I mean everyone. It's a Device; it does everything. All you need."

The wafer-like Device had a wrist strap that was dark gray, extremely thin, and made from some kind of woven metal. A golden cross was embossed on the outside of the band.

He saw me looking at the cross. "For born agains. So you know. You know who you can . . . count on," he said somewhat cryptically. "You a righty?" I nodded. "Put out your left hand, then." He continued, "You can take it off, but you need to keep it with you at all times. Do you understand? It's important. Serious stuff if they find you without it."

I waited patiently over an hour for the clean white ferryboat, bearing the familiar Faith & Freedom Rehabilitation Facility logo on its superstructure, to return to the dock. The ferry ride covering the half mile from Governors Island to the tip of Manhattan took no more than ten minutes, but I was transported by that short trip from one world to another. As I set foot on the ferry, I thought of all the millions of prisoners in human history who stood before the prison gate, watched it open, and then—with the hesitation and reluctance with which we receive all things devoutly sought—stepped through into a place where all their suffering meant nothing.

The Governors Island ferry terminal in Manhattan is directly across the street from my old office building. Walking down the terminal steps, I looked up at the corner windows behind which my former partners still sat, and the middle windows behind which a new generation of associates, who most likely had never heard of me, strived to become the lawyers that the firm wanted them to be. I sat on the step, gazing up, wondering. I saw a few fleeting silhouettes against the glass and remembered a favorite scene from the opera version of *Great Gatsby* where Nick Carraway sits and watches from outside a party under a tent, seeing on the white sides of the tent the shadows of partygoers dancing. I briefly wondered if I always had been an outsider, like Nick, and then realized that it no longer mattered. I had made my decision and had never once regretted it.

I crossed the plaza in front of South Ferry. The taxis were still yellow. The Staten Island ferry was still orange. New Yorkers still wore black. I saw the Nike swoosh. A breeze brought the sweet, salty odor of the nut cart. I sat on a bench. Things seemed completely normal. Secretaries wore sneakers and carried their good shoes in a fashionable bag. Junior bankers and lawyers, looking impossibly young and glowing with confidence and ambition, wore well-shined shoes and new suits and walked with long and purposeful strides. Normal. Tourists poured from the subway, confused about how to get to the Statue of Liberty. All normal. What was I expecting? Women in burkas? Zealots with machine guns? The call to prayer echoing through the canyons of Wall Street? That was what a theocracy was supposed to look like. This looked like the Financial District at the tail end of morning rush hour.

The siege and Battle of the Battery, however, had happened. I looked closely at the plaza in front of the ferry terminal, remembering how it looked the morning we were marched across the same plaza and taken to Governors Island. There had been concrete barricades and rolls of barbed wire, three crashed helicopters, and long black scars on the sides of the office buildings along Battery Place. And every square foot of the plaza was covered with vegetable beds and hoop houses. Lush ripe tomatoes tumbled from a scaffolding made of wire hangers. Spinach grew at the base of the trees. Zucchini squash climbed the columns of the covered walkway where people now waited for uptown buses. All that was gone. I did not see a forgotten bamboo stake, a piece of twine, or a single vegetable seedling forcing its way up through a crack in the concrete. The Manhattan of the siege was eradicated. It might never have happened.

I wandered into Battery Park looking for any sign of the battle fought there just over three years before. I walked over to the East Coast World War II memorial. Surely, no matter how hard they had scrubbed, there would be a faint shadow of the pool of blood in which my friend Matthew had died. I stood below the tall granite slab engraved with the names of the World War II dead, below the same wall of names that had protected me from the first wave of their assault, at the exact place where Matthew lost half his face, and I found no trace of what had happened at that spot. I turned to the wall of names, looking for the pockmarks that would have to remain to tell the story of the bullets that flew that day in August. Again, nothing. The monument appeared pristine. I closed my eyes and touched the wall. And then I felt it. The slight indentations where the bullet holes had been filled. One after another, creating a rippled cratered surface revealing itself to my touch. I stood with my hand on the cool stone caressing the granite surface until I sensed someone nearby and opened my eyes. A well-dressed man, about my age, was standing close by.

"Are you OK, Brother?" I noticed his glance at the golden cross on my Device. He had one too. I pointed with my eyes to a name on the wall near to where I had been touching.

"My great-grandfather," I said, easily dissembling.

He smiled with a superficiality that I soon came to recognize and value. "Quite," he said, staring at my face. He raised his arm and reached forward to shake my hand, unnecessarily thrusting his arm out from the sleeve of his shirt and suit to reveal a deep red scar along the forearm.

"God bless, Brother," he said upon turning to walk away, briefly flashing his eyes to the small gray camera mounted on the side of the adjacent light.

When I arrived at my halfway house in the West Village, I was warmly greeted by my five housemates, three of whom said they had been released from Governors earlier in the month, but only two of whom I recognized. Two of the men were employees of COGA, the Church of God in America, which provided an umbrella organization for all the evangelical and Pentecostal denominations in the country. Although nominally independent from the federal government, it was charged with the supervision of all cultural, academic, and religious institutions. The two COGA employees explained that the church paid little in salary but provided housing for all its not-yet-married employees.

The house, on the charming small Commerce Street, dated from the mid-nineteenth century. It was all wood construction and had settled alarmingly so that no floor was level or wall perpendicular. With its odd angles and low ceilings, it seemed almost whimsical. In back of the house, an old garden, now gone to seed and dominated by weeds and tall grasses, surrounded a small patio with a wrought-iron table and scattered chairs. The pleasure I would have taken in such a place was dulled by the realization that I was doubtless in a house confiscated by the feds from a gay person or family.

The next day after breakfast, when the two COGA heads of house had left for the office, Tom O'Brien, a tall man roughly my age, whom I recognized from GI, asked if I wanted to see the garden. He took two of the chairs and casually positioned them to face away from the sun and the back façade of the house.

"So how much do you know?" he asked.

"Know? About what?" I answered warily.

"About how things are. The Purity Web, for example."

"No. What's that? It sounds good, of course," I answered carefully. "I prayed a great deal on the island that I would find the country cleansed of all the filth we had before."

"Amen. Then you'll be pleased. President Jordan's great insight was that the nation couldn't possibly be redeemed if all the depravity were simply pushed underground—I mean, from the real to the virtual world. Remember, before, what the Internet was? Mostly porn. If that had been allowed to continue, well, how could we expect God's grace and favor as a nation?"

I judged that it was a rhetorical question, and simply nodded.

"Just after the siege began, Congress passed the Purity Web Act, although I understand it was in the works for quite some time before then." That much I remembered.

"Of course porn sites were made illegal, and all immoral content from overseas was stopped at our borders. That was the easy part—I mean, the Chinese and Saudis and others had been doing it for years. But President Jordan's real inspiration was not to stop at eliminating temptation—he realized that since we lived our lives on the web, the web could be an active partner in eradicating evil."

"How so?" I asked, glancing at the Device on my left wrist.

"Yes, the Device is a part of it. Well, the big breakthrough was integration—integration of every webcam, every e-mail and text, every web search, every website visited, every post you make on a social network, everything you watch on TV or listen to on the radio, every video you watch online, every credit card charge, every ATM withdrawal, every cell phone call, every trip in your car or other device with GPS, every digital picture taken—all of it is now integrated and analyzed to discourage and discover evil. It's truly amazing. Jordan reminds everyone that it was divinely inspired—it came to him in a direct revelation from God. Hate the sin."

"Amen to that. Most of those things were already linked to the web one way or another. But what exactly does integration mean? That's a lot of data."

"Every street camera, every security camera in the country, and everyone's Device is linked to the Purity Web. Every bit of GPS data, every keystroke or click on any electronic device is recorded and analyzed by supercomputers. But more than that, they now can recognize a face, they can read handwriting, they can understand speech, they can read lips."

I thought I saw him lift his chin slightly up and to the left, toward the back of the house behind us.

"The big machines look for patterns in the data, changes in your routines, your movements. They look at what you buy, what you say, what you write in your e-mails, what you choose to read, what you search for online. They look for patterns in virtually everything you do. Computers, you know, can predict human behavior better from this data than any person can, and of course only the big machines can handle that volume of information. That part's not new—it was proven technology back in the first decade of the century. What's new are all the data sources, especially the cameras, which are everywhere—their integration on the web and, of course, the big machines themselves. And it wouldn't have been possible without some pretty amazing programming. I heard a rumor that the key algorithms were developed by a Chinese scientist for the Chinese government, but then he was born again and came here and gave it all to the Christian Nation, thank God."

"Thank God," I said with a shadow less enthusiasm than I should have, deliberately, to test his reaction. I had no reason to think he was anything other than a genuine born-again Christian who supported, or at least acquiesced to, the new Christian Nation. He had no reason to think anything other than that about me. To give any hint to the contrary could be fatal for each of us. He paused for only a moment to consider what he had heard.

"Yes. So you see, for our countrymen who are not saved, they have a helping hand to avoid sin and evil. Not really an issue for us, you know. But still, it's helpful to understand. Especially for people like us, from the island. Just remember, they'll know if you don't go to work, they'll know if you are sick, they'll know everything you buy and do and everything you read and write—every word. If your face is pointed toward a camera, they know everything you say. Now the big machines, they're not looking at every person all the time—unless, of course, they identify you as being at particular risk for temptation or evil conduct. When the big machines see something they don't like, you 'go pink.' That's what it's called. It means there's an issue. If that happens, then the machines' analysis is referred to a real person, a deacon, who surveys the data and decides on the next steps. Not a good idea to go pink, my friend. Just so you know. Can be a real hassle. But of course, it's a blessing as well, since the deacons can usually intervene before the sin is actually committed."

"Thanks for the tip. I doubt, though, that I'll be doing anything that could be considered remotely . . . well, pink."

"Of course. And," he said, turning toward the house with a smile that I knew to be artificial and suspected that the big machines did not, "the dream of eradicating evil has been nearly realized. Thank God."

"Thank God," I said, also squarely facing the back of the house.

The *Wall Street Journal* and *USA Today* were delivered each day, via our Devices, to a set of reading tablets in the house. The five of us took turns cooking breakfast and ate together every morning. After a quick prayer, we were left together to read the papers. At first it was an odd feeling knowing that somewhere a big machine was looking at each article I clicked to read and how long I spent with the piece as it searched for patterns and considered what they meant. I learned from the newspapers that the world outside America had changed a great deal during the past three years. Jordan had been true to his word and had terminated all America's treaties and alliances. United States troops were withdrawn from the Korean peninsula, Japan, Europe, and the Middle East. The power vacuum in Asia was filled almost immediately by China, which invited Japan and all of Southeast Asia, including Australia, to join the Greater China Cooperation Area. It was an offer none of those countries was in a position to refuse. In a month, without a shot being fired, China had established a sphere of economic and military domination covering the entirety of the western Pacific. It was nothing less than a new empire, a reprise of the colonial model pioneered by the British, under which all petroleum and minerals in Australia, Indonesia, and elsewhere in the region were reserved to feed China's insatiable demand for energy and resources. In return the "cooperating" countries purchased the products of China's burgeoning manufacturing sector. The Chinese occupied the former US military bases in Japan, the Philippines, and Korea. The Christian Nation seemed to me to be on good terms with China, notwithstanding the fact that every newspaper I read used the adjective "godless" before the word "Chinese." I couldn't figure out this passive acceptance of the Chinese empire, and I wondered what had happened to the evangelistic imperative. But having created a Godly Kingdom in America, the federal government seemed content to allow great swaths of humanity to wallow in atheism and error.

The Middle East had been messier, as Jordan had reiterated America's support for "biblical Israel" as the country's sole international commitment. But having made clear that the Jews must continue to be in control of Jerusalem, Jordan made no effort to protect the Saud family from the Shia revolution that swept the Middle East. The Islamic fundamentalists, with tacit approval from Washington, soon realized their dream of a Shia Islamic Caliphate extending from Pakistan through Iran, Egypt, the entire Gulf, and North Africa. In an attempt to unwind globalization and shock the world economy back to a pre-modern condition, the ayatollahs in charge shut in and abandoned all the oil and gas wells in Saudi Arabia, Iran, Iraq, Kuwait, and the old United Arab Emirates. Within three months, 60 percent of the world's oil production disappeared. Planners in the United States had long assumed that any government in control of the oil fields of the Middle East might threaten to withhold oil from the market—and even do so for a time to achieve some specific objective—but would eventually act in its own economic interest and resume production. This proved incorrect. The Shia Islamic Caliphate decided that the disruption to the Western world and the potential obliteration of modernism in general were far more appealing than the money and power they could have had by continuing to produce and sell petroleum products to the West. As a result, the economies in the developed world other than China and Russia staggered. As a quid pro quo for American acquiescence to the restoration of an Islamic Caliphate, Israel was left alone, and it too realized its destiny as a religious state, with a dramatic revision to its liberal constitution in order to establish the primacy of the Torah and effectively guarantee political domination by the ultra-orthodox Jewish sects.

It was more difficult for me to figure out from the newspapers what had happened in Europe. NATO was gone. The European Community had survived, but it seemed to subsist in a state of Finlandized subservience to Russia, which, through its supply of natural gas and control of the gas pipelines, dominated the western part of the continent both economically and politically. Only the UK and the Scandinavian countries seemed to endure in a state of true political and economic independence. Very little was said of them in the American press.

In Manhattan, fewer cars on the streets appear to be the only symptom of the shock suffered by the country having lost access to half the crude oil it had consumed before. But the newspapers suggest many other changes in the country at large. Shale gas wells linked by a dense web of natural gas pipelines dominate the landscape in a great swath of the country extending from upstate New York down to Texas. Every new car runs on natural gas, and a type of coal-based slurry has replaced fuel oil as the power source for America's home furnaces. Mountain after West Virginia mountain has disappeared to give up its coal, and a hazy smog once again has settled over many cities and suburbs of the country. Politicians appear at each new coal-fired and nuclear plant opening, promising that God will provide and, within a decade, things will return to "normal."

★   ★   ★

MY JOB DID NOT start for a week, so the first few days after my move to Commerce Street I spent wandering around Greenwich Village and, later, the rest of Manhattan. Since I was unable to digest all I was seeing and learning through conversation, my dreams became vivid and memorable. After one of my long walks, I dreamt that a neutron bomb had dispatched all the real New Yorkers and that Stepford Wife–like facsimiles had been installed in their place by the big machines. For a Christian Nation where we were all supposed to be attentive to our souls, the New York I found during these walks was strangely soulless. The absence of the gays was palpable. The West Village, once so animated and irreverent, now had a suburban ambiance. Fast-food outlets and national chain stores, once rare in Manhattan, were ubiquitous. I observed an elevated sense of fashion compared to what we saw on television in the rest of the country, but it was subdued. Nothing outrageous. Nothing revealing. Nothing, really, very interesting.

And then, I slowly realized, there was the lack of foreigners. New

York, a beacon of cosmopolitanism since the seventeenth century, was the one place in the country where walking down any street at any time, you could always hear a language other than English being spoken. Before the war, the population was polyglot, and residents walked the streets with millions of visitors from around the world. But I now found during my walks that the world had stopped coming to New York. While I was on Governors Island, illegal immigrants in the city had joined those from around the country in being detained and repatriated. New Yorkers who had been educated in our schools, who greeted us every day as our doormen and taxi drivers and whose children were born here, were torn from their families and sent back to countries that were for many of them only distant memories. Eventually even those members of their families who were in the United States legally joined their loved ones in exile. New immigration stopped, and hundreds of thousands of Americans from the Rust Belt and the South migrated to New York to fill the shoes of the missing immigrants.

My new job was a short walk across Greenwich Village to the old NYU Bobst Library building on the south side of Washington Square. As I entered the building, it suddenly occurred to me that this was only the third job I'd held in my life: the firm, TW, and now the Christian Nation Archives. I was greeted by my direct supervisor, a corpulent middle-aged woman with a helmet of carefully composed hair, an engagingly warm smile, and an accent that suggested the southern reaches of the Midwest.

"I am Mrs. Scott," she said, "but I hope you will call me Lurlene. No need to stand on formality here—like my Dale used to say, God rest his soul. After all, we are all . . . Well, yes. So now. I know you were at the, um, the facility. . . . I just want you to know it makes no difference. You know, we are now all together despite, you know—"

"Don't worry about it," I interrupted. "I understand. I'm here now and anxious to get to work."

"Oh good. And so important, you know. Our work. Really, I mean, you know how much trouble all that, well, trash caused. So much trouble. So it's up to us to sort it all out. What's left, that is."

The old NYU library is unlike the Classical or Gothic palaces of the great Ivy League universities. The building is urban and modern with a tall glass atrium at its center. It had been one of the larger open-stack research libraries in the country, with fourteen stories of books and reading areas.

Lurlene walked me down to the second sub level of the building where dozens of tables were positioned in neat rows in the center of a large room. I was thrilled to find that the room smelled of old books. The index clerk at each table received books from the open stacks in old-fashioned metal book carts. His job was to inspect each book, reading only as much of the content as was necessary. The clerk then chose from stacks of coded index cards the approximate size of old-fashioned bookmarks and inserted the chosen card behind the cover of the book. The clerk then placed the indexed book onto an empty cart.

"That will be your desk," said Lurlene, pointing to an empty table. "But first you must learn the alphabet." She saw my look of confusion. "Oh dear, of course, silly me. My husband—now with the Lord— always said, 'Lordy, Lurlene, folks don't understand a thing you say. For heaven's sake, slow down.' Have you lost someone, Greg?"

"Yes, but as you say, they are with the Lord."

"Still. So, well, yes. Here, alphabet means the letters—you know, A-C means approved Christian literature. The prefix D means books to destroy, so D-D, for example, means books to destroy that have to do with some kind of deviancy. But there are more than twenty-six letter combinations actually, and they're a bit tough to learn. So for a day or so you'll work with Mr. Thornton . . ." She then lowered her voice, whispering conspiratorially, "who is a bit, let's say, stiff. You'll see."

Mr. Thornton informed the group of three workers who were starting that Monday that he had been chief librarian at Patrick Henry College. He told us that immediately after the end of the Holy War he had been selected personally by President Jordan to organize the Christian Nation Archives around the country where those physical books not selected for destruction were to be preserved for the use of COGA-approved historians and other scholars. No physical books, of course, were required any longer by the general public, who had access to the entirety of the COGA-approved canon through their Devices.

"As saved Christians, you all understand just how urgently God requires us to rid His kingdom of all traces of smut, filth, and evil. Our redemption as a nation is conditional—conditional on our following through and eradicating evil the way God wants. Think of it this way, Gentlemen: Every ungodly book was a paving stone in that wicked road of human-centered, egotistical arrogance that led this nation off the path of righteousness. As long as such books still exist, they have the potential to exercise their evil influence on the fragile and flawed minds of man. God calls us to their eradication. So, job one, so to speak, is to ensure that not a single such book remains. Do you understand? You might think, what does it matter if a couple old books remain on a shelf somewhere? But sin is like a virus. It worms its way out of the pockets where you try to keep it hidden and then it waits, silently, for the chance to strike. Understand?"

The three of us nodded silently. I was surprised by the depth of the anger directed at the humble book. This was a rhetoric I had not heard before Governors. Mr. Thornton continued:

"So the D codes are by far the most important. Any code starting with a D means the book requires destruction. This is your prime objective. Take your time. Obviously any book that contains the text of a false religion or is sympathetic to a false religion or asserts or even explains heretical teachings at odds with the truths of The Blessing— these are D-F. We have chosen letters you can remember—so think 'F for false.' Ridding the nation of false teaching or confusing untruth is one of our highest priorities. Understand?"

Again we nodded.

"Then you must also consider whether the book promotes so-called humanism, any basis for morality that is not based on God's word or asserts the primacy of reason over faith. These are all D-H; here H is for humanism. Or perhaps the book promotes the theory of evolution or argues the existence of geological or biological evidence that con- tradicts the Bible; this is all D-S—anything that assumes that pure science can exist separately from revelation and other types of godly knowledge. Then we have D-D—you can probably guess, with D for deviancy. These we call 'double D's.' Few of these escaped from the purges of three years ago, but you will be shocked how many are still floating around, and in places you would not expect. So everything written by a known or suspected homosexual that promotes, excuses, or justifies the homosexual lifestyle or includes homosexual characters is D-D. Similar to that is D-A, for adultery, which of course includes anything involving divorce, sex before marriage, or other sexual sins."

Mr. Thornton looked both disgusted and exhilarated by this litany of enemy texts. He wanted us to understand the immense burden and responsibility that was his.

"Can you imagine, all those years, all those novels where characters casually dissolved marriages made by God, had affairs, committed adultery. Books where people flaunted homosexual lifestyles. They disrespected God, trashed Christians. What were children to think other than that it was all OK?"

He went on in a similar vein and then had us practice with a stack of twenty books. When he visited my table late on the second day to check my work, he looked skeptical. When it turned out that I was the only worker to index each of my test books exactly right, he stared at me with interest, and then spoke in a low voice, with his back to the two small cameras on the far wall of the room.

"I know who you are, you know. From before. They thought I should know. But they told me they were certain that your call to Christ was strong and deep. But I plan to watch you. More closely than the others. No one else has ever gotten a perfect score. Not the most devout and dedicated deacon. Only you saw the insidious undercurrents hidden beneath seemingly acceptable texts. That really takes . . . If He can open a heart like yours . . ." He stared at me again with a searching intensity. "Well, praise God is all I can say."

On the second day at work, Lurlene casually mentioned at lunch that as much as she loathed filth, she found it sad that her grandchildren would never know what it was to hold and read a physical book.

I then learned that all new books were required to be published only in electronic form, delivered through a Device and read on tablets or screens, or heard through readers.

"No big deal," another indexer said when I asked how this had happened. "The industry went electronic years ago. The physical book was all but dead even before the all-digital rule. Who cares?"

And yet I was chilled by the obvious. Nothing now could be written or read in private. All digital text could be centrally edited, censored, or deleted. The written word no longer could be hidden behind walls or tucked away in the attic. With all new words in the maw of the Purity Web, no wonder they were obsessed with eradicating the old words on paper that conflicted with their version of history and truth.

Sanjay and I had understood the anger directed at intellectuals. We knew the deep resentment at the secular universities. But even after Sarah Palin's Christian Nation resolution was celebrated with spontaneous book burnings around the country, we had not grasped the anger at the book itself. The book was the ultimate symbol of the great divide between faith, which depends on a single authoritative book, and reason, which challenges the very idea of revealed wisdom and celebrates books for their subversion of authority. And here I was. It was bad enough that I fraudulently pretended to their belief to save my life, but now I did their work, spending my days eradicating the only seeds from which a counterrevolution could emerge. I was slowly, a book at a time, eradicating both memory and hope.

The relief I initially felt upon leaving Governors Island alive was soon eclipsed by a sense of profound lethargy. I should have felt revulsion, anger, frustration, and despair at the new Christian Nation that I found. I did not. I mustered enough attention to my work to more than satisfy my bosses at the archives. I allowed Lurlene to mother me a bit. I ate lunch with some of the other indexers, but I trusted none of them. None trusted me. And if I had trusted them, what would I have said? The ubiquitous Purity Web listened and watched and knew everything.

Time passed slowly, but I was patient. No events of any meaning occurred to mark the passage of time. One of my housemates became engaged, and we had a dull party. He was almost thirty, approaching the time when any "yet-to-be-married Christians," known colloquially as "YC's," needed to make the transition to "married Christians," or "MC's." No man or woman risked turning thirty as a YC. At the party I watched him with his twenty-nine-year-old fiancée. I saw no signs of affection.

Sometime after the second anniversary of my release from the island, I was working as usual at the archives. Early on, I had disciplined myself to pick books from each day's cart strictly in the order in which they were presented. I might spy an intriguing spine or from time to time a title that was familiar, but I resisted the temptation to pluck it from the cart and instead worked my way methodically from left to right and top shelf to bottom. That day, I noticed, first thing in the morning, the name "E. O. Wilson" on the spine of a small book on the middle shelf. I worked patiently all morning and then finally I retrieved the book and set it on my table. I instantly understood how this particular book, by a prominent entomologist, biologist, and environmentalist, could have survived the previous purges. Its title was *The Creation*, so those to whom the author's name meant nothing would have mistaken it as a creationist screed and reshelved it with reverence. It was a book I had read twenty-three years before, after it had been given to me by Sanjay. E. O. Wilson was one of his heroes.

It was difficult for me to keep my composure as I read the first few pages of the book, which took the form of a letter written by the famous scientist to an imagined Southern Baptist pastor. Wilson was seeking to build a bridge across the great divide based on mutual reverence for the natural world that is the creation:

Dear Pastor: We have not met, yet I feel I know you well enough to call you friend. First of all, we grew up in the same faith. As a boy I too answered the altar call; I went under the water. Although I no longer belong to that faith, I am confident that if we met and spoke privately of our deepest beliefs, it would be in a spirit of

mutual respect and good will. I know we share many precepts of
moral behavior. Perhaps it also matters that we are both Americans
and, insofar as it might still affect civility and good manners, we
are both Southerners.

There it was. Wilson, relying on shared American values, mutual
respect, goodwill, civility, and good manners, reached across the divide,
confident that common ground can be found. History's verdict: a decent
man betrayed and a magnificent gesture rebuffed. Unsettled, I pulled
an A-C card out of the box, incorrectly coded the subversive text as
"Approved Christian," and placed it on the outgoing cart. I figured I
could pull it off the cart later in the afternoon.

The rest of the day the book sat there, haunting me. If my work were
checked, would I have any excuse or explanation, or would it mean the
end? They must not check every book, I thought. Perhaps one in ten?
So it was, probably, a roll of the dice. I would decide before the end of
the day. But when I returned from a bathroom break at 3:30 p.m., my
outgoing cart was gone and an empty one was in its place. I panicked.
As casually as I could, I asked the indexer at the next table why the cart
had been collected before the usual time of 5:00 p.m.

"Sam promised his wife he would be at his daughter's birthday
party. Lurlene said it was fine; he could make up the time next week.
There a problem?"

"No, not at all. He's such a creature of habit. I was just wondering
what could have thrown him off his schedule." I have become a smooth
and accomplished liar.

There was nothing I could do. One month later, when there had
been no consequence of my rash act, I woke up in the middle of the
night with the idea that I could do it again. It was, I realized, within my
power to save books by deliberately mis-indexing them. An A-C card
was a free pass to the future. With one small act, I could guarantee that
the logic, the passion, the poetry, or the conviction of an author could
take a ride to immortality on the dusty shelves of the Christian Nation
Archives. Once shelved in the permanent archives, my imposter books

almost certainly would not be discovered. There, in the custody of the mighty COGA itself, would reside the seeds for the American culture that would subvert and succeed it. Tucked among novels of banal edification, expositions of intelligent design, and theology dense with its own self-referential illogic—I could plant these subversive gems.

In that still wide-open space of nighttime wakefulness, the act seemed to me to be enormously consequential. In the narrowing light of dawn, I was not so sure. How much can be asked of one person, my left brain protested while I brushed my teeth that morning. I had already walked away from my career to follow a friend and fight the Holies. I had already stood up in front of charging United States marines expecting to die. Wasn't that enough? And who, my left brain insisted, who exactly would I do this thing for?

Two years passed. And then, only six months ago, a new indexer named Adam was greeted by Lurlene, instructed by Mr. Thornton, and settled in to work two rows behind me. He was the only African American in our group, and his glasses, dress, and speech suggested that he had been a teacher or scholar. For the first two weeks, he ignored me nearly to the point of rudeness. Then, during his second week, seeing that I was heading to Washington Square Park for lunch, Adam casually asked if he could join me.

"Let's sit here instead," he said, "I insist." We walked to an out-of-the-way bench facing a large block of shrubs.

Adam asked me lots of questions about work. He dodged most of my questions about him. When we rose from the bench, he glanced to see that no one was near and then said simply, "Greg, you need to know that I am here because of you." Before I could respond, he shook my hand, giving it that distinctive extra squeeze I had felt from a few others, and then turned to walk back to the library by himself. It was only six weeks after that day that the two of us, new friends, left for a vacation—my first in five years.

"You go, Honey," said Lurlene. "You deserve it. Camping is good for the soul. My Dale loved to camp. 'Outdoors,' he said, 'is the only place I can think.' Think and pray. So have yourself some fun."

CHAPTER TWENTY-ONE

Ripples

2029

And the day will come when the mystical generation of Jesus, by the supreme being as his father in the womb of a virgin, will be classed with the fable of the generation of Minerva in the brain of Jupiter.
—Thomas Jefferson, April 11, 1823

But there remains also the truth that every end in history necessarily contains a new beginning; this beginning is the promise, the only "message" which the end can ever produce. Beginning, before it becomes an historical event, is the supreme capacity of man.
—Hannah Arendt,
The Origins of Totalitarianism

Darkness cannot drive out darkness; only light can do that. Hate cannot drive out hate; only love can do that.
—Martin Luther King, Jr.

I HEARD A SPLASH THROUGH the open window and looked up to see two ducks that had just landed in the lake. They both lifted their heads, straightened their bodies with a front-to-back shake, and paddled forward, leaving a well-ordered wake, its ripples spreading gently toward the banks.

"You know," Adam said during our conversation early yesterday morning, "this will probably get you killed. Or at least get you put back in prison for life. Maybe worse. You're still a young man. You have a choice."

"You didn't give me that choice when you asked me to come up here. You didn't give me that choice when I started to write. Why not?"

"It would have been a lot to ask," he said.

I didn't disagree. Since leaving Governors, I had not thought about my future. Honestly, not once. But now, with the past safety tucked into this book, my mind has once again started to drift into forward time. I imagine staying here, swimming every day in the summer, sitting on the big rock watching the ducks. Smelling the fallen leaves. Reveling in the blankness of the snow. That would be happiness of a sort. A natural coda to an eventful life.

Yesterday I finally learned what they are asking of me. Sitting at the small breakfast table, Adam raised the subject.

"The book is almost done. We should talk about what comes next."

"Enlighten me," I said a bit acidly.

"Free Minds works on the cell system. A cell is four people. Every cell has an originator, called the 'point,' and the others are members. Everyone is in two cells. You are recruited by the point of your first cell, and that becomes your base cell. Once that cell is established, each of the members—assuming the role of a new point—has to go out and organize his or her own cell. You get it? The point is the only link between cells. And all any one person knows is the members of two cells—the original base cell of which he is a member, and the new one that he has formed as point."

"So how many cells are there?"

"No one knows. At least I have no idea. I don't know who formed the original cell. It's like a chain letter—you are tapped and you tap three more people. Over time, it should produce huge numbers. It's about the power of exponential numbers."

"But you don't know that. There could be only two cells in the whole country."

Adam stared at the ceiling as if considering the possibility for the first time.

"Yes, you're right. It's possible. But I don't think so. I think there are thousands, maybe even hundreds of thousands. There has to be."

"But how can anything get done? Do all cells act independently, or in pairs?"

"Mostly independently. But not in this," he answered.

"This?"

"You. The memoir. This is . . . different," Adam said, pausing. I waited. I am now nothing if not patient.

"Well, all I really know is that the plan came from somewhere above or outside my point's base cell. Far above, I think. My point received a specific message for me. A message from someone who knew about you but also knew about me. Knew about this place. My point was told that I was to get to you and told how I was to do it. I was instructed to apply for the job at the archives. When I was hired, I knew that other FMs must be at work. I was told exactly what to do. I was told what to ask you to do. That's all I know."

"The woman who came a few weeks ago?"

"My point."

"So what now?" I asked.

"The system in reverse. We have access to old copiers that are not networked. I will make six copies of the book, one for each other member of the cell where I am the point and also one for everyone in the cell where I am a member. Up and down. Each one of them will do the same. Many, many people, Greg, will read it. Exponential numbers."

He did not seem to want to say the obvious. "But of course . . ."

I waited.

"Well, eventually a copy will come into their hands. They will know what you have done. They will come and get you."

"And what about you and Sarah?" I asked. "What about the movement itself? This place? The book reveals it all. Should I take that out?"

"No. FM will do its best to take care of us, but both of us, and Sarah, will be fugitives for as long as the Christian Nation endures. This place will be sacrificed. There are lots more like it, and we want them to know that. We want them to know that FM is real. We want them to know what we can do. We want them to know we're organized. We want them to fear us, and we want them to crack down harder. Each time they do, they take one step forward toward their own destruction. All authoritarian regimes, Greg, all of them, eventually collapse under the weight of their own contradictions."

"I don't see it," I said. "Not this time. They control everything. There's never been technology like the Purity Web. That changes everything. I'm not sure a little bit of cognitive dissonance will bring it all down." I saw his right hand grip the table edge.

"That is *not* what I'm saying. Surely you of all people understand that ideas matter. They rule in the name of a religion that has love as its core value, and yet they came to power on a wave of hate. They preach peace, and came to power by violence. They venerate the Constitution, but subverted its core principle of individual rights. They say they love freedom but have created a technology that holds us all in its bondage. They say their core ideology is small government, but they have created the most intrusive and comprehensive authoritarian rule ever to exist. For God's sake, Greg, that's hardly a little bit of cognitive dissonance."

It had been, of course, Sanjay's argument as to why they should not succeed. Should, not would. He was always careful to distinguish between the two. If a movement based on such contradictions could take power, why couldn't it maintain power? Adam continued.

"Greg, I know it's hard to believe when they seem to hold all the cards. But believe me, they will self-destruct. Each time we show our hand, they crack down harder. The harder they crack down, the more people are turned to the opposition. Each turn of the screw is a step closer to the end. It's just a question of whether it takes years or decades. And that matters a lot. So for FM, it's all about accelerating the process."

★   ★   ★

I CANNOT HELP wondering who you are. You, the reader. My reader. Who are you? Will I bring you anything more than danger? I honestly have no fear for myself. I am sorry for Adam and Sarah. I am sorry to leave this magical place. But I am certain that I have not done the wrong thing. I read once that the struggle of man against power is the struggle of memory against forgetting. So I have done my best to remember. Remembering is one of only two things that Sanjay ever asked me to do.

"Is it all true?" Adam asked this morning.

"It's factual, as factual as I can make it. That is to say, it's as I experienced it and as I remember it."

"Then it is a powerful thing," he said.

"Maybe, if truth still has power—if truth ever had power. But maybe truth is really a fragile thing, even impotent against the really big lie. I don't know."

"No," Adam said, "we don't know. But at least we'll have it. Like the books hidden away in plain sight in the archives. They're not read, but they're not lost. That's something."

Last night at dinner, Adam asked me whether I hated the Holies.

"Do you?" I asked.

"Yes," he answered. "I do. Very much. More than anything. I would give my life to destroy them. You must too, Greg. You have to hate them. Not hating them is too passive . . . it's a kind of death. But . . . it's not entirely clear, from the book I mean, that you do. Do you?"

"I don't know," I answered carefully. "I really don't know."

But I do know. I do not hate them. How could I, when hate is what destroyed my life and my world? Actually, I could hate them. I'm not Sanjay. But I don't. And perhaps Adam is right, perhaps I *should* hate them. But I don't. Socrates, I think, said that deep desire is at the root of all hate. And I desire nothing. It's true. Nothing. So perhaps that's why I don't hate them. I can hear Sanjay saying, as he often did, that only by setting aside desire can we find freedom. I used to think that his non-attachment was hollowness. A cop-out. But now I'm starting to understand. I wish he were here to talk to.

When Adam, Sarah, and I left the cabin, I did not look back. We walked down the rough path and clambered over the rocky ridge that served as a gate between our sanctuary and the harsh reality of the Christian Nation outside. We walked into the back door of the small guesthouse in Putnam Valley that we had left only three weeks before.

★　★　★

"HOW WAS YOUR camping trip?" the innkeeper asked.

"Very nice," said Adam. "Terrific weather. Lots of deer. No bears, though."

"I'm glad," the innkeeper said, handing us our Devices from the drawer under the counter.

He gave us a ride down to the train station in the small village of Garrison. The train back to New York City runs at water level along the east bank of the Hudson River.

"Did you know," asked Adam, "that the Indians called it The River That Flows Both Ways? The Hudson is tidal. Twice a day, it reverses direction and flows upstream. Twice a day, a chance to recover lost ground."

I looked out the window, and as the train lumbered south I watched the water flow slowly north around a large stone near the bank. It left a well-ordered wake, as if it were the stone, and not the water, that was moving. Adam continued his explanation.

"When the tide comes in, the fresh water flowing downstream is no match for the ocean. An invisible tide of salt water comes up from a trench deep below the surface, strong and dense enough to reverse the flow of the river above. Did you know that?"

"No," I said. "I didn't know that. But I do now."

AFTERWORD

CRITICS OF THIS BOOK may suggest that it overstates the influence of the dominionist and reconstructionist theologies within the evangelical movement as a whole, and thus exaggerates the probability of theocracy should the Christian right obtain the political power it has long sought. Were this novel intended as a prediction about the most likely outcome of the "culture wars," that criticism might be deserved. But this novel is not such a prediction; instead, it is intended as a warning that such an outcome is *possible*. And because this possible outcome would be so catastrophic were it to occur, the resulting risk demands our vigilant attention. By illustrating what our homegrown fundamentalists mean when they say America should be a "Christian Nation," I hope this book will cause its readers to think twice about politicians who justify their public policy agenda on the basis of the Bible or who sprinkle their political speech with references to the desires of God. Support for the constitutional design of a secular state, with no religious belief receiving preference over any other, should be common ground for all Americans, conservative and liberal, religious and secular.

ACKNOWLEDGMENTS

I GRATEFULLY ACKNOWLEDGE the fine books by journalists and scholars that first alerted me to the danger to our democracy posed by Christian fundamentalism. These include, among others, *American Fascists: The Christian Right and the War on America* and *Empire of Illusion: The End of Literacy and the Triumph of Spectacle*, both by Chris Hedges; *Kingdom Coming: The Rise of Christian Nationalism*, by Michelle Goldberg; *The Family: The Secret Fundamentalism at the Heart of American Power*, by Jeff Sharlet; *American Theocracy*, by Kevin Philips; and *Republican Gomorrah*, by Max Blumenthal. I acknowledge and credit these works as my primary sources for the theology and ambitions of Christian nationalism, its totalitarian precedents and authoritarian tendencies, and many of the historical quotes and incidents that illustrate the power of the movement prior to 2008.

I am grateful to legendary editor Star Lawrence for his faith in this book and superb editorial direction. I also owe a debt to his assistant, Ryan Harrington, and to all their colleagues at Norton who worked with alacrity and professionalism to bring this work to readers.

Many friends assisted me on the long journey from initial idea to finished book. These include Lauren Belfer, Devendra Chauhan, Elliot Figman and his colleagues at *Poets & Writers*, Ham Fish, David Foster, Pat Hass, Rick and Carol Hamlin, Don Lamm, Jeanette Limondjian,

Elinor Lipman, Caroline Niemczyk, Ru Rauch, Ted Rogers, Jonathan Rose, and Theresa Volpe. And most of all, I am grateful to my law partners, who are the finest colleagues one could imagine and who have given me ample scope to pursue my many interests while at the same time providing a professional practice of unparalleled interest and challenge.

CREDITS